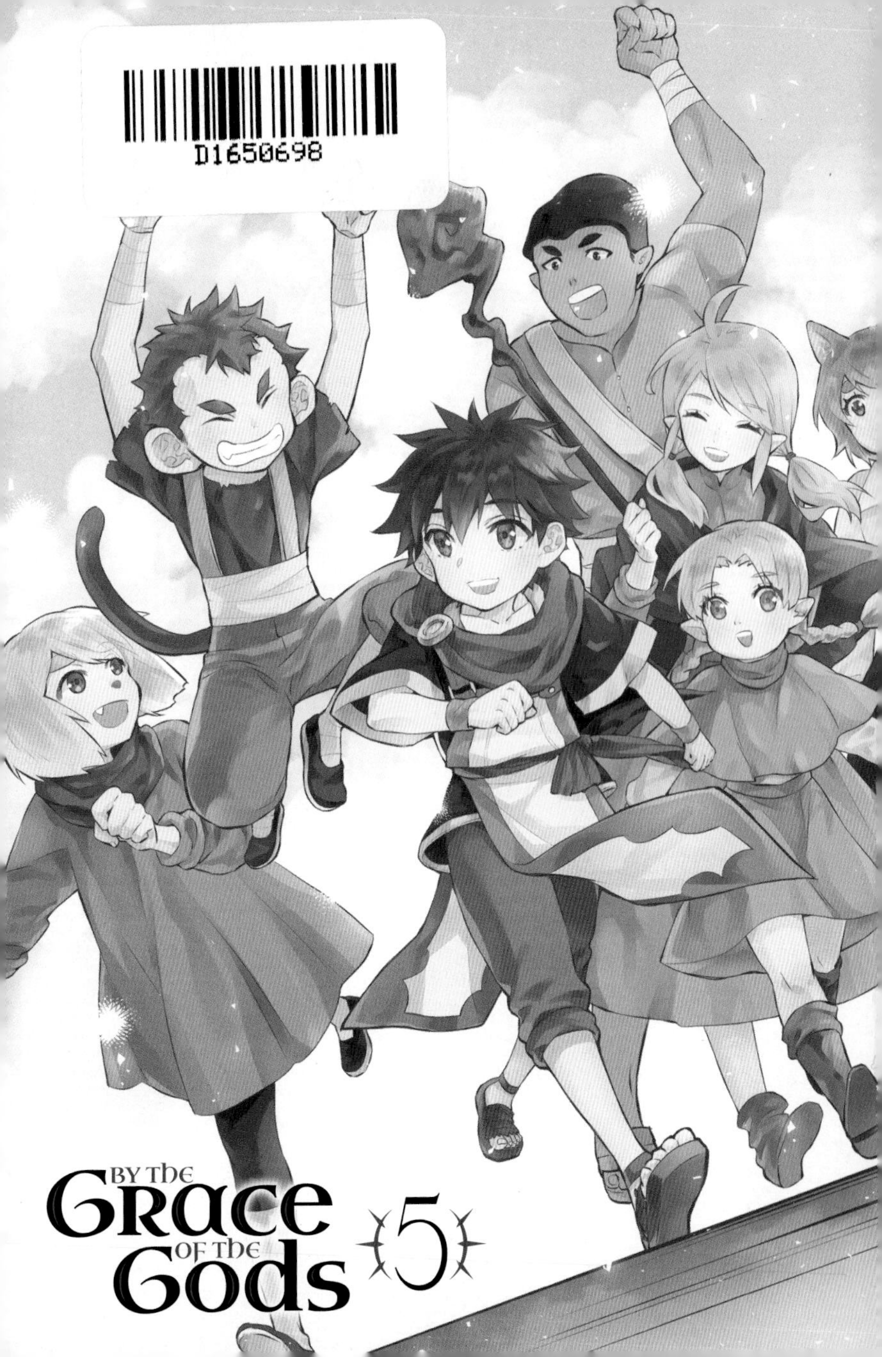
By the Grace of the Gods
5

CONTENTS

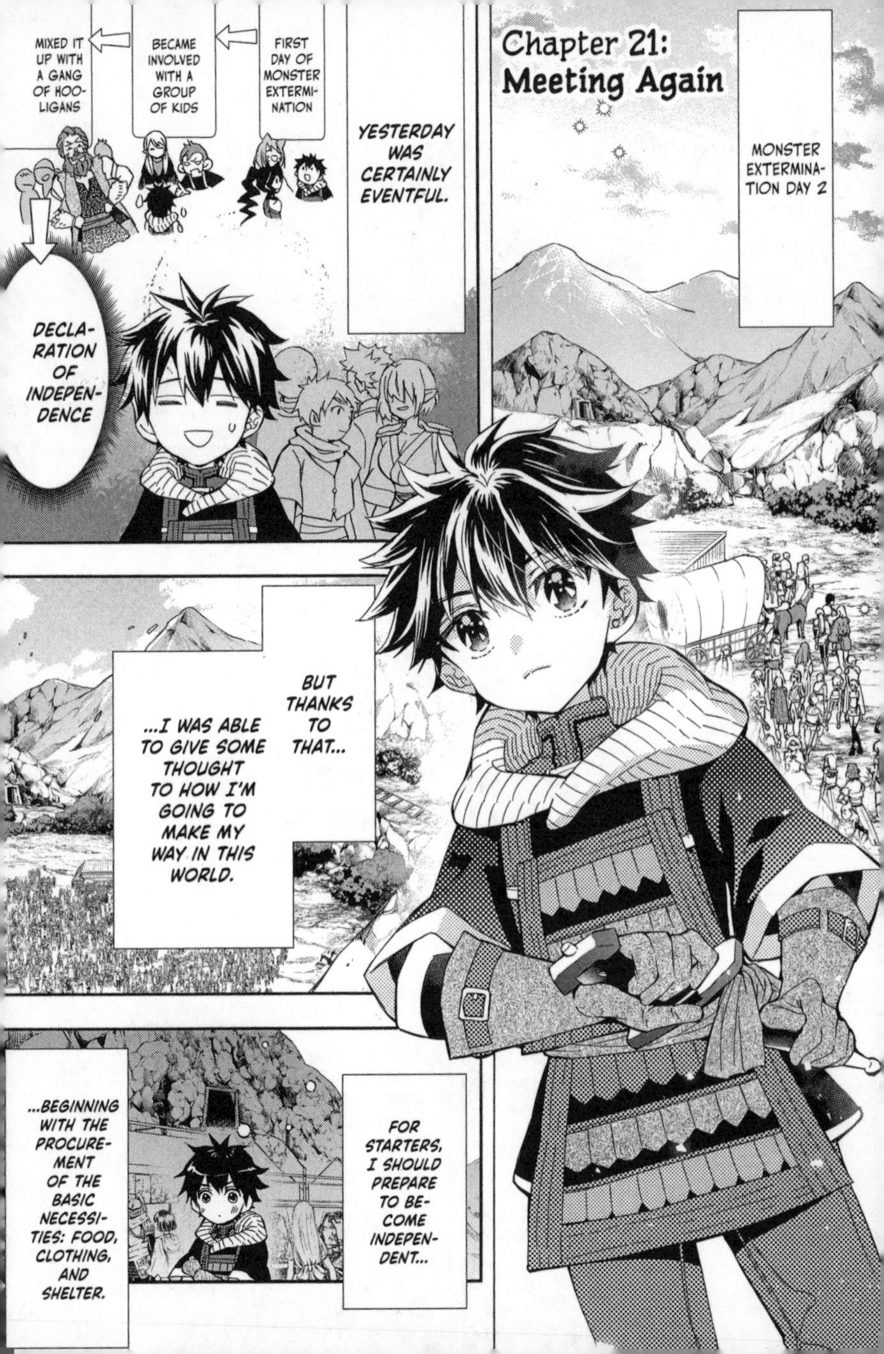

Chapter 21: Meeting Again
MONSTER EXTERMINATION DAY 2
YESTERDAY WAS CERTAINLY EVENTFUL.
FIRST DAY OF MONSTER EXTERMINATION
BECAME INVOLVED WITH A GROUP OF KIDS
MIXED IT UP WITH A GANG OF HOOLIGANS
DECLARATION OF INDEPENDENCE
BUT THANKS TO THAT...
...I WAS ABLE TO GIVE SOME THOUGHT TO HOW I'M GOING TO MAKE MY WAY IN THIS WORLD.
FOR STARTERS, I SHOULD PREPARE TO BECOME INDEPENDENT...
...BEGINNING WITH THE PROCUREMENT OF THE BASIC NECESSITIES: FOOD, CLOTHING, AND SHELTER.

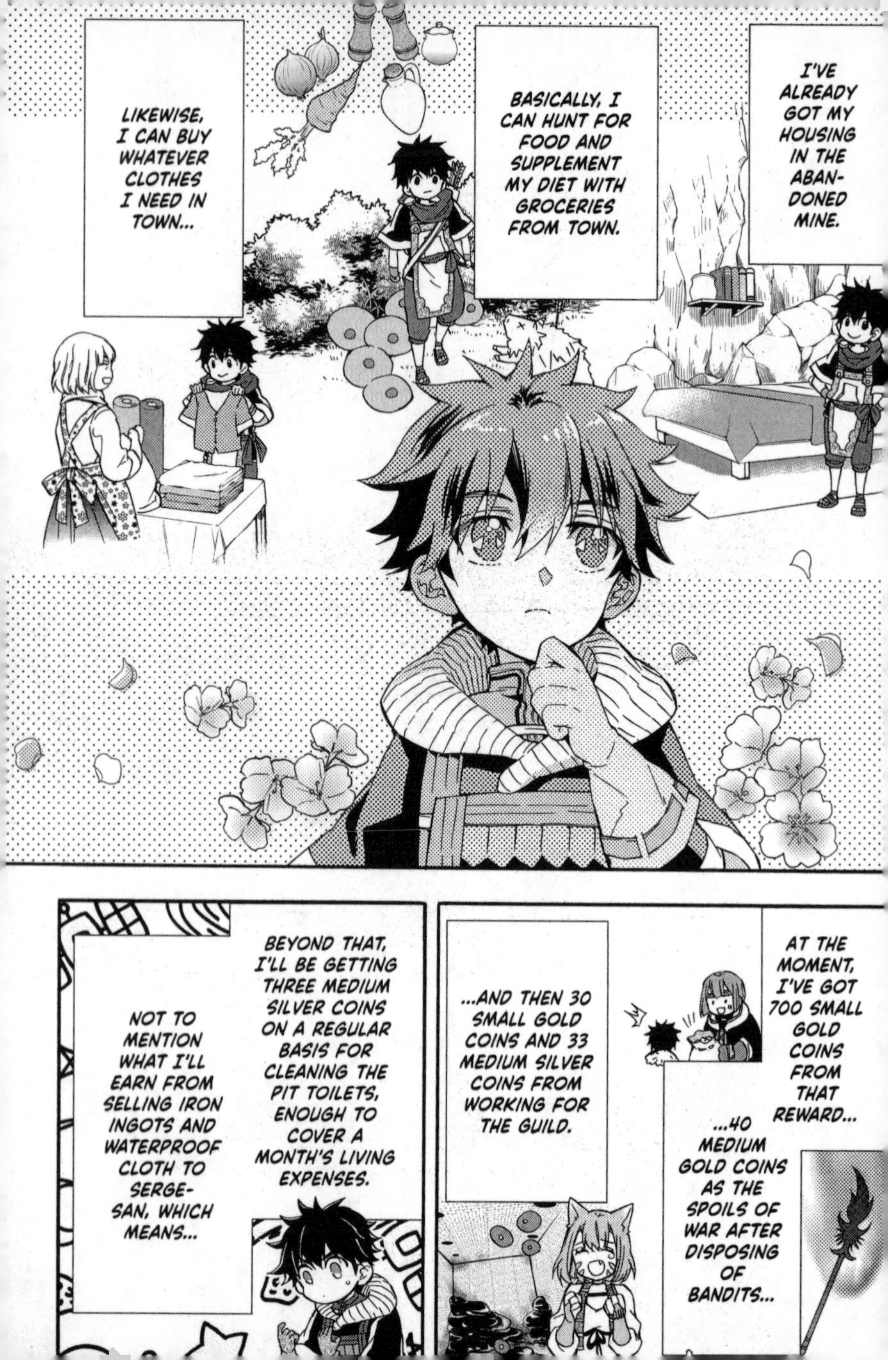
I'VE ALREADY GOT MY HOUSING IN THE ABANDONED MINE.
BASICALLY, I CAN HUNT FOR FOOD AND SUPPLEMENT MY DIET WITH GROCERIES FROM TOWN.
LIKEWISE, I CAN BUY WHATEVER CLOTHES I NEED IN TOWN...
AT THE MOMENT, I'VE GOT 700 SMALL GOLD COINS FROM THAT REWARD...
...40 MEDIUM GOLD COINS AS THE SPOILS OF WAR AFTER DISPOSING OF BANDITS...
...AND THEN 30 SMALL GOLD COINS AND 33 MEDIUM SILVER COINS FROM WORKING FOR THE GUILD.
BEYOND THAT, I'LL BE GETTING THREE MEDIUM SILVER COINS ON A REGULAR BASIS FOR CLEANING THE PIT TOILETS, ENOUGH TO COVER A MONTH'S LIVING EXPENSES.
NOT TO MENTION WHAT I'LL EARN FROM SELLING IRON INGOTS AND WATERPROOF CLOTH TO SERGE-SAN, WHICH MEANS...

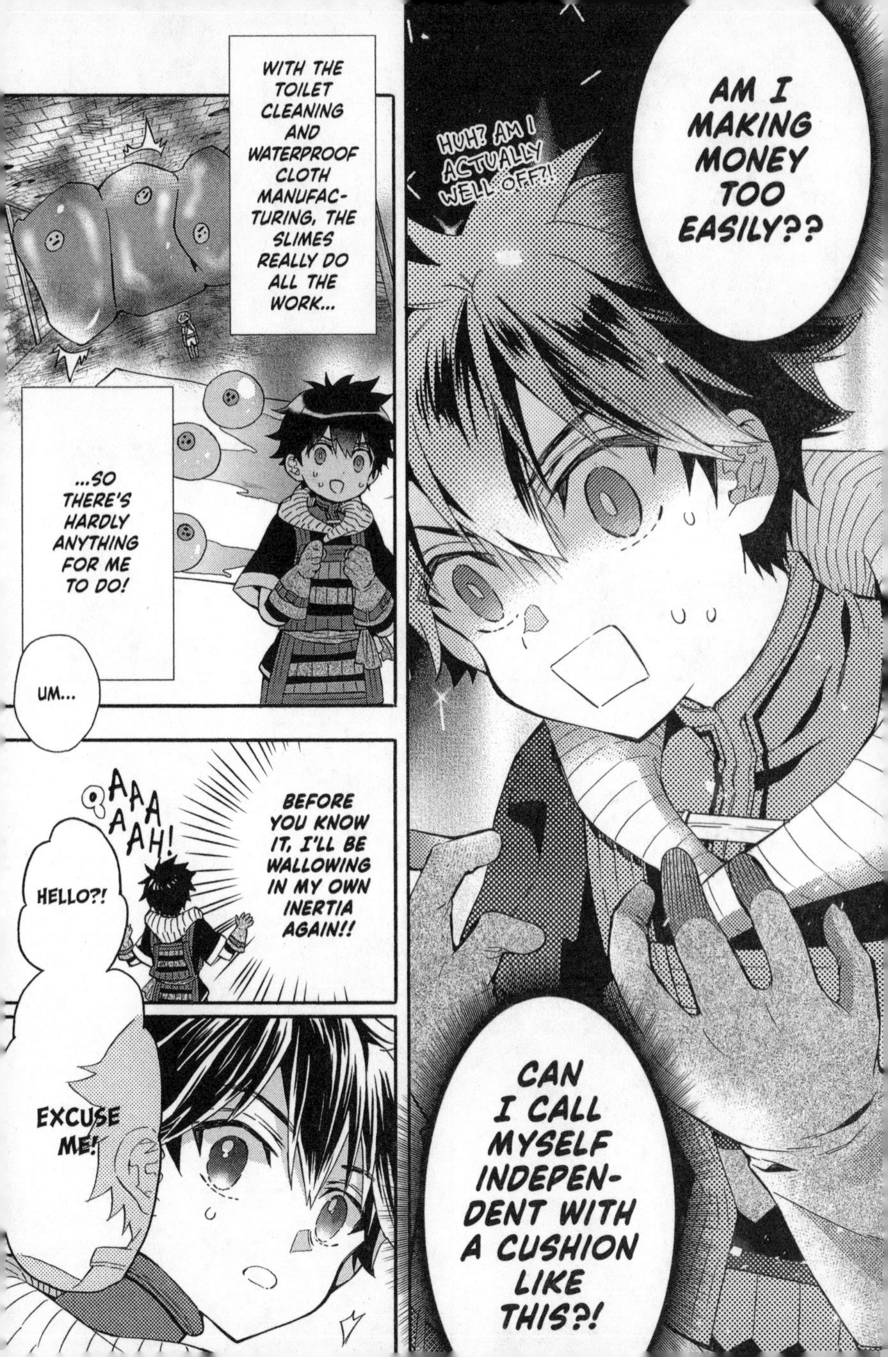
AM I MAKING MONEY TOO EASILY??
HUH? AM I ACTUALLY WELL OFF?!
CAN I CALL MYSELF INDEPEN-DENT WITH A CUSHION LIKE THIS?!
WITH THE TOILET CLEANING AND WATERPROOF CLOTH MANUFAC-TURING, THE SLIMES REALLY DO ALL THE WORK...
...SO THERE'S HARDLY ANYTHING FOR ME TO DO!
UM...
BEFORE YOU KNOW IT, I'LL BE WALLOWING IN MY OWN INERTIA AGAIN!!
AAAAAH!
HELLO?!
EXCUSE ME!

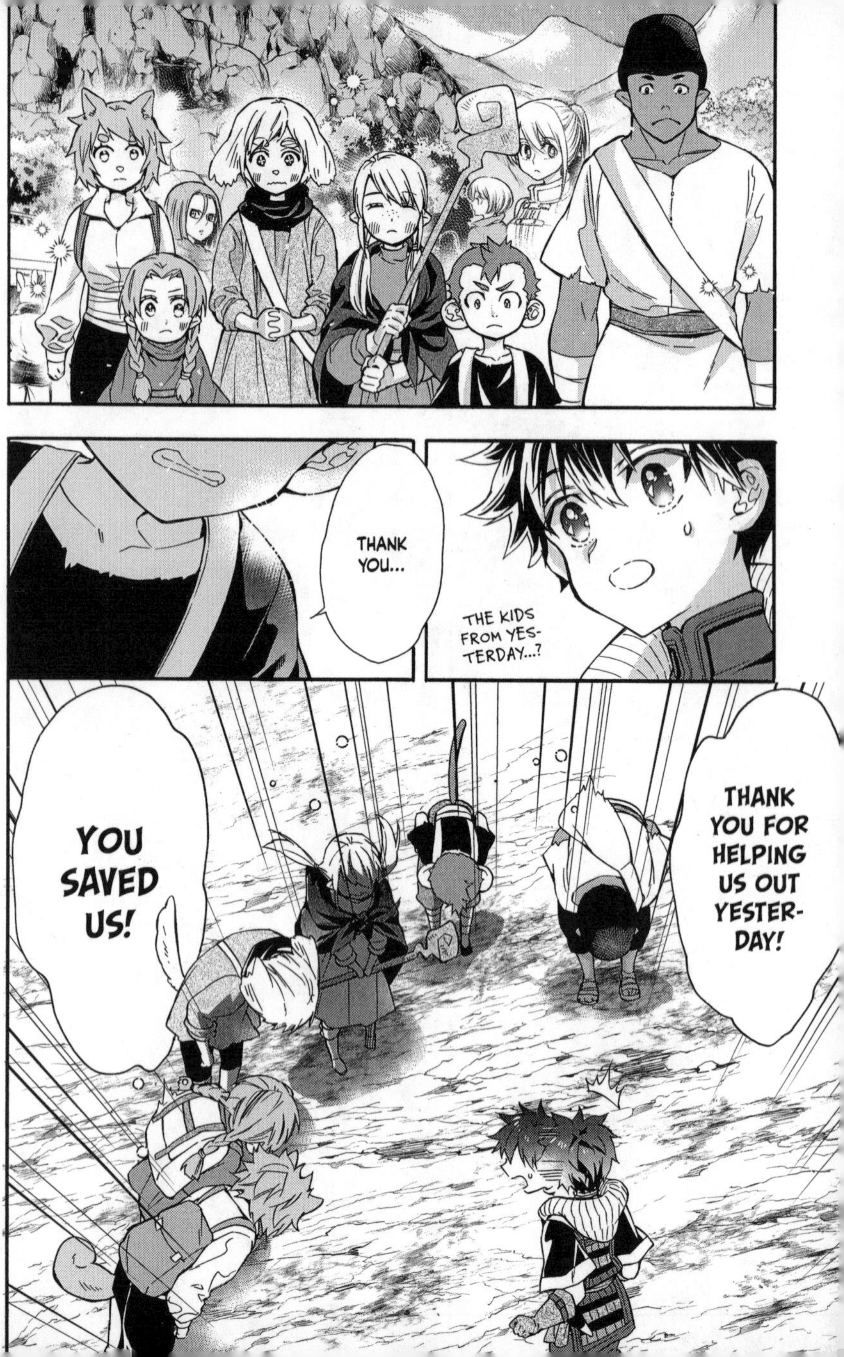
THE KIDS FROM YES-TERDAY...?
THANK YOU...
THANK YOU FOR HELPING US OUT YESTER-DAY!
YOU SAVED US!

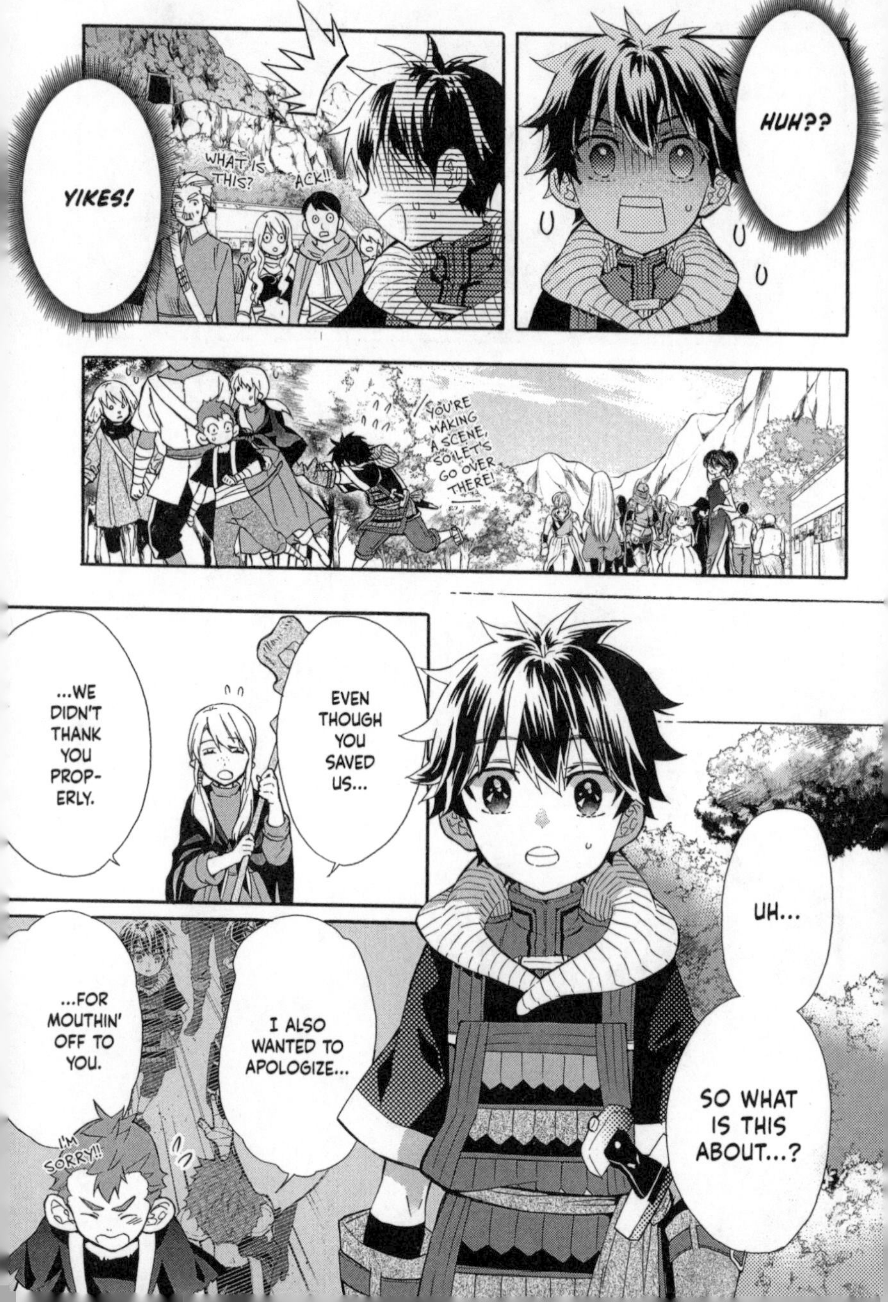
HUH??
ACK!!
WHAT IS THIS?
YIKES!
YOU'RE MAKING A SCENE, SO LET'S GO OVER THERE!
UH...
SO WHAT IS THIS ABOUT...?
EVEN THOUGH YOU SAVED US...
...WE DIDN'T THANK YOU PROP-ERLY.
I ALSO WANTED TO APOLOGIZE...
...FOR MOUTHIN' OFF TO YOU.
I'M SORRY!!

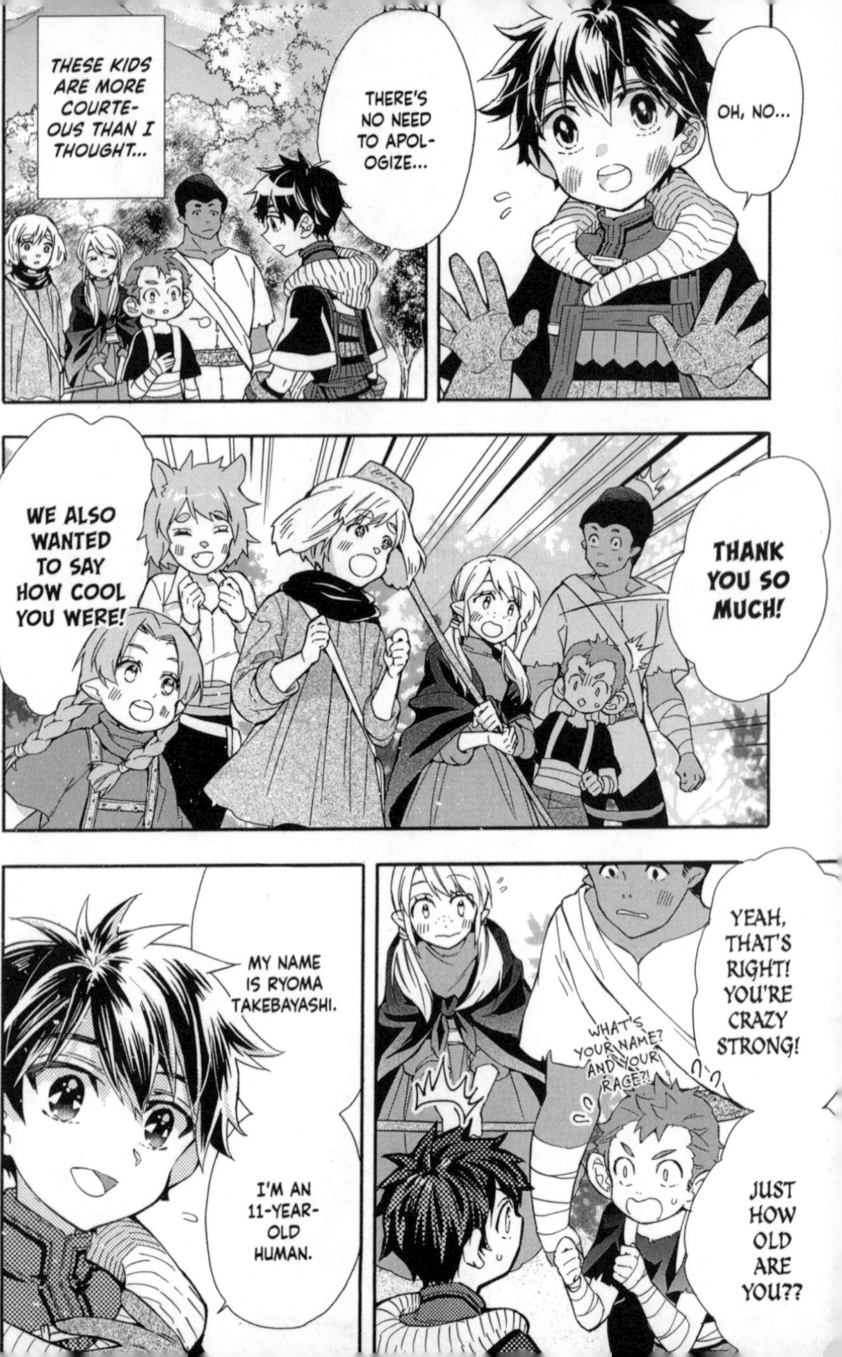

OH, NO...
THERE'S NO NEED TO APOLOGIZE...
THESE KIDS ARE MORE COURTEOUS THAN I THOUGHT...
THANK YOU SO MUCH!
WE ALSO WANTED TO SAY HOW COOL YOU WERE!
YEAH, THAT'S RIGHT! YOU'RE CRAZY STRONG!
WHAT'S YOUR NAME? AND YOUR RACE?!
JUST HOW OLD ARE YOU??
MY NAME IS RYOMA TAKEBAYASHI.
I'M AN 11-YEAR-OLD HUMAN.

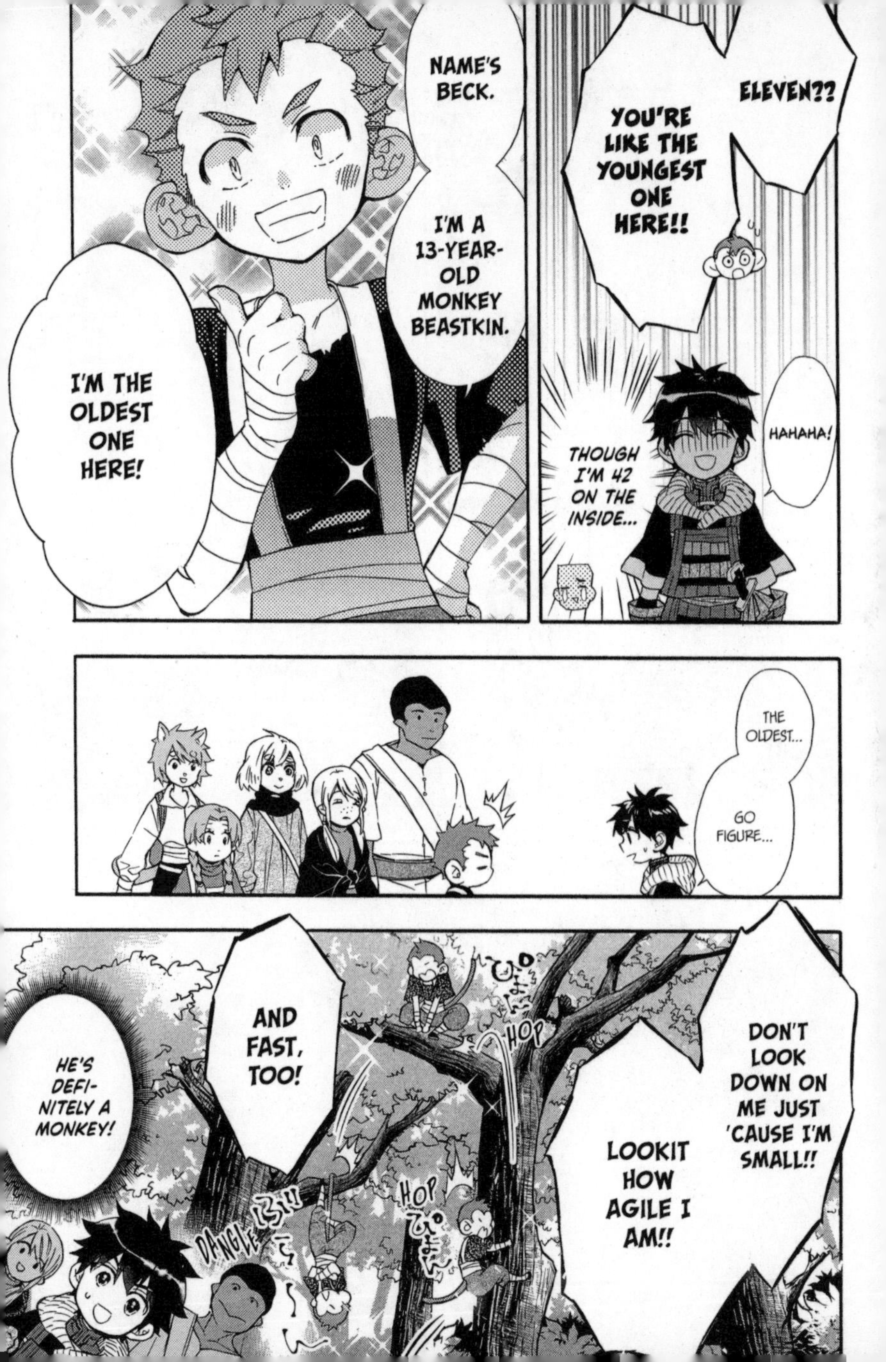
ELEVEN??
YOU'RE LIKE THE YOUNGEST ONE HERE!!
HAHAHA!
THOUGH I'M 42 ON THE INSIDE...
NAME'S BECK.
I'M A 13-YEAR-OLD MONKEY BEASTKIN.
I'M THE OLDEST ONE HERE!
THE OLDEST...
GO FIGURE...
DON'T LOOK DOWN ON ME JUST 'CAUSE I'M SMALL!!
LOOKIT HOW AGILE I AM!!
HOP
AND FAST, TOO!
HOP
DANGLE
HE'S DEFI-NITELY A MONKEY!

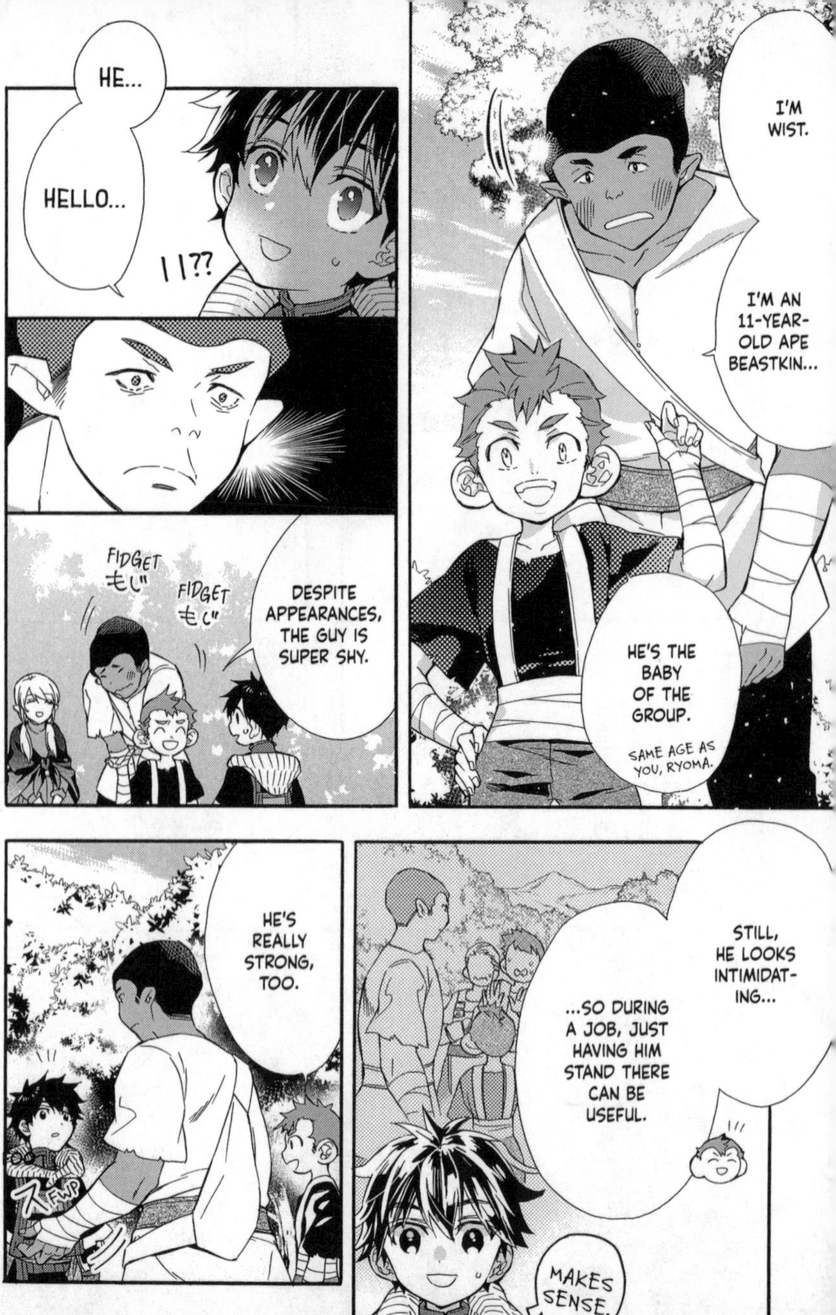
I'M WIST.
I'M AN 11-YEAR-OLD APE BEASTKIN...
HE'S THE BABY OF THE GROUP.
SAME AGE AS YOU, RYOMA.
HE...
HELLO...
!!??
FIDGET もじ
FIDGET もじ
DESPITE APPEARANCES, THE GUY IS SUPER SHY.
STILL, HE LOOKS INTIMIDATING...
...SO DURING A JOB, JUST HAVING HIM STAND THERE CAN BE USEFUL.
MAKES SENSE.
HE'S REALLY STRONG, TOO.
ス FWP

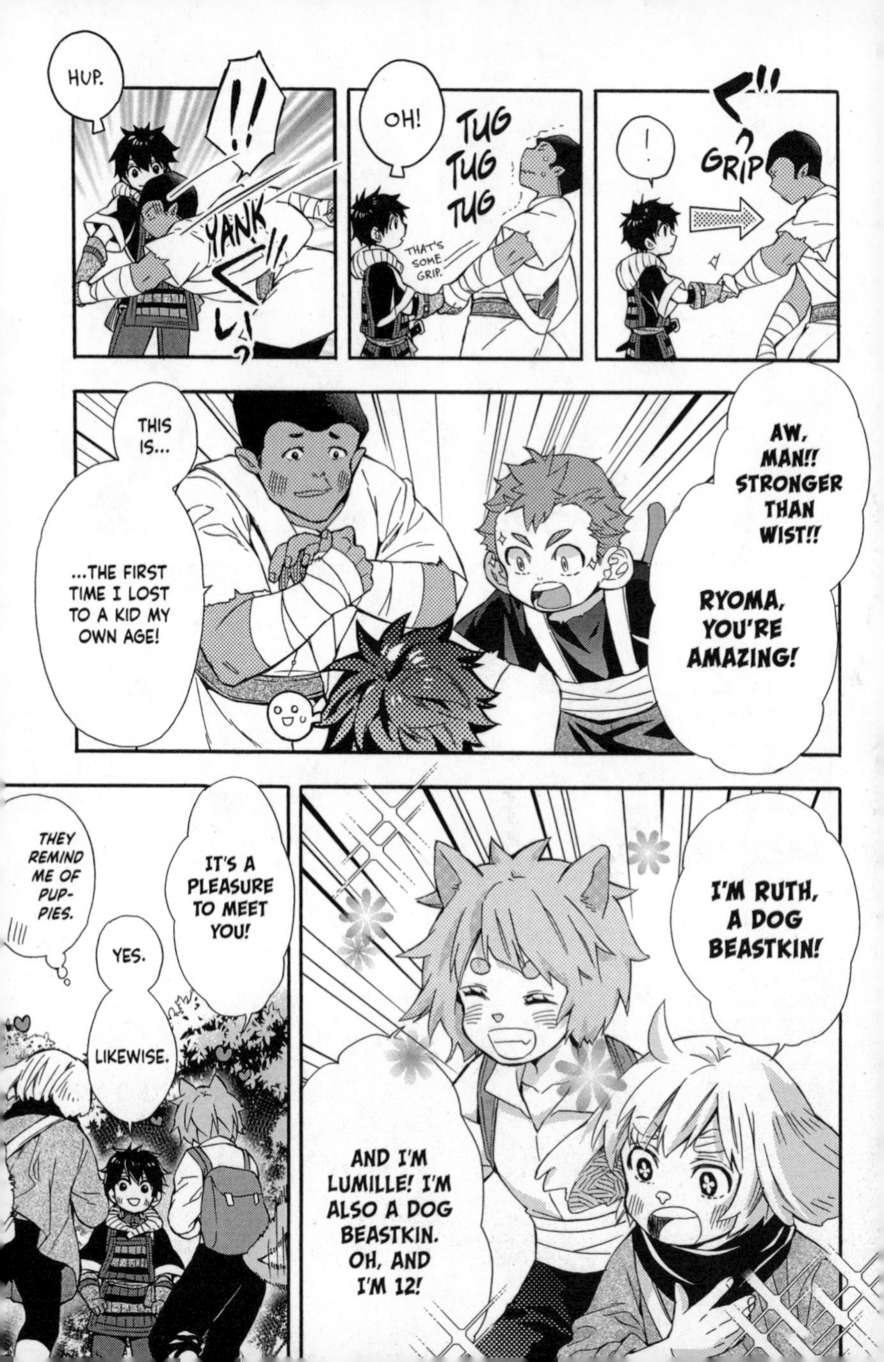

!
GRIP
OH!
TUG TUG TUG
THAT'S SOME GRIP.
HUP.
!!
YANK
AW, MAN!! STRONGER THAN WIST!!
RYOMA, YOU'RE AMAZING!
THIS IS...
...THE FIRST TIME I LOST TO A KID MY OWN AGE!
I'M RUTH, A DOG BEASTKIN!
AND I'M LUMILLE! I'M ALSO A DOG BEASTKIN. OH, AND I'M 12!
IT'S A PLEASURE TO MEET YOU!
THEY REMIND ME OF PUPPIES.
YES.
LIKEWISE.

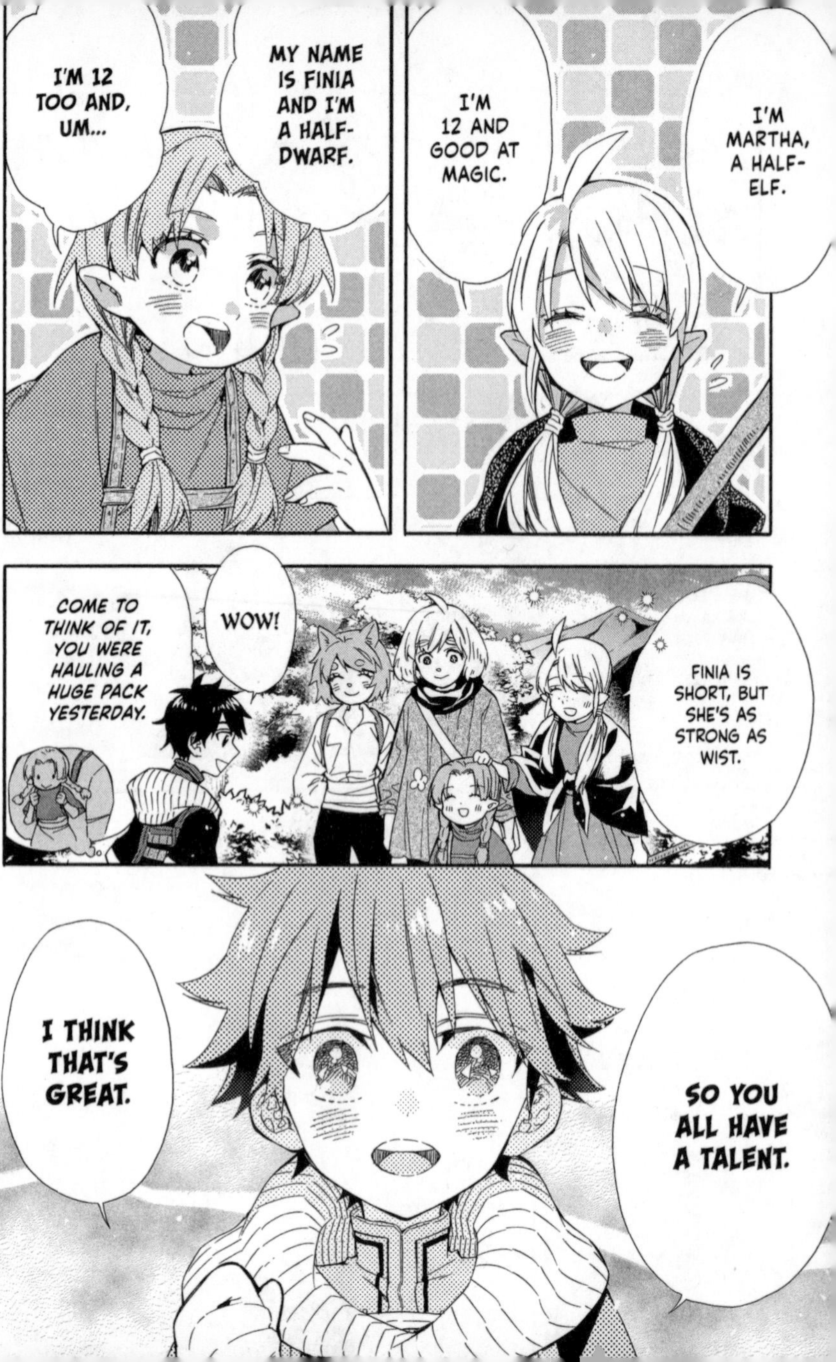
I'M MARTHA, A HALF-ELF.
I'M 12 AND GOOD AT MAGIC.
MY NAME IS FINIA AND I'M A HALF-DWARF.
I'M 12 TOO AND, UM...
FINIA IS SHORT, BUT SHE'S AS STRONG AS WIST.
WOW!
COME TO THINK OF IT, YOU WERE HAULING A HUGE PACK YESTERDAY.
SO YOU ALL HAVE A TALENT.
I THINK THAT'S GREAT.

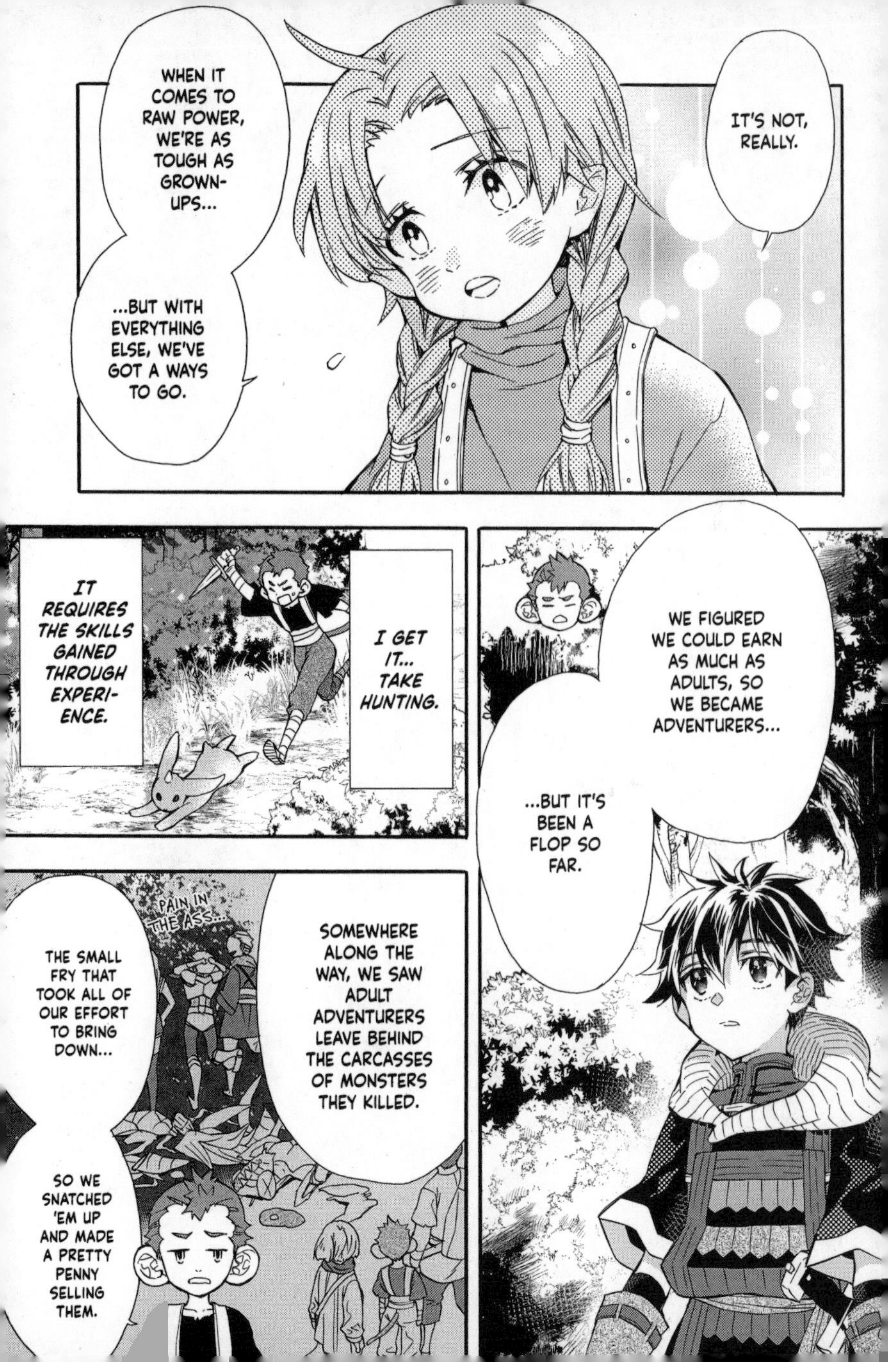
IT'S NOT, REALLY.
WHEN IT COMES TO RAW POWER, WE'RE AS TOUGH AS GROWN-UPS...
...BUT WITH EVERYTHING ELSE, WE'VE GOT A WAYS TO GO.
WE FIGURED WE COULD EARN AS MUCH AS ADULTS, SO WE BECAME ADVENTURERS...
...BUT IT'S BEEN A FLOP SO FAR.
I GET IT... TAKE HUNTING.
IT REQUIRES THE SKILLS GAINED THROUGH EXPERI-ENCE.
SOMEWHERE ALONG THE WAY, WE SAW ADULT ADVENTURERS LEAVE BEHIND THE CARCASSES OF MONSTERS THEY KILLED.
PAIN IN THE ASS...
THE SMALL FRY THAT TOOK ALL OF OUR EFFORT TO BRING DOWN...
SO WE SNATCHED 'EM UP AND MADE A PRETTY PENNY SELLING THEM.

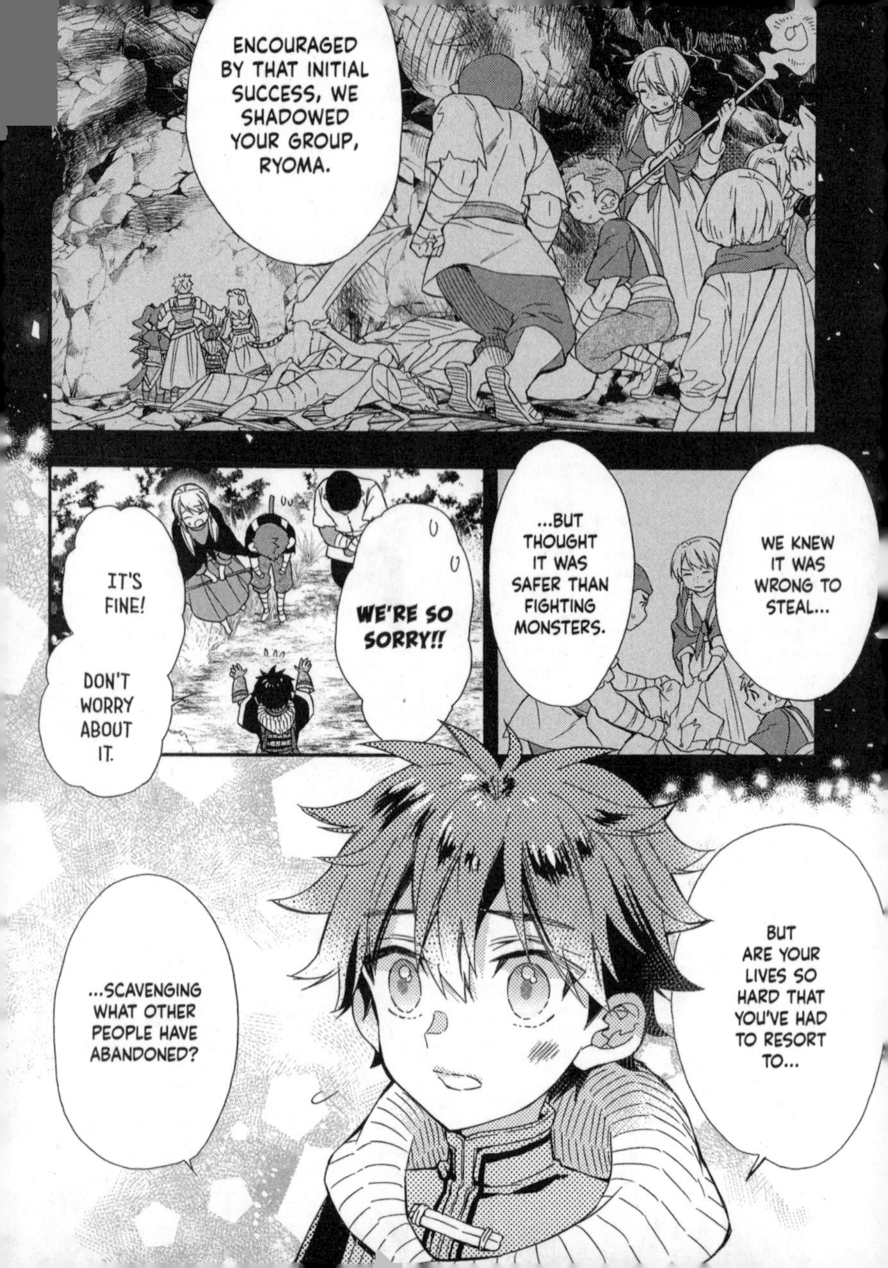
ENCOURAGED BY THAT INITIAL SUCCESS, WE SHADOWED YOUR GROUP, RYOMA.
WE KNEW IT WAS WRONG TO STEAL...
...BUT THOUGHT IT WAS SAFER THAN FIGHTING MONSTERS.
WE'RE SO SORRY!!
IT'S FINE!
DON'T WORRY ABOUT IT.
BUT ARE YOUR LIVES SO HARD THAT YOU'VE HAD TO RESORT TO...
...SCAVENGING WHAT OTHER PEOPLE HAVE ABANDONED?

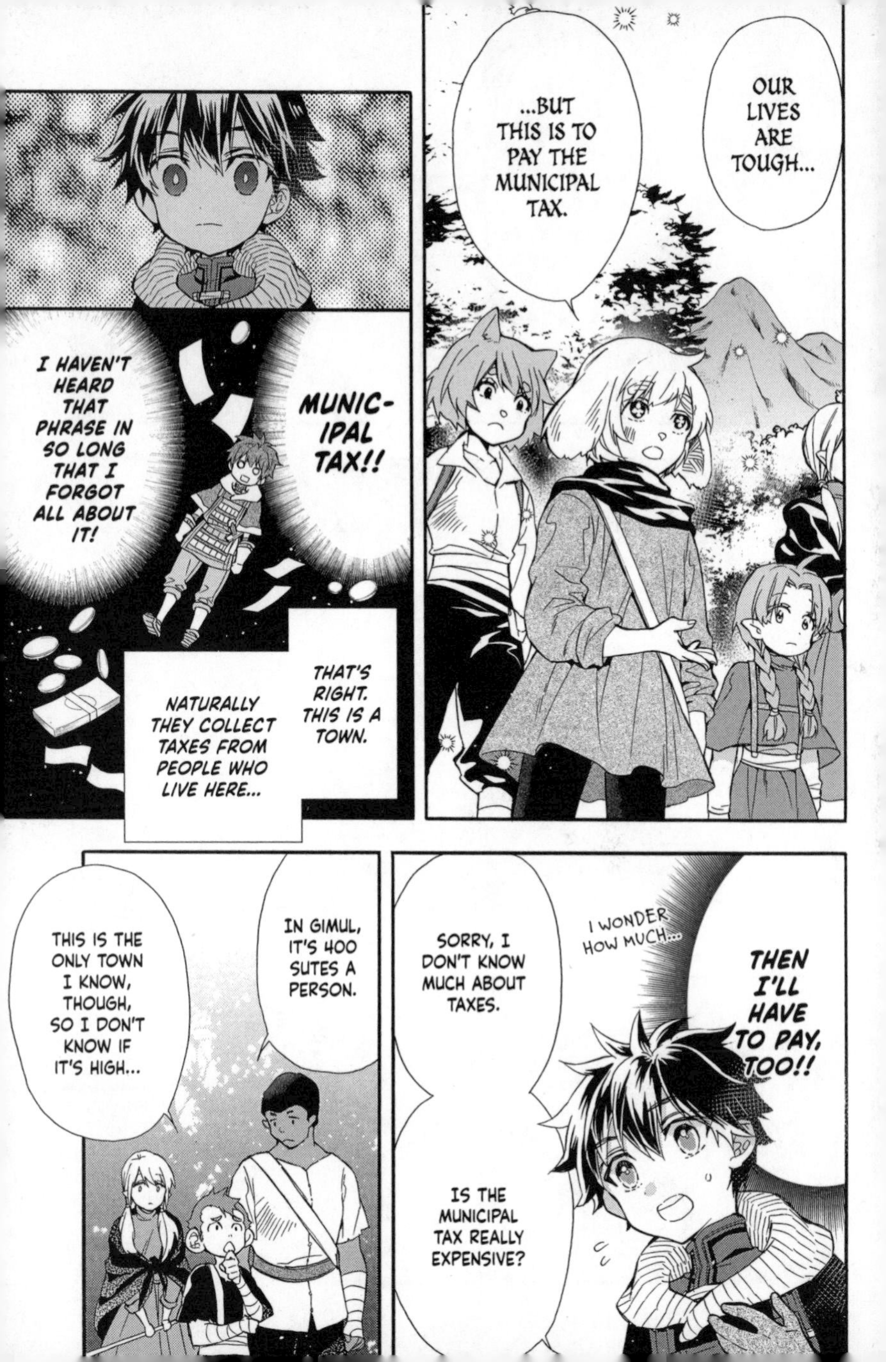
OUR LIVES ARE TOUGH...
...BUT THIS IS TO PAY THE MUNICIPAL TAX.
MUNIC-IPAL TAX!!
I HAVEN'T HEARD THAT PHRASE IN SO LONG THAT I FORGOT ALL ABOUT IT!
THAT'S RIGHT. THIS IS A TOWN.
NATURALLY THEY COLLECT TAXES FROM PEOPLE WHO LIVE HERE...
THEN I'LL HAVE TO PAY, TOO!!
I WONDER HOW MUCH...
IS THE MUNICIPAL TAX REALLY EXPENSIVE?
SORRY, I DON'T KNOW MUCH ABOUT TAXES.
IN GIMUL, IT'S 400 SUTES A PERSON.
THIS IS THE ONLY TOWN I KNOW, THOUGH, SO I DON'T KNOW IF IT'S HIGH...

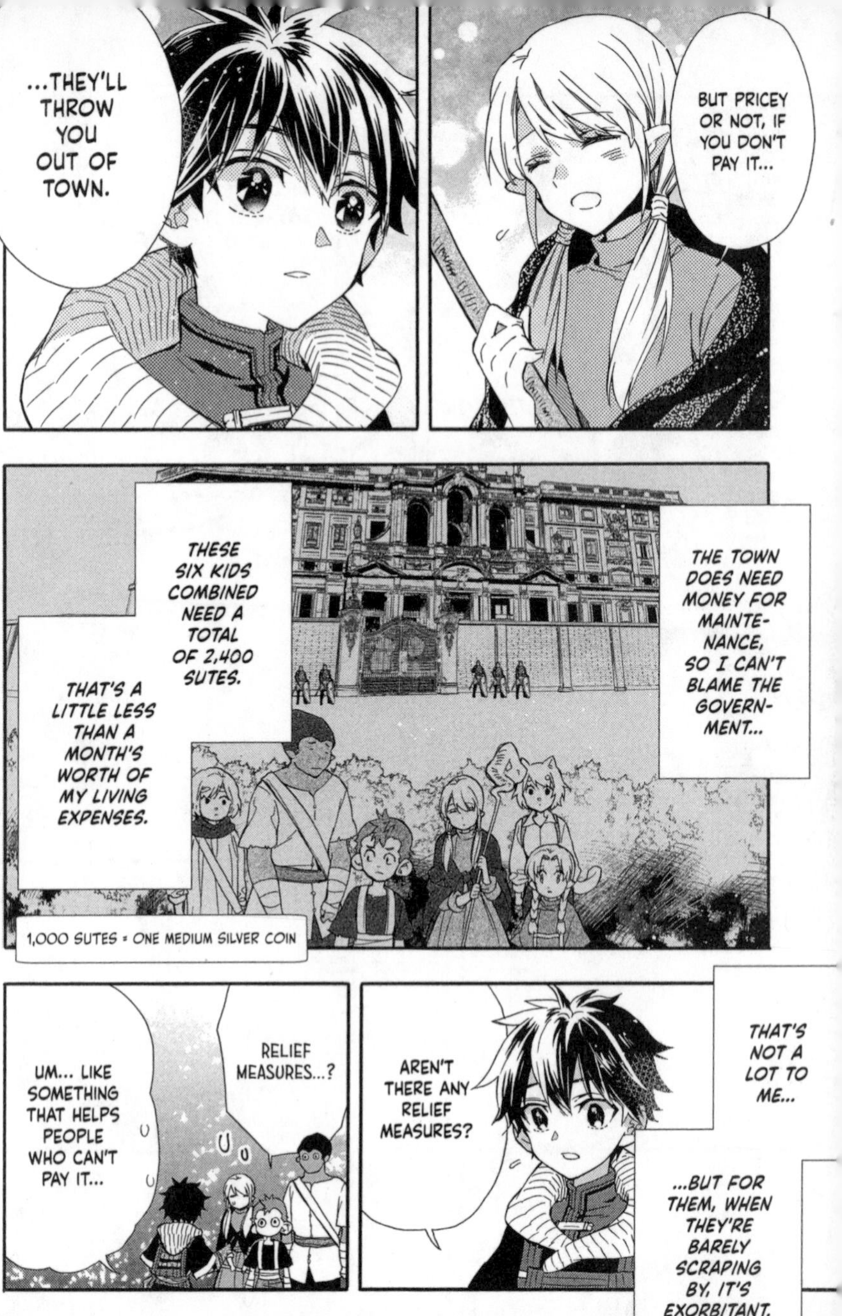
BUT PRICEY OR NOT, IF YOU DON'T PAY IT...
...THEY'LL THROW YOU OUT OF TOWN.
THE TOWN DOES NEED MONEY FOR MAINTE-NANCE, SO I CAN'T BLAME THE GOVERN-MENT...
THESE SIX KIDS COMBINED NEED A TOTAL OF 2,400 SUTES.
THAT'S A LITTLE LESS THAN A MONTH'S WORTH OF MY LIVING EXPENSES.
1,000 SUTES = ONE MEDIUM SILVER COIN
THAT'S NOT A LOT TO ME...
...BUT FOR THEM, WHEN THEY'RE BARELY SCRAPING BY, IT'S EXORBITANT.
AREN'T THERE ANY RELIEF MEASURES?
RELIEF MEASURES...?
UM... LIKE SOMETHING THAT HELPS PEOPLE WHO CAN'T PAY IT...

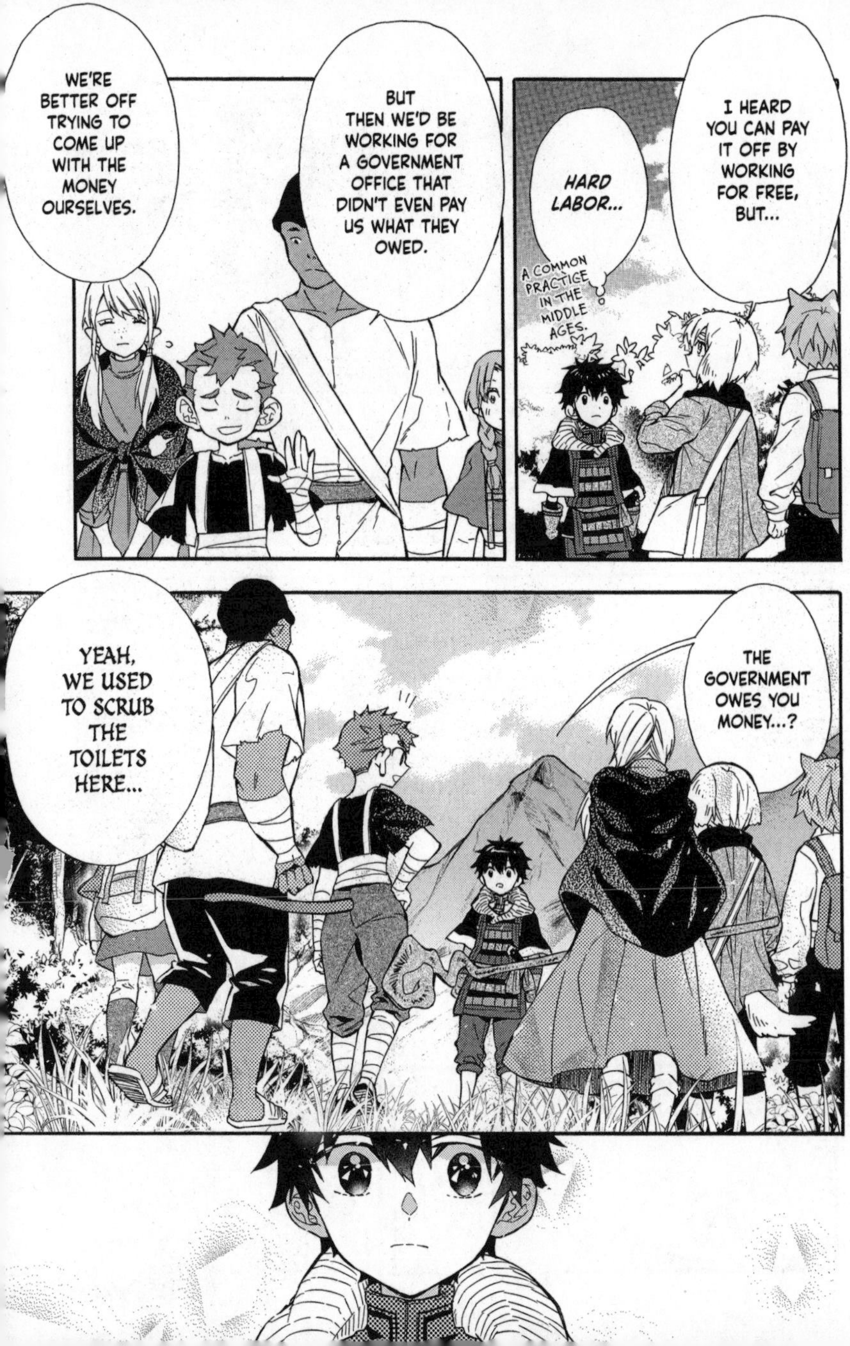
I HEARD YOU CAN PAY IT OFF BY WORKING FOR FREE, BUT...
HARD LABOR...
A COMMON PRACTICE IN THE MIDDLE AGES.
BUT THEN WE'D BE WORKING FOR A GOVERNMENT OFFICE THAT DIDN'T EVEN PAY US WHAT THEY OWED.
WE'RE BETTER OFF TRYING TO COME UP WITH THE MONEY OURSELVES.
THE GOVERNMENT OWES YOU MONEY...?
YEAH, WE USED TO SCRUB THE TOILETS HERE...

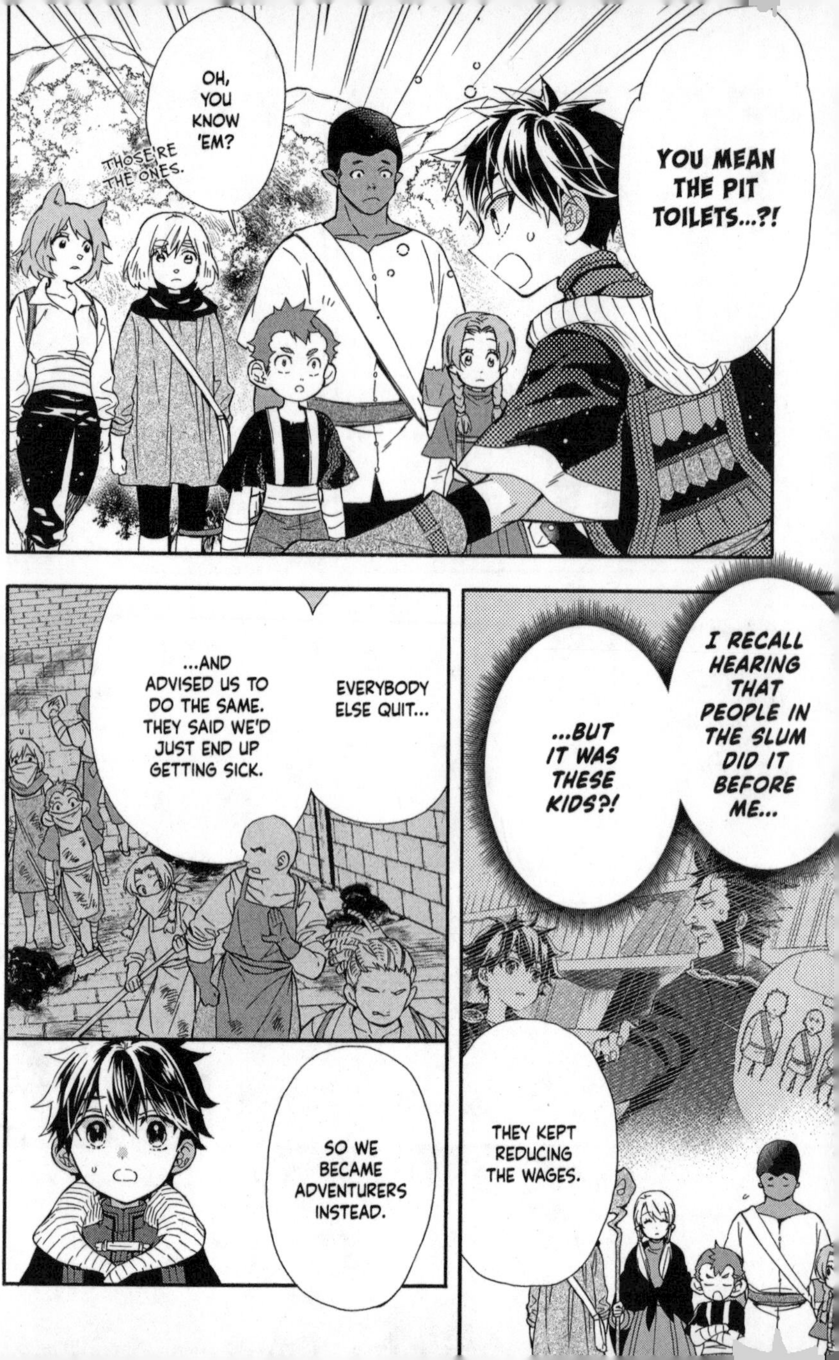
YOU MEAN THE PIT TOILETS...?!
OH, YOU KNOW 'EM?
THOSE'RE THE ONES.
I RECALL HEARING THAT PEOPLE IN THE SLUM DID IT BEFORE ME...
...BUT IT WAS THESE KIDS?!
EVERYBODY ELSE QUIT...
...AND ADVISED US TO DO THE SAME. THEY SAID WE'D JUST END UP GETTING SICK.
THEY KEPT REDUCING THE WAGES.
SO WE BECAME ADVENTURERS INSTEAD.

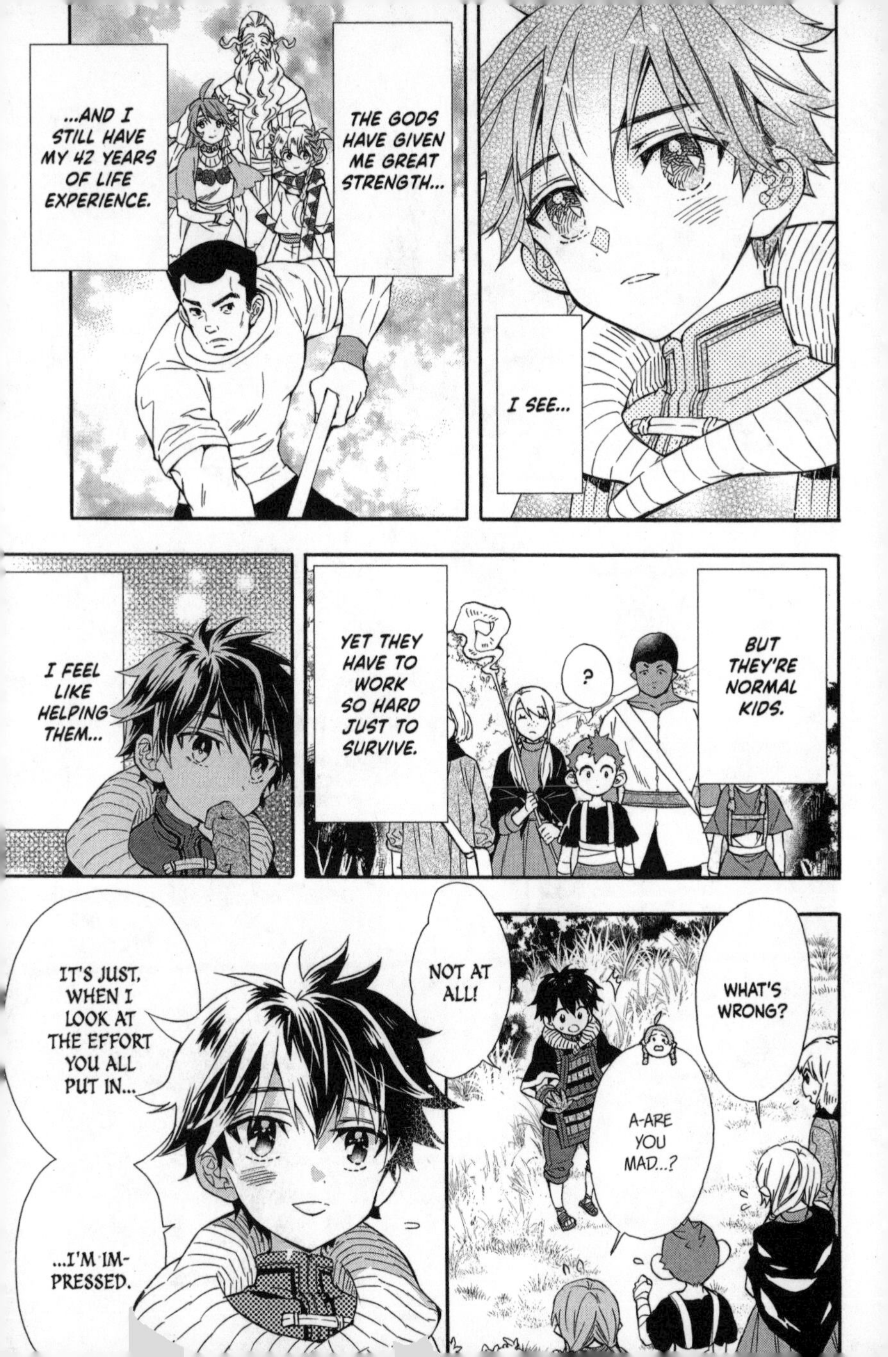
I SEE...
THE GODS HAVE GIVEN ME GREAT STRENGTH...
...AND I STILL HAVE MY 42 YEARS OF LIFE EXPERIENCE.
BUT THEY'RE NORMAL KIDS.
?
YET THEY HAVE TO WORK SO HARD JUST TO SURVIVE.
I FEEL LIKE HELPING THEM...
WHAT'S WRONG?
A-ARE YOU MAD...?
NOT AT ALL!
IT'S JUST, WHEN I LOOK AT THE EFFORT YOU ALL PUT IN...
...I'M IM-PRESSED.

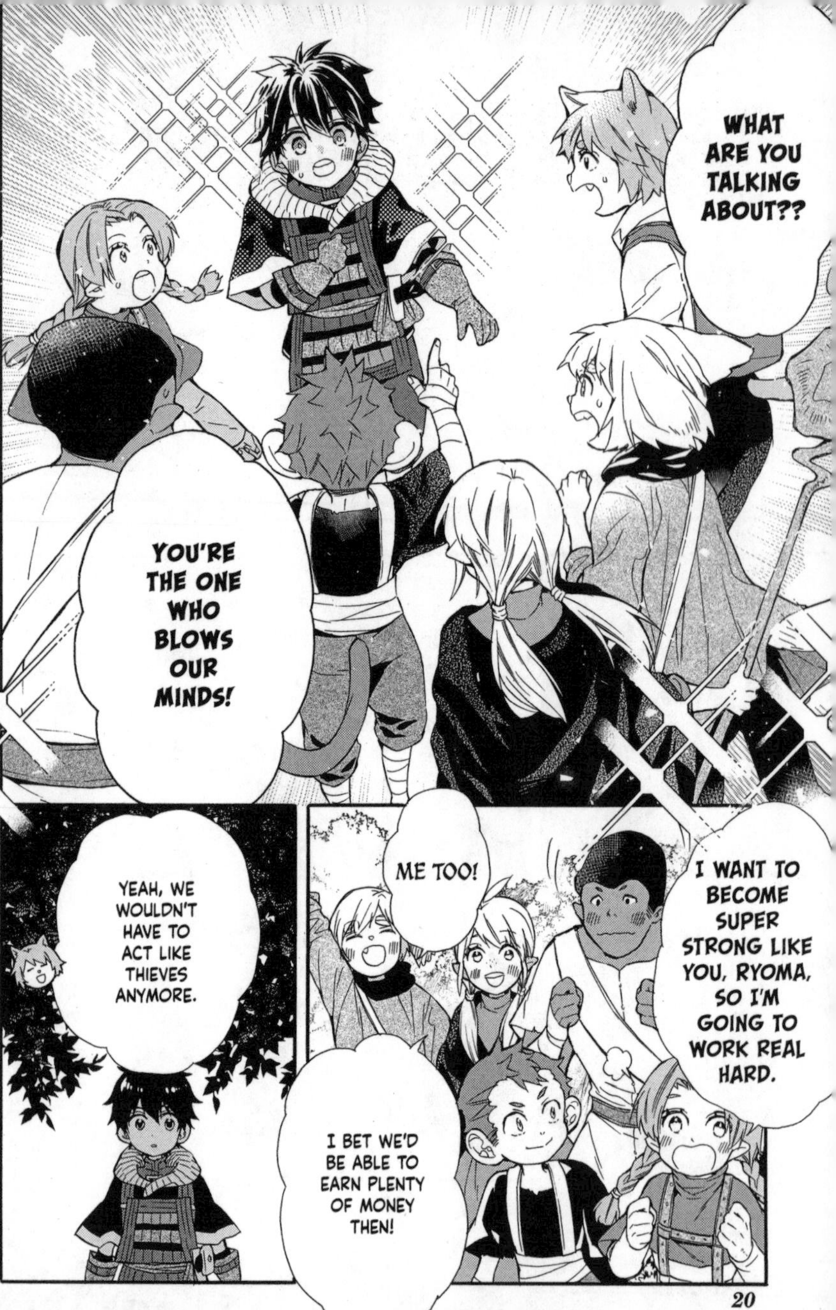
WHAT ARE YOU TALKING ABOUT??
YOU'RE THE ONE WHO BLOWS OUR MINDS!
I WANT TO BECOME SUPER STRONG LIKE YOU, RYOMA, SO I'M GOING TO WORK REAL HARD.
ME TOO!
I BET WE'D BE ABLE TO EARN PLENTY OF MONEY THEN!
YEAH, WE WOULDN'T HAVE TO ACT LIKE THIEVES ANYMORE.

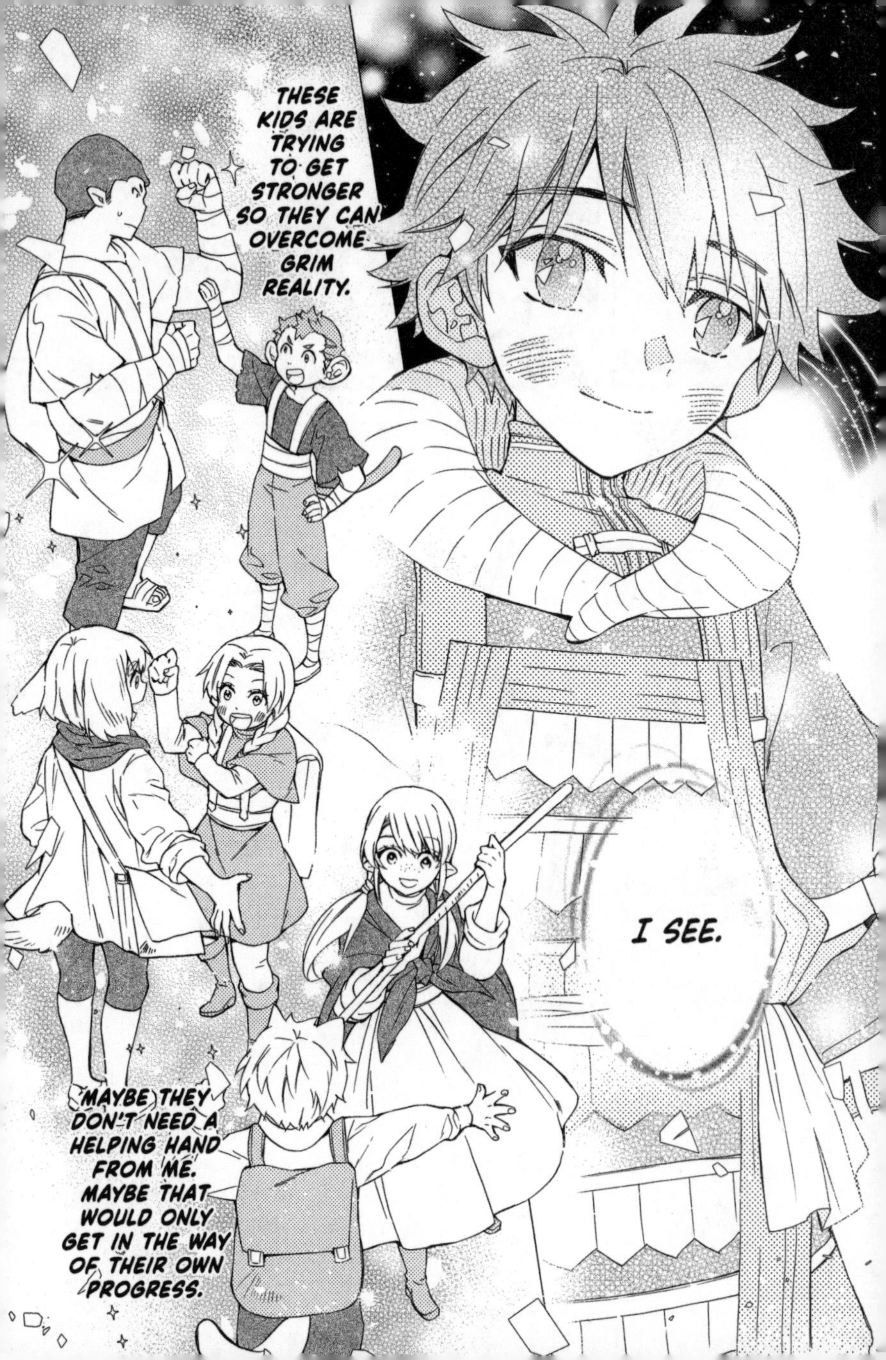
THESE KIDS ARE TRYING TO GET STRONGER SO THEY CAN OVERCOME GRIM REALITY.
I SEE.
MAYBE THEY DON'T NEED A HELPING HAND FROM ME. MAYBE THAT WOULD ONLY GET IN THE WAY OF THEIR OWN PROGRESS.

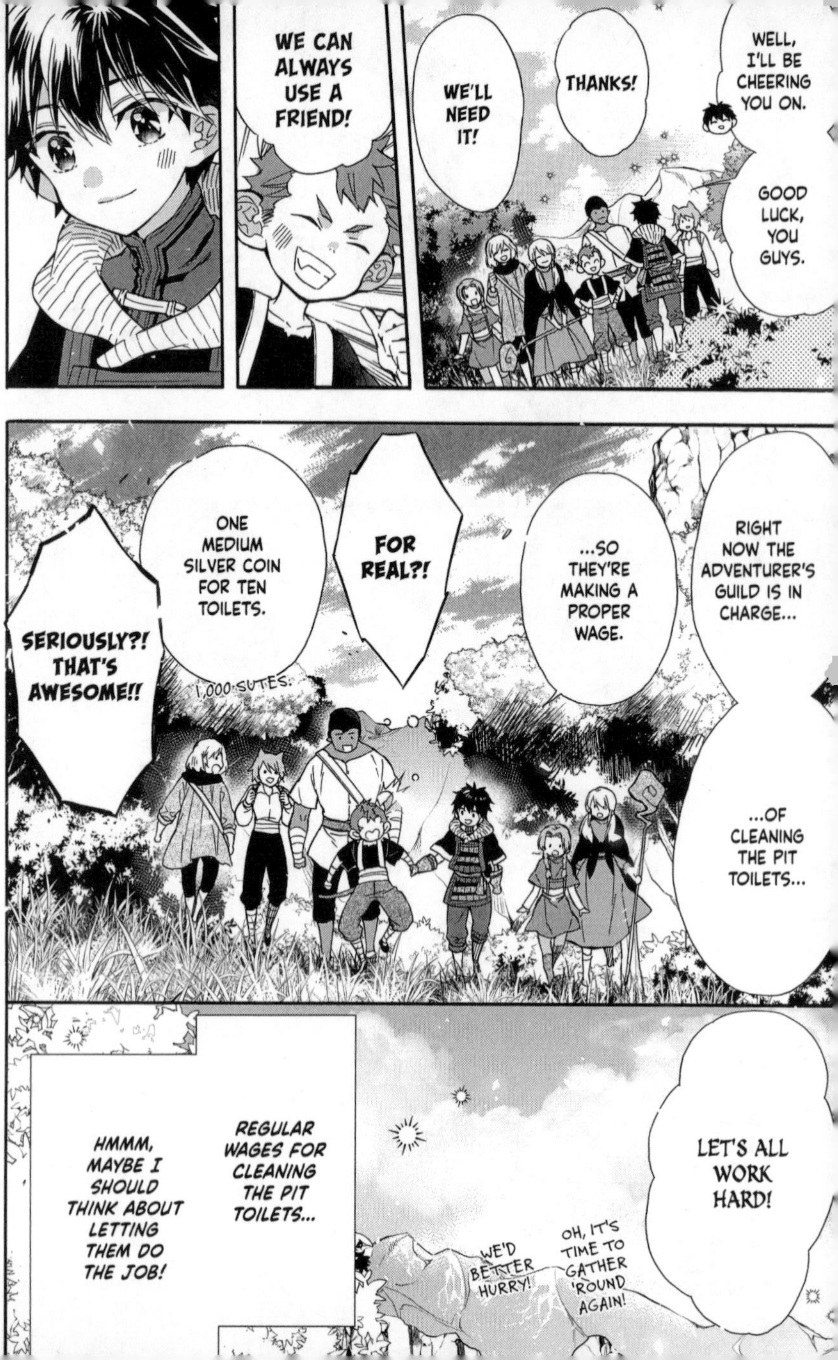

WELL, I'LL BE CHEERING YOU ON.
GOOD LUCK, YOU GUYS.
THANKS!
WE'LL NEED IT!
WE CAN ALWAYS USE A FRIEND!
RIGHT NOW THE ADVENTURER'S GUILD IS IN CHARGE...
...OF CLEANING THE PIT TOILETS...
...SO THEY'RE MAKING A PROPER WAGE.
FOR REAL?!
ONE MEDIUM SILVER COIN FOR TEN TOILETS.
1,000 SUTES.
SERIOUSLY?! THAT'S AWESOME!!
LET'S ALL WORK HARD!
OH, IT'S TIME TO GATHER 'ROUND AGAIN!
WE'D BETTER HURRY!
REGULAR WAGES FOR CLEANING THE PIT TOILETS...
HMMM, MAYBE I SHOULD THINK ABOUT LETTING THEM DO THE JOB!

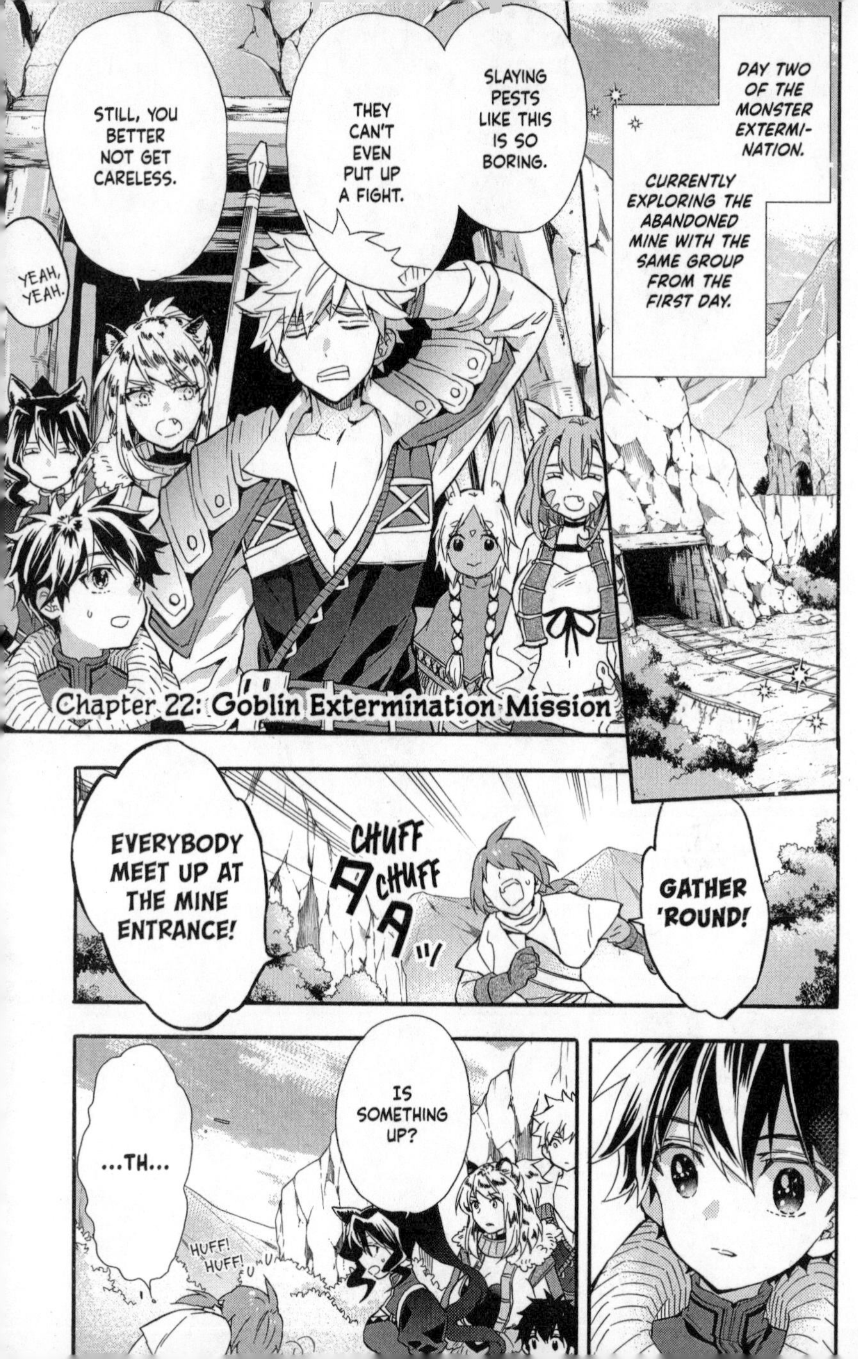
DAY TWO OF THE MONSTER EXTERMI-NATION.
CURRENTLY EXPLORING THE ABANDONED MINE WITH THE SAME GROUP FROM THE FIRST DAY.
SLAYING PESTS LIKE THIS IS SO BORING.
THEY CAN'T EVEN PUT UP A FIGHT.
STILL, YOU BETTER NOT GET CARELESS.
YEAH, YEAH.
Chapter 22: Goblin Extermination Mission
GATHER 'ROUND!
CHUFF CHUFF
EVERYBODY MEET UP AT THE MINE ENTRANCE!
IS SOMETHING UP?
...TH...
HUFF! HUFF!

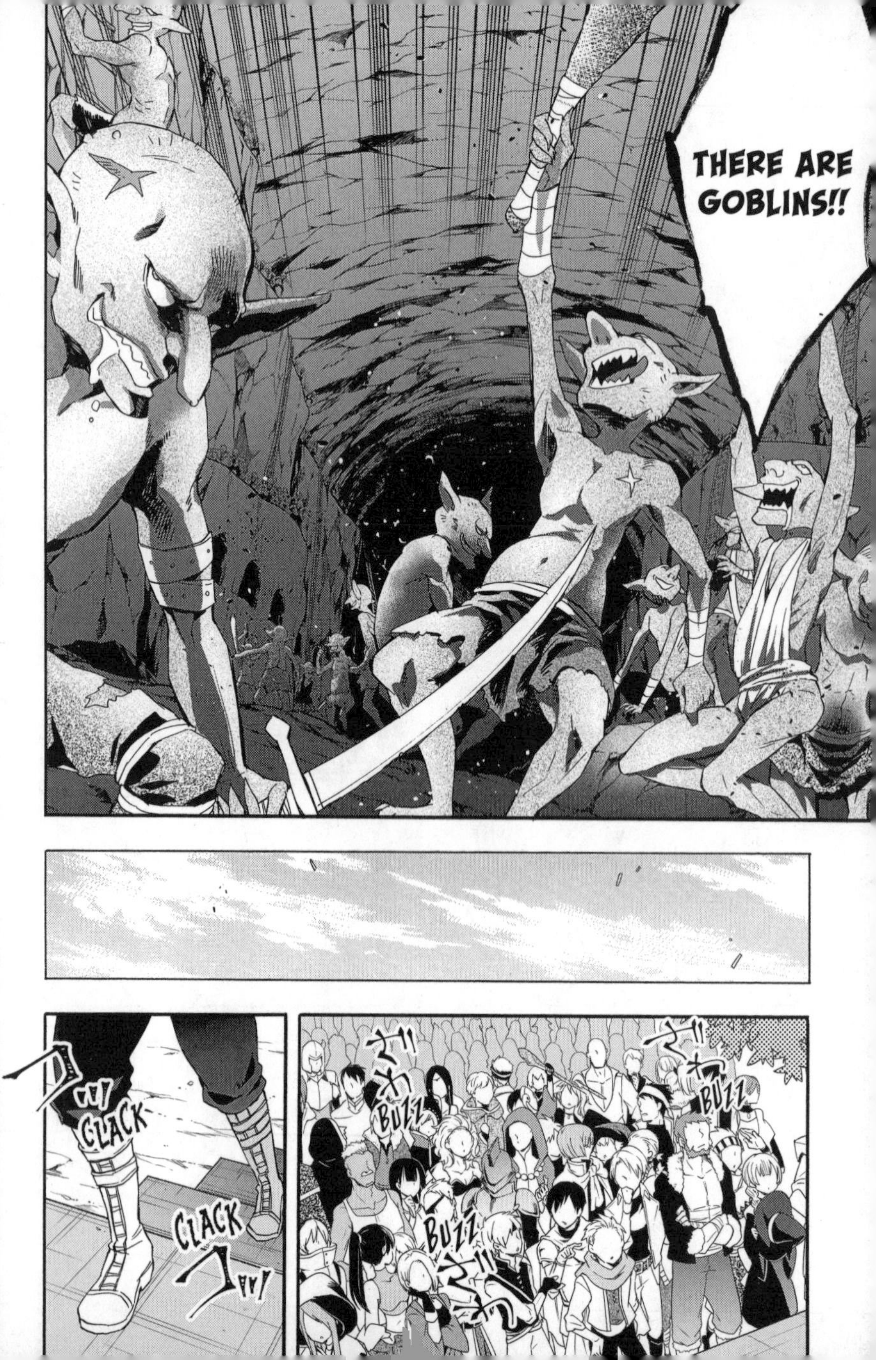
THERE ARE GOBLINS!!
BUZZ
BUZZ
BUZZ
CLACK
CLACK

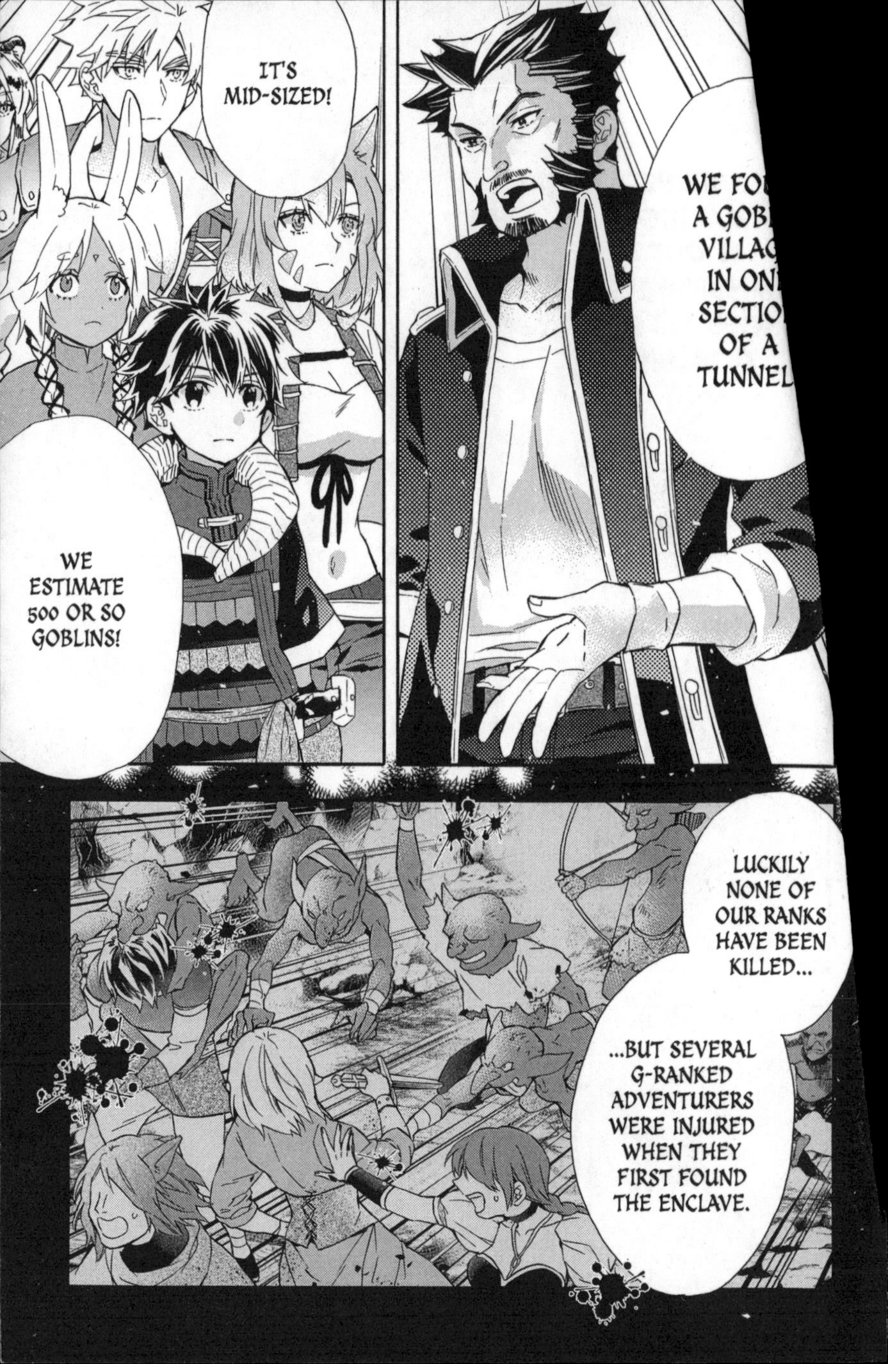
WE FO A GOB VILLAG IN ON SECTIO OF A TUNNEL
IT'S MID-SIZED!
WE ESTIMATE 500 OR SO GOBLINS!
LUCKILY NONE OF OUR RANKS HAVE BEEN KILLED...
...BUT SEVERAL G-RANKED ADVENTURERS WERE INJURED WHEN THEY FIRST FOUND THE ENCLAVE.

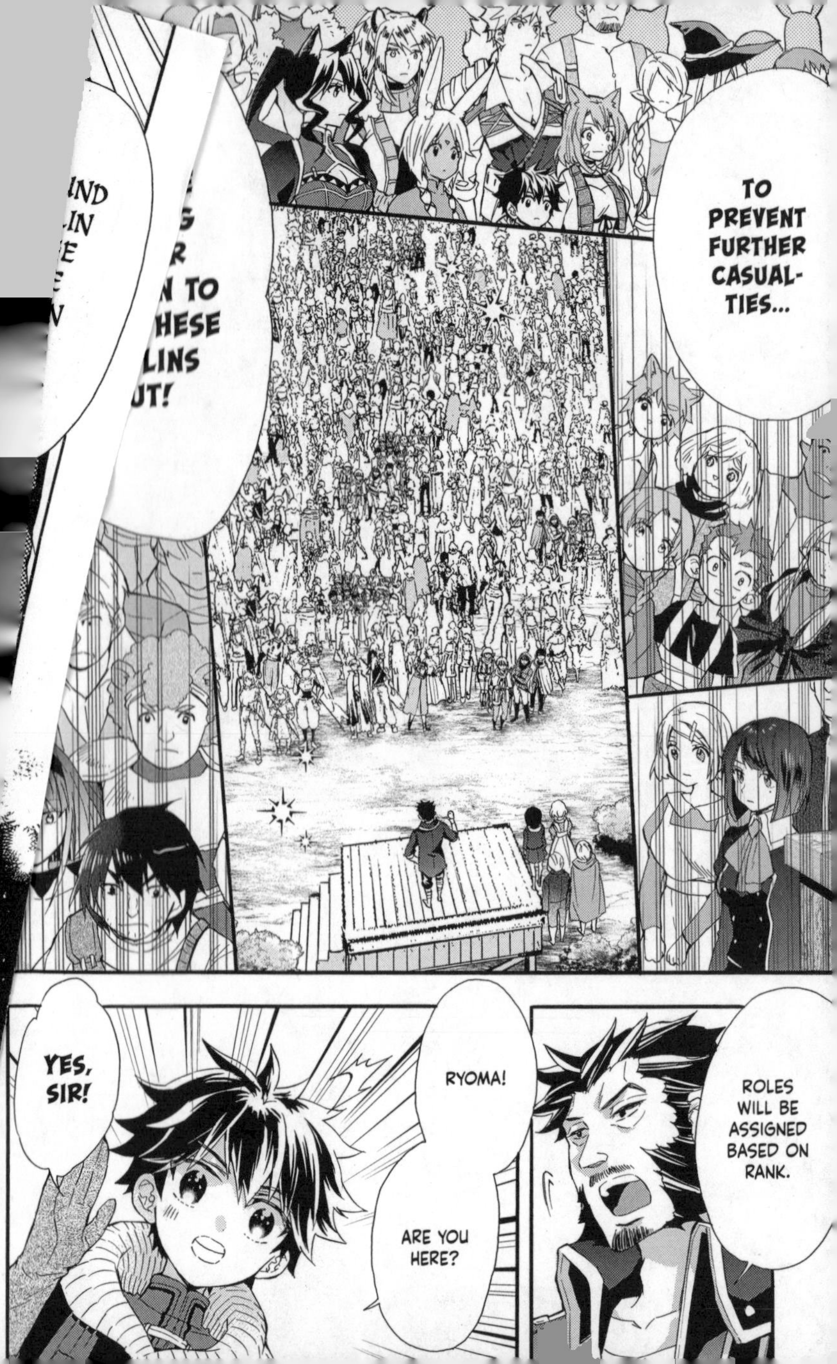
TO PREVENT FURTHER CASUAL-TIES...
ROLES WILL BE ASSIGNED BASED ON RANK.
RYOMA!
ARE YOU HERE?
YES, SIR!

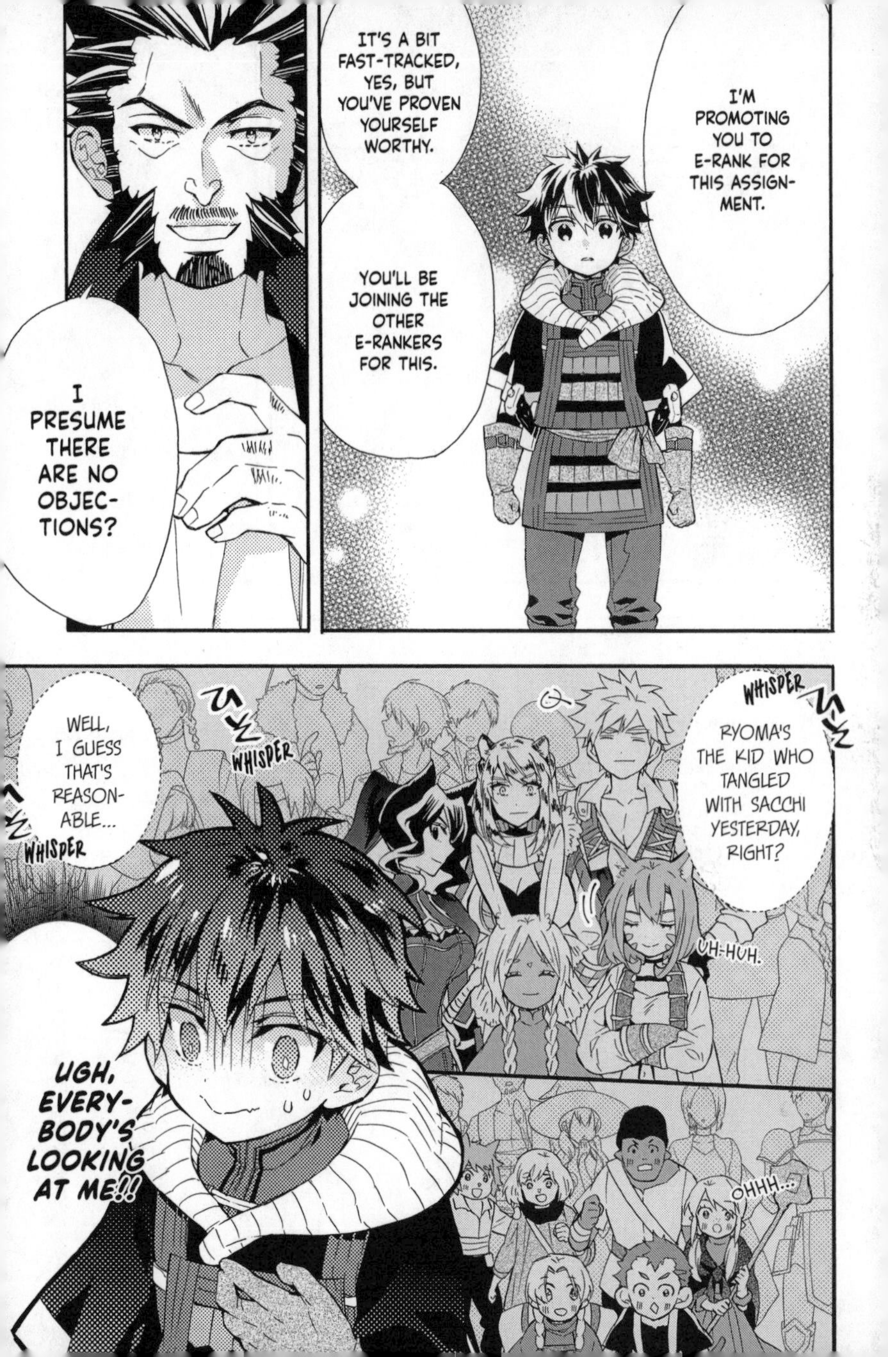
I'M PROMOTING YOU TO E-RANK FOR THIS ASSIGNMENT.
IT'S A BIT FAST-TRACKED, YES, BUT YOU'VE PROVEN YOURSELF WORTHY.
YOU'LL BE JOINING THE OTHER E-RANKERS FOR THIS.
I PRESUME THERE ARE NO OBJECTIONS?
WHISPER
RYOMA'S THE KID WHO TANGLED WITH SACCHI YESTERDAY, RIGHT?
UH-HUH.
WHISPER
WELL, I GUESS THAT'S REASONABLE...
WHISPER
UGH, EVERYBODY'S LOOKING AT ME!!
OHHH...

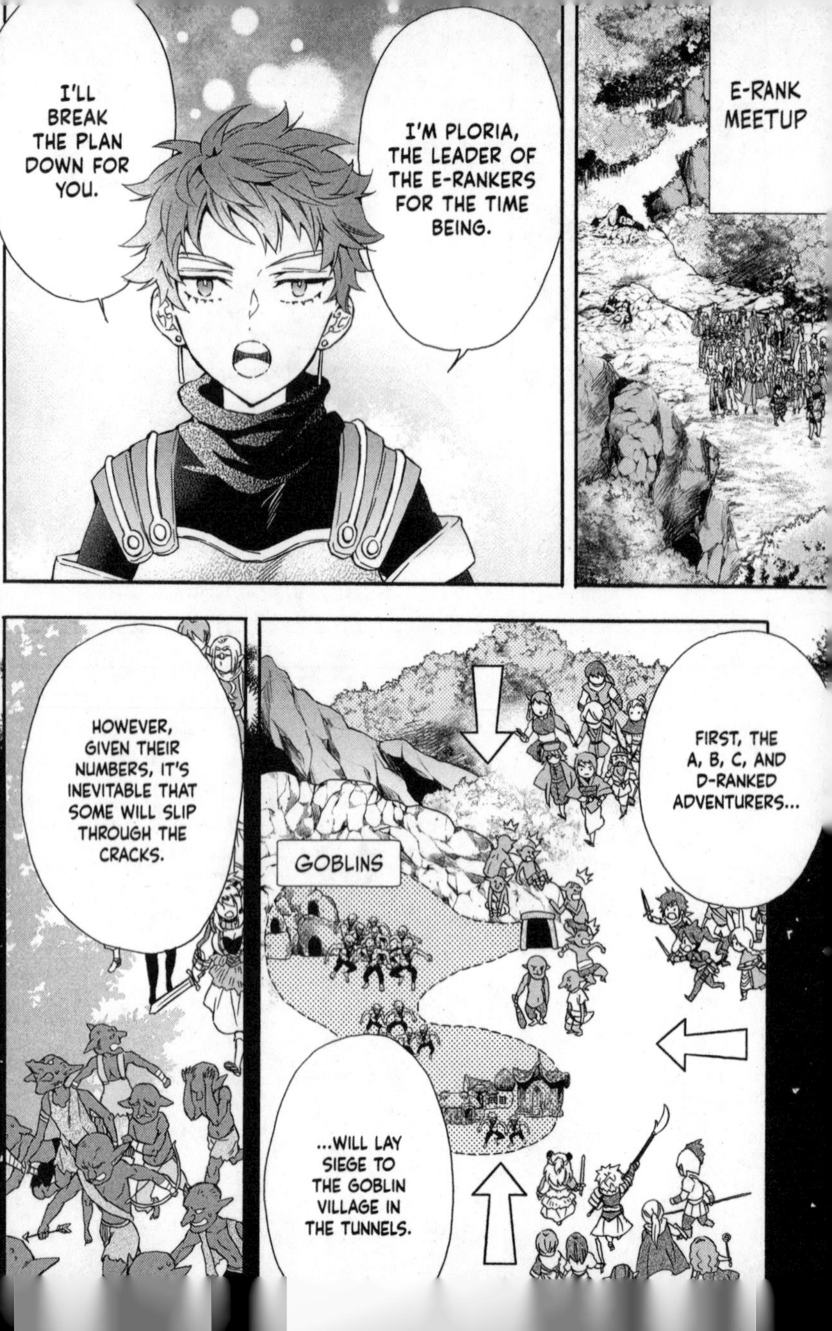
E-RANK MEETUP
I'M PLORIA, THE LEADER OF THE E-RANKERS FOR THE TIME BEING.
I'LL BREAK THE PLAN DOWN FOR YOU.
FIRST, THE A, B, C, AND D-RANKED ADVENTURERS...
GOBLINS
...WILL LAY SIEGE TO THE GOBLIN VILLAGE IN THE TUNNELS.
HOWEVER, GIVEN THEIR NUMBERS, IT'S INEVITABLE THAT SOME WILL SLIP THROUGH THE CRACKS.

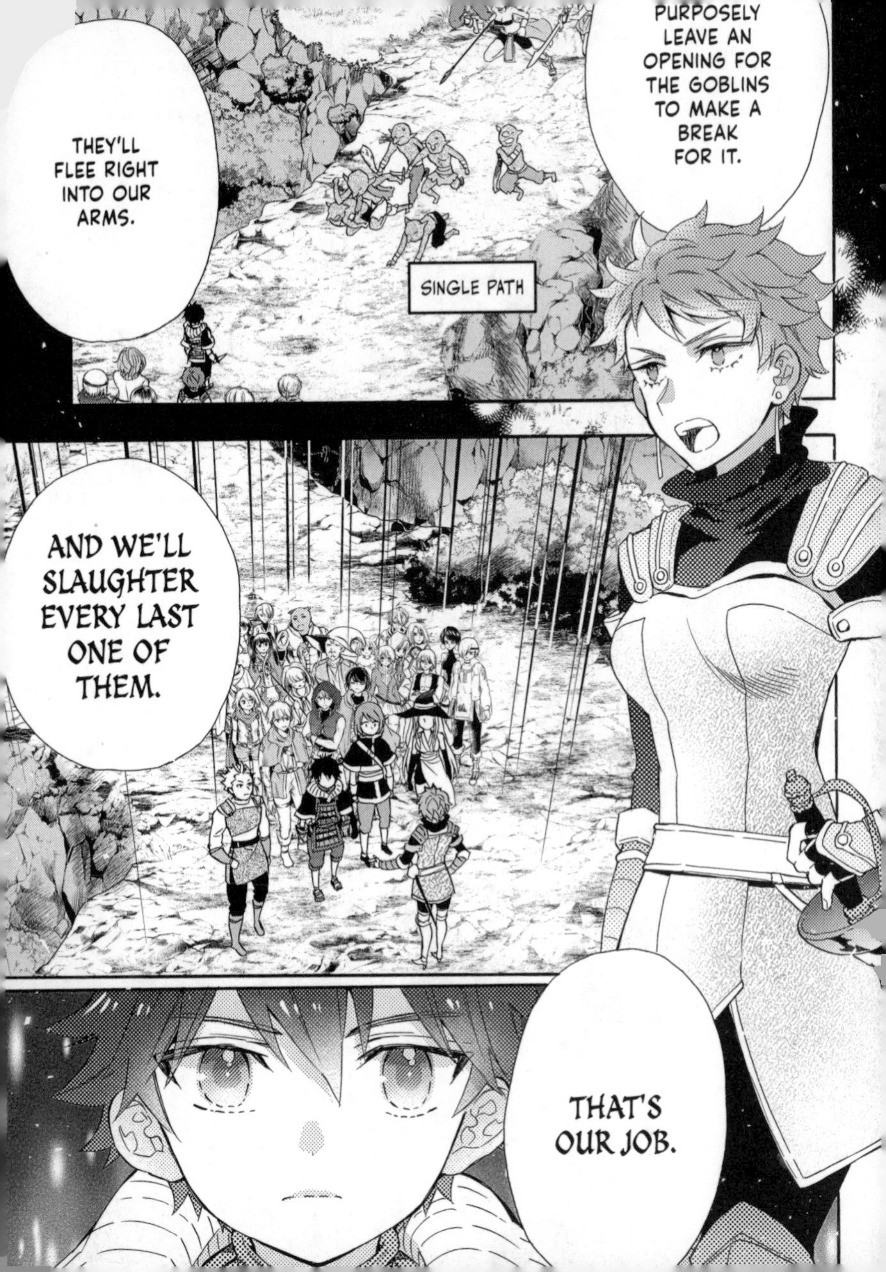
PURPOSELY LEAVE AN OPENING FOR THE GOBLINS TO MAKE A BREAK FOR IT.
THEY'LL FLEE RIGHT INTO OUR ARMS.
SINGLE PATH
AND WE'LL SLAUGHTER EVERY LAST ONE OF THEM.
THAT'S OUR JOB.

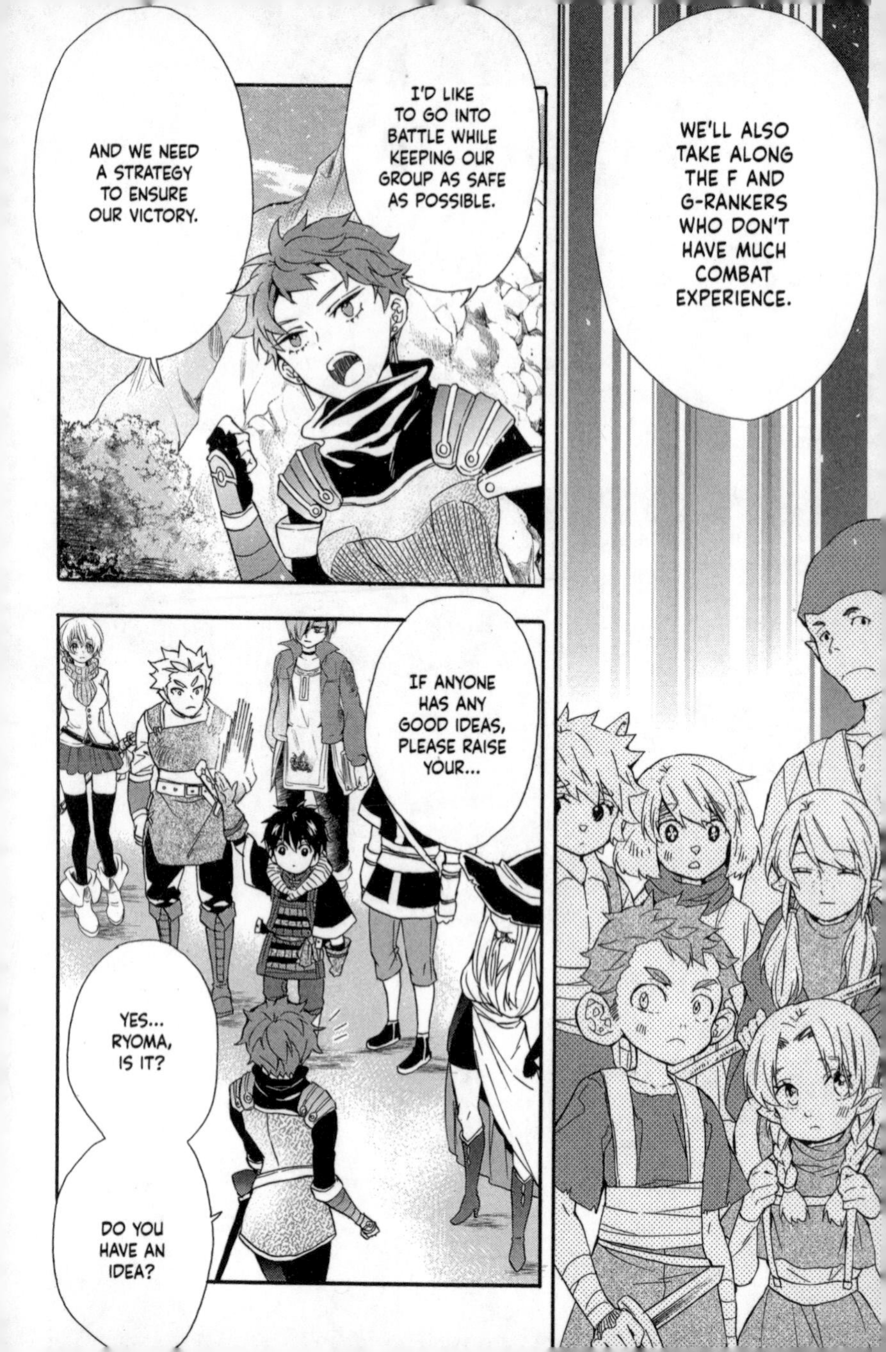
WE'LL ALSO TAKE ALONG THE F AND G-RANKERS WHO DON'T HAVE MUCH COMBAT EXPERIENCE.
I'D LIKE TO GO INTO BATTLE WHILE KEEPING OUR GROUP AS SAFE AS POSSIBLE.
AND WE NEED A STRATEGY TO ENSURE OUR VICTORY.
IF ANYONE HAS ANY GOOD IDEAS, PLEASE RAISE YOUR...
YES... RYOMA, IS IT?
DO YOU HAVE AN IDEA?

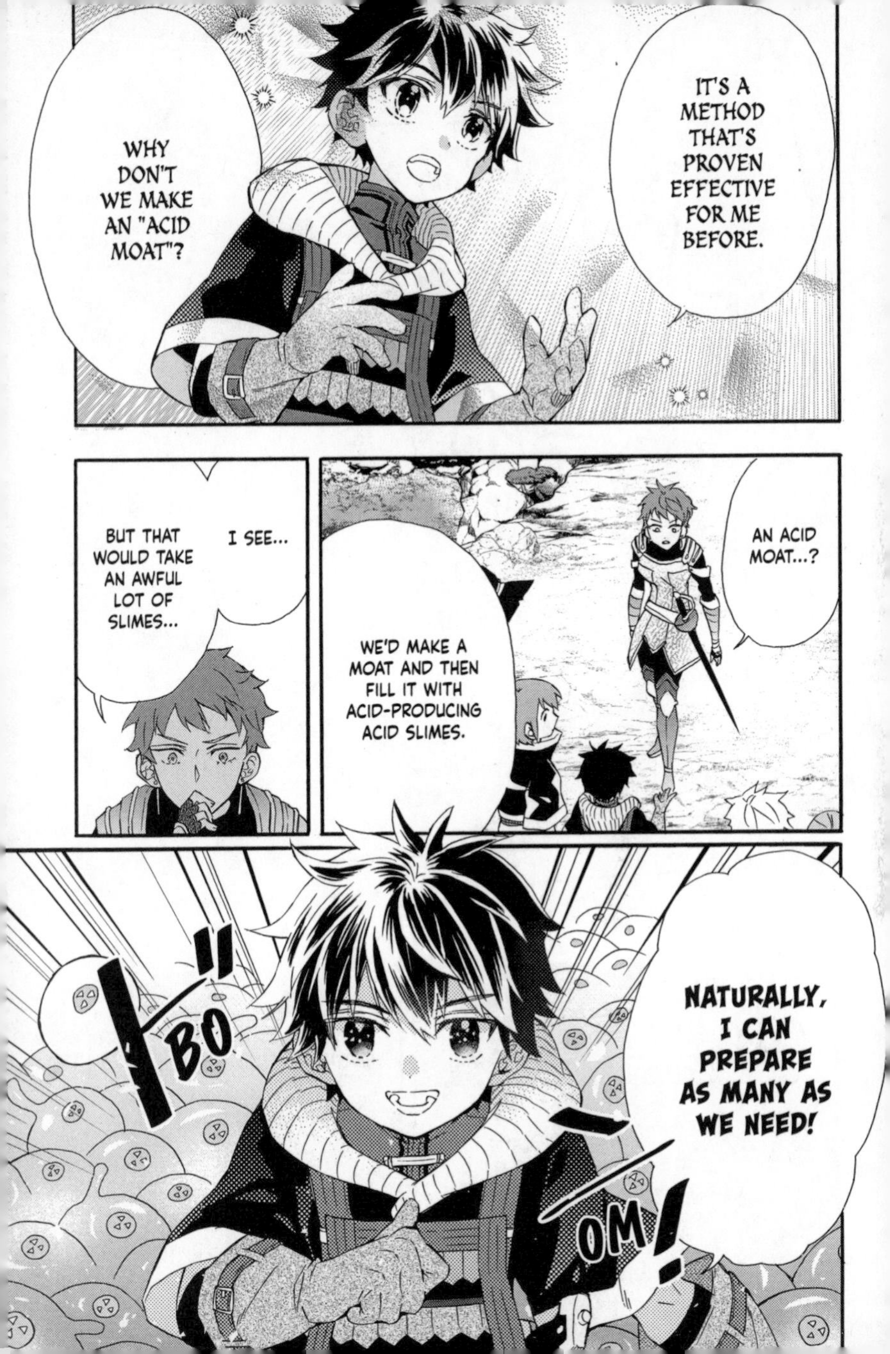
IT'S A METHOD THAT'S PROVEN EFFECTIVE FOR ME BEFORE.
WHY DON'T WE MAKE AN "ACID MOAT"?
AN ACID MOAT...?
WE'D MAKE A MOAT AND THEN FILL IT WITH ACID-PRODUCING ACID SLIMES.
I SEE...
BUT THAT WOULD TAKE AN AWFUL LOT OF SLIMES...
NATURALLY, I CAN PREPARE AS MANY AS WE NEED!
BO
OM!

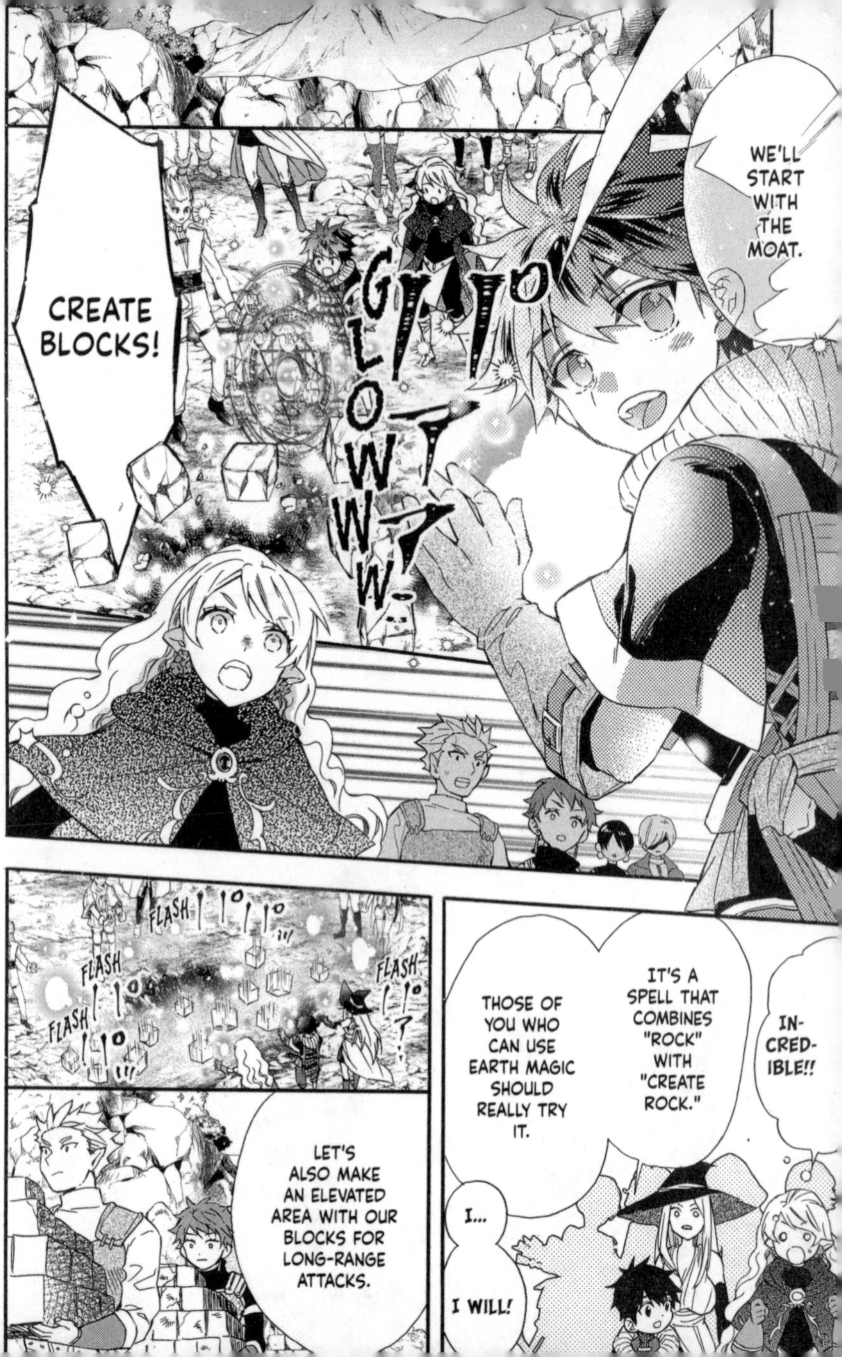
WE'LL START WITH THE MOAT.
CREATE BLOCKS!
GLOWWW
INCRED-IBLE!!
IT'S A SPELL THAT COMBINES "ROCK" WITH "CREATE ROCK."
THOSE OF YOU WHO CAN USE EARTH MAGIC SHOULD REALLY TRY IT.
I...
I WILL!
FLASH
FLASH
FLASH
FLASH
LET'S ALSO MAKE AN ELEVATED AREA WITH OUR BLOCKS FOR LONG-RANGE ATTACKS.

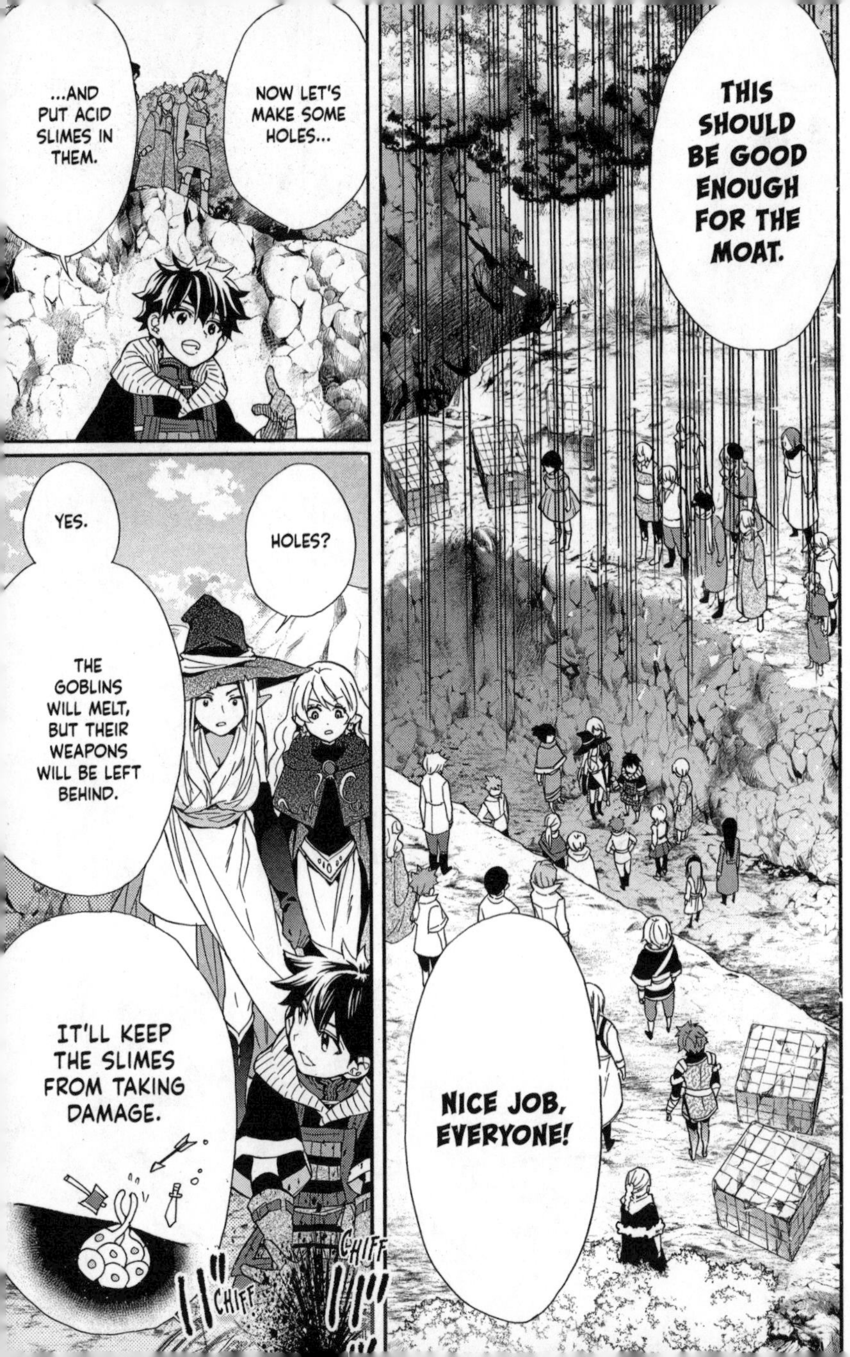
THIS SHOULD BE GOOD ENOUGH FOR THE MOAT.
NICE JOB, EVERYONE!
NOW LET'S MAKE SOME HOLES...
...AND PUT ACID SLIMES IN THEM.
HOLES?
YES.
THE GOBLINS WILL MELT, BUT THEIR WEAPONS WILL BE LEFT BEHIND.
IT'LL KEEP THE SLIMES FROM TAKING DAMAGE.
CHIFF
CHIFF

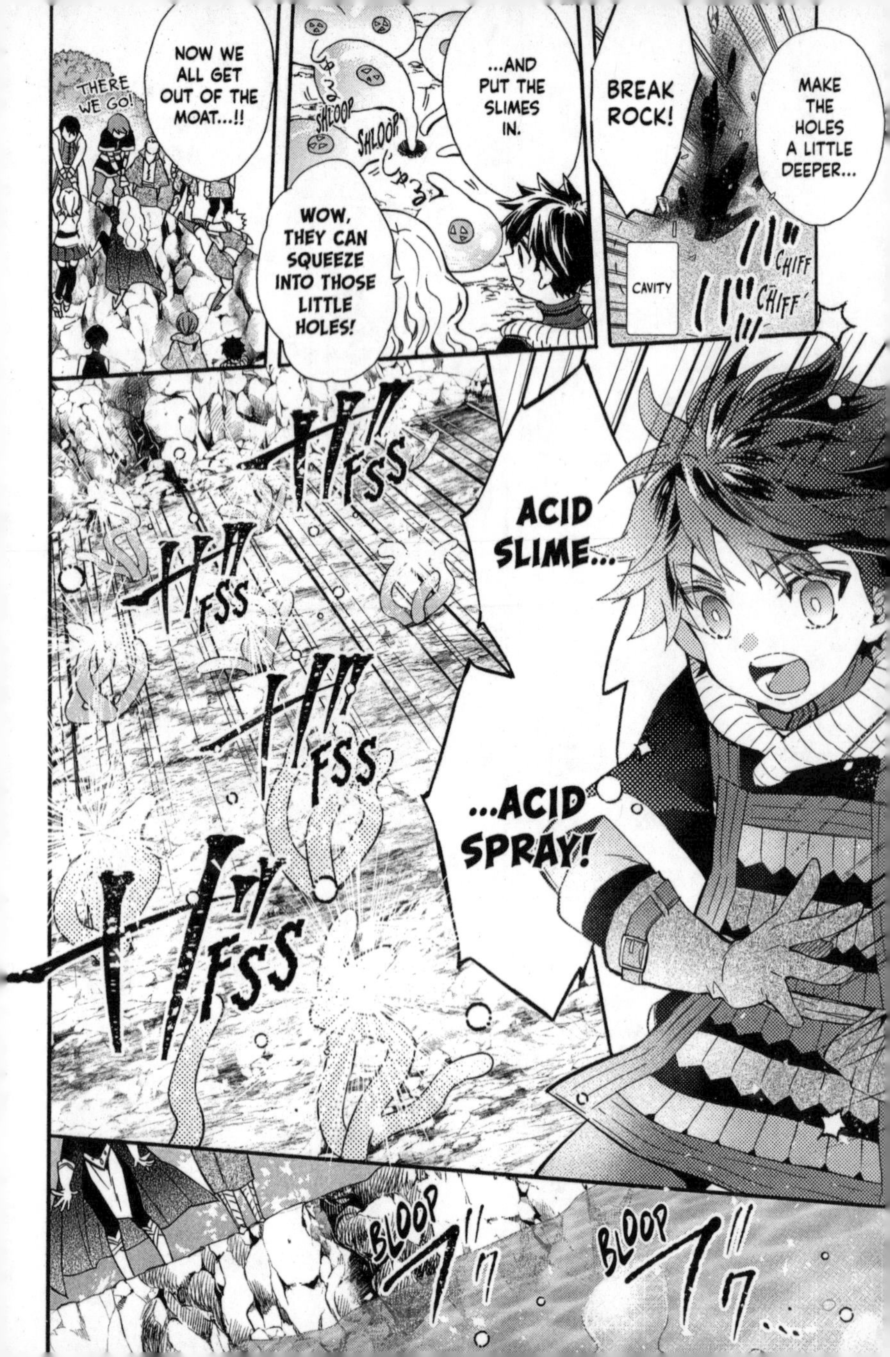
MAKE THE HOLES A LITTLE DEEPER...
BREAK ROCK!
CAVITY
CHIFF
CHIFF
...AND PUT THE SLIMES IN.
SHLOOP
SHLOOP
WOW, THEY CAN SQUEEZE INTO THOSE LITTLE HOLES!
NOW WE ALL GET OUT OF THE MOAT...!!
THERE WE GO!
ACID SLIME...
...ACID SPRAY!
FSS
FSS
FSS
FSS
BLOOP
BLOOP

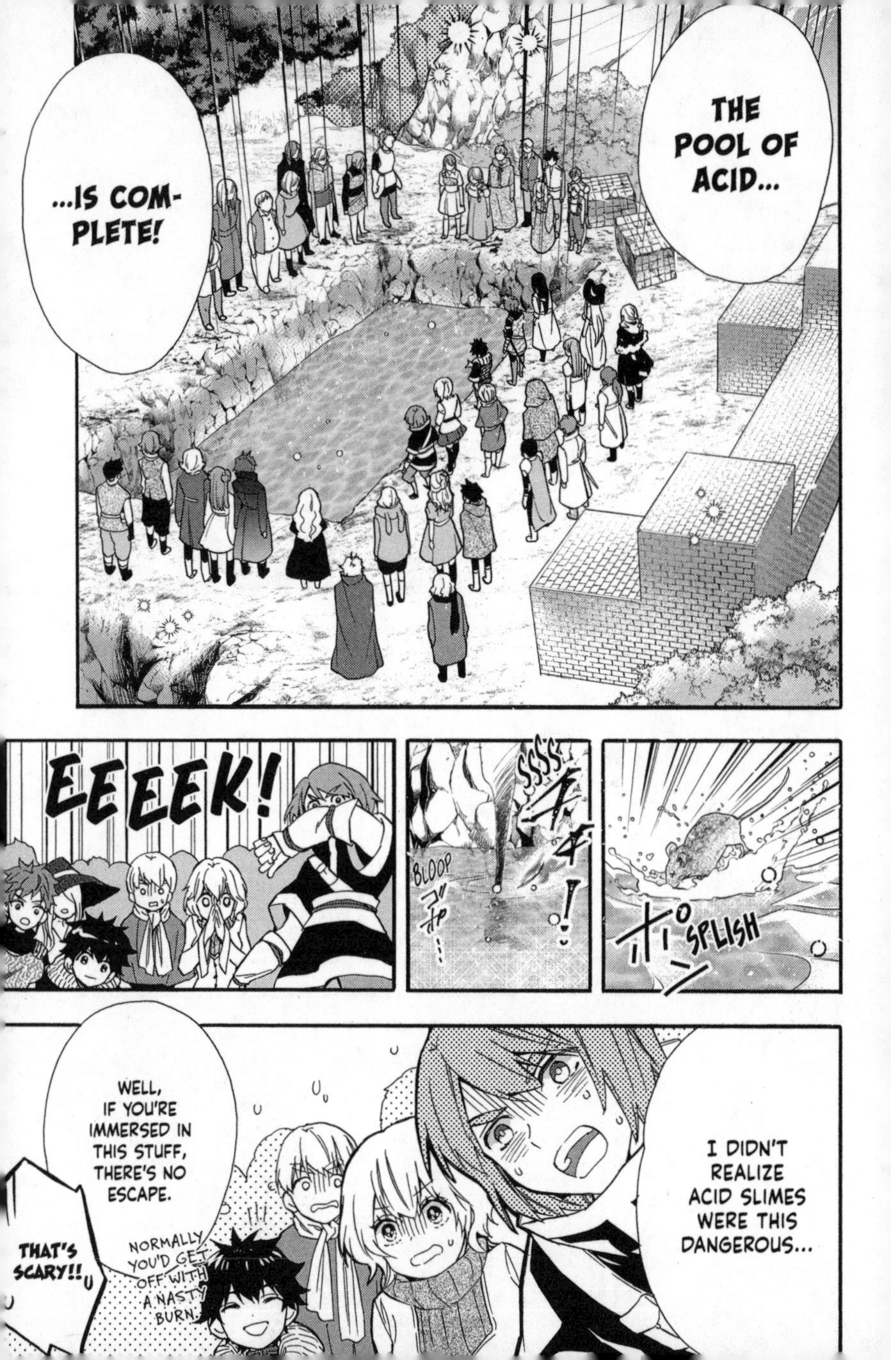

THE POOL OF ACID...
...IS COMPLETE!
SPLISH
BLOOP
EEEEK!
I DIDN'T REALIZE ACID SLIMES WERE THIS DANGEROUS...
WELL, IF YOU'RE IMMERSED IN THIS STUFF, THERE'S NO ESCAPE.
NORMALLY YOU'D GET OFF WITH A NASTY BURN.
THAT'S SCARY!!

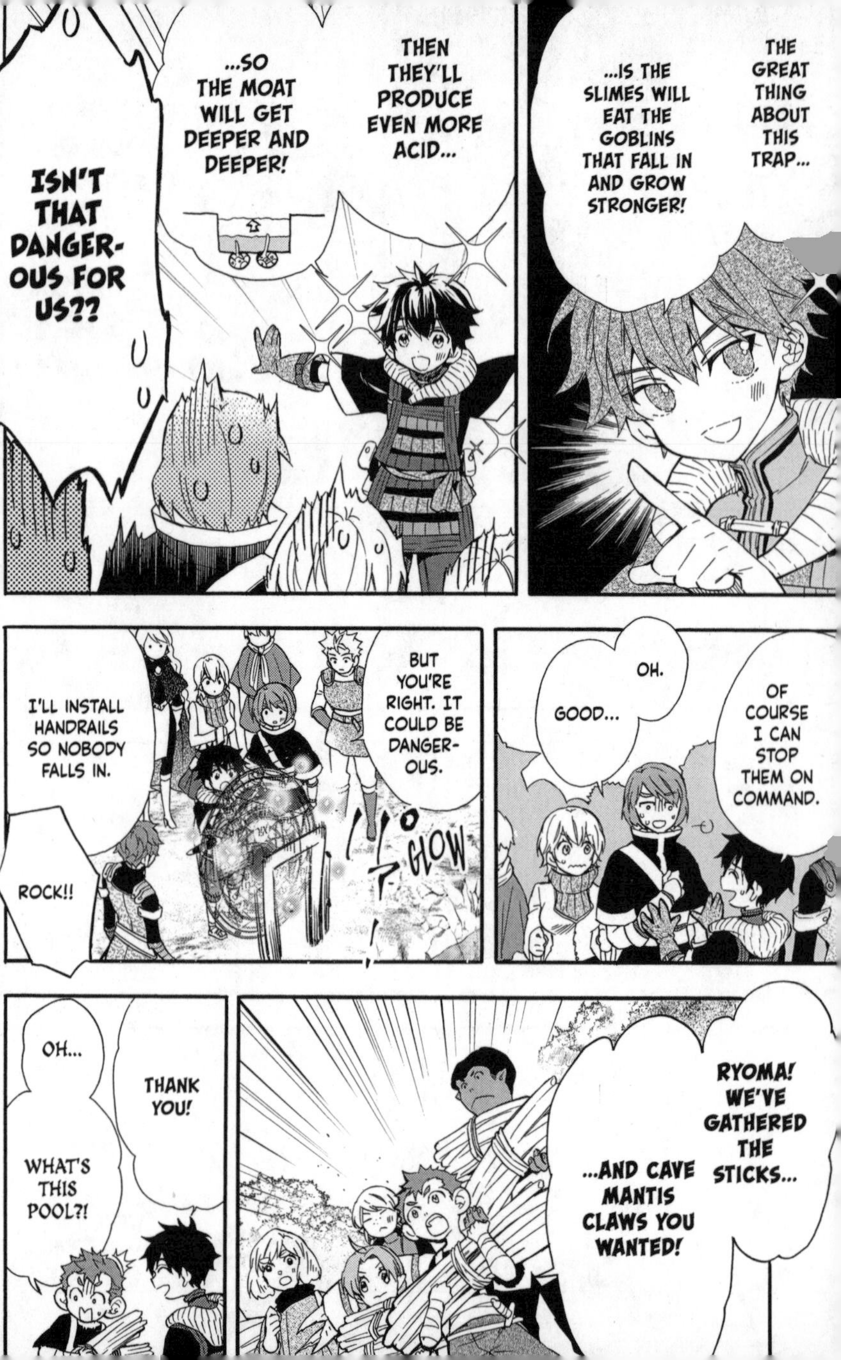
THE GREAT THING ABOUT THIS TRAP...
...IS THE SLIMES WILL EAT THE GOBLINS THAT FALL IN AND GROW STRONGER!
THEN THEY'LL PRODUCE EVEN MORE ACID...
...SO THE MOAT WILL GET DEEPER AND DEEPER!
ISN'T THAT DANGER-OUS FOR US??
OF COURSE I CAN STOP THEM ON COMMAND.
OH.
GOOD...
BUT YOU'RE RIGHT. IT COULD BE DANGER-OUS.
I'LL INSTALL HANDRAILS SO NOBODY FALLS IN.
ROCK!!
GLOW
RYOMA! WE'VE GATHERED THE STICKS...
...AND CAVE MANTIS CLAWS YOU WANTED!
THANK YOU!
OH...
WHAT'S THIS POOL?!

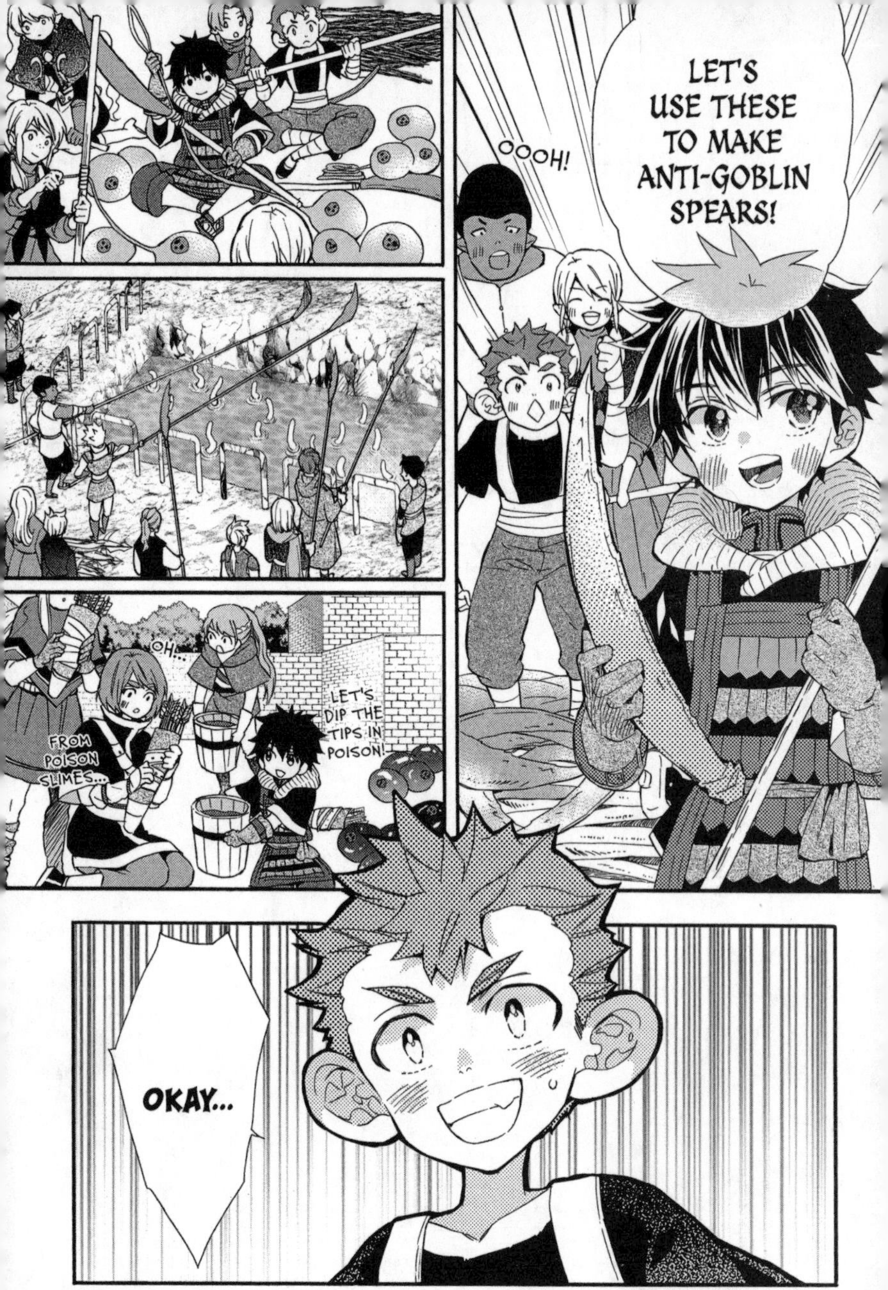
LET'S USE THESE TO MAKE ANTI-GOBLIN SPEARS!
OOOH!
LET'S DIP THE TIPS IN POISON!
OH...
FROM POISON SLIMES...
OKAY...

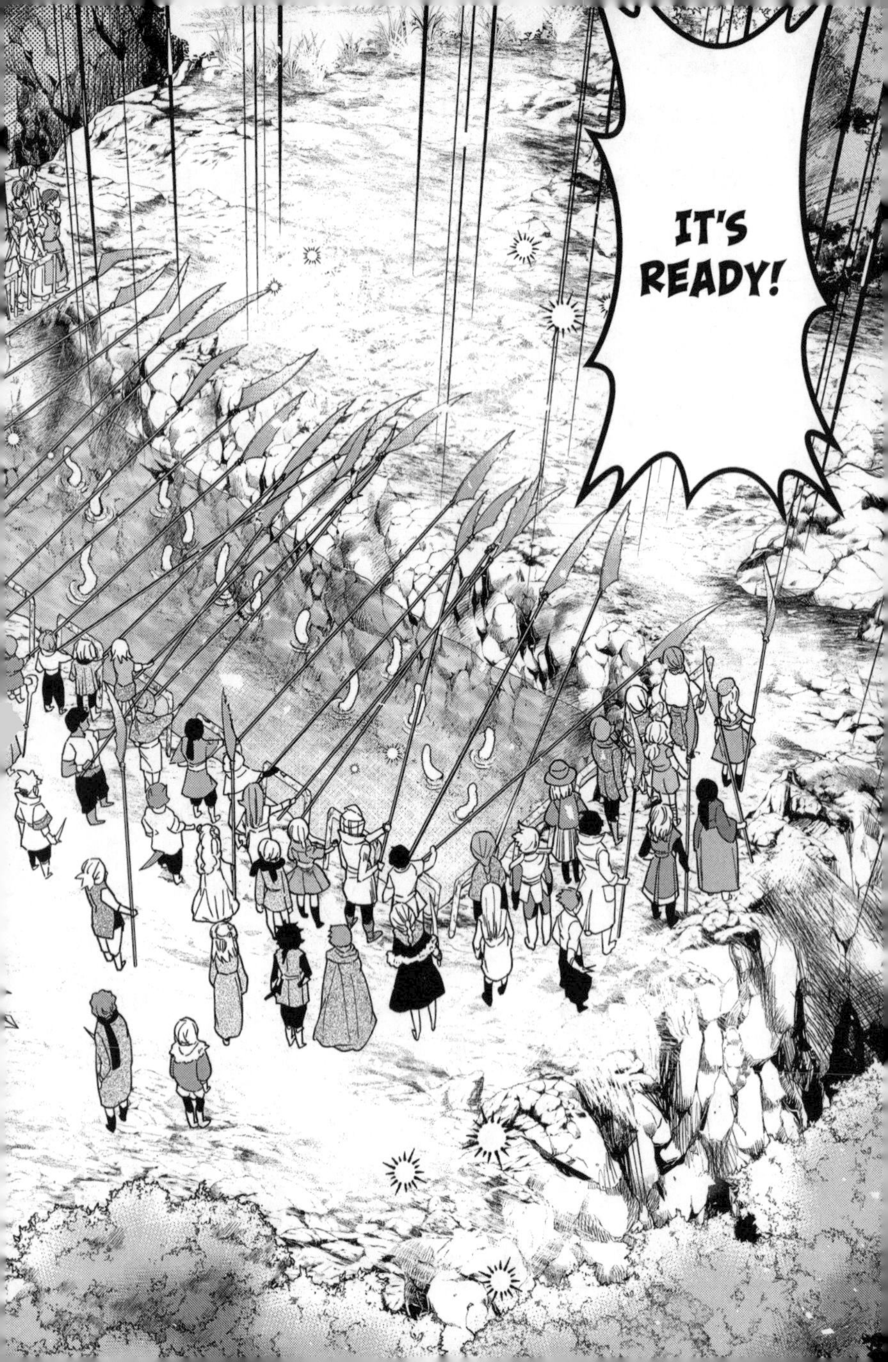
IT'S READY!

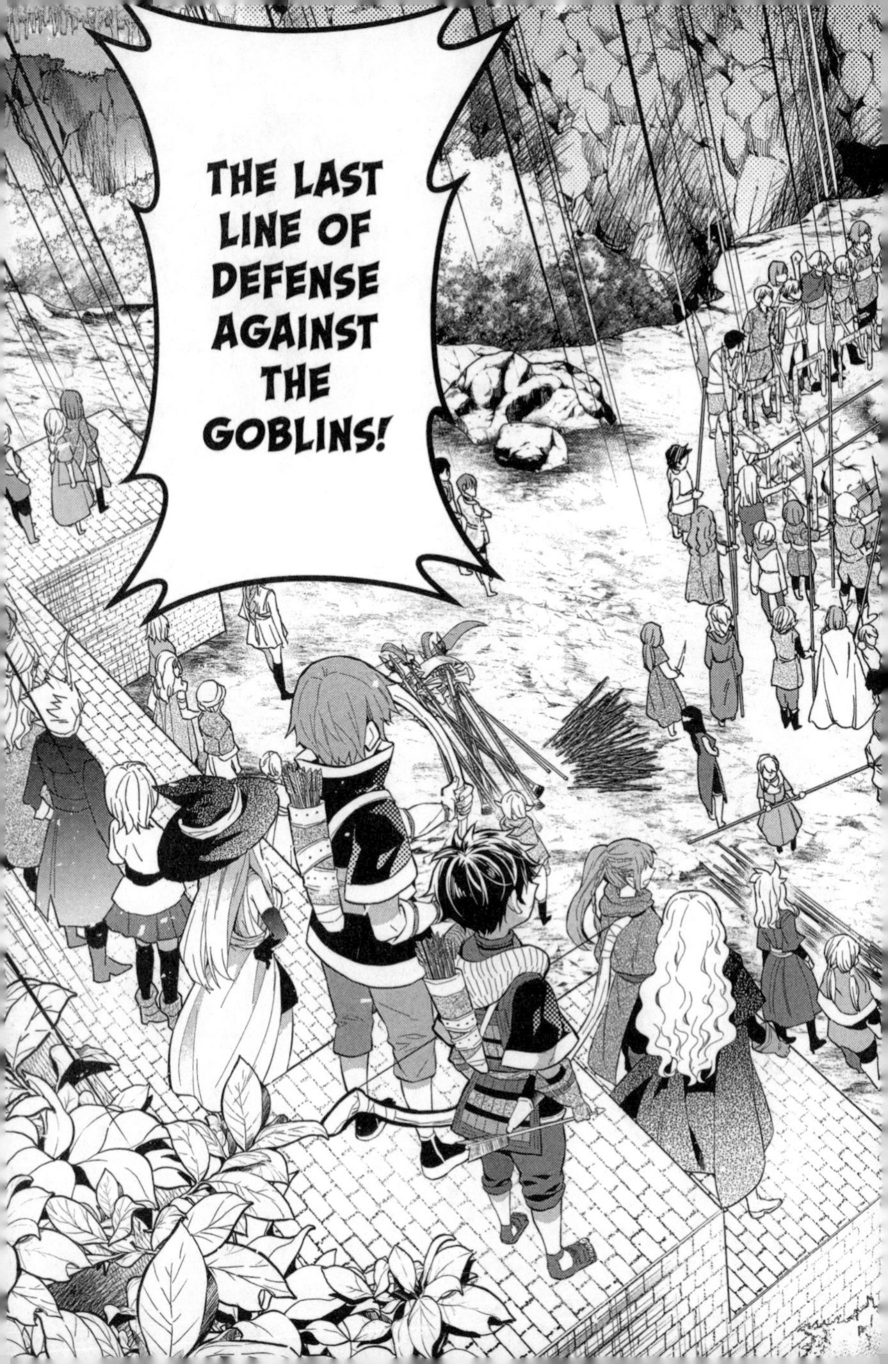
THE LAST LINE OF DEFENSE AGAINST THE GOBLINS!

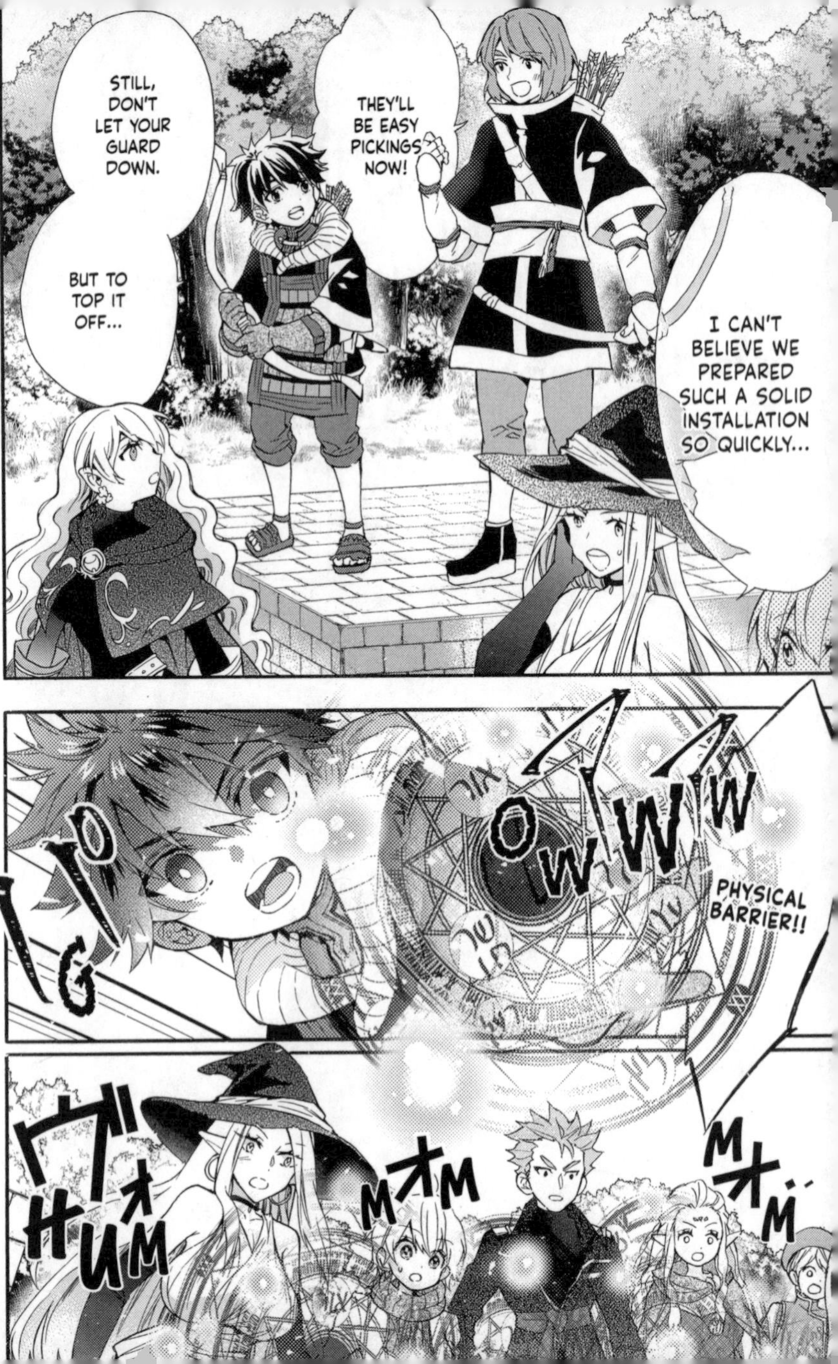
I CAN'T BELIEVE WE PREPARED SUCH A SOLID INSTALLATION SO QUICKLY...
THEY'LL BE EASY PICKINGS NOW!
STILL, DON'T LET YOUR GUARD DOWN.
BUT TO TOP IT OFF...
PHYSICAL BARRIER!!
MM
MM
HUM

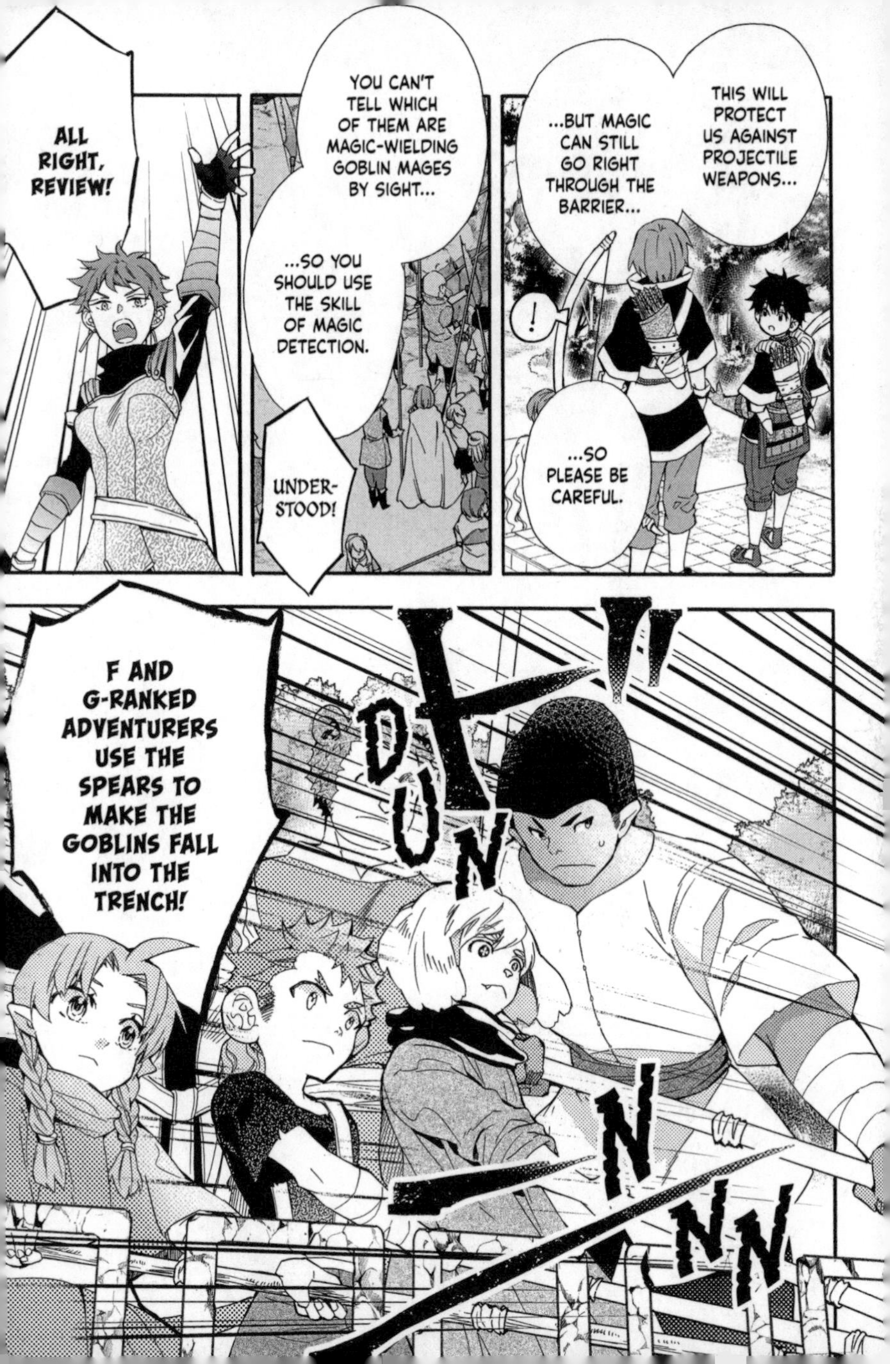

THIS WILL PROTECT US AGAINST PROJECTILE WEAPONS...
...BUT MAGIC CAN STILL GO RIGHT THROUGH THE BARRIER...
!
...SO PLEASE BE CAREFUL.
YOU CAN'T TELL WHICH OF THEM ARE MAGIC-WIELDING GOBLIN MAGES BY SIGHT...
...SO YOU SHOULD USE THE SKILL OF MAGIC DETECTION.
UNDER-STOOD!
ALL RIGHT, REVIEW!
DUNNNN
F AND G-RANKED ADVENTURERS USE THE SPEARS TO MAKE THE GOBLINS FALL INTO THE TRENCH!

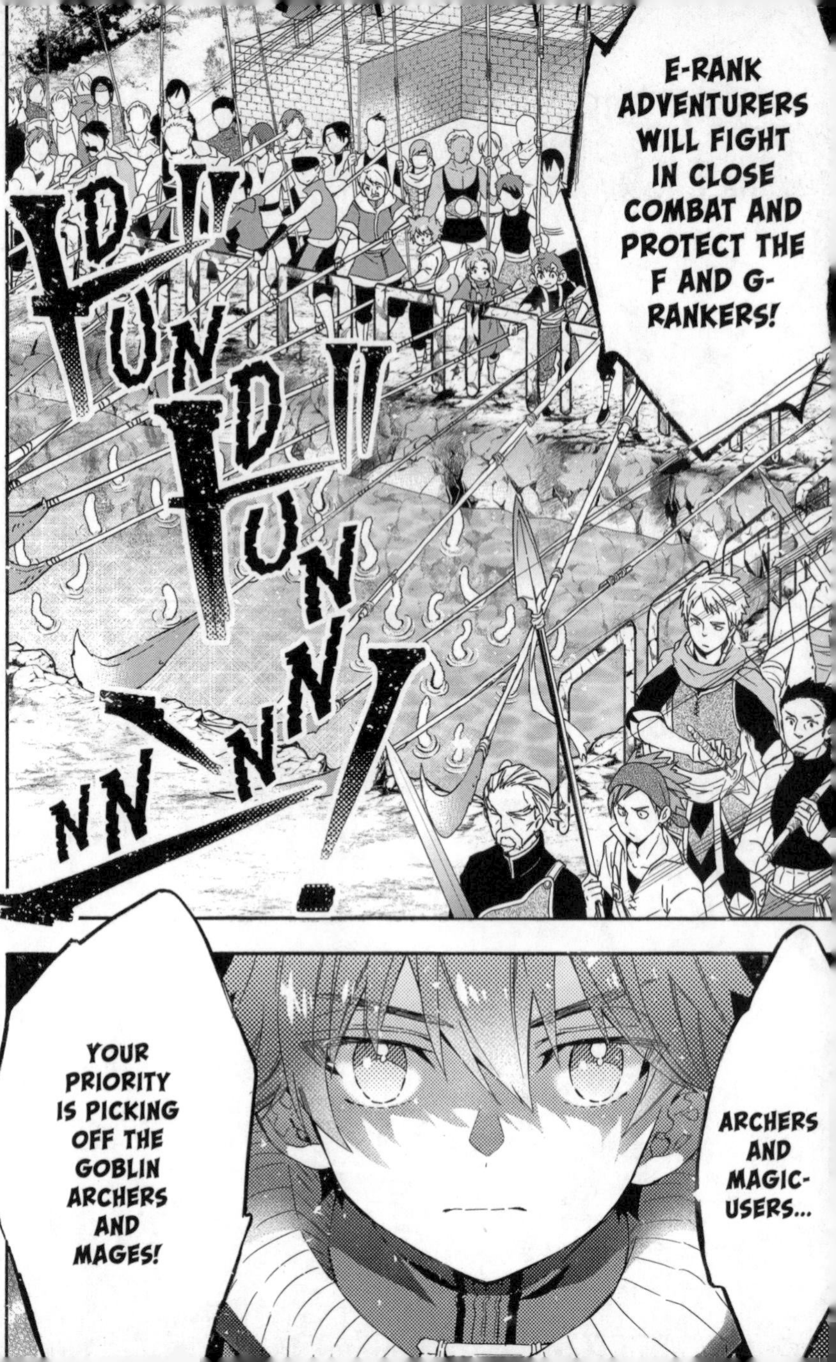
E-RANK ADVENTURERS WILL FIGHT IN CLOSE COMBAT AND PROTECT THE F AND G-RANKERS!
DUN DUN DUNNNN...
ARCHERS AND MAGIC-USERS...
YOUR PRIORITY IS PICKING OFF THE GOBLIN ARCHERS AND MAGES!

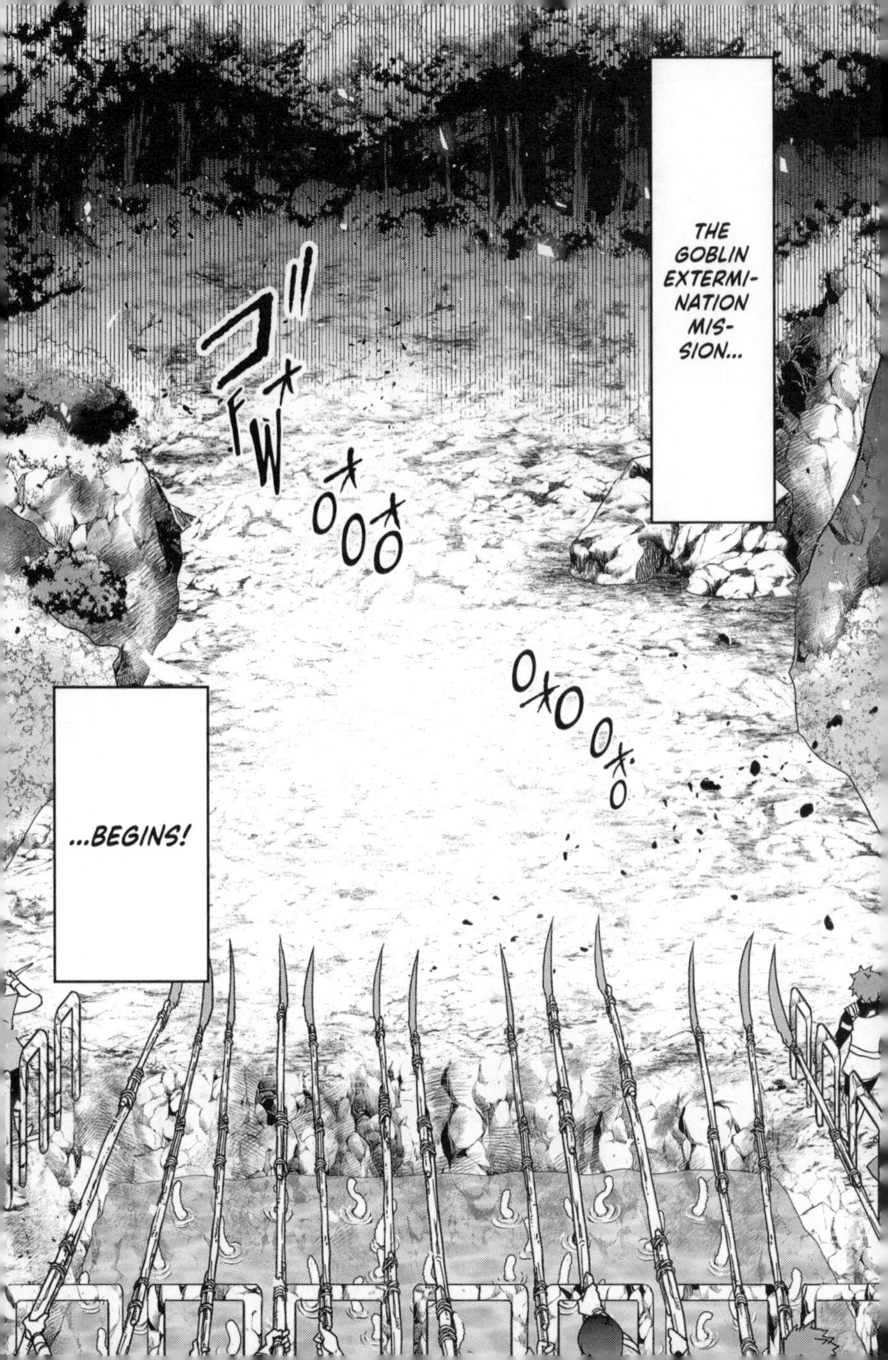
THE GOBLIN EXTERMI-NATION MIS-SION...
...BEGINS!

BY THE
GRACE
OF THE
GODS

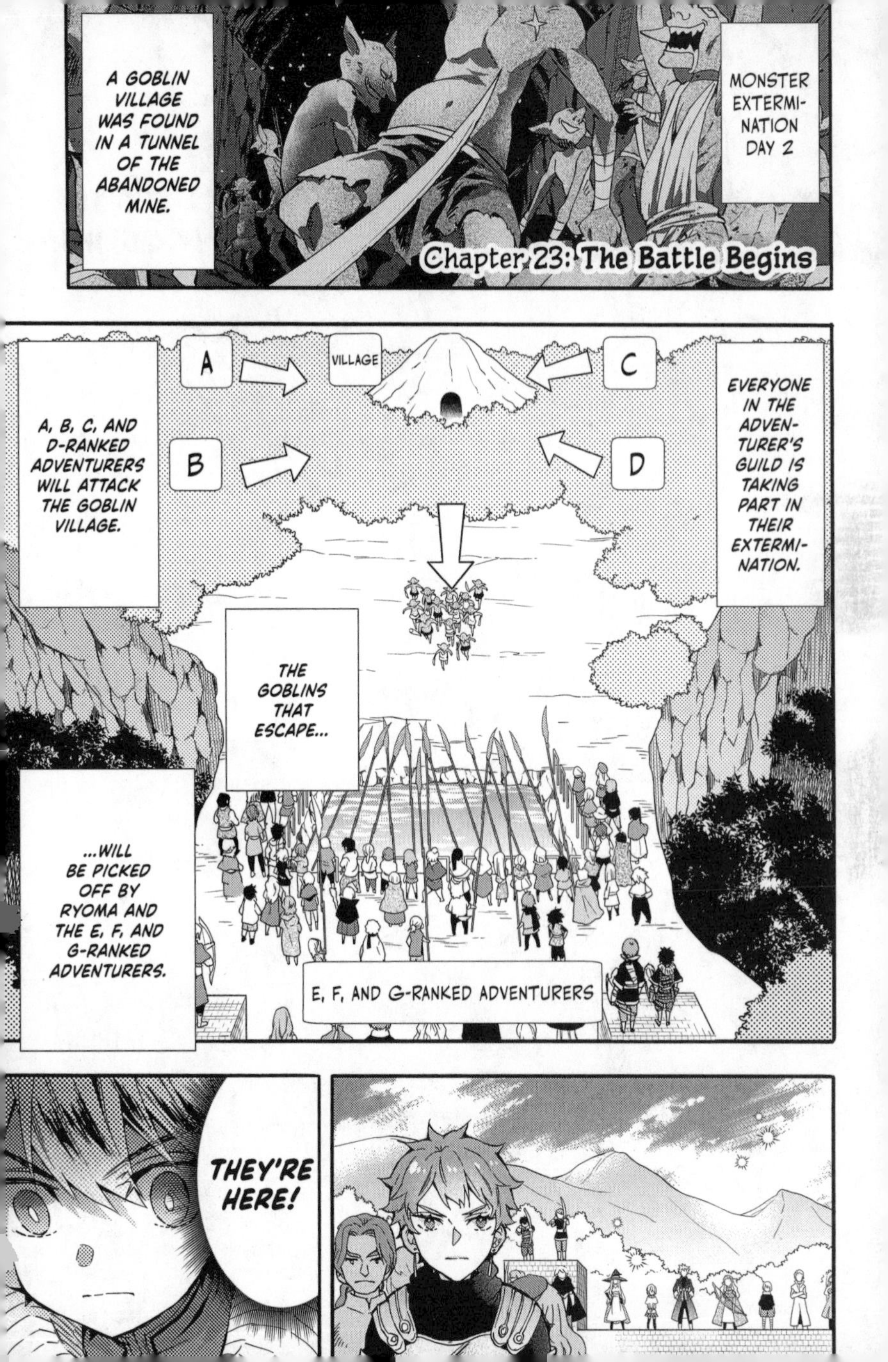
MONSTER EXTERMINATION DAY 2
A GOBLIN VILLAGE WAS FOUND IN A TUNNEL OF THE ABANDONED MINE.
Chapter 23: The Battle Begins
EVERYONE IN THE ADVENTURER'S GUILD IS TAKING PART IN THEIR EXTERMINATION.
C
VILLAGE
A
D
B
A, B, C, AND D-RANKED ADVENTURERS WILL ATTACK THE GOBLIN VILLAGE.
THE GOBLINS THAT ESCAPE...
...WILL BE PICKED OFF BY RYOMA AND THE E, F, AND G-RANKED ADVENTURERS.
E, F, AND G-RANKED ADVENTURERS
THEY'RE HERE!

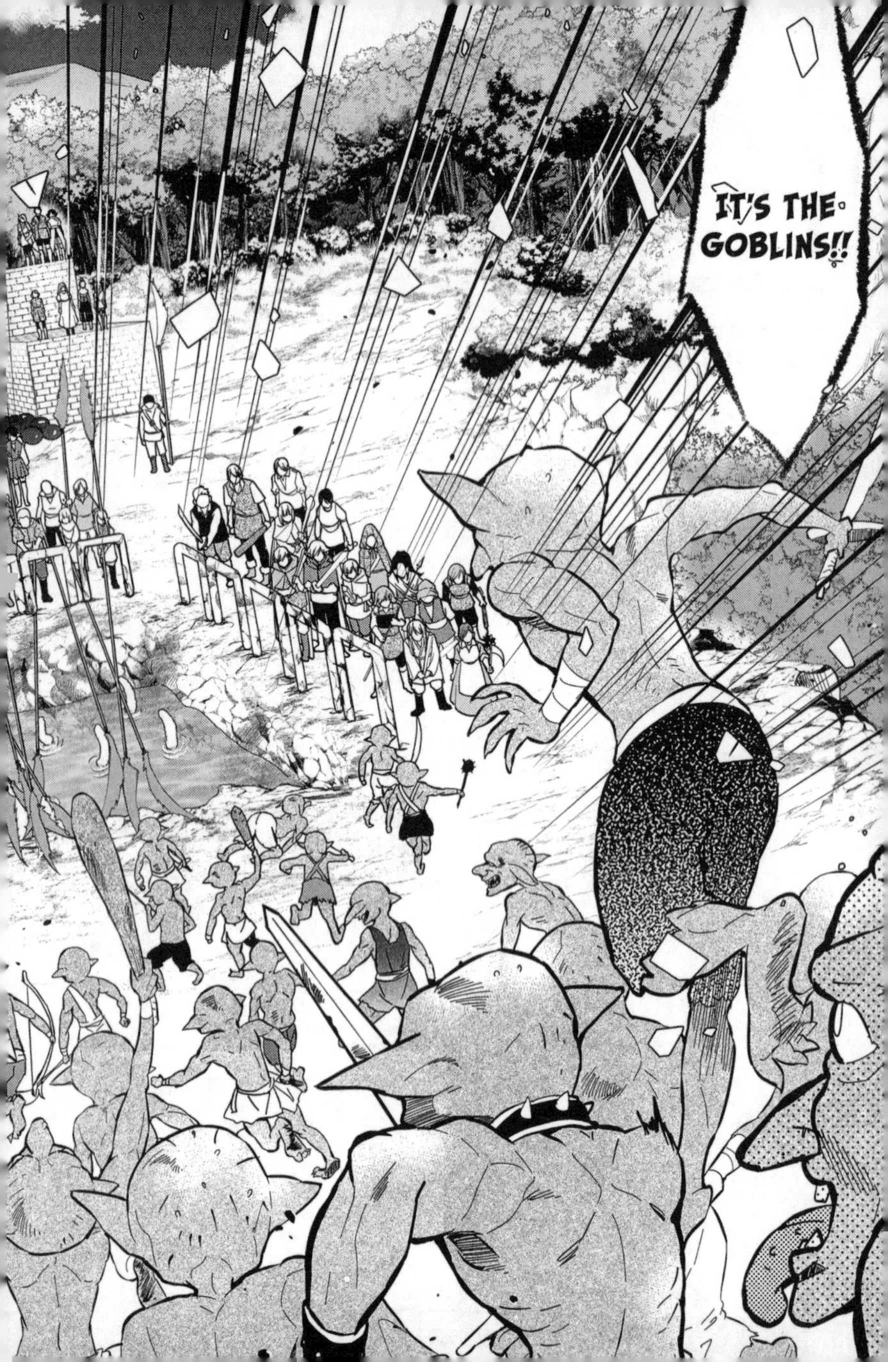
IT'S THE GOBLINS!!

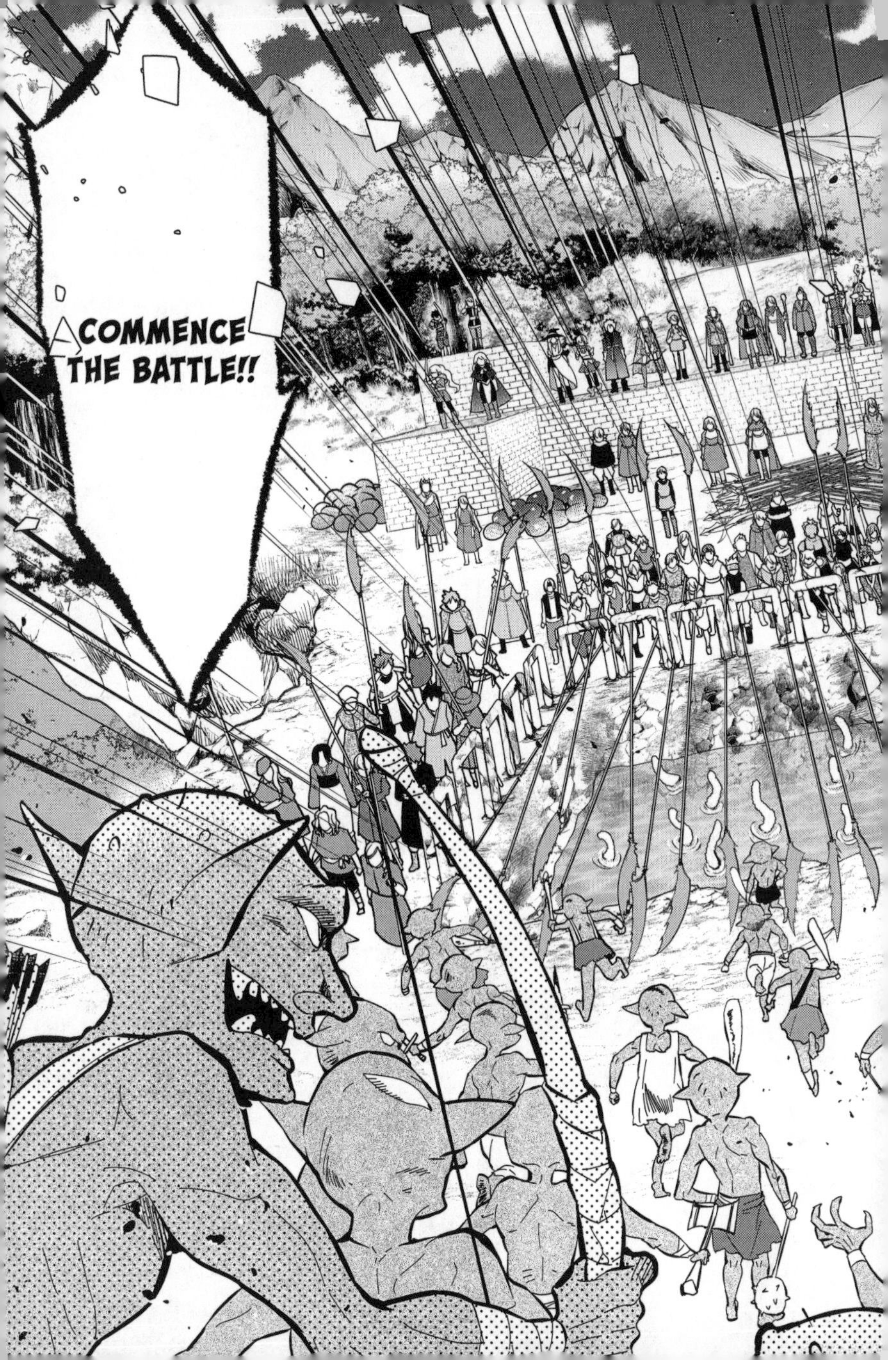
COMMENCE THE BATTLE!!

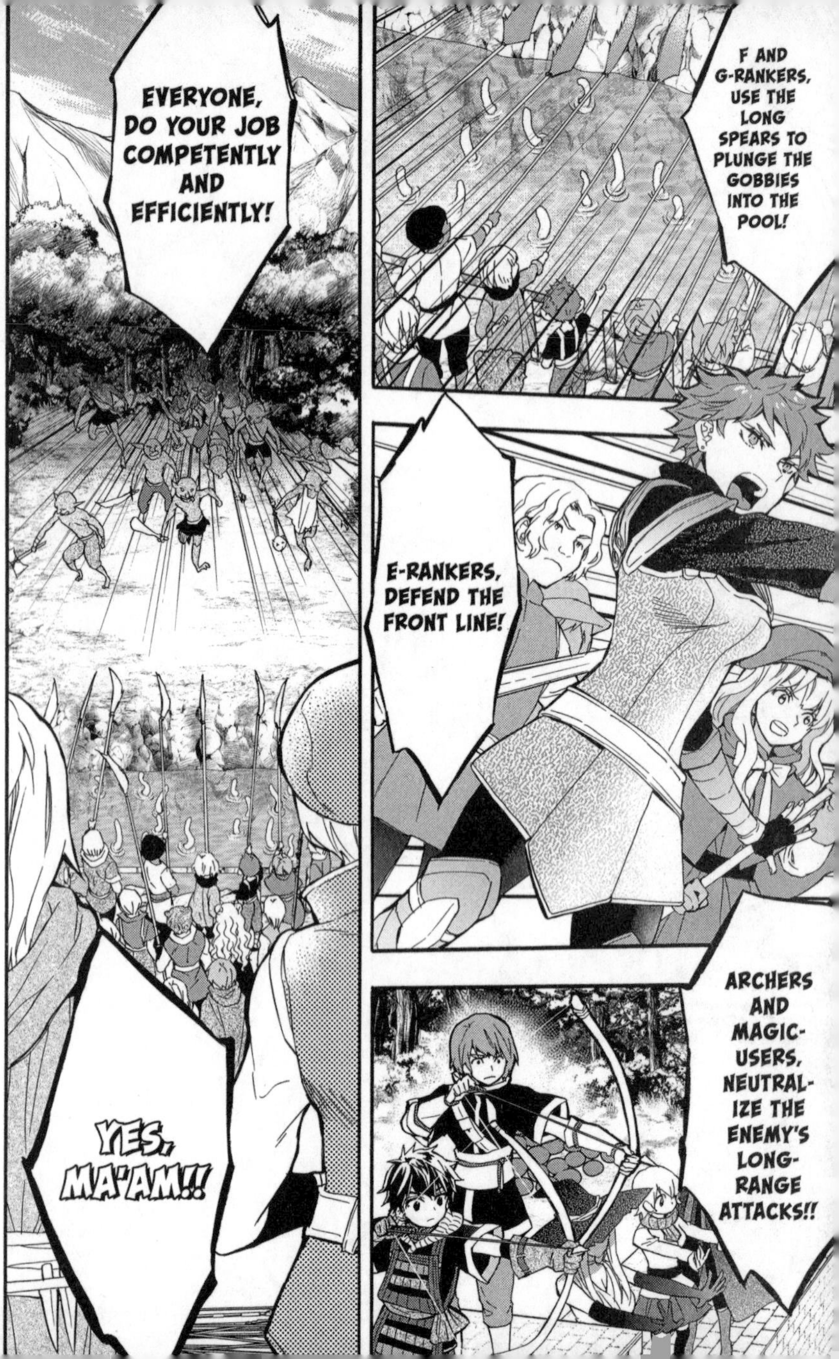
F AND G-RANKERS, USE THE LONG SPEARS TO PLUNGE THE GOBBIES INTO THE POOL!
E-RANKERS, DEFEND THE FRONT LINE!
ARCHERS AND MAGIC-USERS, NEUTRAL-IZE THE ENEMY'S LONG-RANGE ATTACKS!!
EVERYONE, DO YOUR JOB COMPETENTLY AND EFFICIENTLY!
YES, MA'AM!!

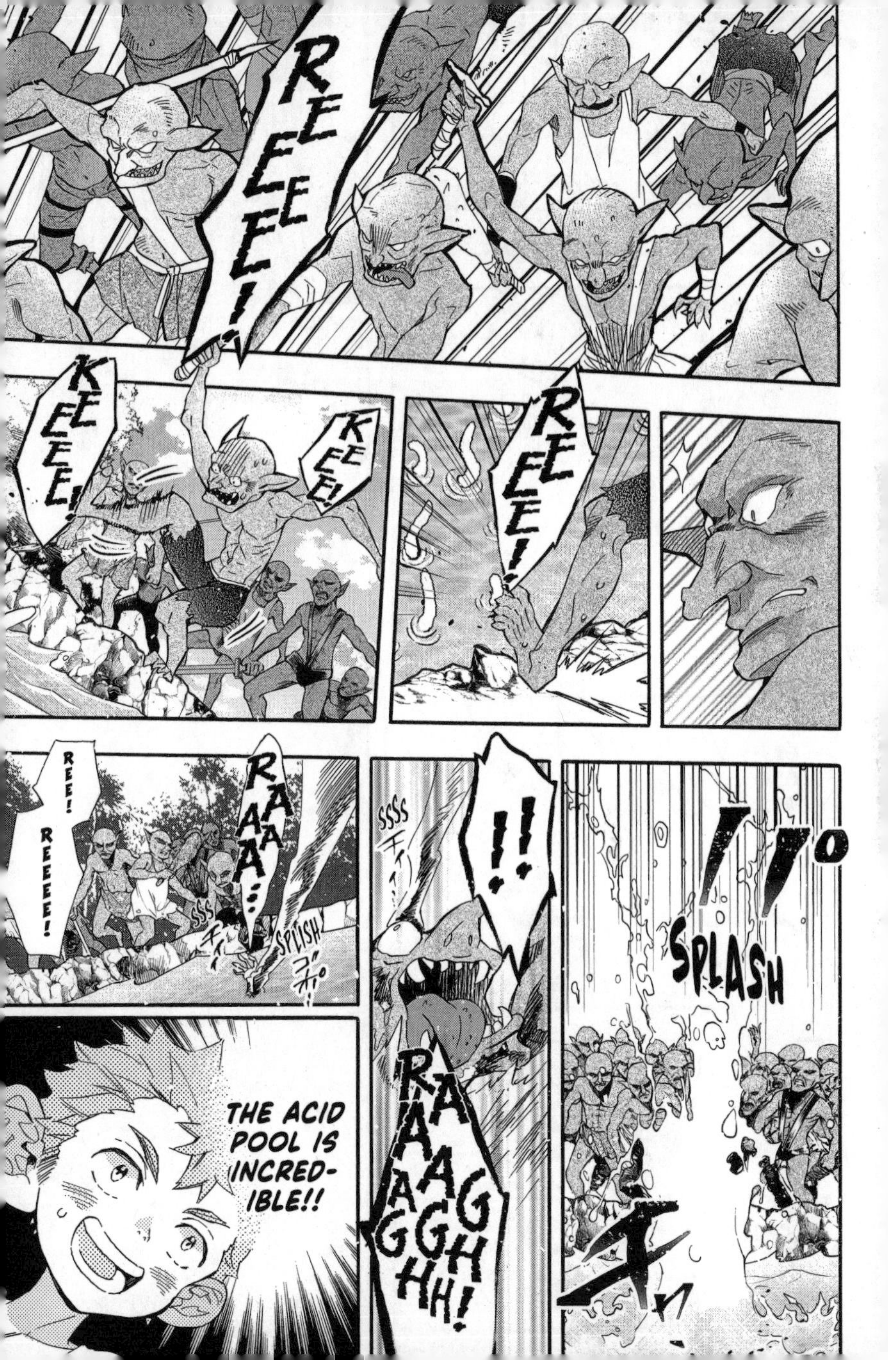
REEEEE!!
REEE!!
KEE!
KEEEE!
SPLASH
!!
SSSS
RAAAAGGGHHH!
RAAA..!
SSS
SPLISH
REE! REEEEE!
THE ACID POOL IS INCRED-IBLE!!

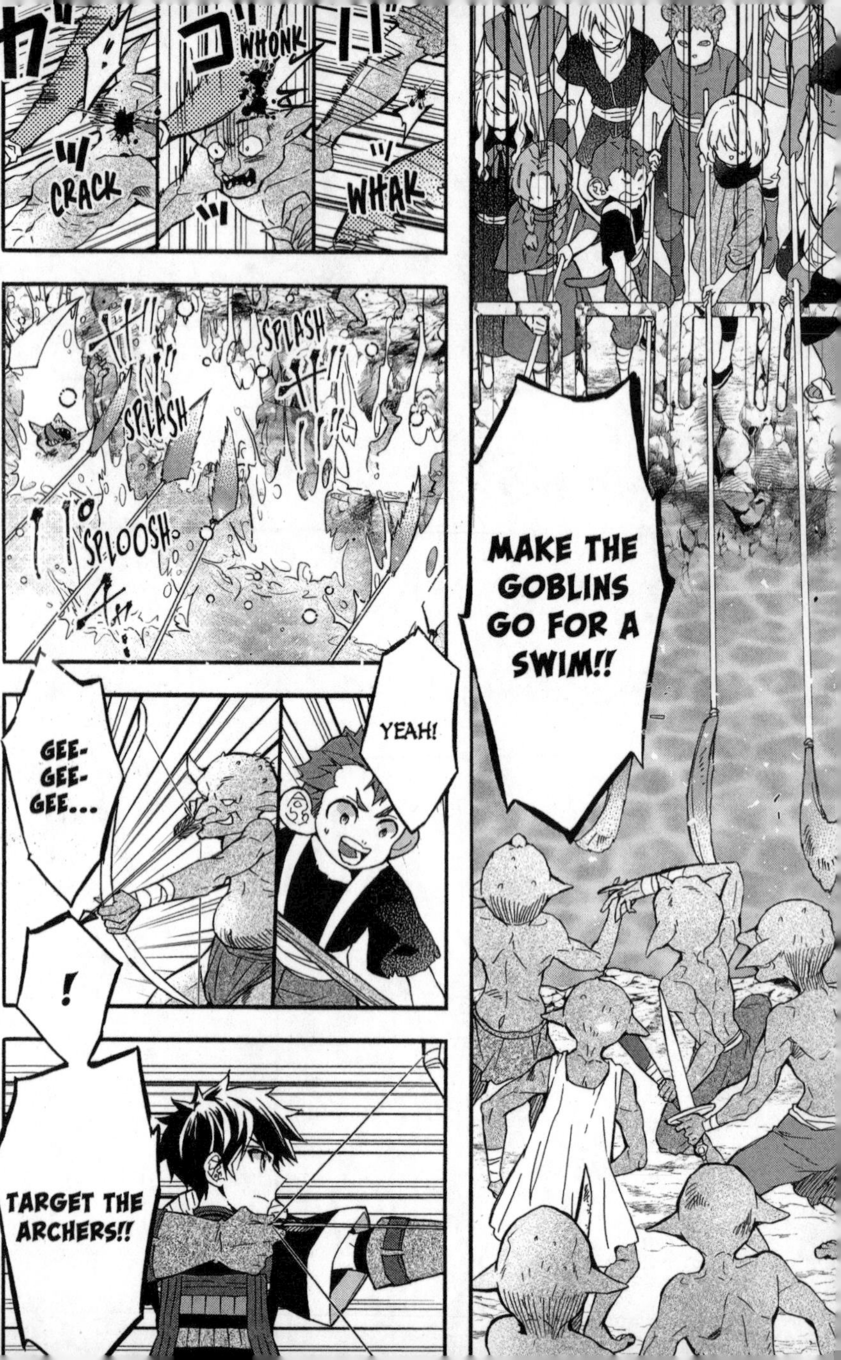
MAKE THE GOBLINS GO FOR A SWIM!!
WHAK
WHONK
CRACK
SPLASH
SPLASH
SPLOOSH
YEAH!
GEE-GEE-GEE...
!
TARGET THE ARCHERS!!

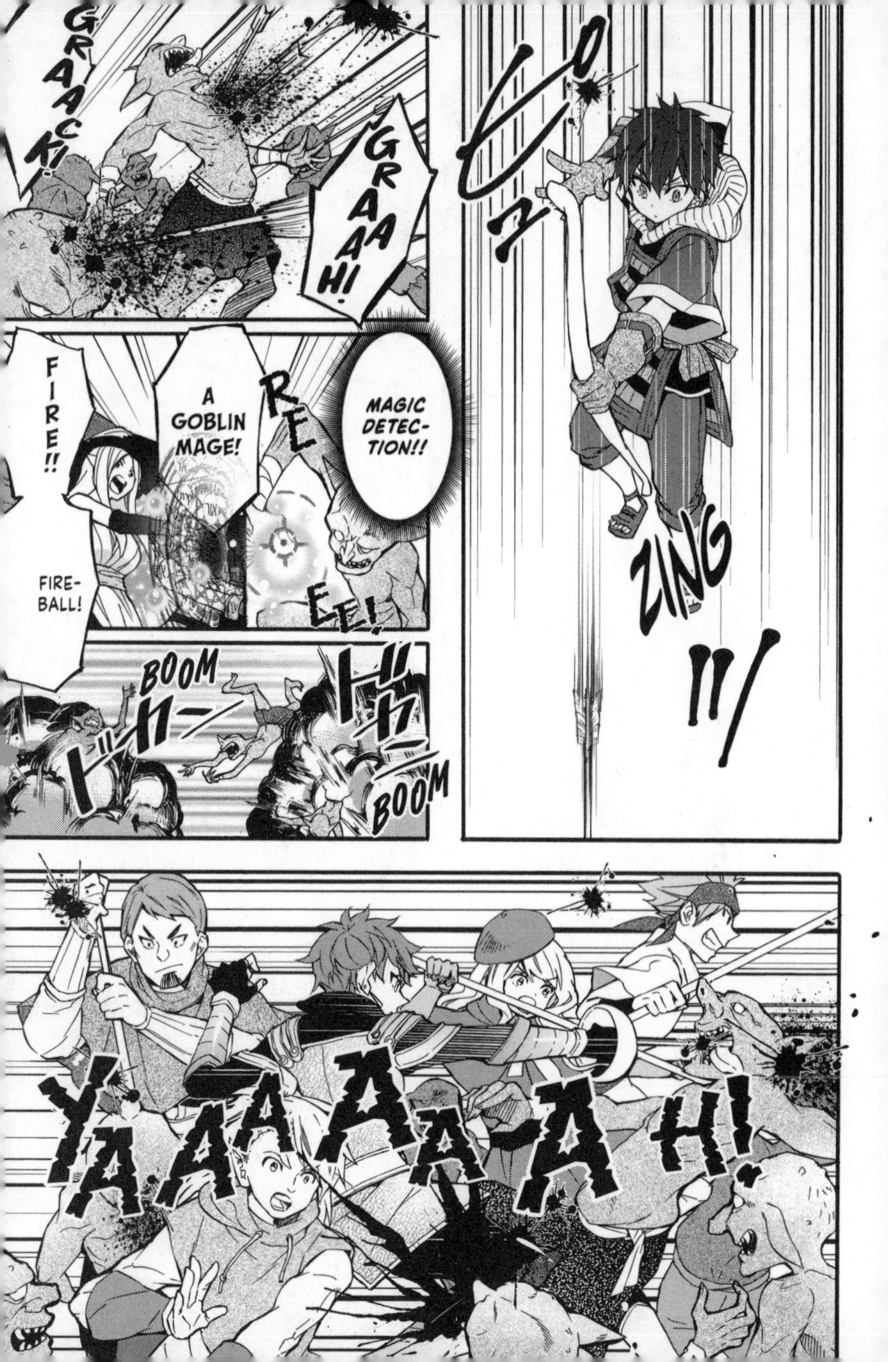
ZING!!
GRAAAH!
GRAAACK!
MAGIC DETECTION!!
REEE!
A GOBLIN MAGE!
FIRE!!
FIRE-BALL!
BOOM
BOOM
YAAAA-AH!

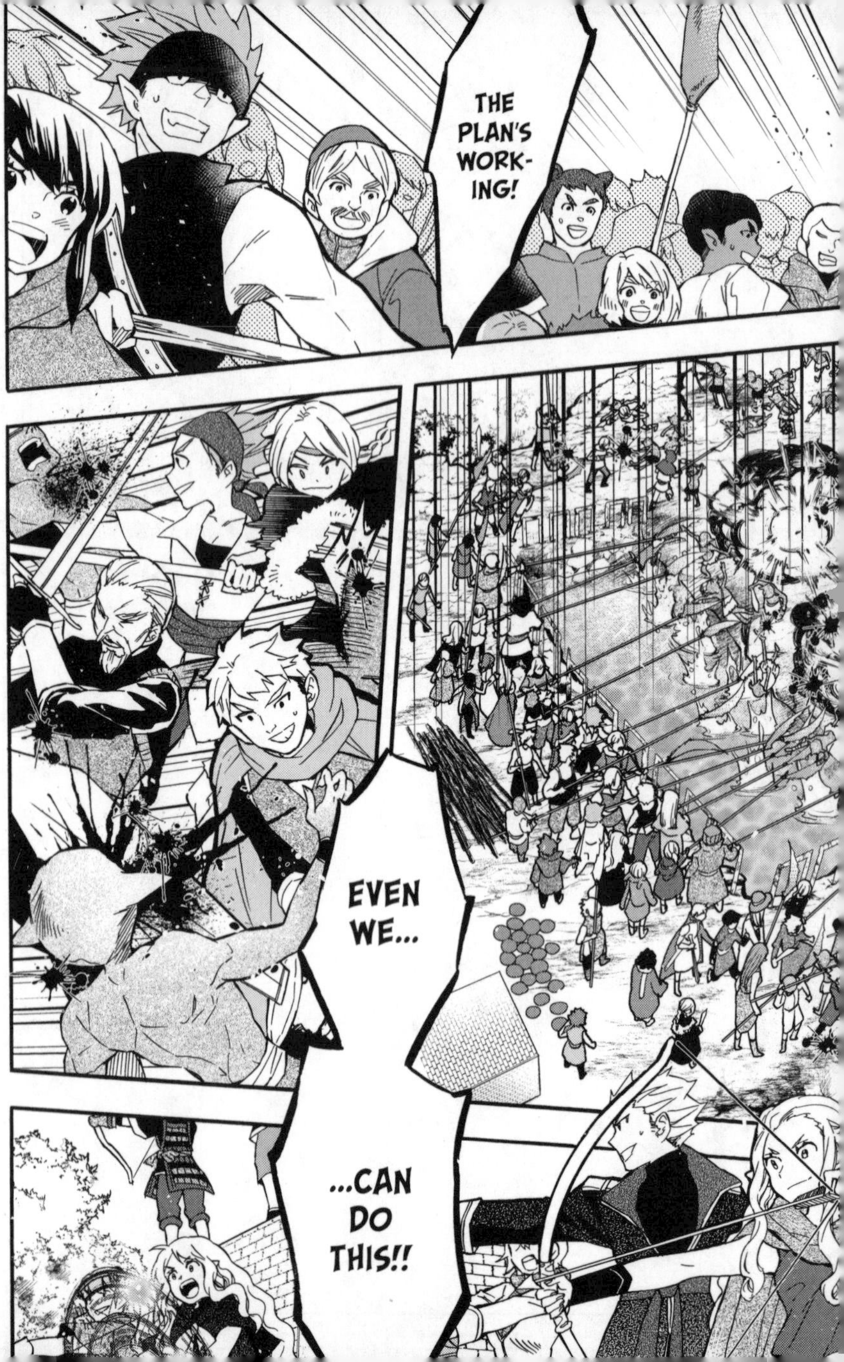
THE PLAN'S WORKING!
EVEN WE...
...CAN DO THIS!!

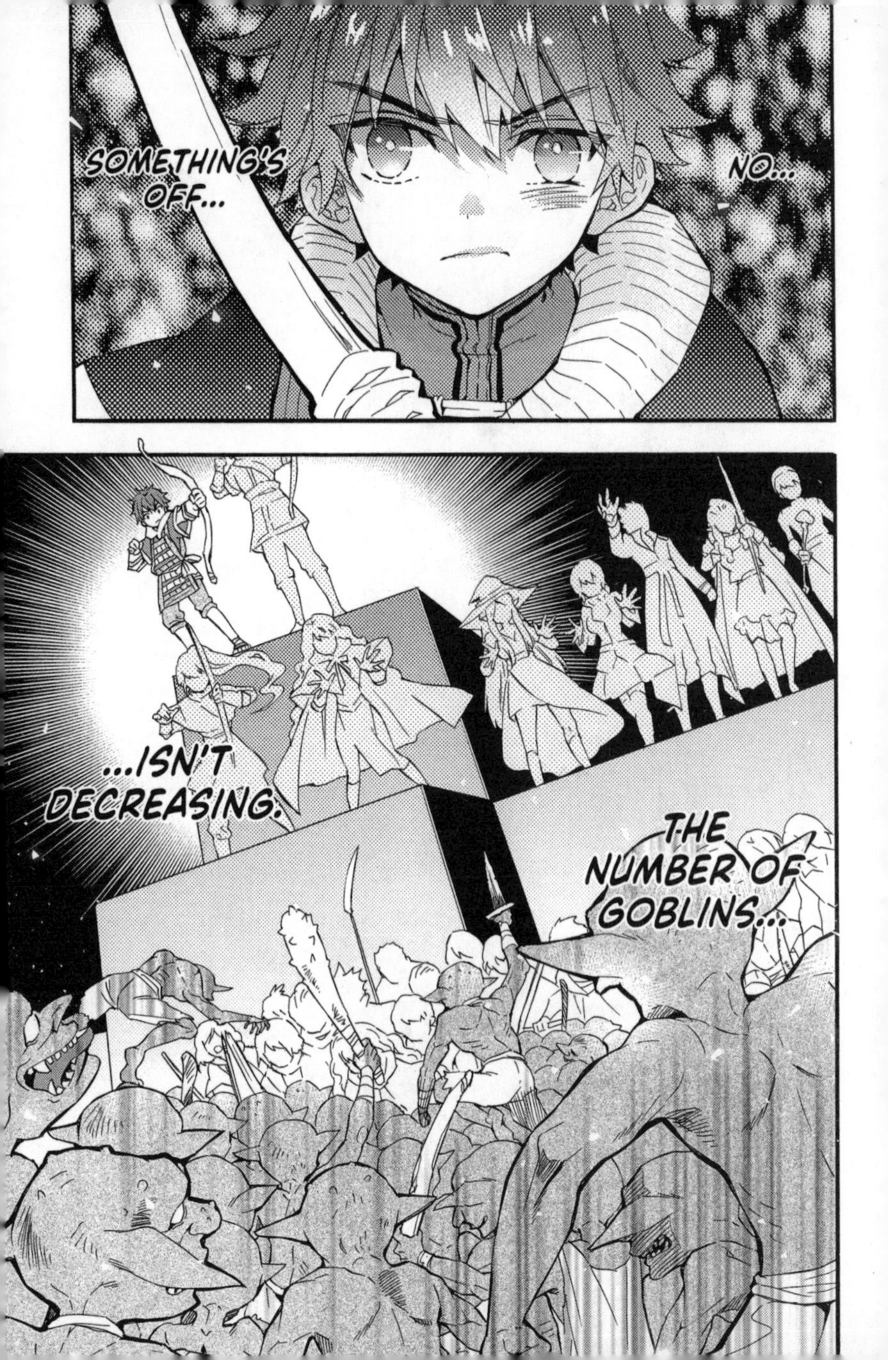
NO...
SOMETHING'S OFF...
THE NUMBER OF GOBLINS...
...ISN'T DECREASING.

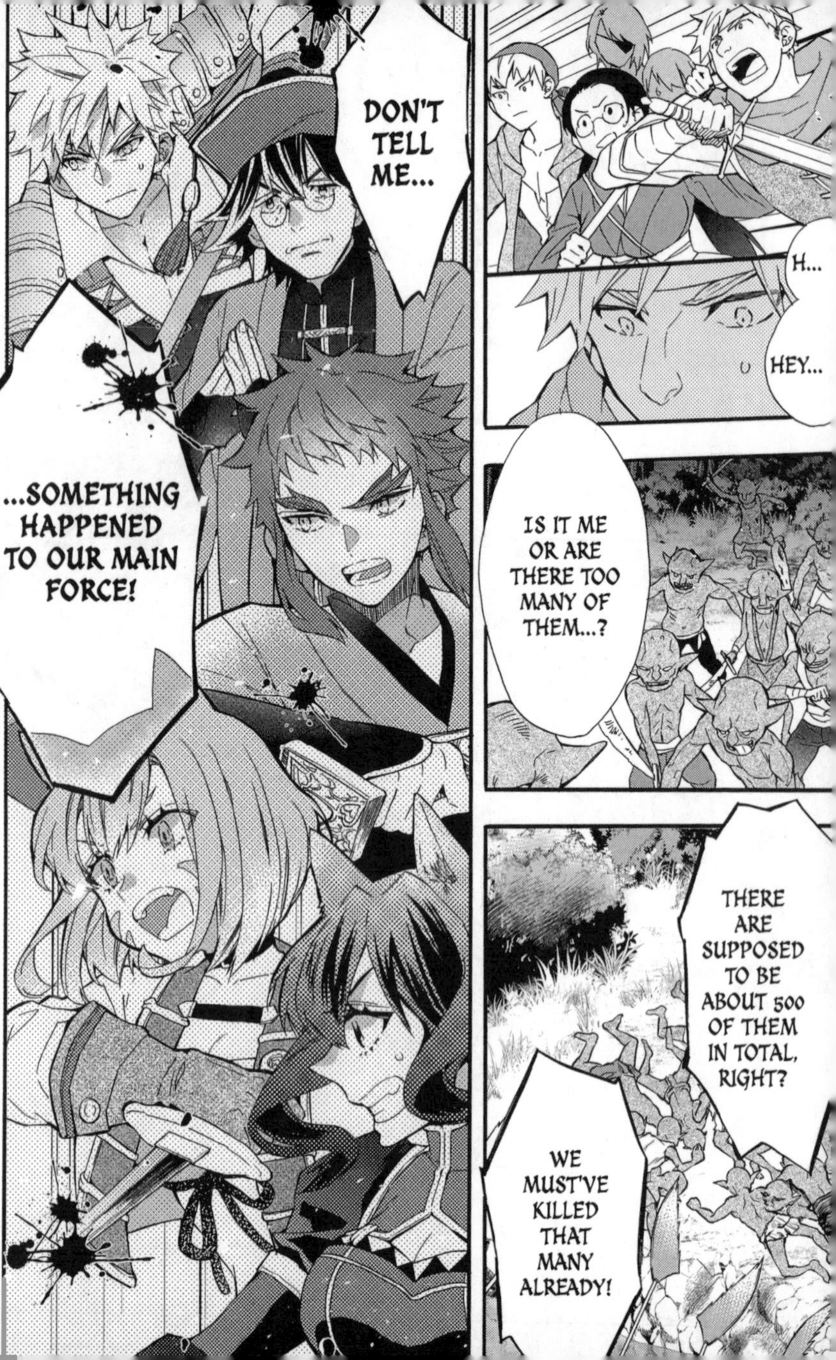
H...
HEY...
IS IT ME OR ARE THERE TOO MANY OF THEM...?
THERE ARE SUPPOSED TO BE ABOUT 500 OF THEM IN TOTAL, RIGHT?
WE MUST'VE KILLED THAT MANY ALREADY!
DON'T TELL ME...
...SOMETHING HAPPENED TO OUR MAIN FORCE!

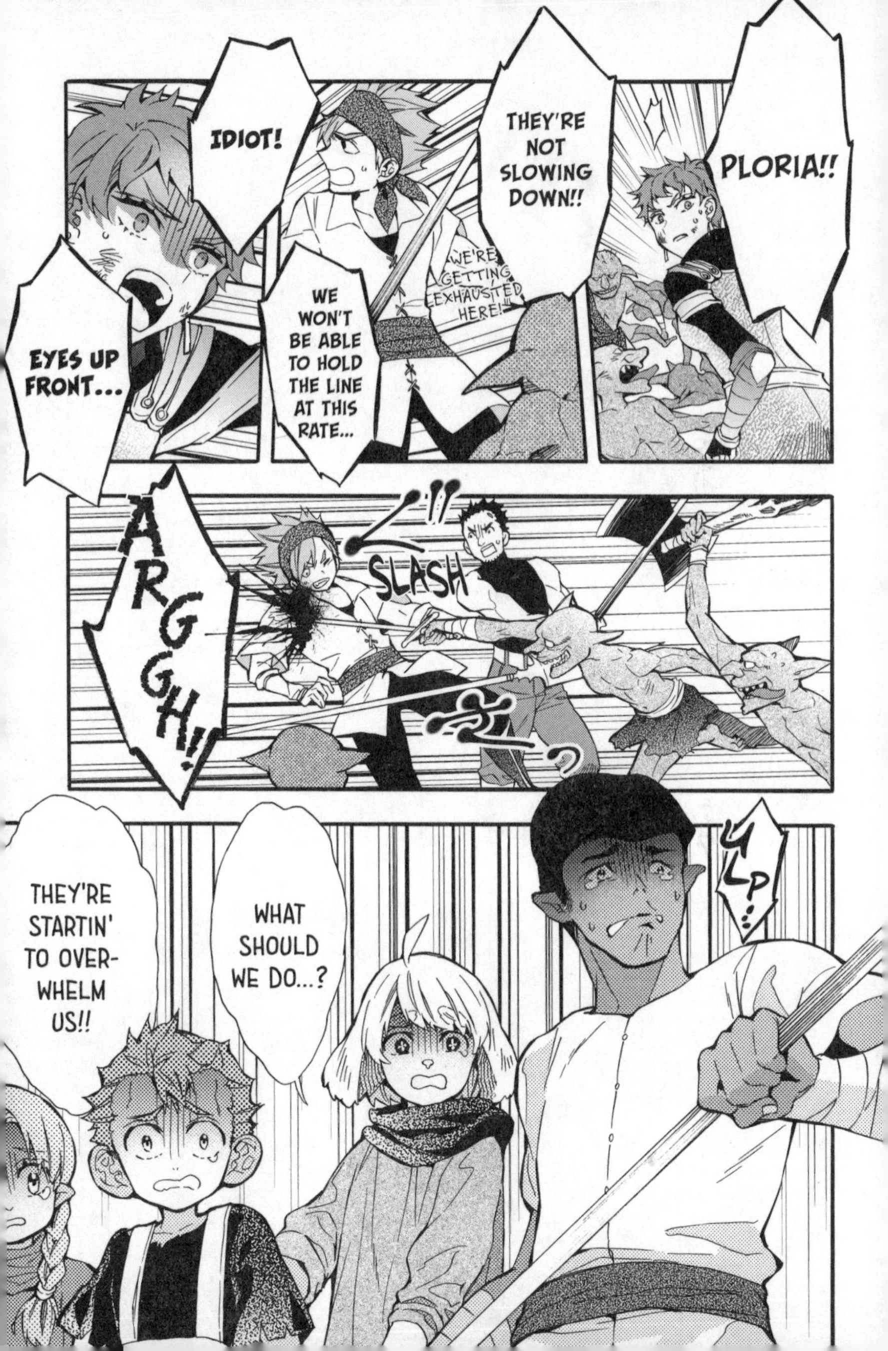
PLORIA!!
THEY'RE NOT SLOWING DOWN!!
WE'RE GETTING EXHAUSTED HERE!
WE WON'T BE ABLE TO HOLD THE LINE AT THIS RATE...
IDIOT!
EYES UP FRONT...
!!
SLASH
ARGH!!
ULP...
WHAT SHOULD WE DO...?
THEY'RE STARTIN' TO OVER-WHELM US!!

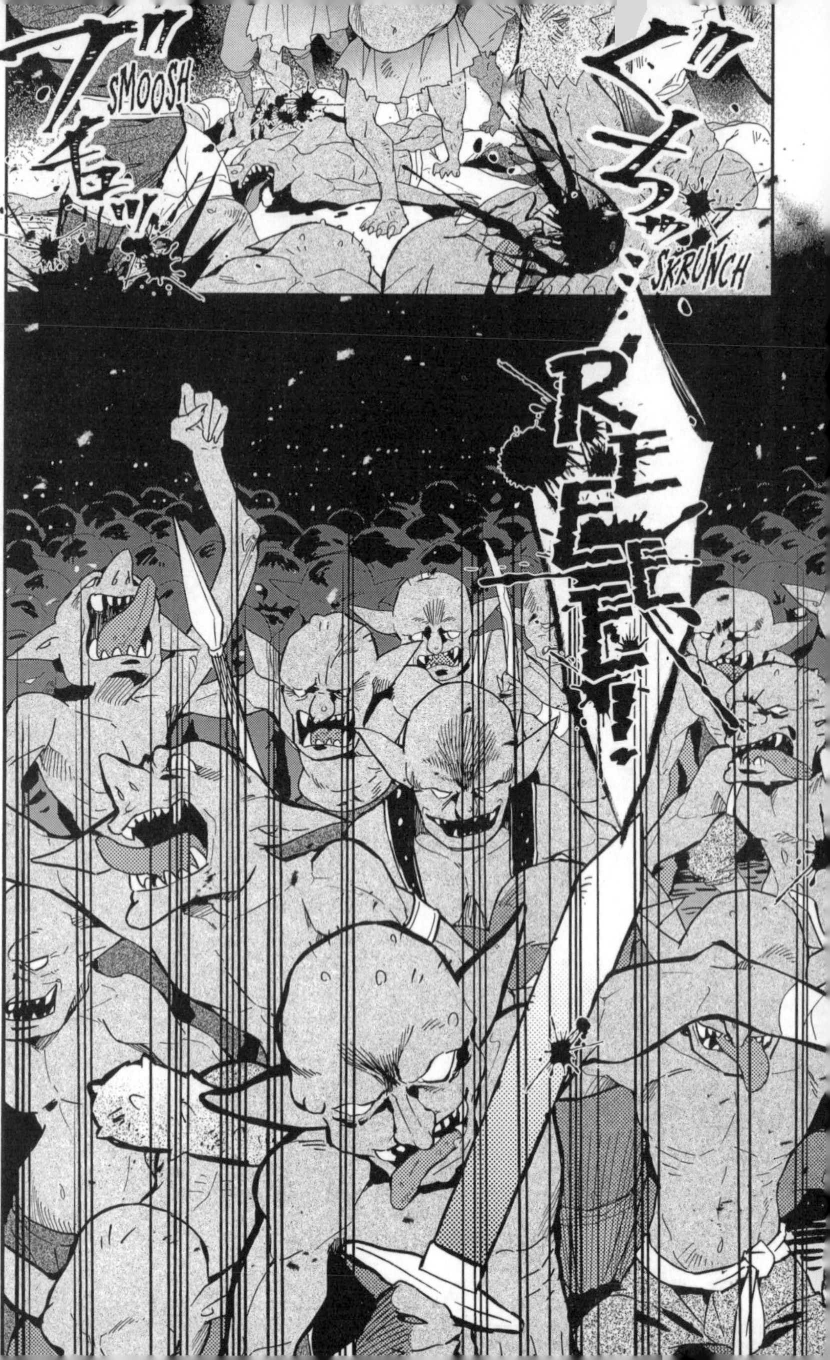
SKRUNCH
SMOOSH
REEEE!

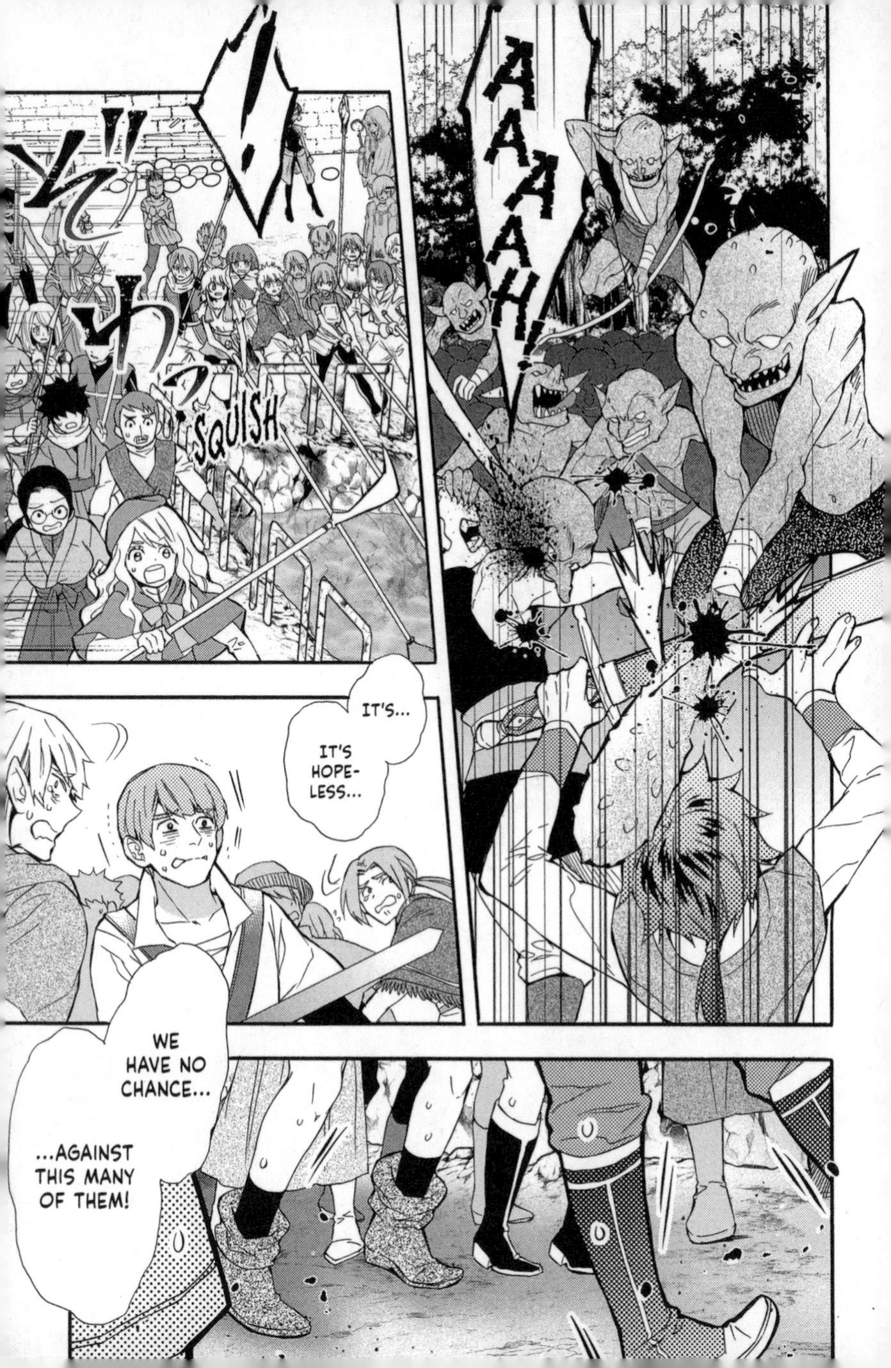
AAAAH!!
SQUISH
IT'S...
IT'S HOPE-LESS...
WE HAVE NO CHANCE...
...AGAINST THIS MANY OF THEM!

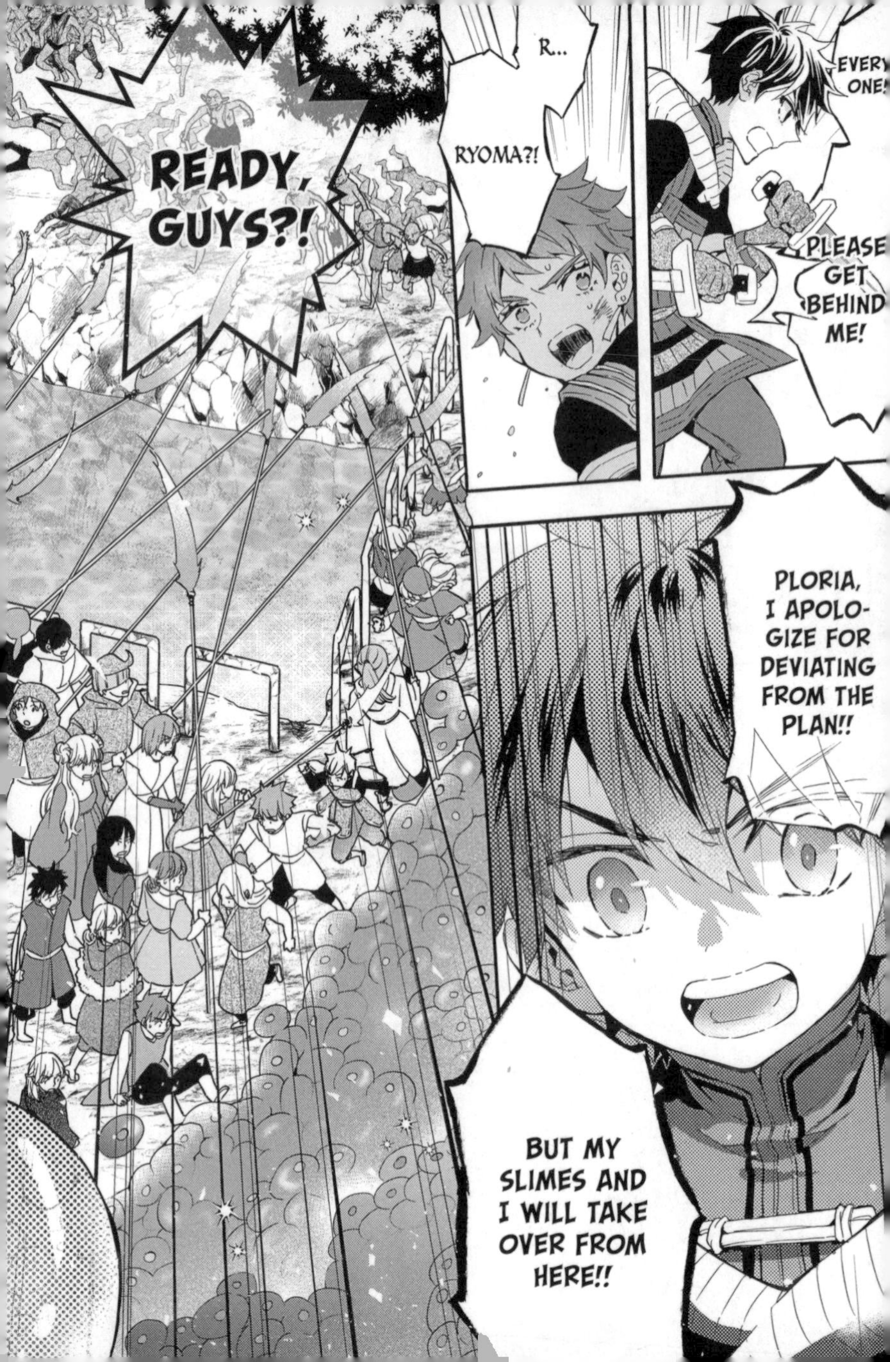
EVERY ONE!
PLEASE GET BEHIND ME!
R...
RYOMA?!
PLORIA, I APOLOGIZE FOR DEVIATING FROM THE PLAN!!
BUT MY SLIMES AND I WILL TAKE OVER FROM HERE!!
READY, GUYS?!

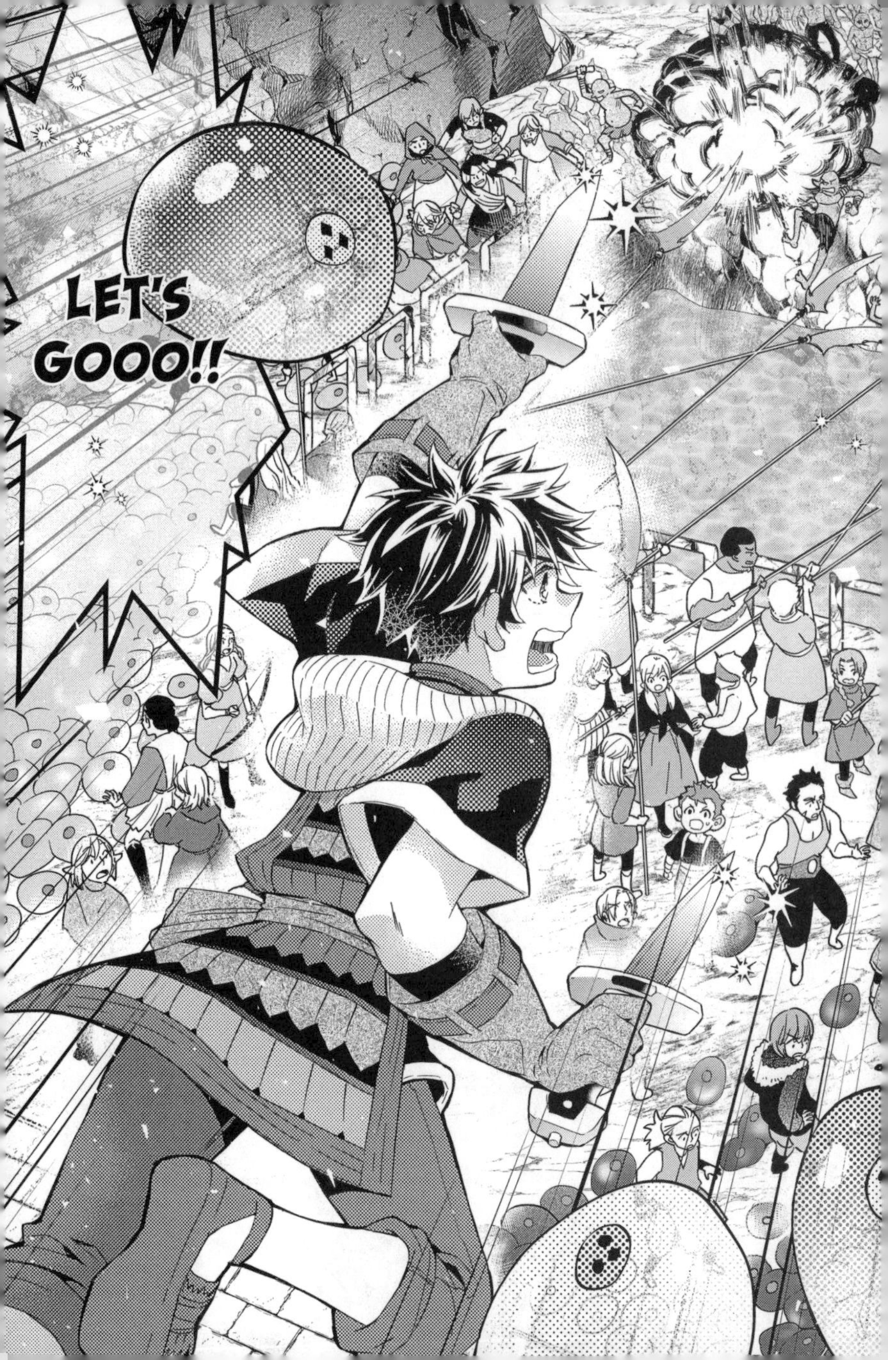
LET'S GOOO!!

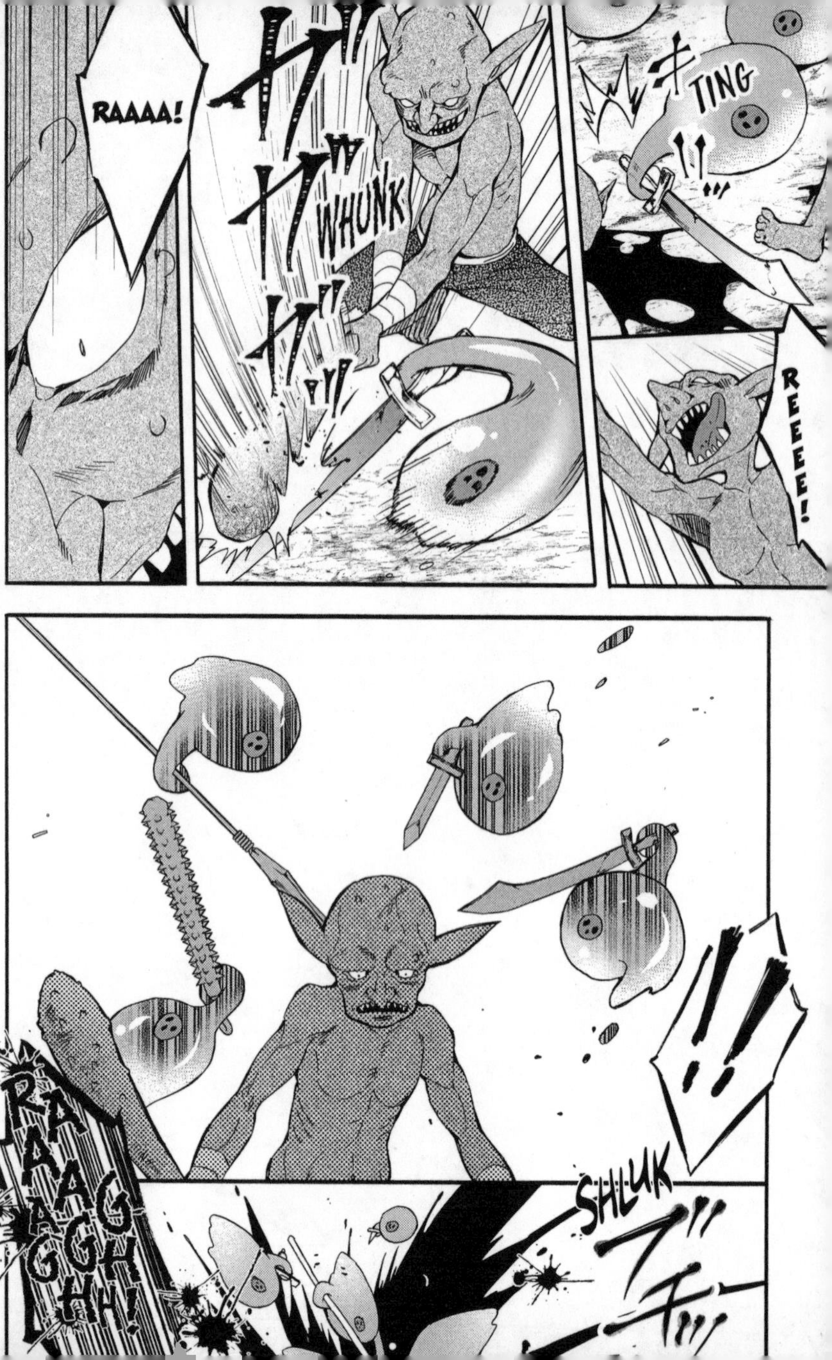
TING
REEEEE!
WHUNK
RAAAA!
!!
SHLUK
RAAAGGGHHH!

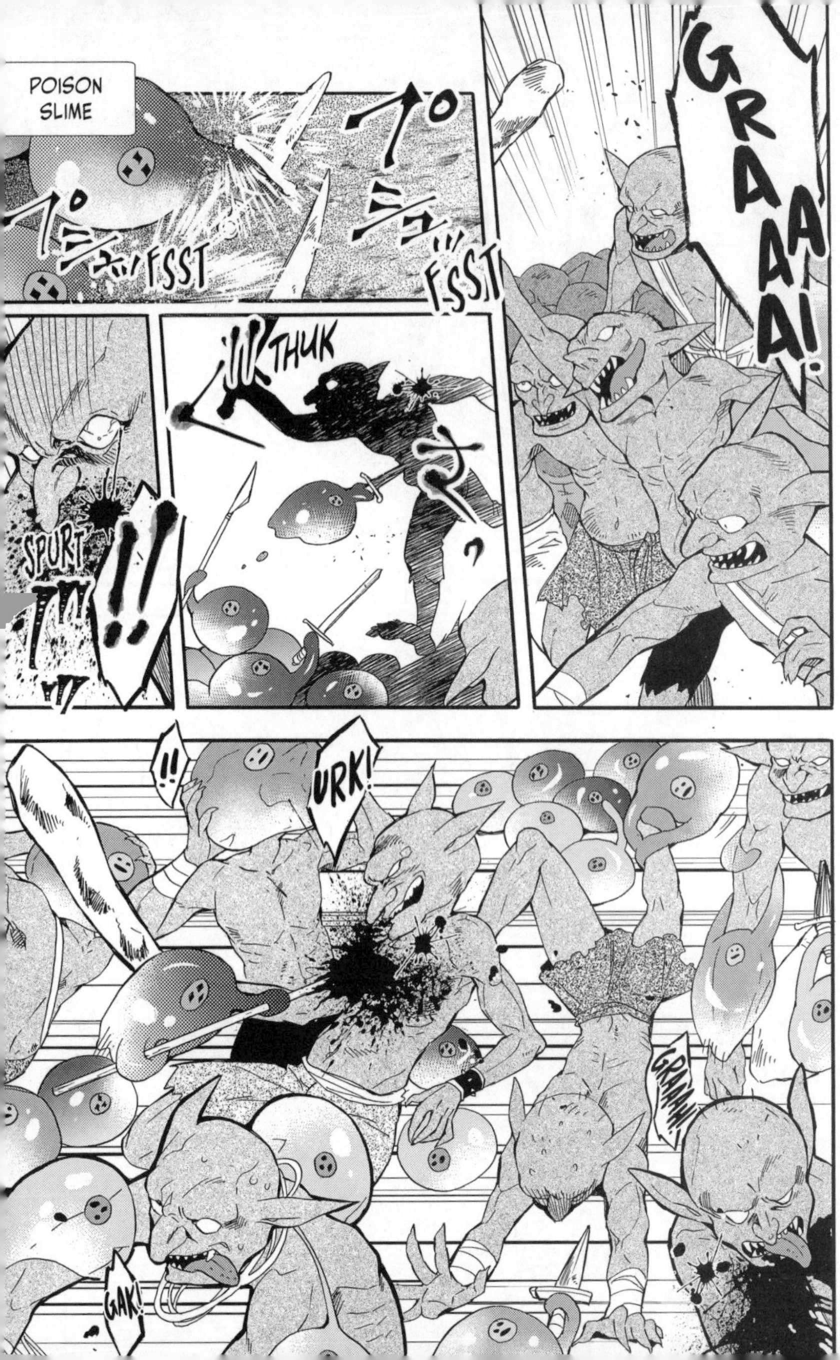

GRAAAAAI!
FSST
POISON SLIME
FSST
THUK
!!
SPURT
URK!
!!
GRAAAAH!
GAK!

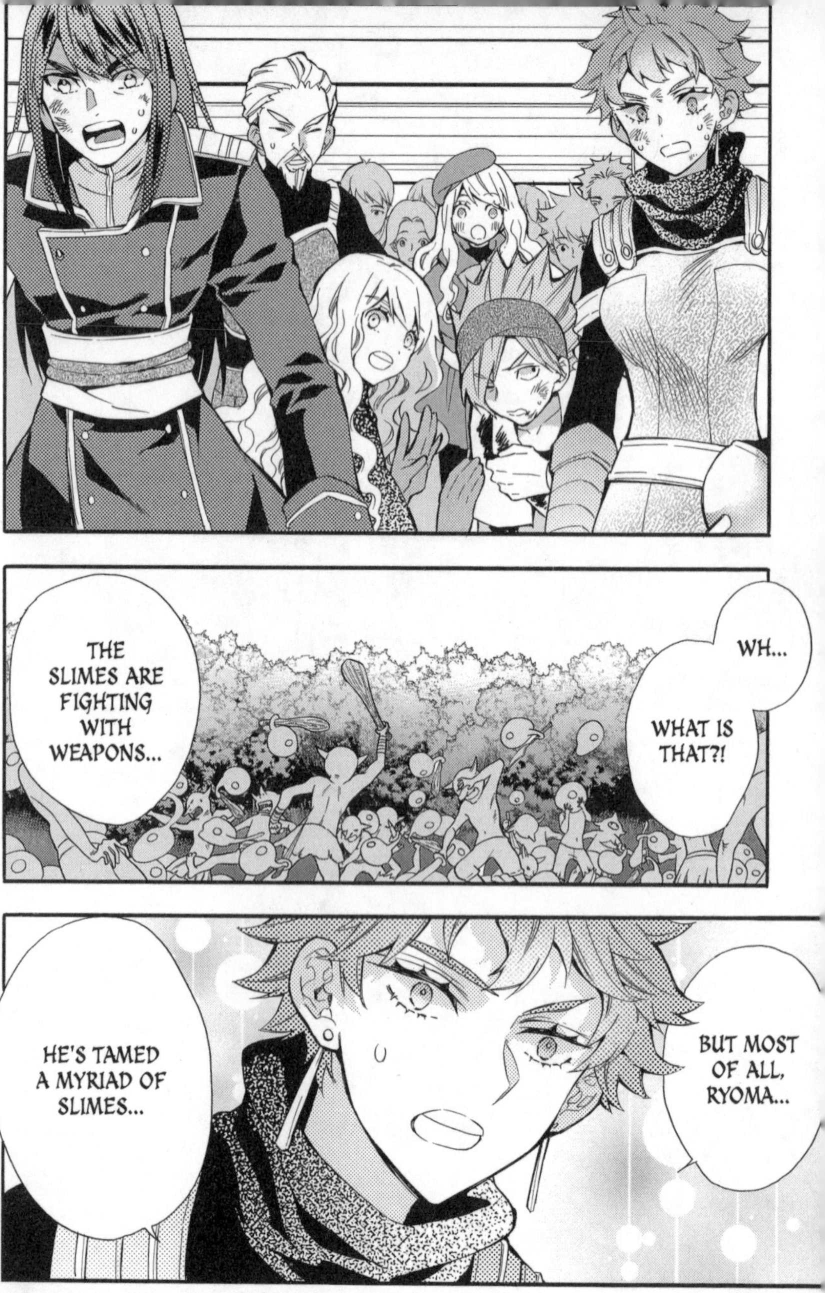
WH...
WHAT IS THAT?!
THE SLIMES ARE FIGHTING WITH WEAPONS...
BUT MOST OF ALL, RYOMA...
HE'S TAMED A MYRIAD OF SLIMES...

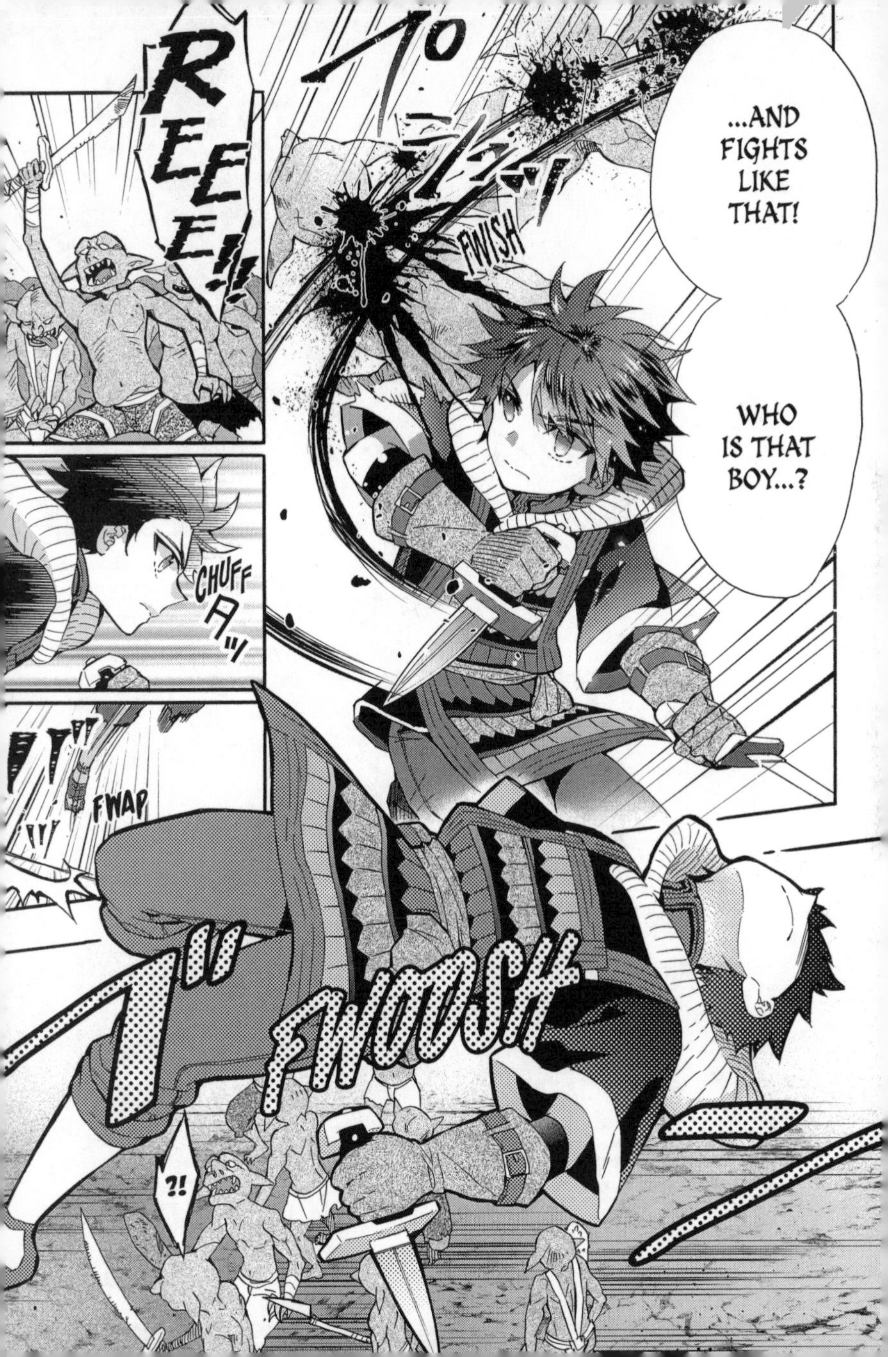
...AND FIGHTS LIKE THAT!
WHO IS THAT BOY...?
FWISH
REEE!!!
CHUFF
FWAP
FWOOSH
?!

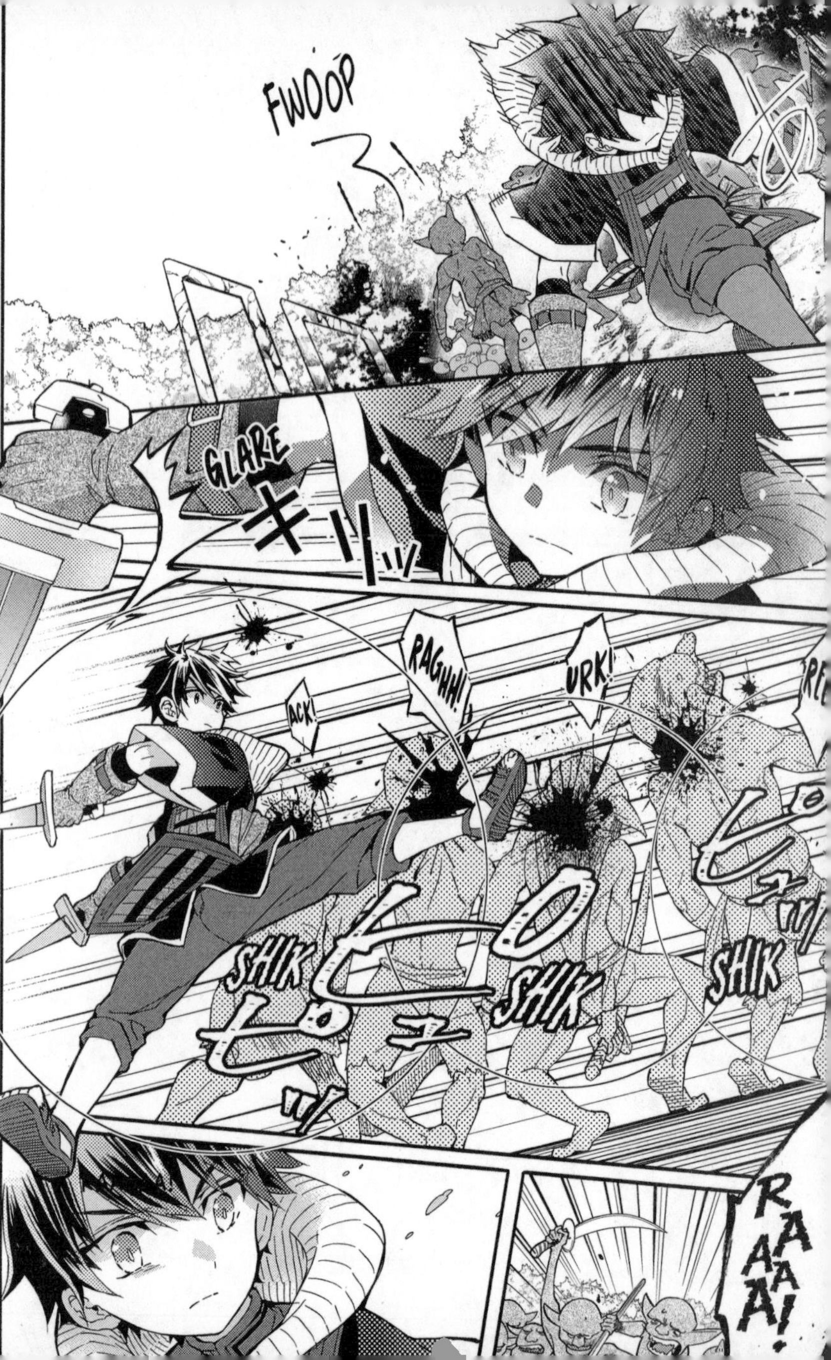
FWOOP
GLARE
URK!
RAGHH!
ACK!
SHIK
SHIK
SHIK
RAAAA!

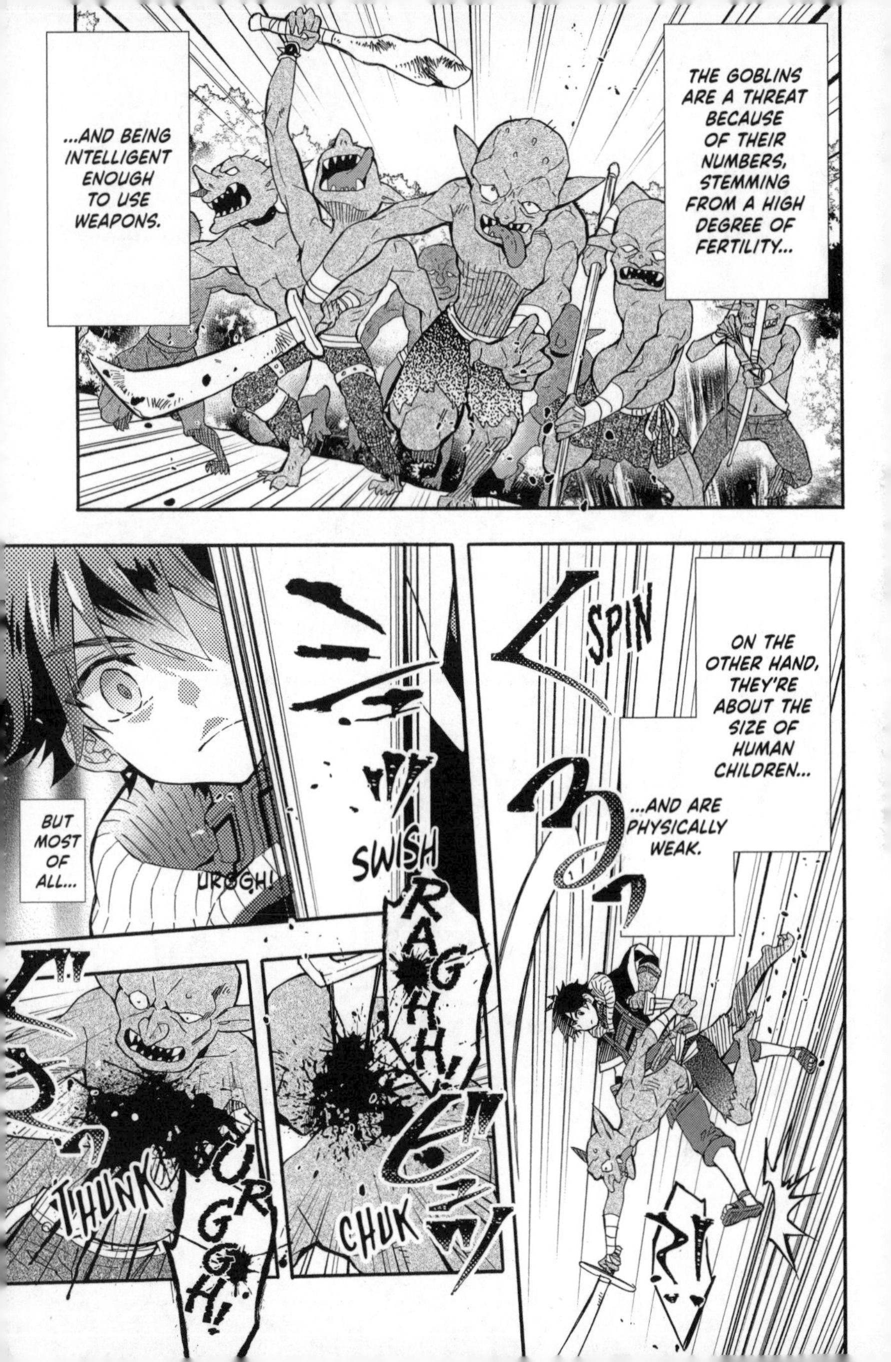
THE GOBLINS ARE A THREAT BECAUSE OF THEIR NUMBERS, STEMMING FROM A HIGH DEGREE OF FERTILITY...
...AND BEING INTELLIGENT ENOUGH TO USE WEAPONS.
SPIN
ON THE OTHER HAND, THEY'RE ABOUT THE SIZE OF HUMAN CHILDREN...
...AND ARE PHYSICALLY WEAK.
R!
SWISH
URGH!
BUT MOST OF ALL...
RAGHH!
CHUK
THUNK
GURRGGH!

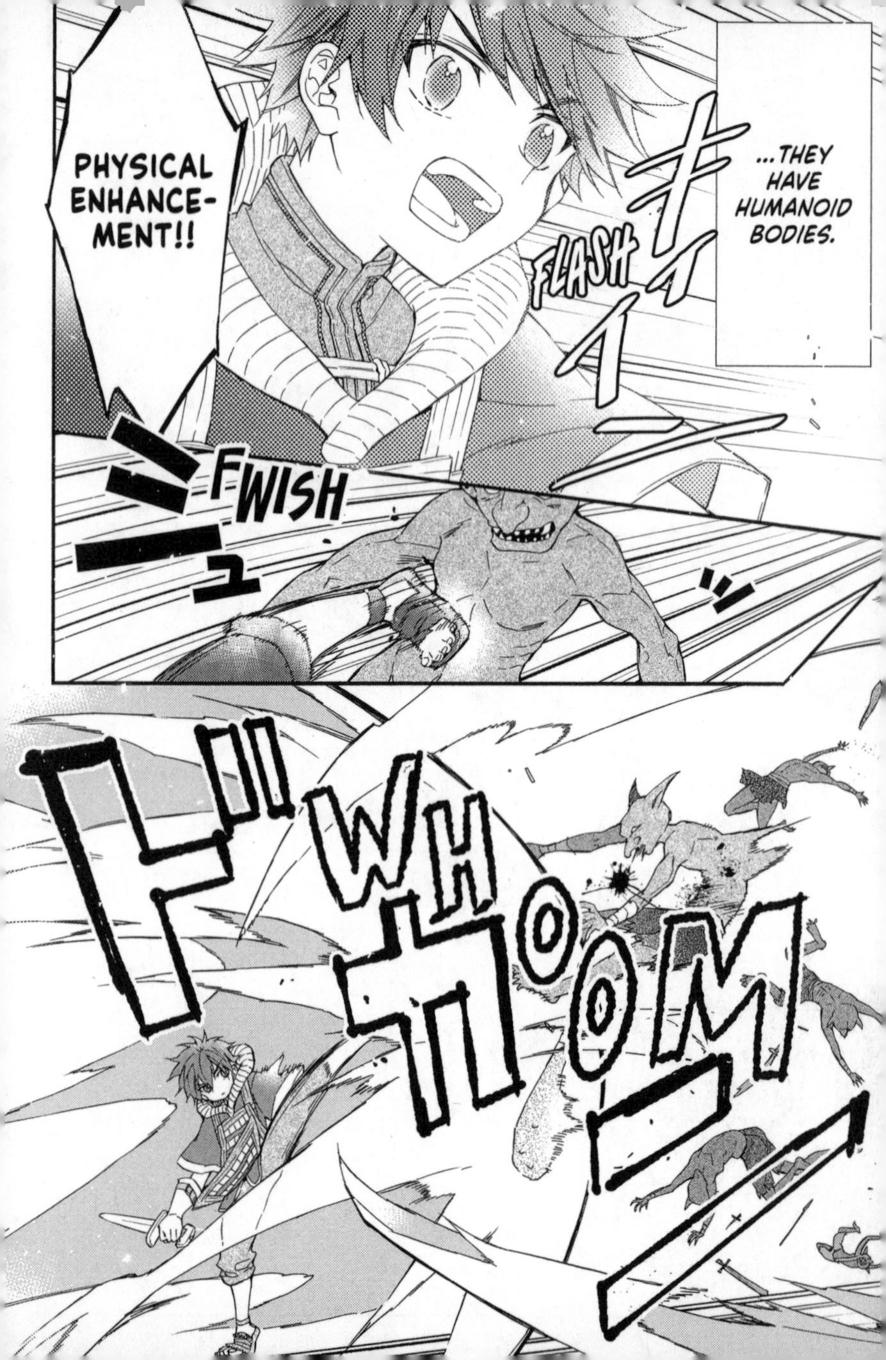
...THEY HAVE HUMANOID BODIES.
FLASH
PHYSICAL ENHANCE-MENT!!
FWISH
WHOOM

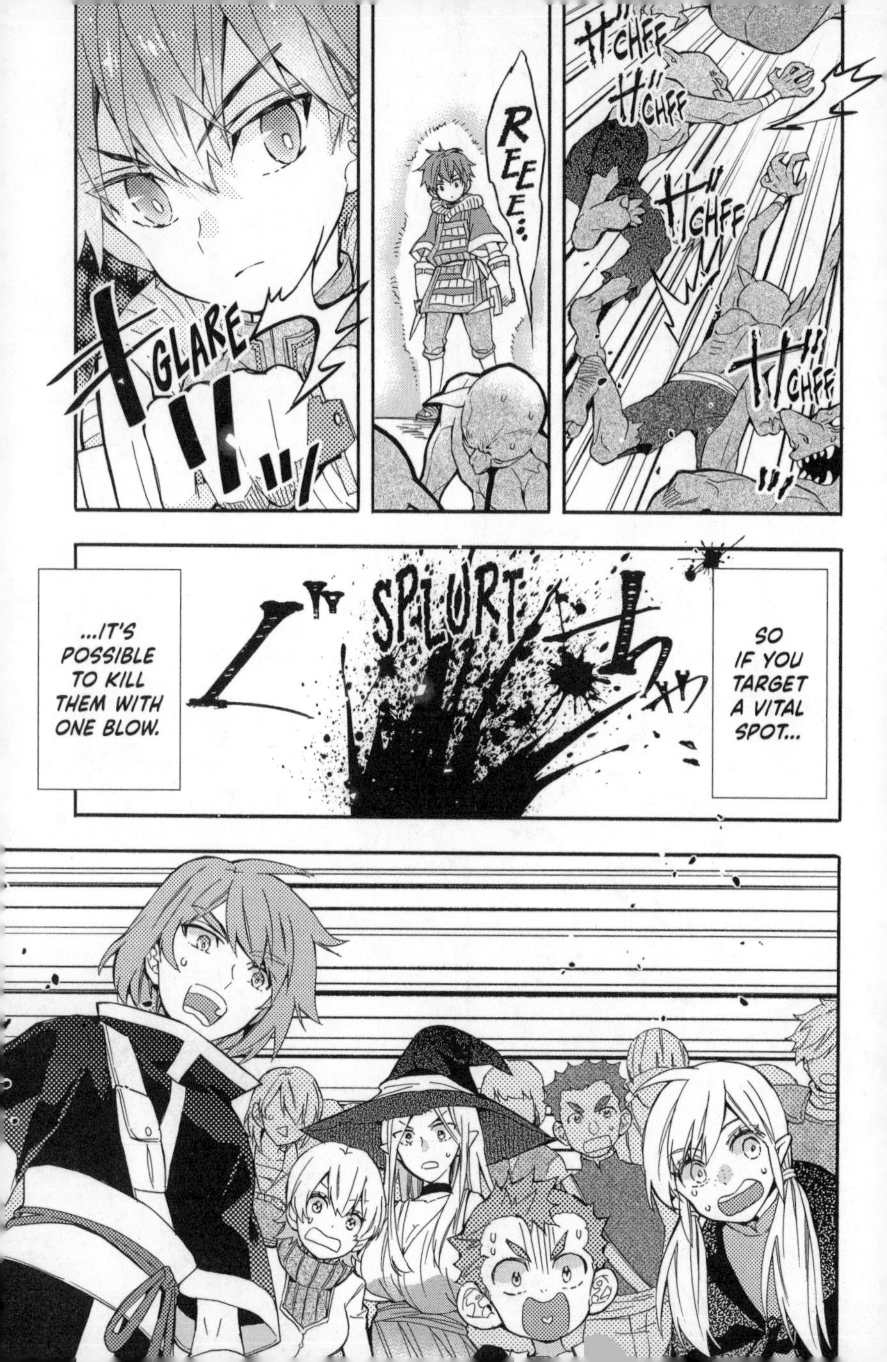
CHFF
CHFF
CHFF
CHFF
REEE...
GLARE
SO IF YOU TARGET A VITAL SPOT...
SPLURT
...IT'S POSSIBLE TO KILL THEM WITH ONE BLOW.

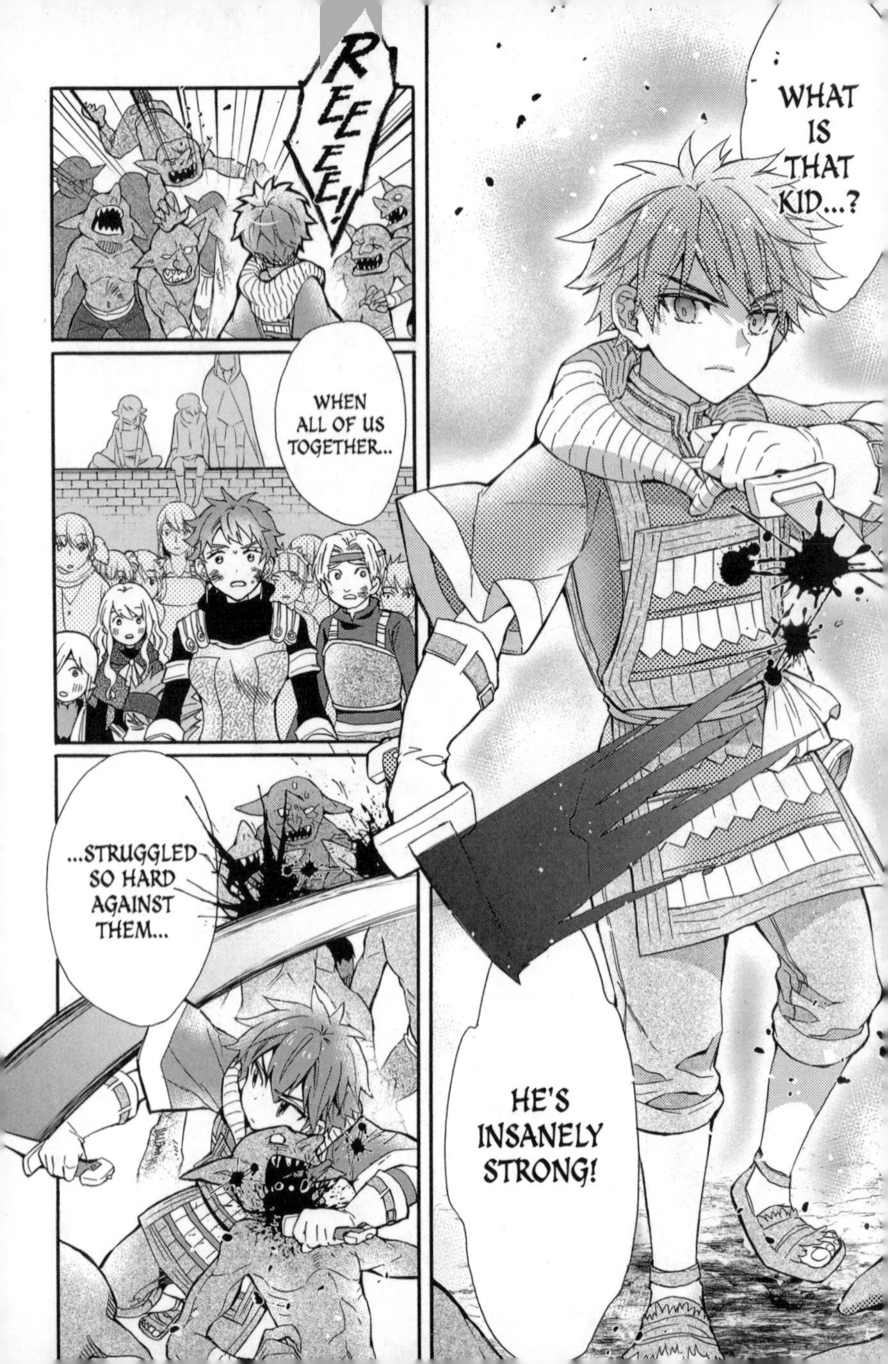
WHAT IS THAT KID...?
HE'S INSANELY STRONG!
REEEEE!
WHEN ALL OF US TOGETHER...
...STRUGGLED SO HARD AGAINST THEM...

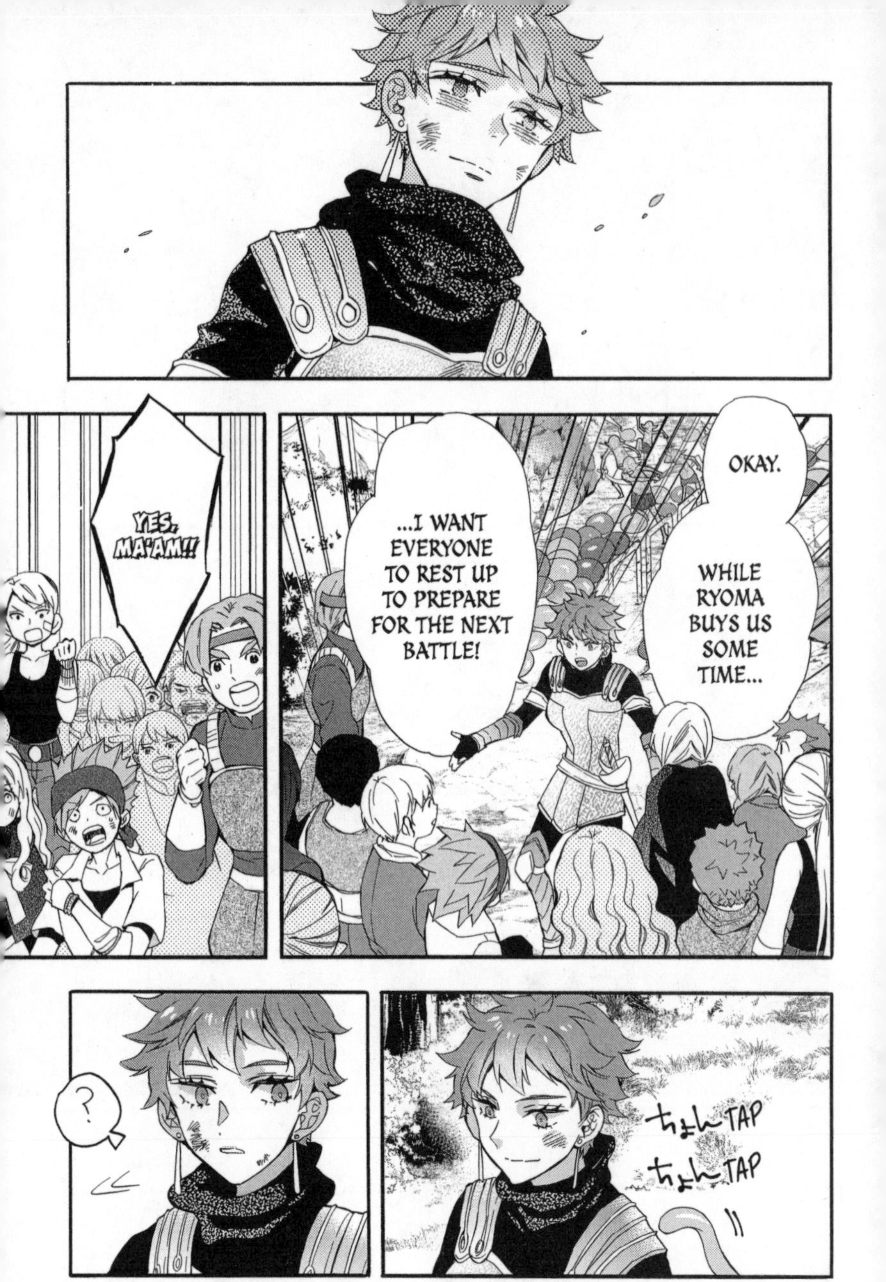
OKAY.
WHILE RYOMA BUYS US SOME TIME...
...I WANT EVERYONE TO REST UP TO PREPARE FOR THE NEXT BATTLE!
YES, MA'AM!!
ちょん TAP
ちょん TAP
?

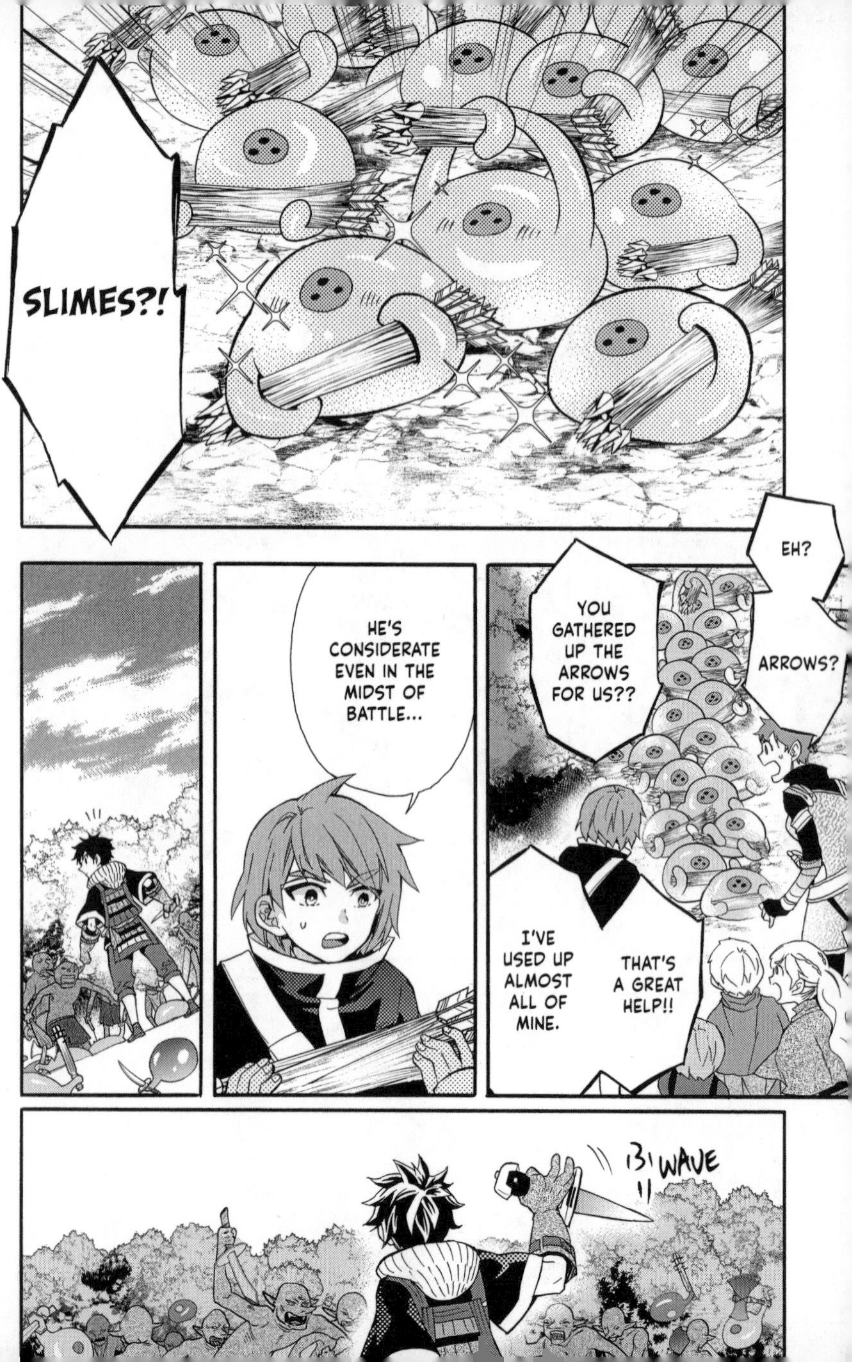
SLIMES?!
EH?
ARROWS?
YOU GATHERED UP THE ARROWS FOR US??
THAT'S A GREAT HELP!!
I'VE USED UP ALMOST ALL OF MINE.
HE'S CONSIDERATE EVEN IN THE MIDST OF BATTLE...
WAVE

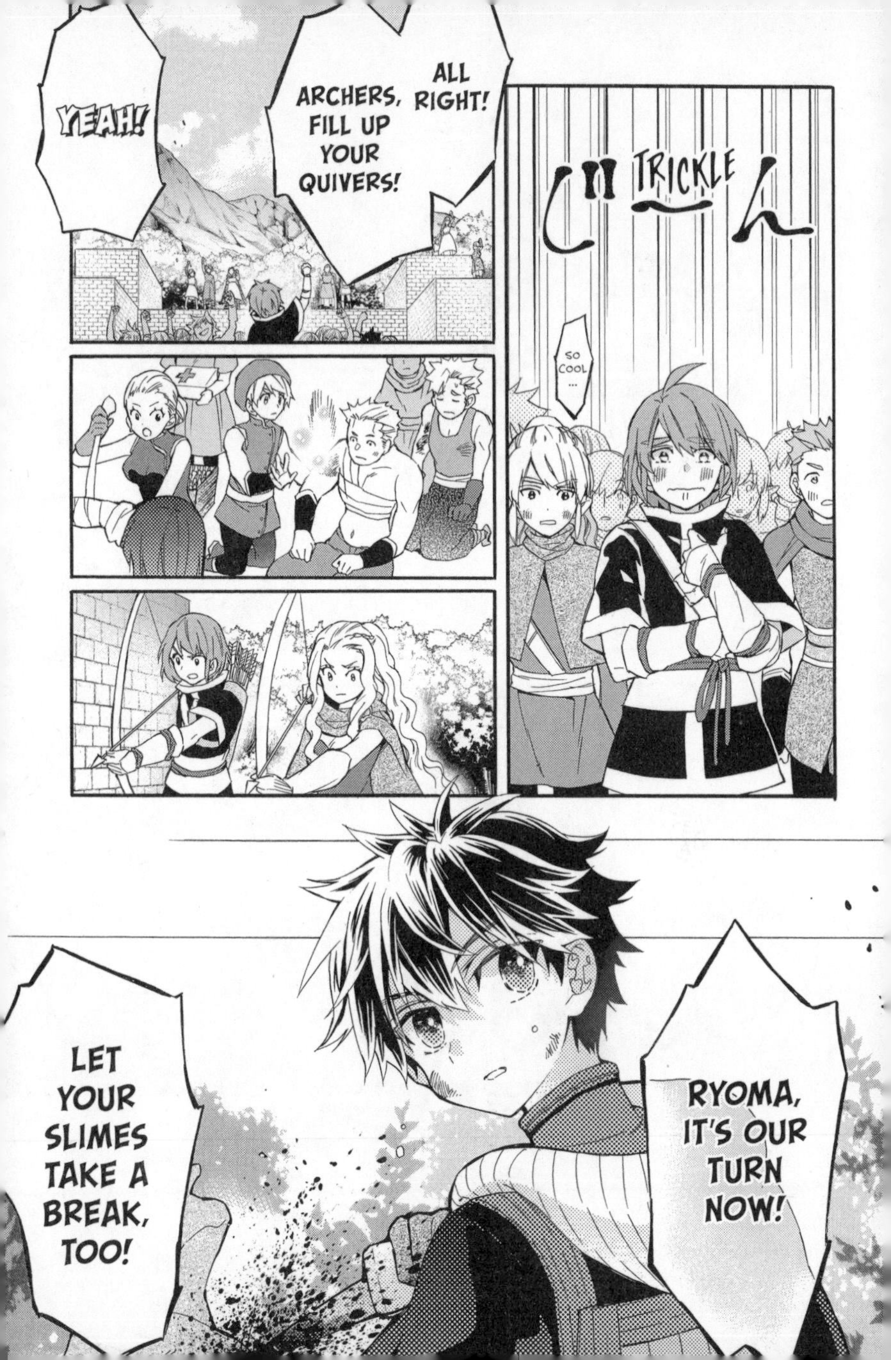
TRICKLE
SO COOL...
ALL RIGHT! ARCHERS, FILL UP YOUR QUIVERS!
YEAH!
RYOMA, IT'S OUR TURN NOW!
LET YOUR SLIMES TAKE A BREAK, TOO!

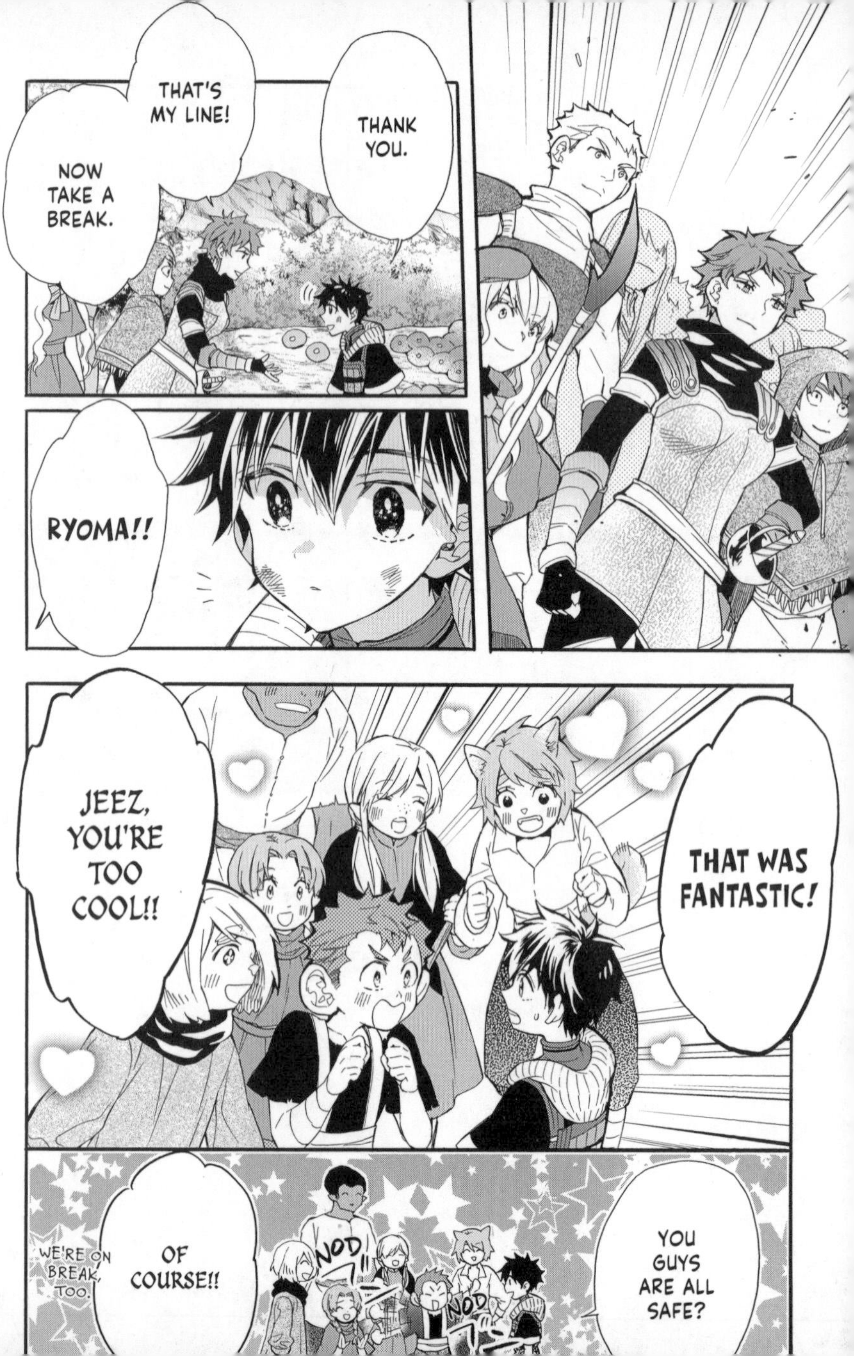
THANK YOU.
THAT'S MY LINE!
NOW TAKE A BREAK.
RYOMA!!
THAT WAS FANTASTIC!
JEEZ, YOU'RE TOO COOL!!
YOU GUYS ARE ALL SAFE?
NOD
NOD
OF COURSE!!
WE'RE ON BREAK, TOO.

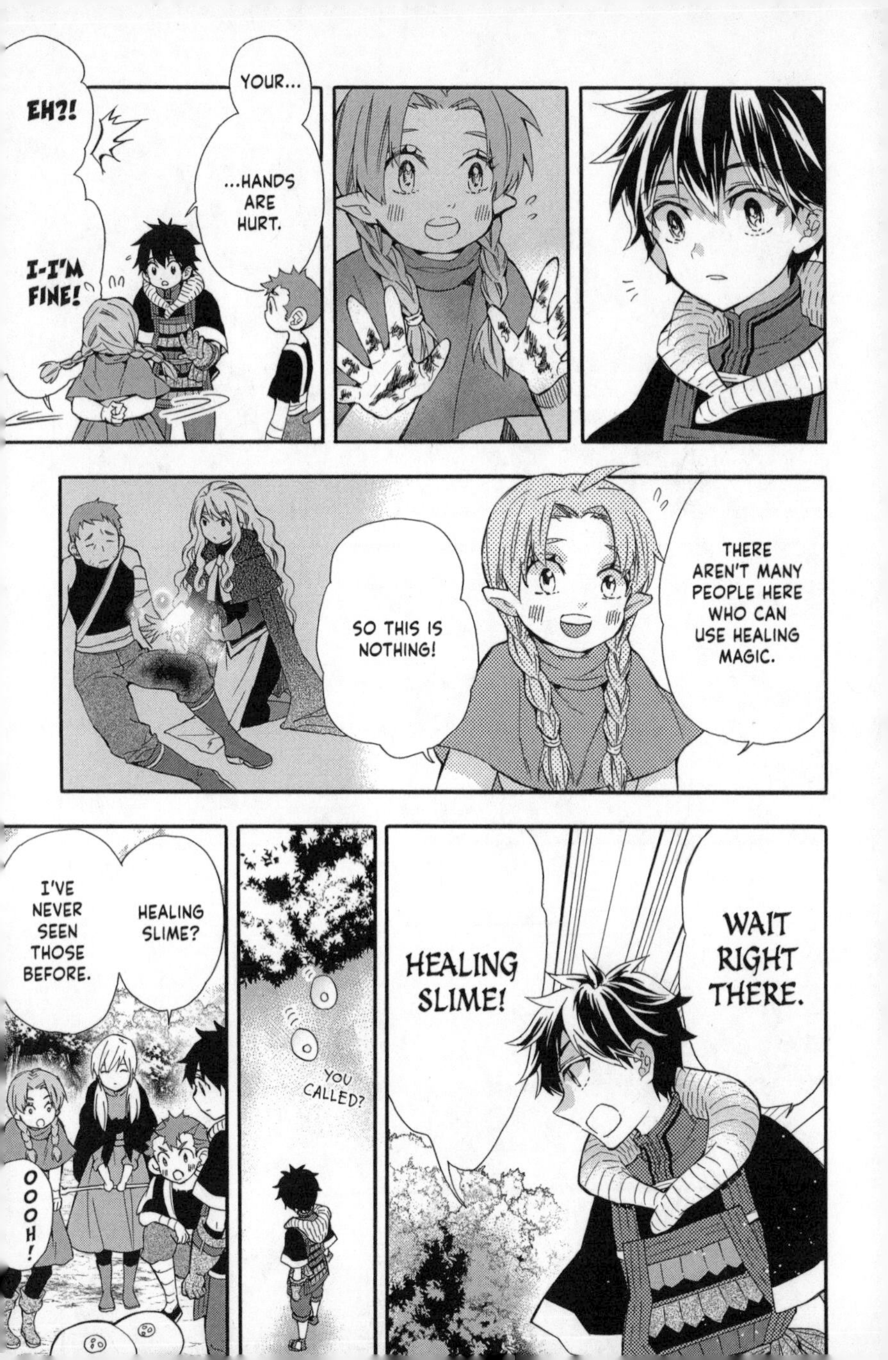
YOUR...
...HANDS ARE HURT.
EH?!
I-I'M FINE!
THERE AREN'T MANY PEOPLE HERE WHO CAN USE HEALING MAGIC.
SO THIS IS NOTHING!
WAIT RIGHT THERE.
HEALING SLIME!
YOU CALLED?
HEALING SLIME?
I'VE NEVER SEEN THOSE BEFORE.
OOOH!

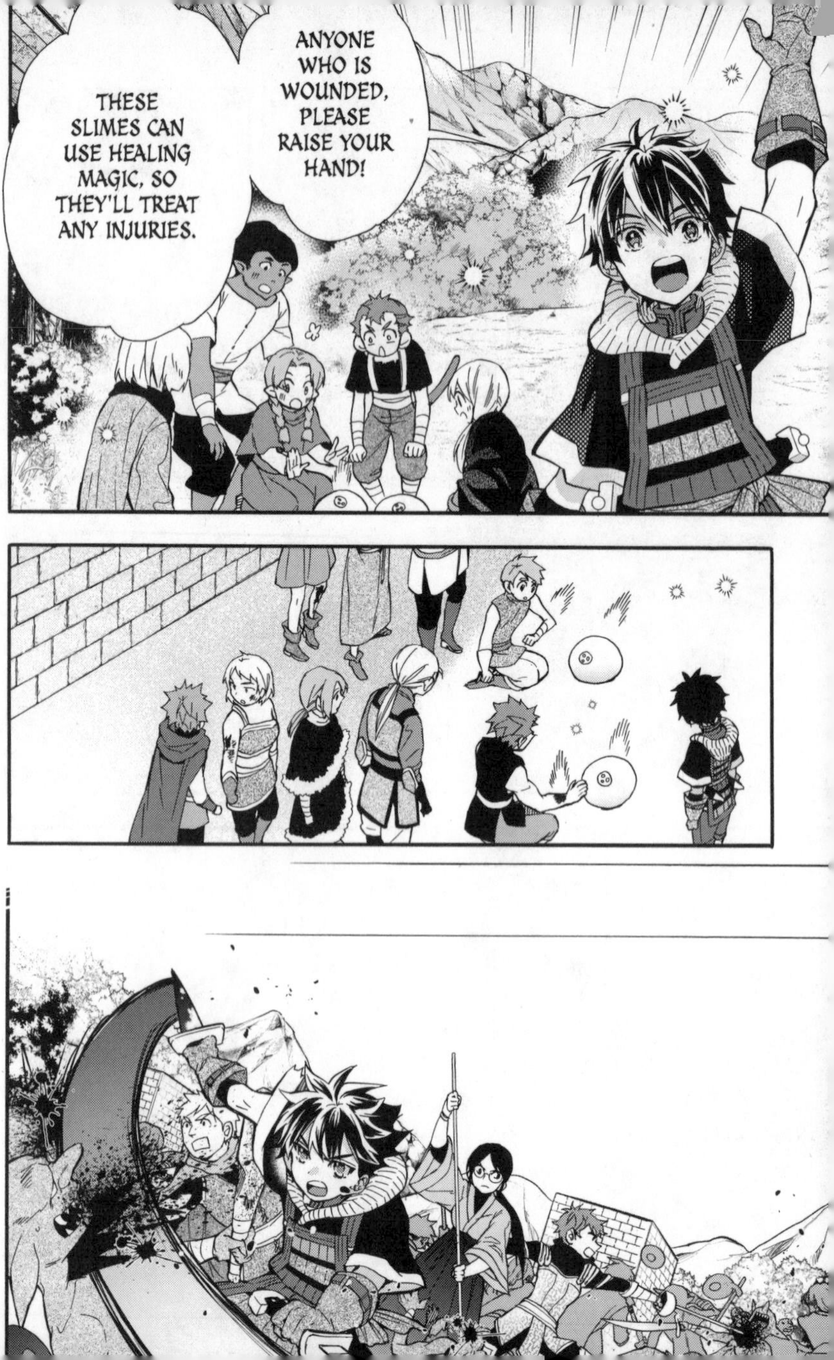
ANYONE WHO IS WOUNDED, PLEASE RAISE YOUR HAND!
THESE SLIMES CAN USE HEALING MAGIC, SO THEY'LL TREAT ANY INJURIES.

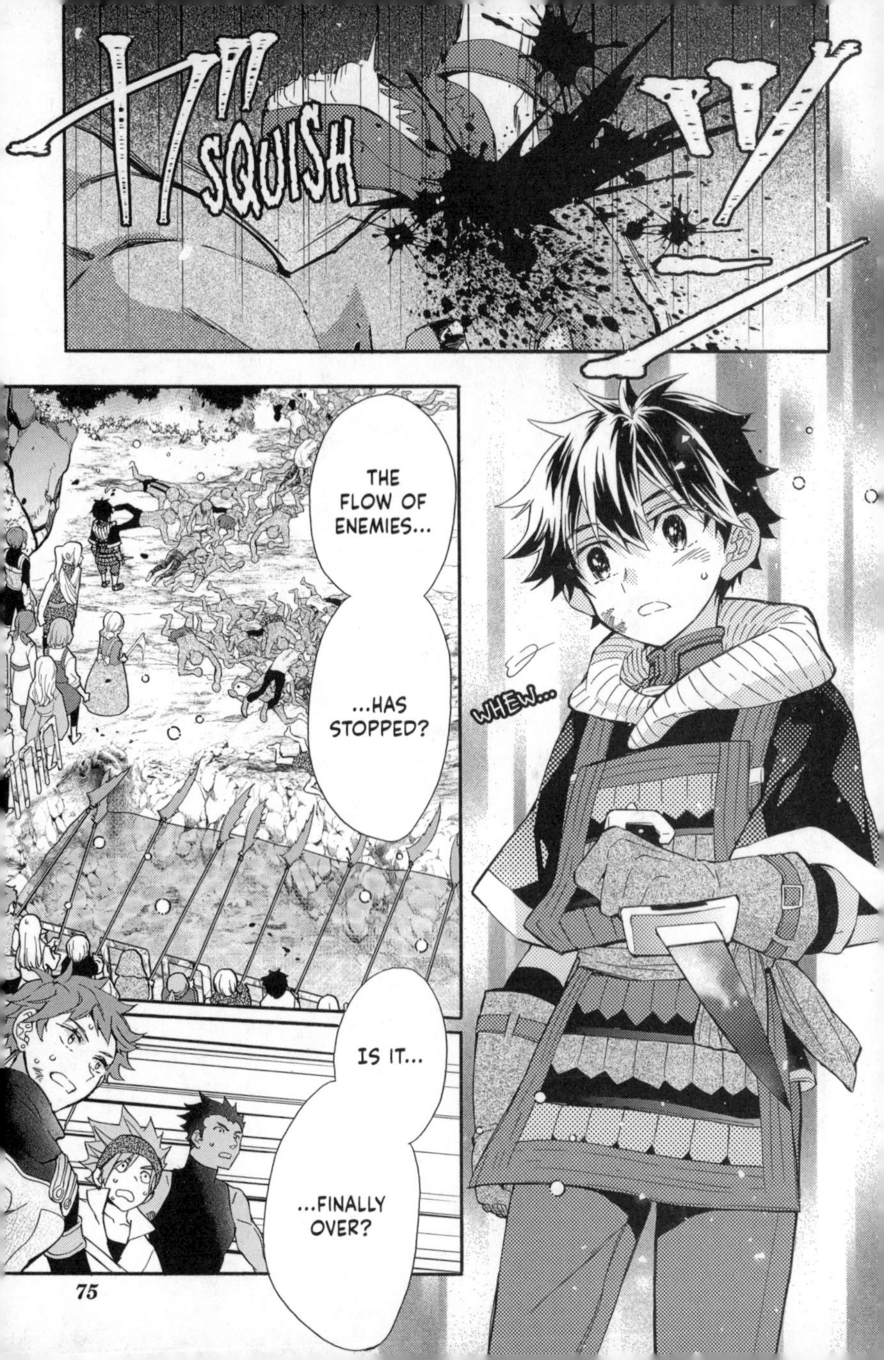
SQUISH
WHEW...
THE FLOW OF ENEMIES...
...HAS STOPPED?
IS IT...
...FINALLY OVER?

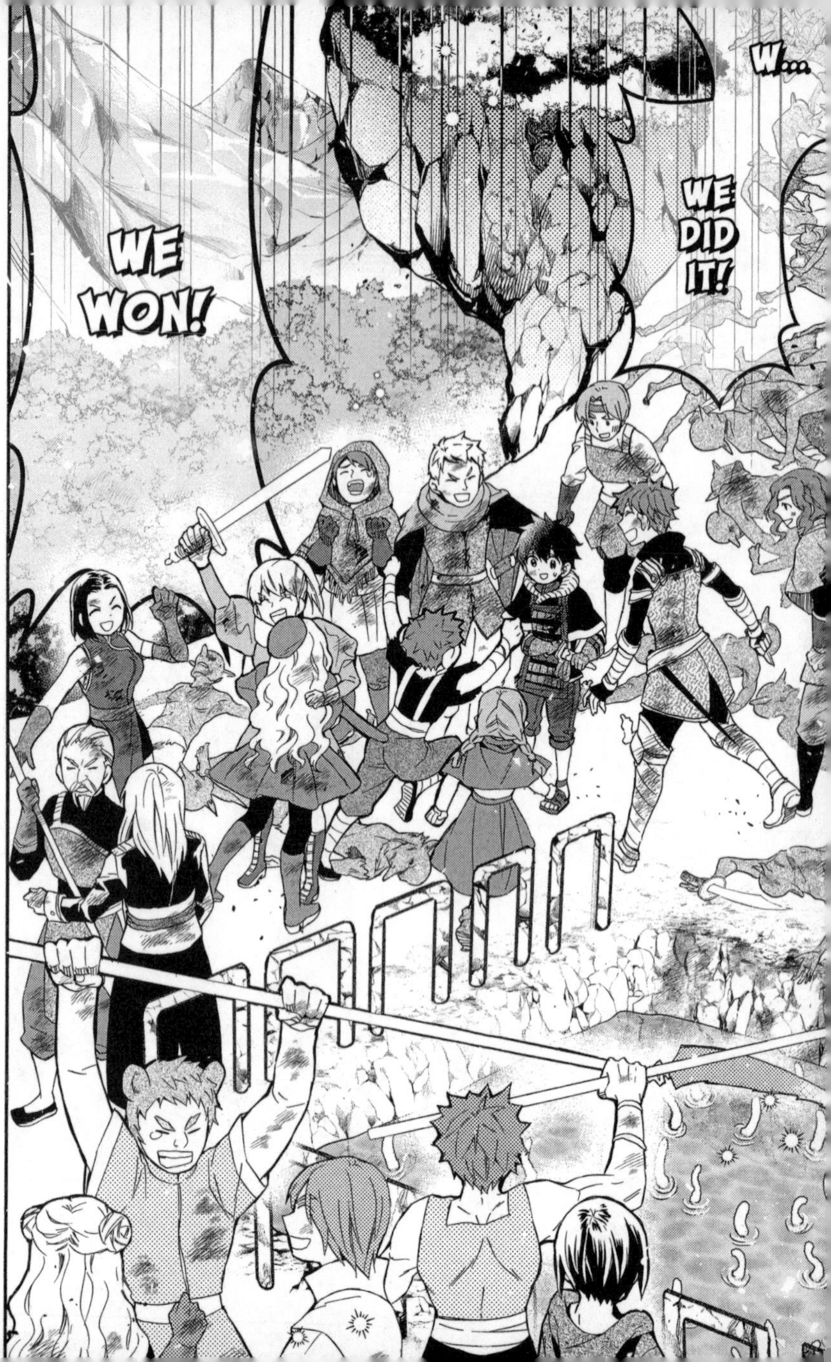

W...
WE DID IT!
WE WON!

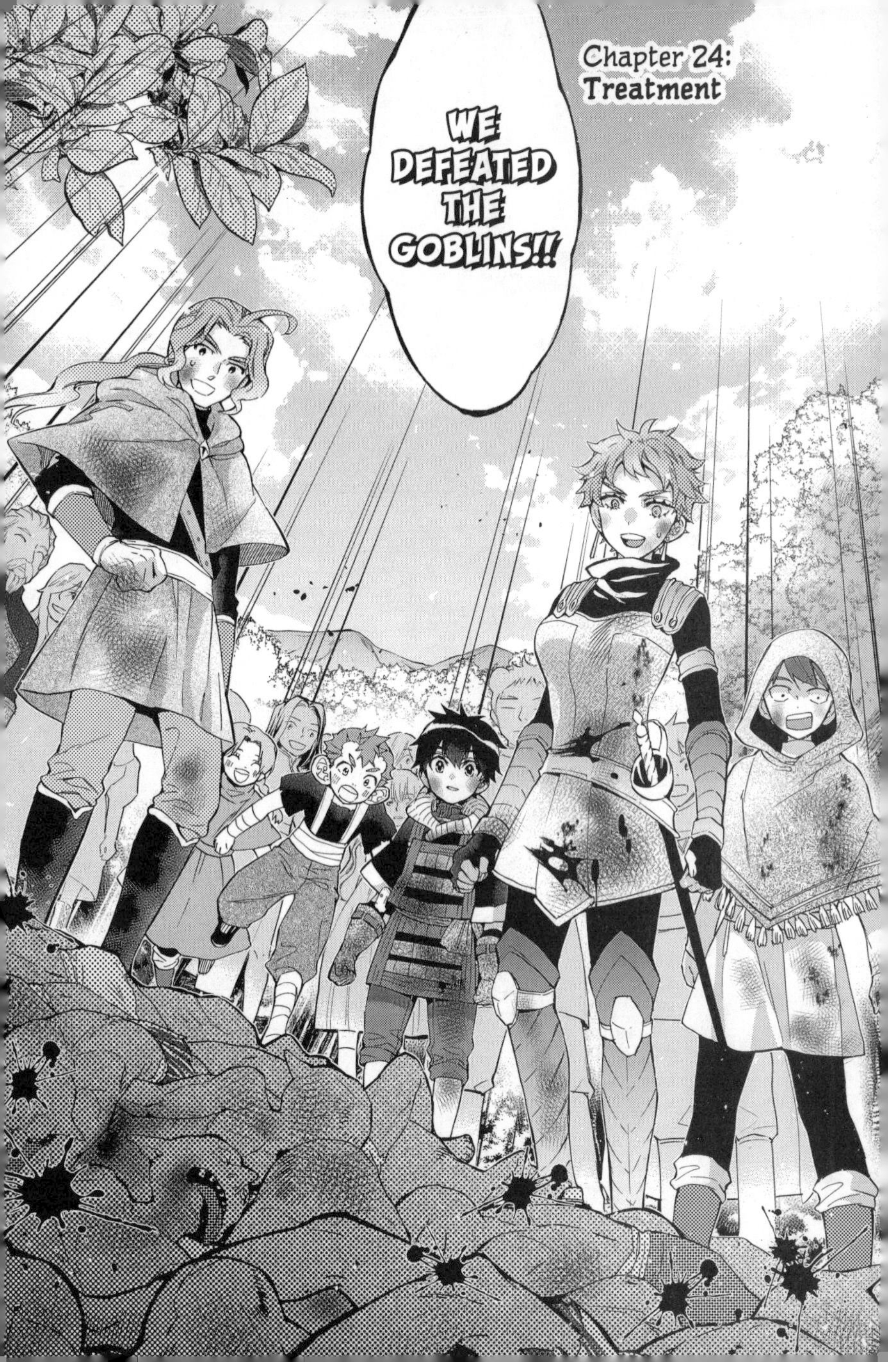
Chapter 24: Treatment
WE DEFEATED THE GOBLINS!!

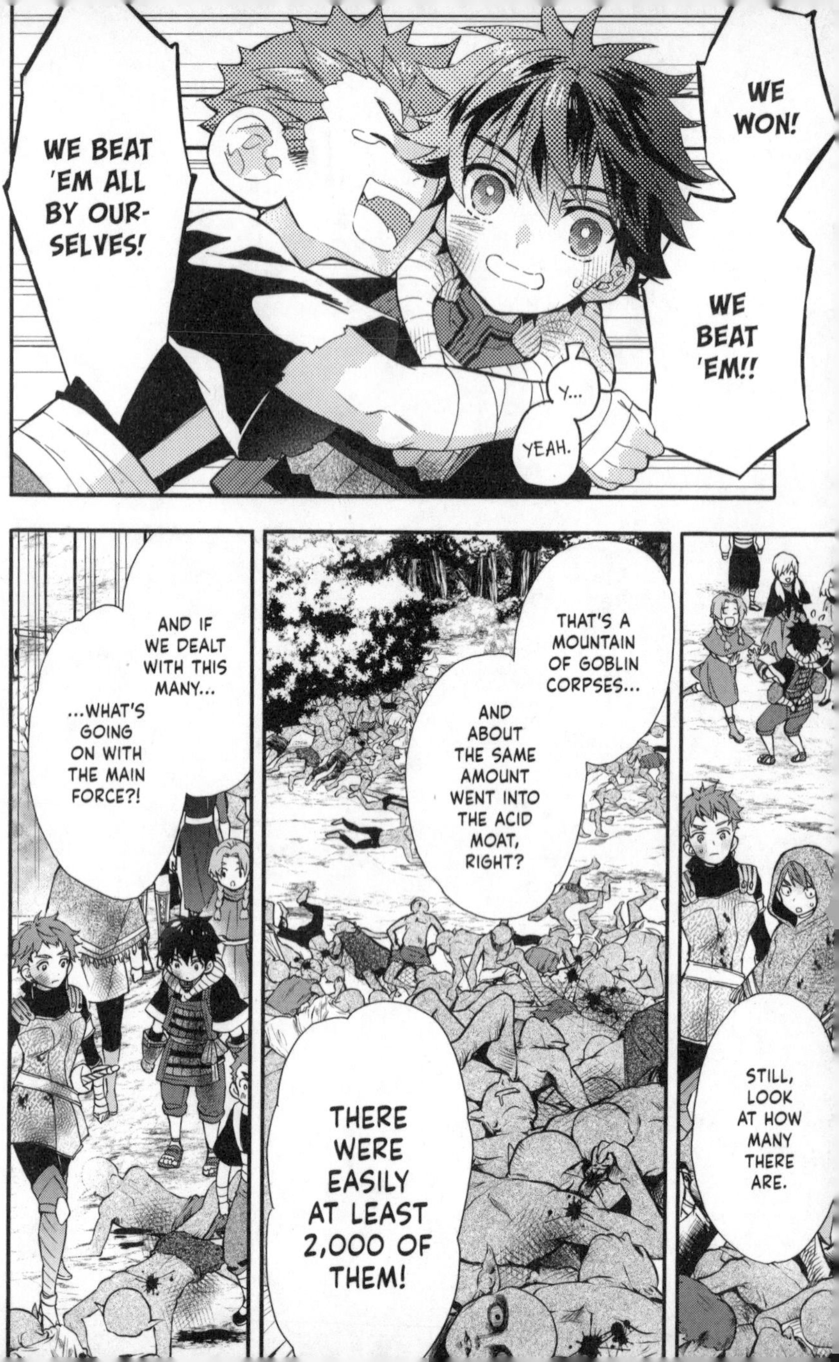
WE WON!
WE BEAT 'EM!!
Y...
YEAH.
WE BEAT 'EM ALL BY OURSELVES!
STILL, LOOK AT HOW MANY THERE ARE.
THAT'S A MOUNTAIN OF GOBLIN CORPSES...
AND ABOUT THE SAME AMOUNT WENT INTO THE ACID MOAT, RIGHT?
THERE WERE EASILY AT LEAST 2,000 OF THEM!
AND IF WE DEALT WITH THIS MANY...
...WHAT'S GOING ON WITH THE MAIN FORCE?!

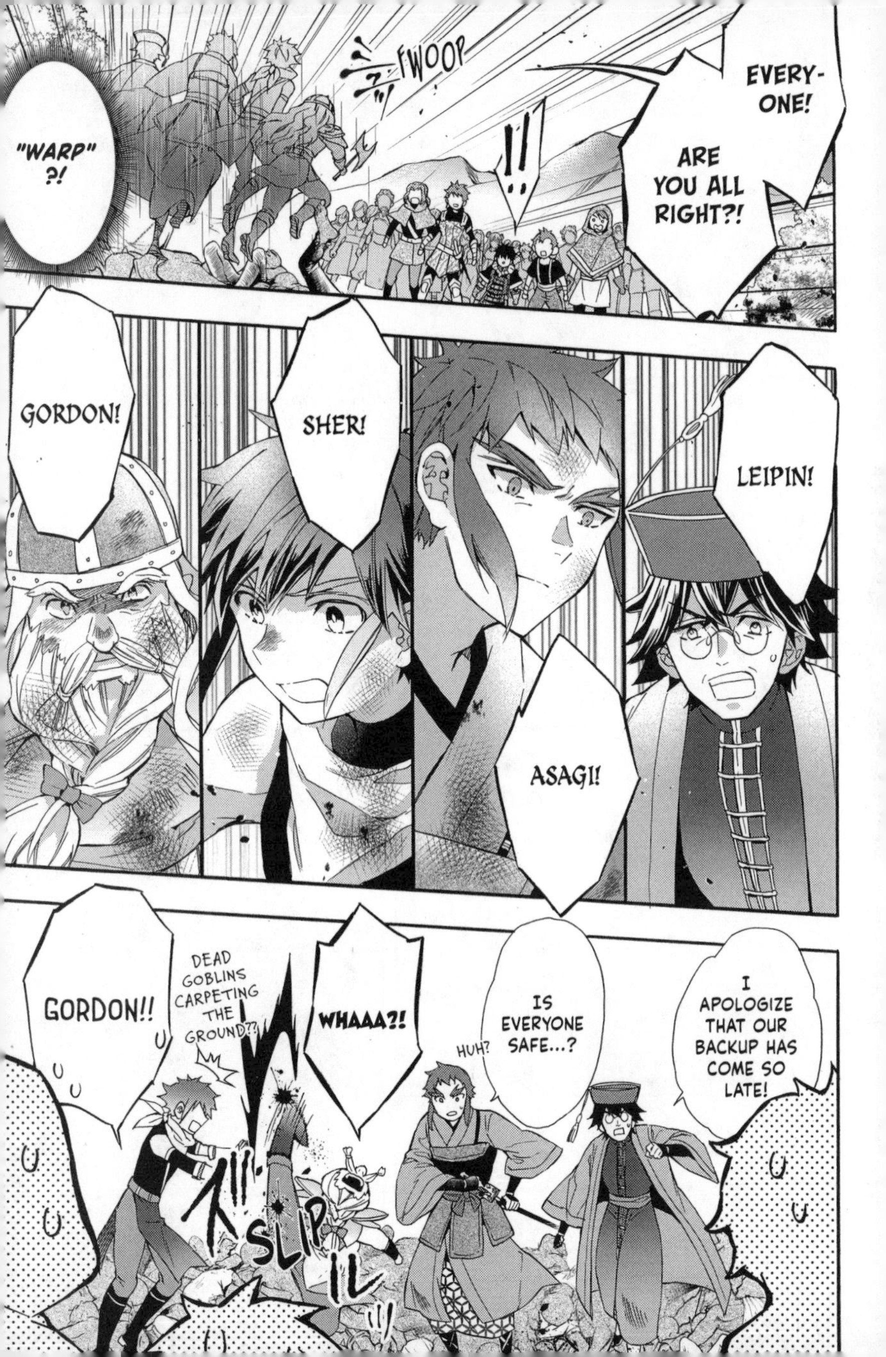
EVERY-ONE!
ARE YOU ALL RIGHT?!
FWOOP
!!
"WARP" ?!
LEIPIN!
ASAGI!
SHER!
GORDON!
I APOLOGIZE THAT OUR BACKUP HAS COME SO LATE!
IS EVERYONE SAFE...?
HUH?
WHAAA?!
SLIP
DEAD GOBLINS CARPETING THE GROUND??
GORDON!!

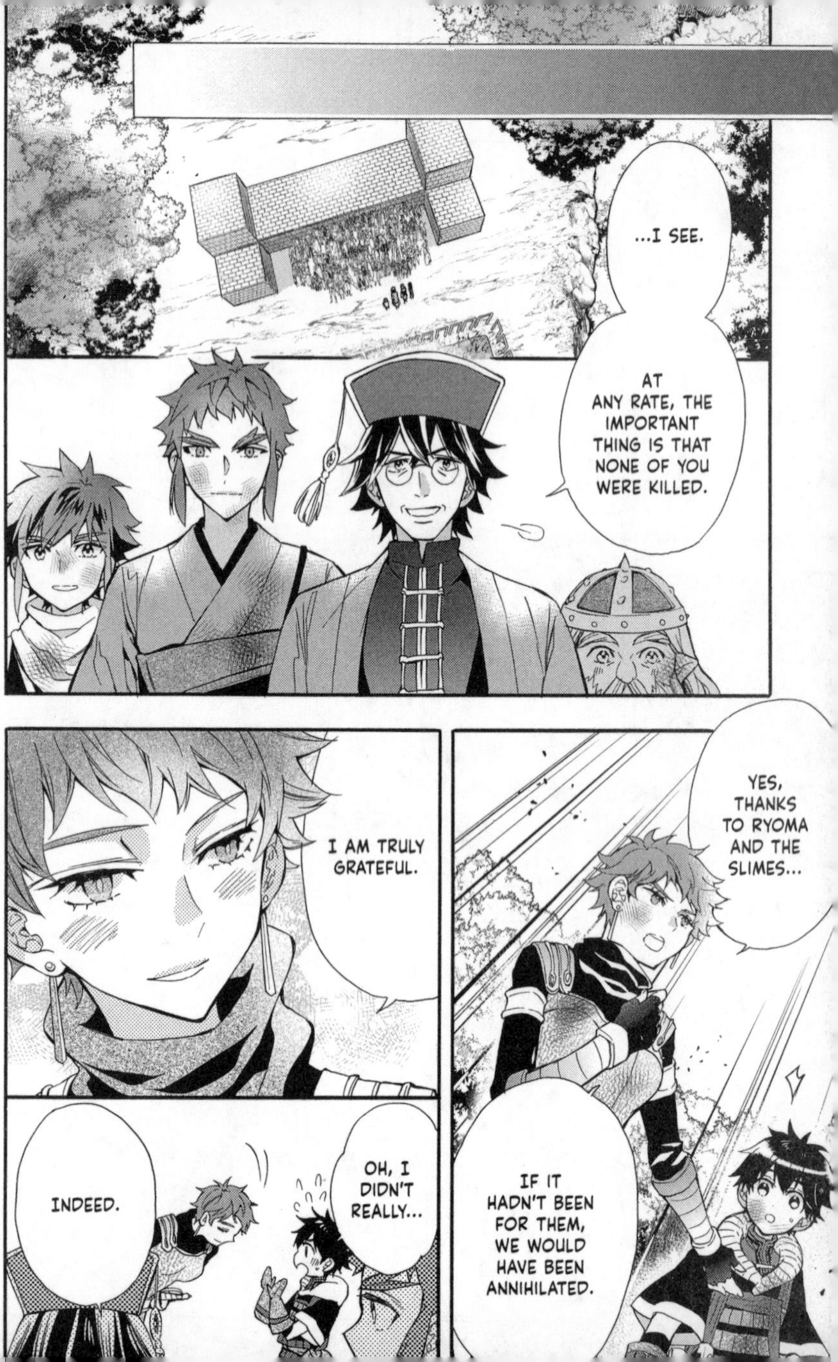
...I SEE.
AT ANY RATE, THE IMPORTANT THING IS THAT NONE OF YOU WERE KILLED.
YES, THANKS TO RYOMA AND THE SLIMES...
IF IT HADN'T BEEN FOR THEM, WE WOULD HAVE BEEN ANNIHILATED.
I AM TRULY GRATEFUL.
OH, I DIDN'T REALLY...
INDEED.

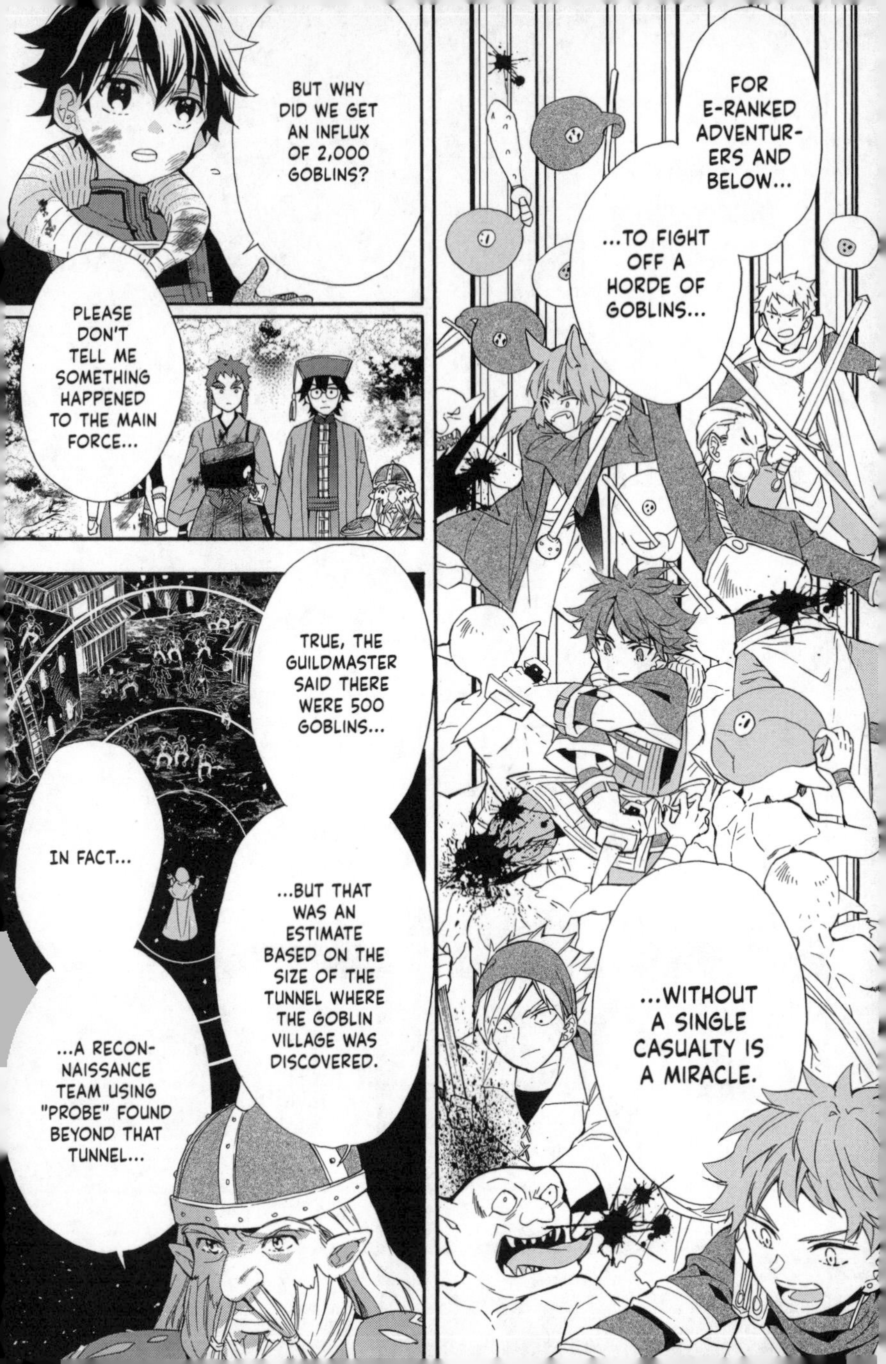
FOR E-RANKED ADVENTURER-ERS AND BELOW...
...TO FIGHT OFF A HORDE OF GOBLINS...
...WITHOUT A SINGLE CASUALTY IS A MIRACLE.
BUT WHY DID WE GET AN INFLUX OF 2,000 GOBLINS?
PLEASE DON'T TELL ME SOMETHING HAPPENED TO THE MAIN FORCE...
TRUE, THE GUILDMASTER SAID THERE WERE 500 GOBLINS...
...BUT THAT WAS AN ESTIMATE BASED ON THE SIZE OF THE TUNNEL WHERE THE GOBLIN VILLAGE WAS DISCOVERED.
IN FACT...
...A RECON-NAISSANCE TEAM USING "PROBE" FOUND BEYOND THAT TUNNEL...

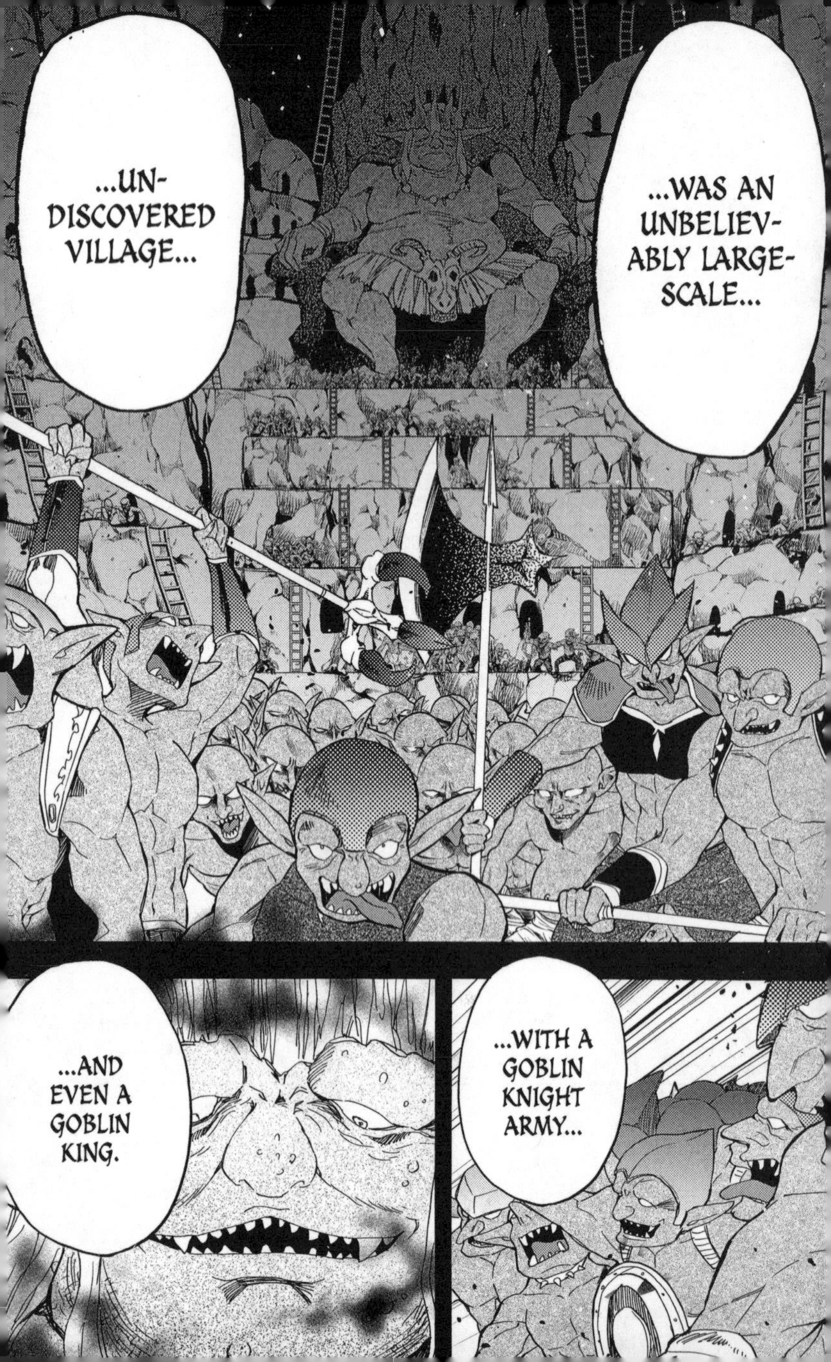
...WAS AN UNBELIEV-ABLY LARGE-SCALE...
...UN-DISCOVERED VILLAGE...
...WITH A GOBLIN KNIGHT ARMY...
...AND EVEN A GOBLIN KING.

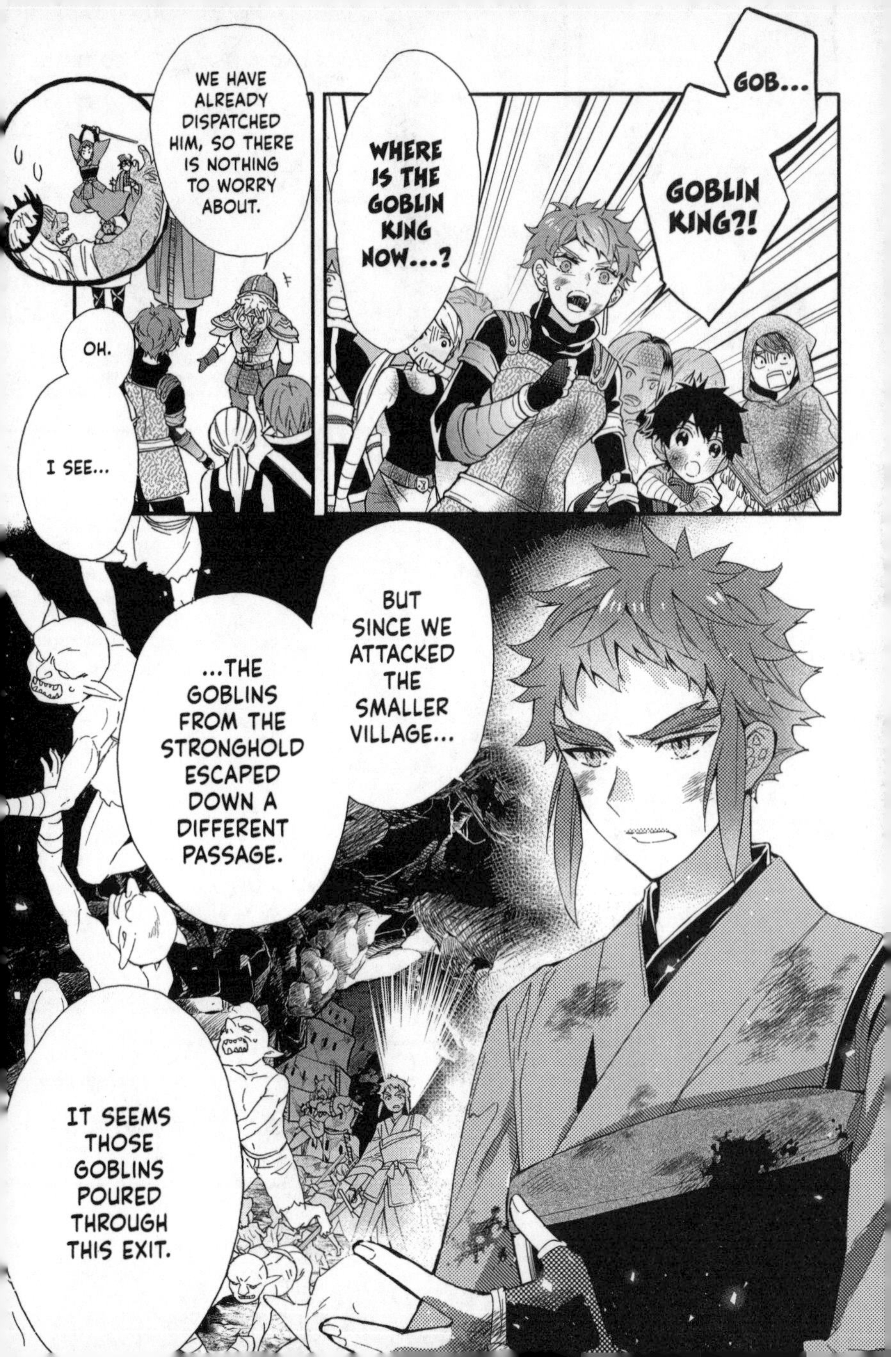
GOB...
GOBLIN KING?!
WHERE IS THE GOBLIN KING NOW...?
WE HAVE ALREADY DISPATCHED HIM, SO THERE IS NOTHING TO WORRY ABOUT.
OH. I SEE...
BUT SINCE WE ATTACKED THE SMALLER VILLAGE...
...THE GOBLINS FROM THE STRONGHOLD ESCAPED DOWN A DIFFERENT PASSAGE.
IT SEEMS THOSE GOBLINS POURED THROUGH THIS EXIT.

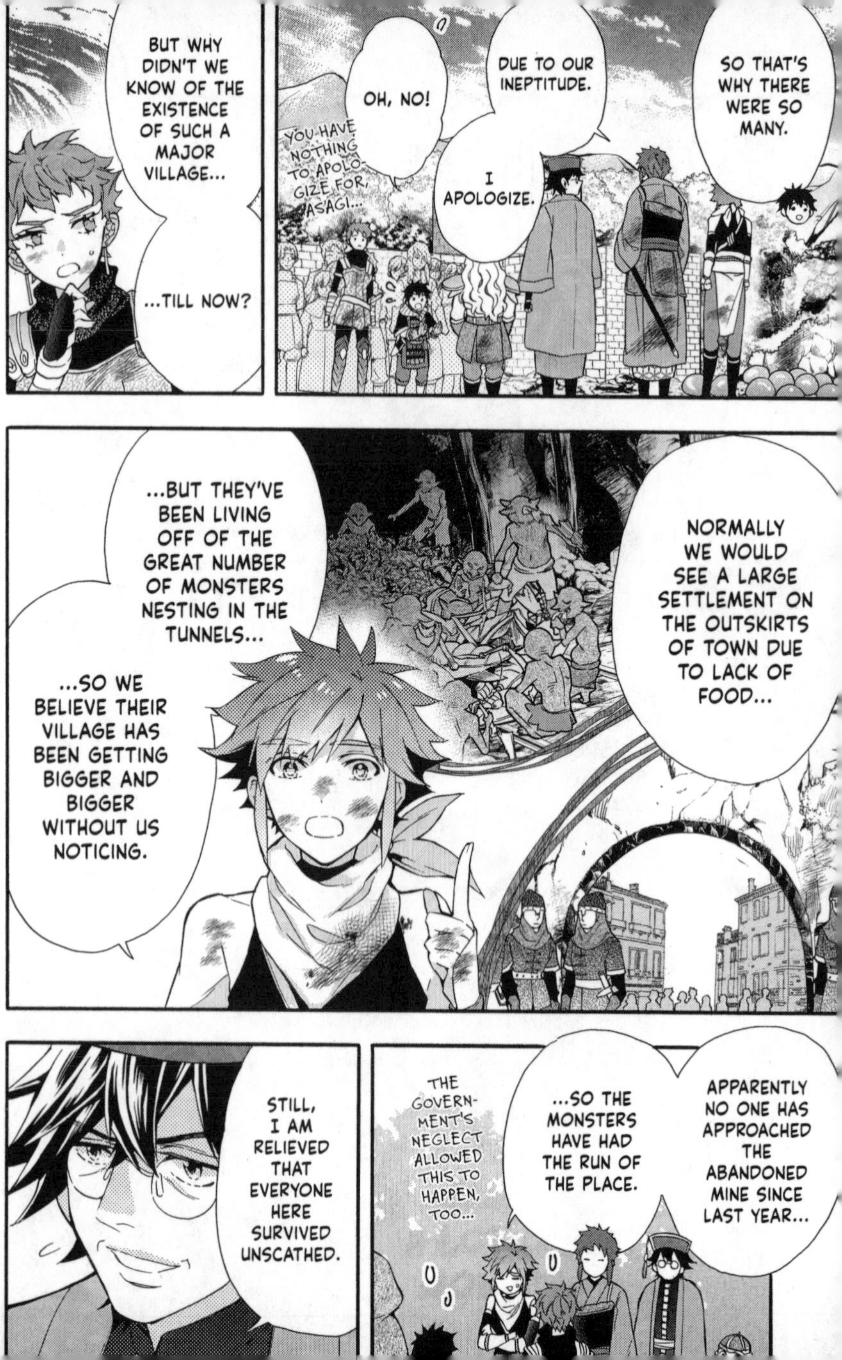
SO THAT'S WHY THERE WERE SO MANY.
DUE TO OUR INEPTITUDE.
I APOLOGIZE.
OH, NO!
YOU HAVE NOTHING TO APOLOGIZE FOR, ASAGI...
BUT WHY DIDN'T WE KNOW OF THE EXISTENCE OF SUCH A MAJOR VILLAGE...
...TILL NOW?
NORMALLY WE WOULD SEE A LARGE SETTLEMENT ON THE OUTSKIRTS OF TOWN DUE TO LACK OF FOOD...
...BUT THEY'VE BEEN LIVING OFF OF THE GREAT NUMBER OF MONSTERS NESTING IN THE TUNNELS...
...SO WE BELIEVE THEIR VILLAGE HAS BEEN GETTING BIGGER AND BIGGER WITHOUT US NOTICING.
APPARENTLY NO ONE HAS APPROACHED THE ABANDONED MINE SINCE LAST YEAR...
...SO THE MONSTERS HAVE HAD THE RUN OF THE PLACE.
THE GOVERNMENT'S NEGLECT ALLOWED THIS TO HAPPEN, TOO...
STILL, I AM RELIEVED THAT EVERYONE HERE SURVIVED UNSCATHED.

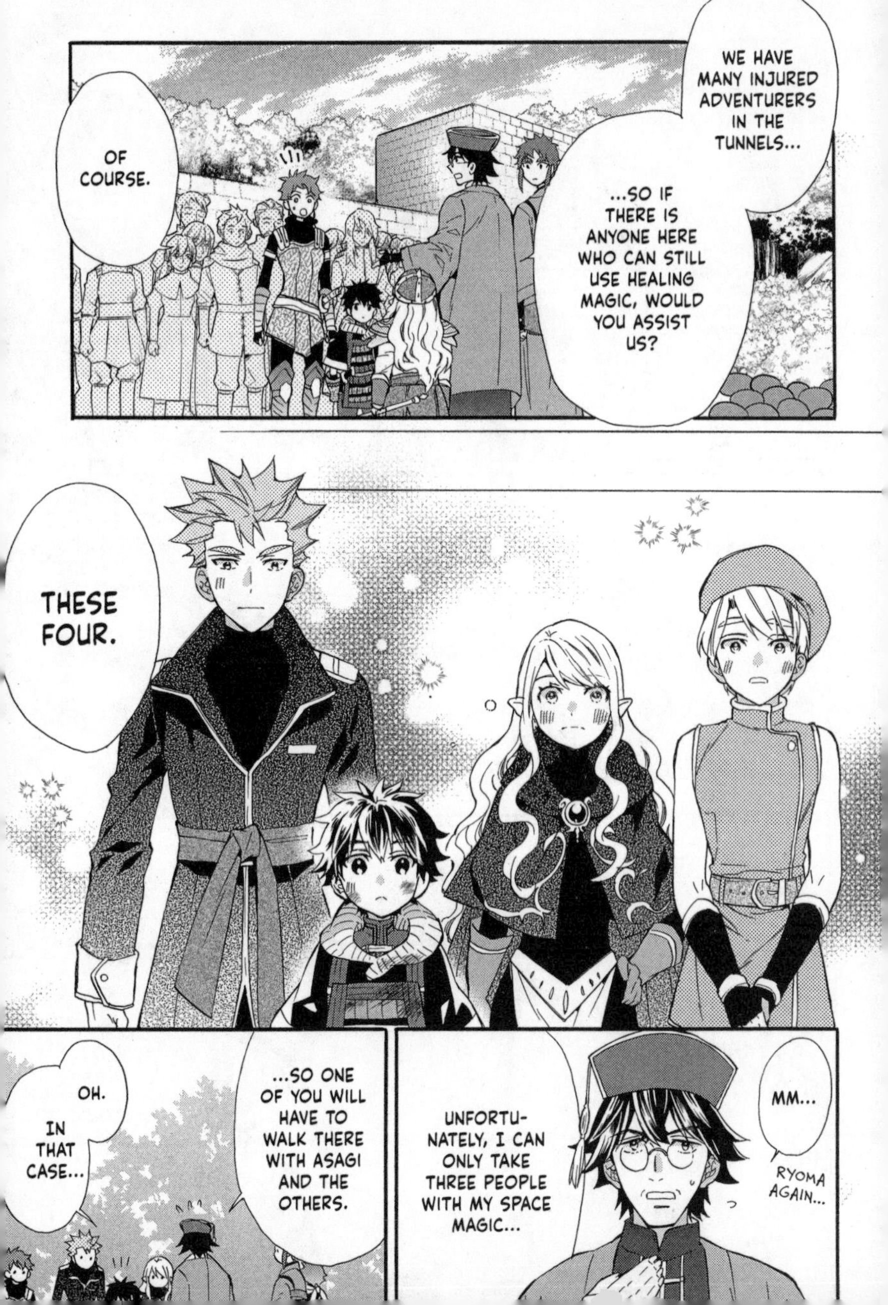
WE HAVE MANY INJURED ADVENTURERS IN THE TUNNELS...
...SO IF THERE IS ANYONE HERE WHO CAN STILL USE HEALING MAGIC, WOULD YOU ASSIST US?
OF COURSE.
THESE FOUR.
MM...
RYOMA AGAIN...
UNFORTU-NATELY, I CAN ONLY TAKE THREE PEOPLE WITH MY SPACE MAGIC...
...SO ONE OF YOU WILL HAVE TO WALK THERE WITH ASAGI AND THE OTHERS.
OH.
IN THAT CASE...

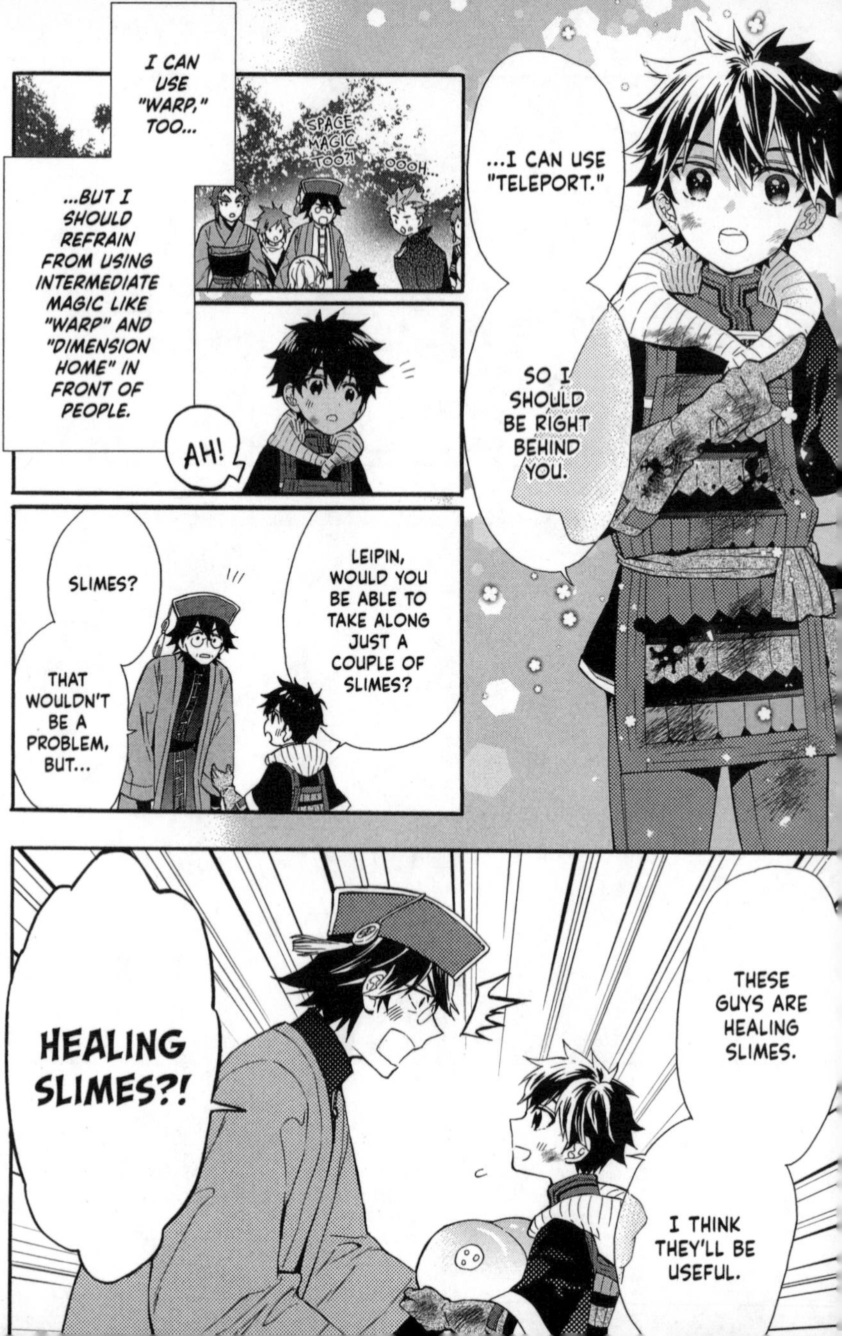
...I CAN USE "TELEPORT."
SO I SHOULD BE RIGHT BEHIND YOU.
I CAN USE "WARP," TOO...
SPACE MAGIC TOO?!
OOOH...
...BUT I SHOULD REFRAIN FROM USING INTERMEDIATE MAGIC LIKE "WARP" AND "DIMENSION HOME" IN FRONT OF PEOPLE.
AH!
LEIPIN, WOULD YOU BE ABLE TO TAKE ALONG JUST A COUPLE OF SLIMES?
SLIMES?
THAT WOULDN'T BE A PROBLEM, BUT...
THESE GUYS ARE HEALING SLIMES.
I THINK THEY'LL BE USEFUL.
HEALING SLIMES?!

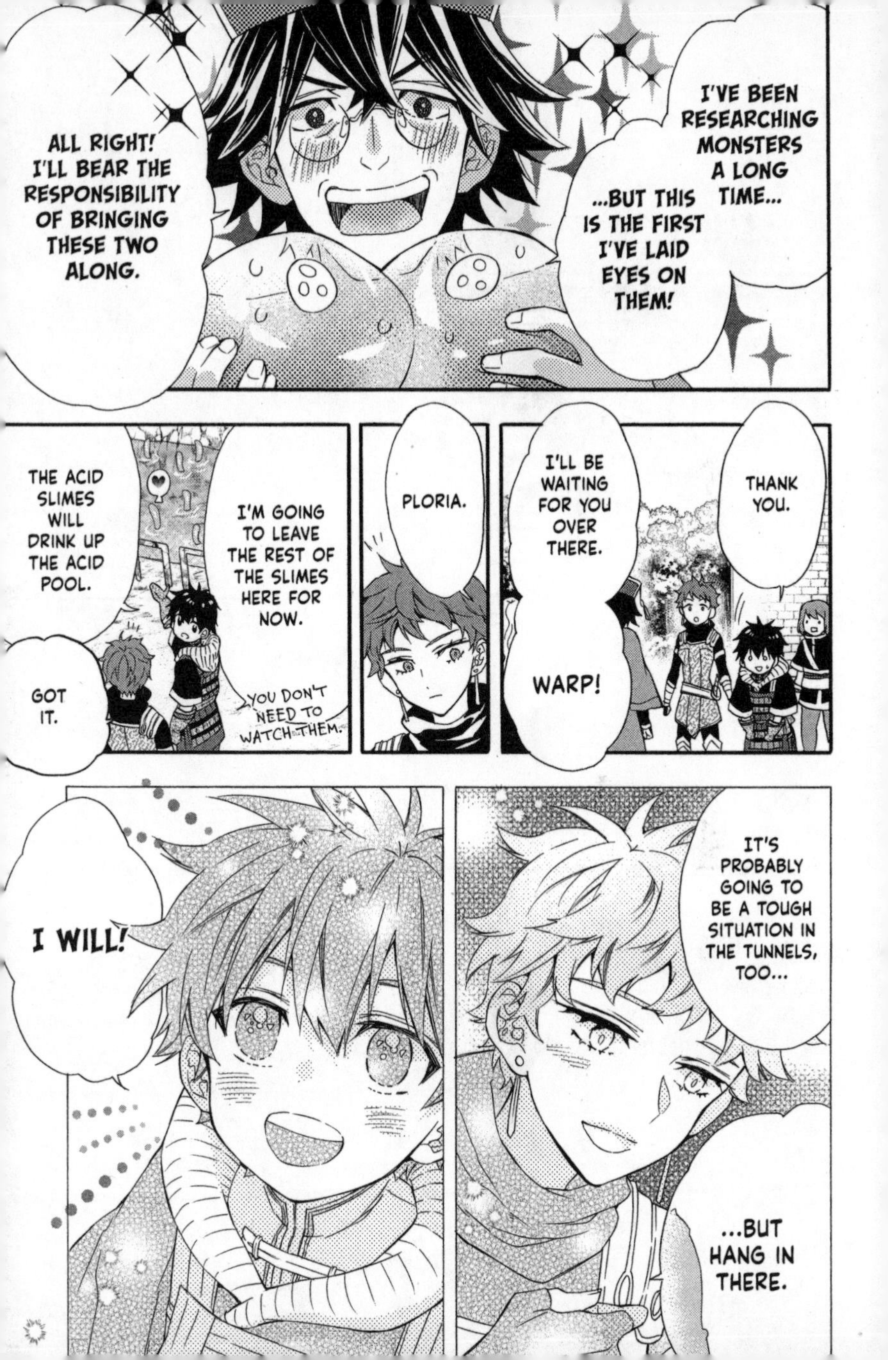
I'VE BEEN RESEARCHING MONSTERS A LONG TIME...
...BUT THIS IS THE FIRST I'VE LAID EYES ON THEM!
ALL RIGHT! I'LL BEAR THE RESPONSIBILITY OF BRINGING THESE TWO ALONG.
THANK YOU.
I'LL BE WAITING FOR YOU OVER THERE.
WARP!
PLORIA.
I'M GOING TO LEAVE THE REST OF THE SLIMES HERE FOR NOW.
THE ACID SLIMES WILL DRINK UP THE ACID POOL.
YOU DON'T NEED TO WATCH THEM.
GOT IT.
IT'S PROBABLY GOING TO BE A TOUGH SITUATION IN THE TUNNELS, TOO...
...BUT HANG IN THERE.
I WILL!

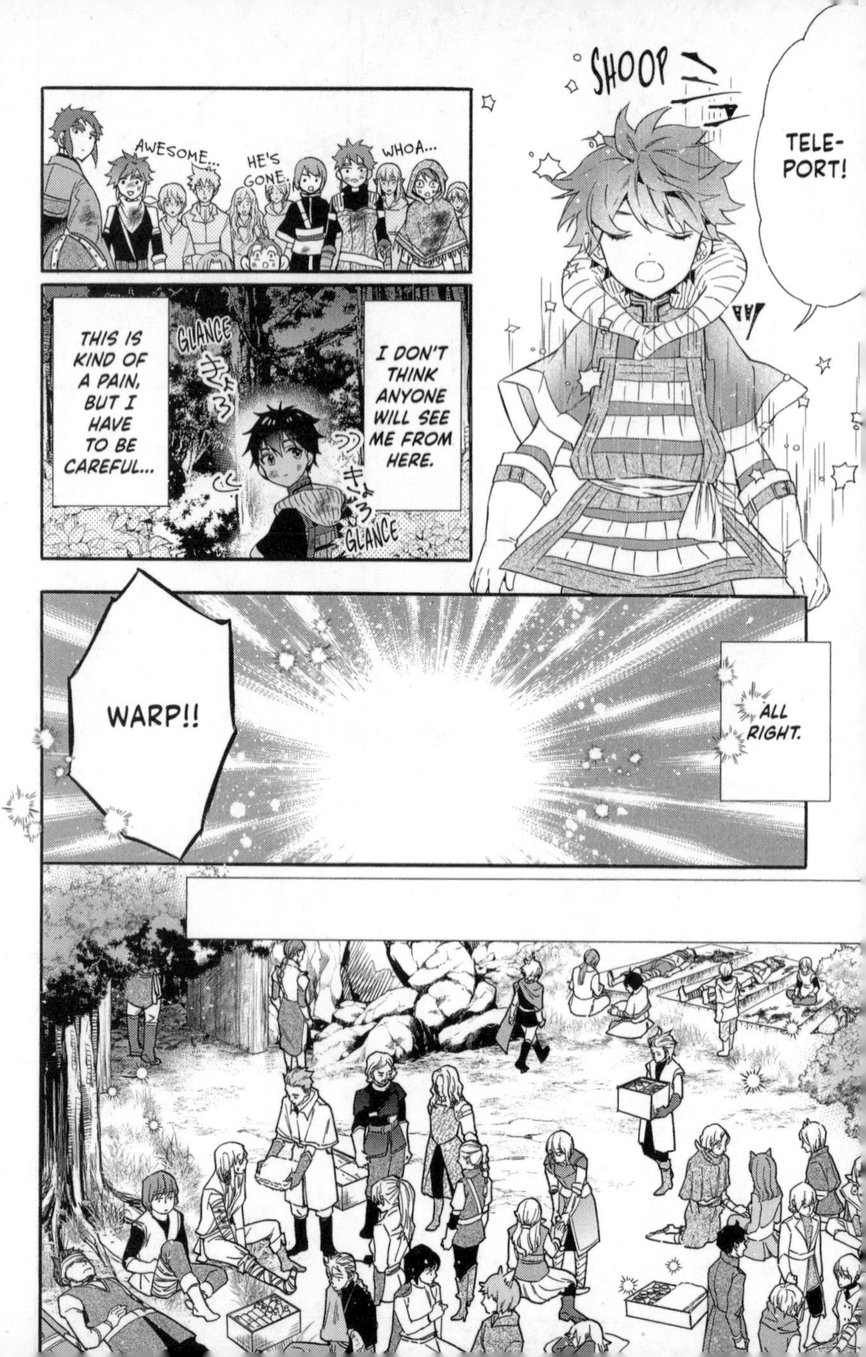
SHOOP
TELE-PORT!
WHOA...
HE'S GONE.
AWESOME...
I DON'T THINK ANYONE WILL SEE ME FROM HERE.
GLANCE
GLANCE
THIS IS KIND OF A PAIN, BUT I HAVE TO BE CAREFUL...
ALL RIGHT.
WARP!!

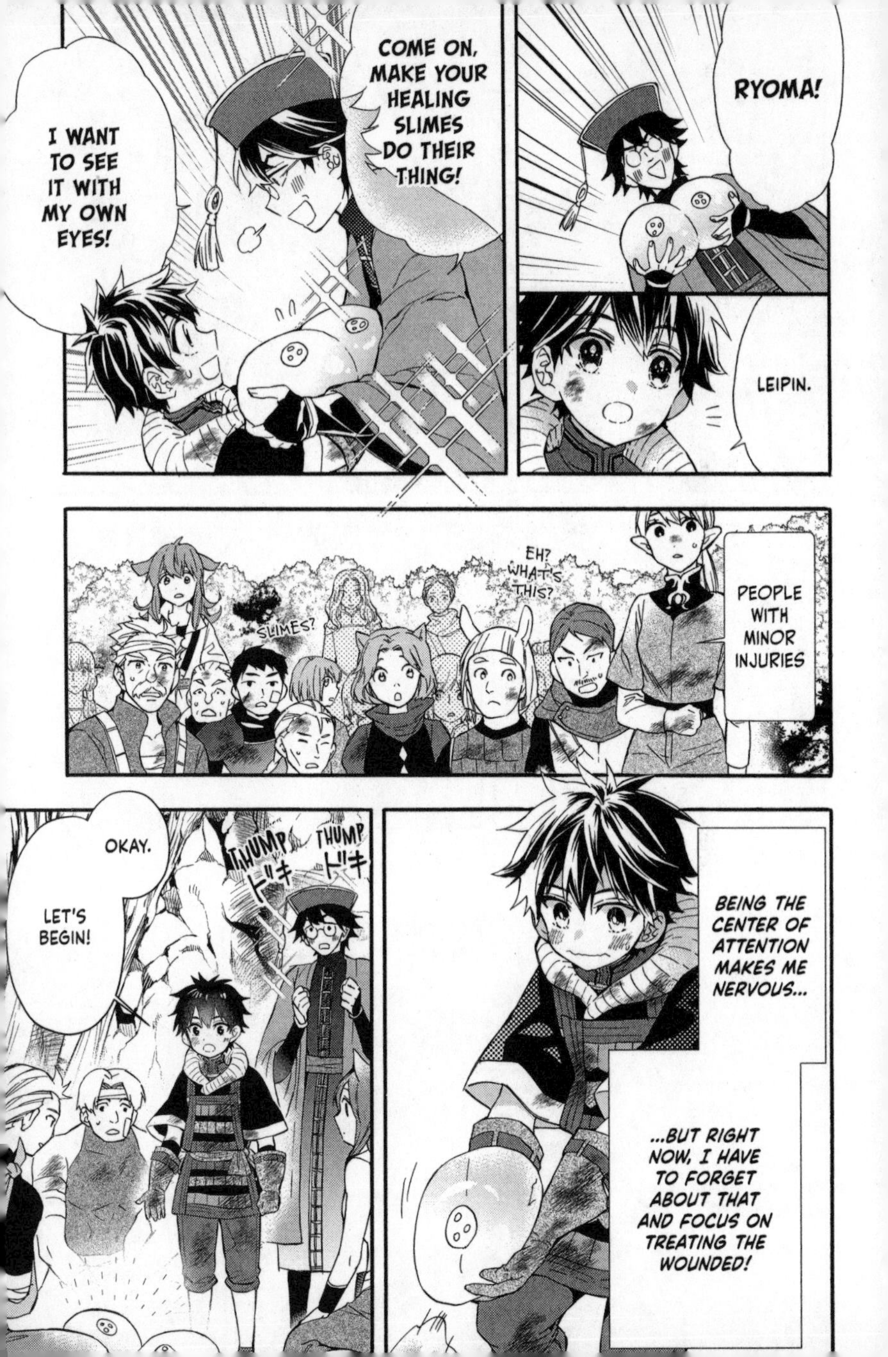
RYOMA!
LEIPIN.
COME ON, MAKE YOUR HEALING SLIMES DO THEIR THING!
I WANT TO SEE IT WITH MY OWN EYES!
PEOPLE WITH MINOR INJURIES
EH? WHAT'S THIS?
SLIMES?
BEING THE CENTER OF ATTENTION MAKES ME NERVOUS...
...BUT RIGHT NOW, I HAVE TO FORGET ABOUT THAT AND FOCUS ON TREATING THE WOUNDED!
THUMP ドキ
THUMP ドキ
OKAY.
LET'S BEGIN!

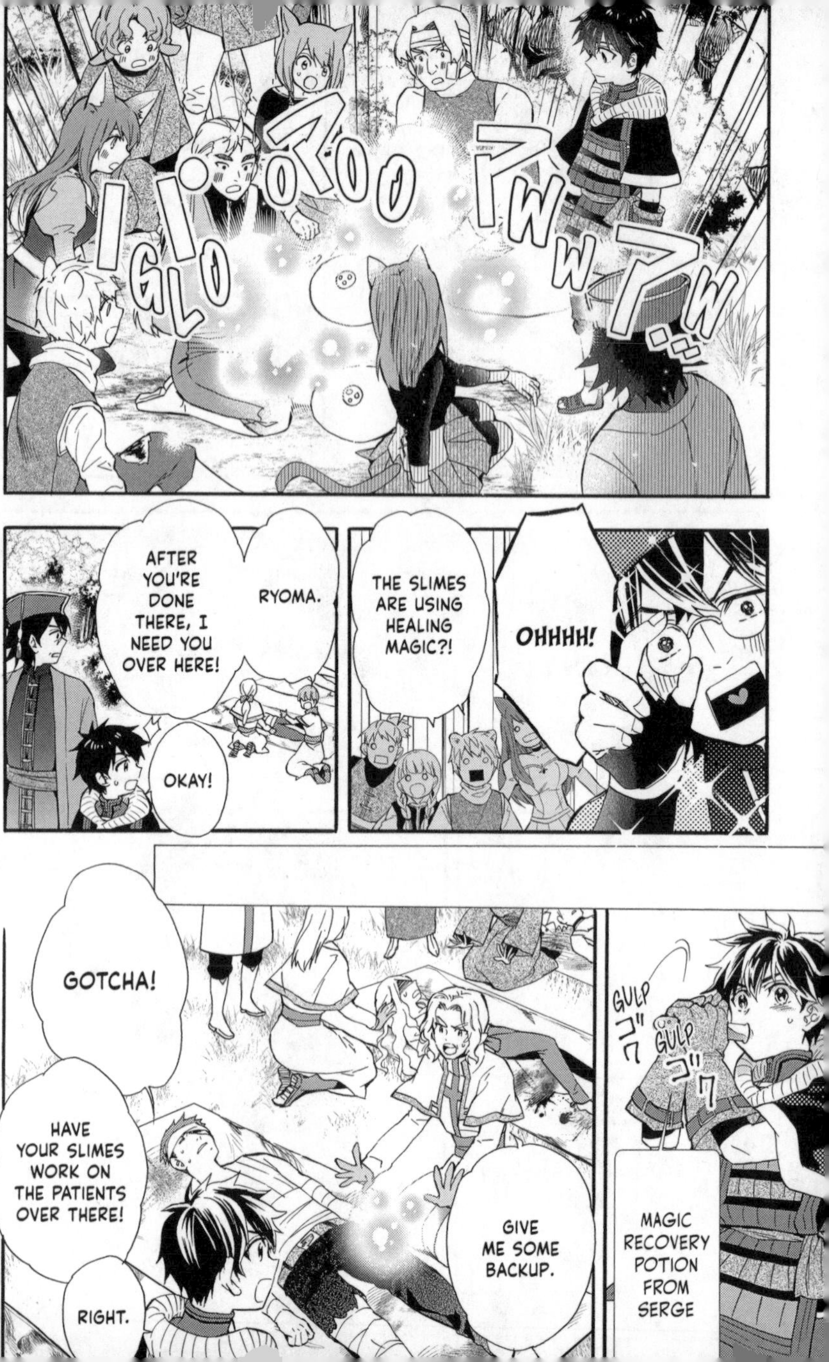
GLOOOO
WWW
OHHHH!
THE SLIMES ARE USING HEALING MAGIC?!
RYOMA.
AFTER YOU'RE DONE THERE, I NEED YOU OVER HERE!
OKAY!
GULP
GULP
MAGIC RECOVERY POTION FROM SERGE
GIVE ME SOME BACKUP.
GOTCHA!
HAVE YOUR SLIMES WORK ON THE PATIENTS OVER THERE!
RIGHT.

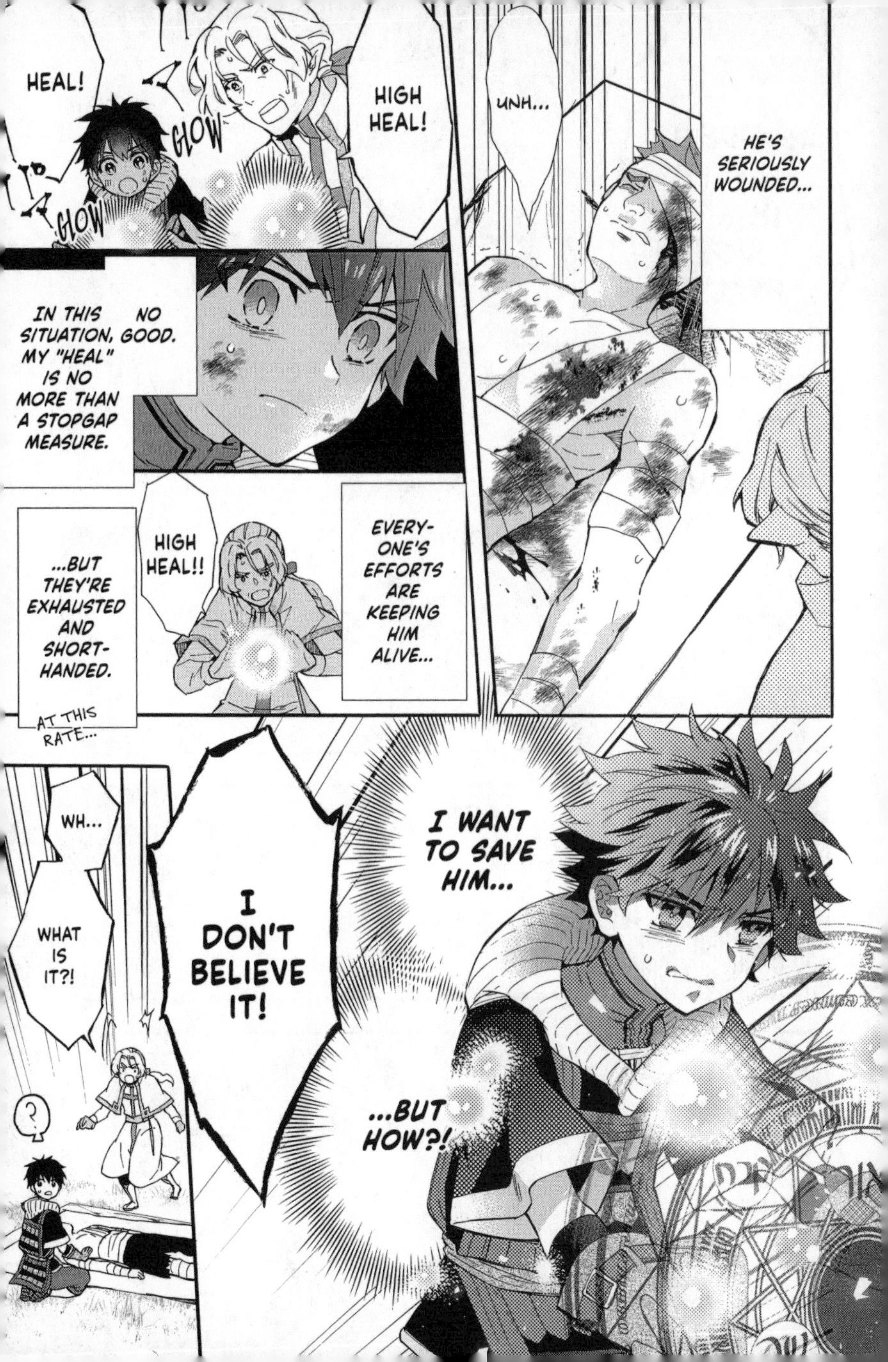
UNH...
HE'S SERIOUSLY WOUNDED...
HIGH HEAL!
GLOW
HEAL!
GLOW
NO GOOD.
IN THIS SITUATION, MY "HEAL" IS NO MORE THAN A STOPGAP MEASURE.
EVERYONE'S EFFORTS ARE KEEPING HIM ALIVE...
HIGH HEAL!!
...BUT THEY'RE EXHAUSTED AND SHORT-HANDED.
AT THIS RATE...
I WANT TO SAVE HIM...
...BUT HOW?!
I DON'T BELIEVE IT!
WH...
WHAT IS IT?!
?

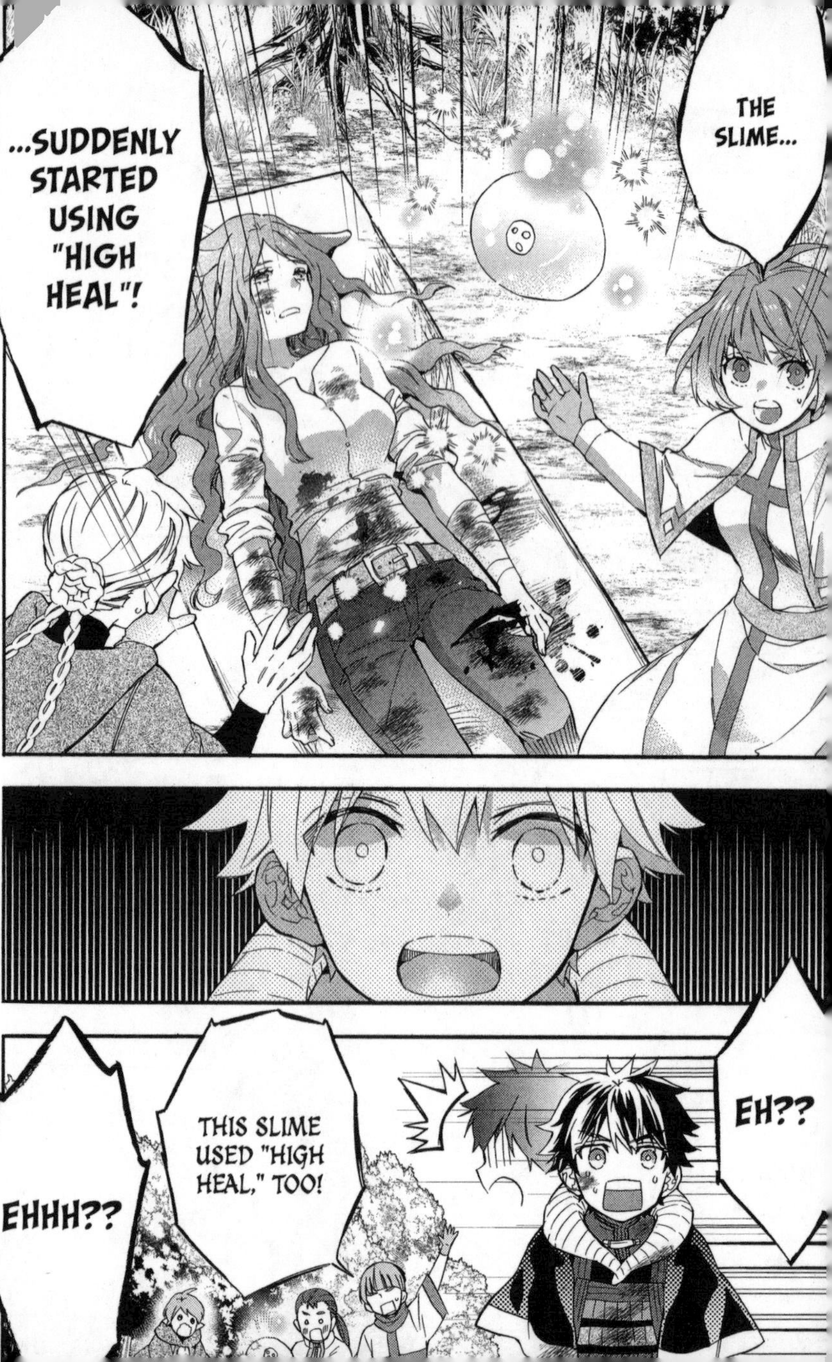
THE SLIME...
...SUDDENLY STARTED USING "HIGH HEAL"!
EH??
THIS SLIME USED "HIGH HEAL," TOO!
EHHH??

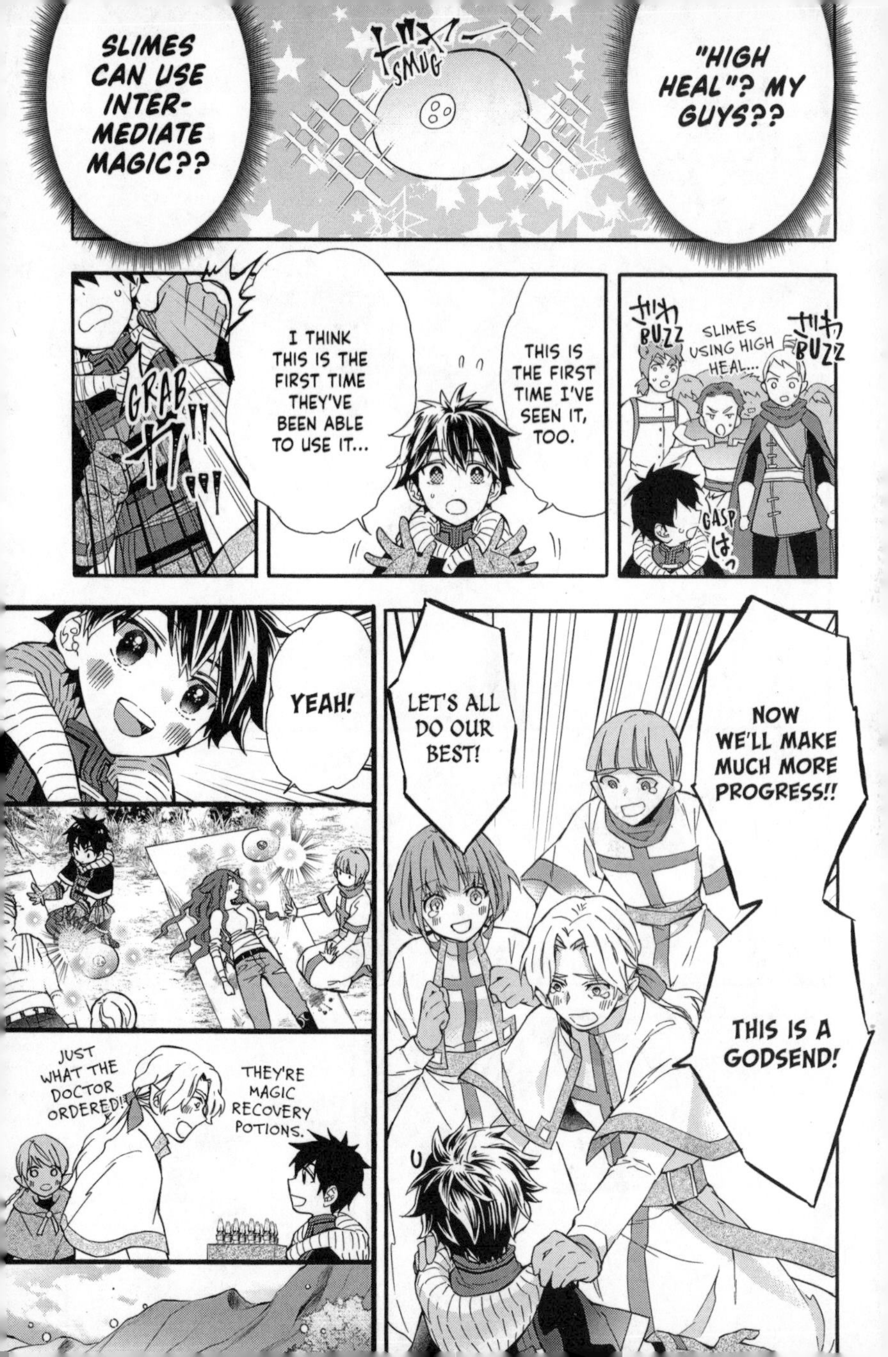
"HIGH HEAL"? MY GUYS??
SMUG
SLIMES CAN USE INTER-MEDIATE MAGIC??
BUZZ
SLIMES USING HIGH HEAL...
BUZZ
GASP
THIS IS THE FIRST TIME I'VE SEEN IT, TOO.
I THINK THIS IS THE FIRST TIME THEY'VE BEEN ABLE TO USE IT...
GRAB
NOW WE'LL MAKE MUCH MORE PROGRESS!!
THIS IS A GODSEND!
LET'S ALL DO OUR BEST!
YEAH!
THEY'RE MAGIC RECOVERY POTIONS.
JUST WHAT THE DOCTOR ORDERED!

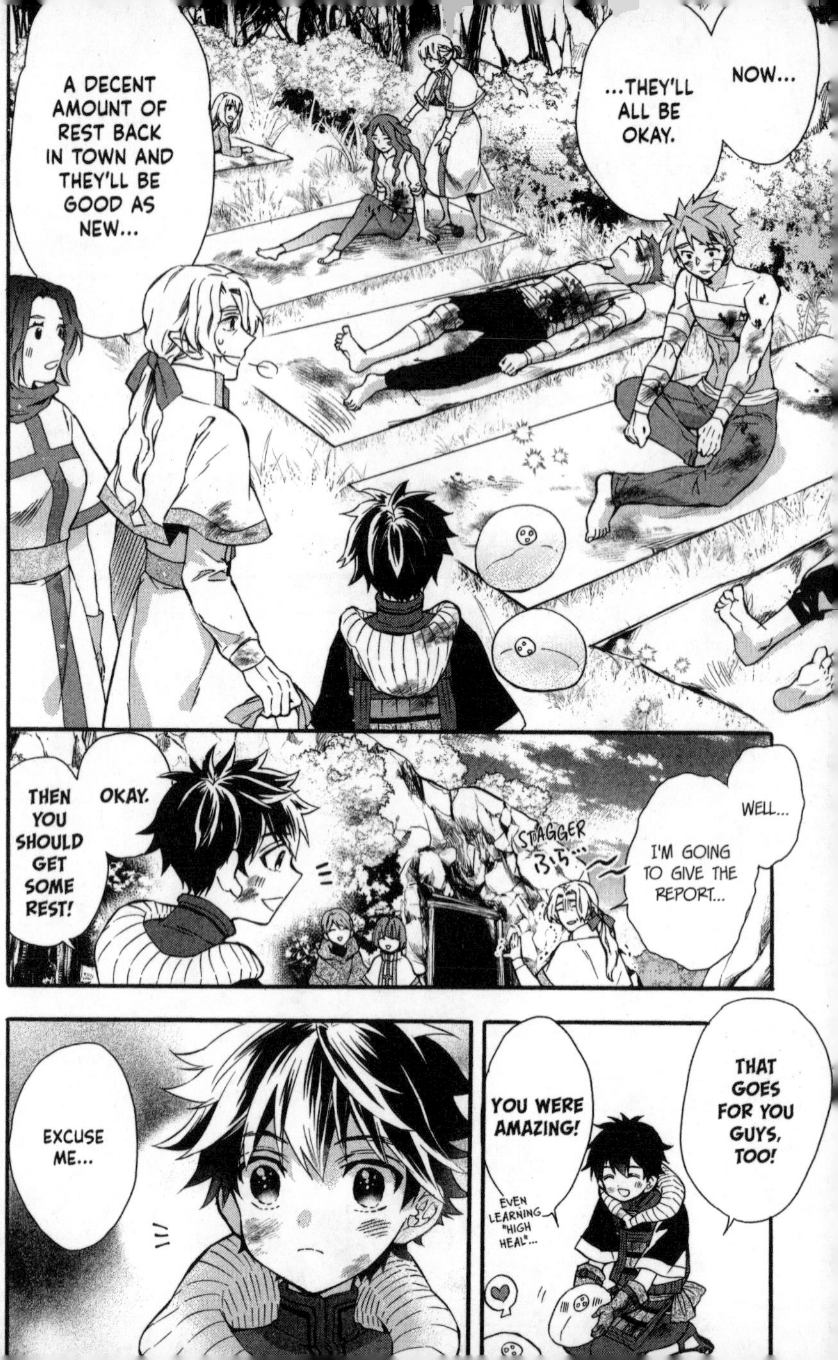
NOW...
...THEY'LL ALL BE OKAY.
A DECENT AMOUNT OF REST BACK IN TOWN AND THEY'LL BE GOOD AS NEW...
WELL...
I'M GOING TO GIVE THE REPORT...
STAGGER
ふら…
OKAY.
THEN YOU SHOULD GET SOME REST!
THAT GOES FOR YOU GUYS, TOO!
YOU WERE AMAZING!
EVEN LEARNING "HIGH HEAL"...
EXCUSE ME...

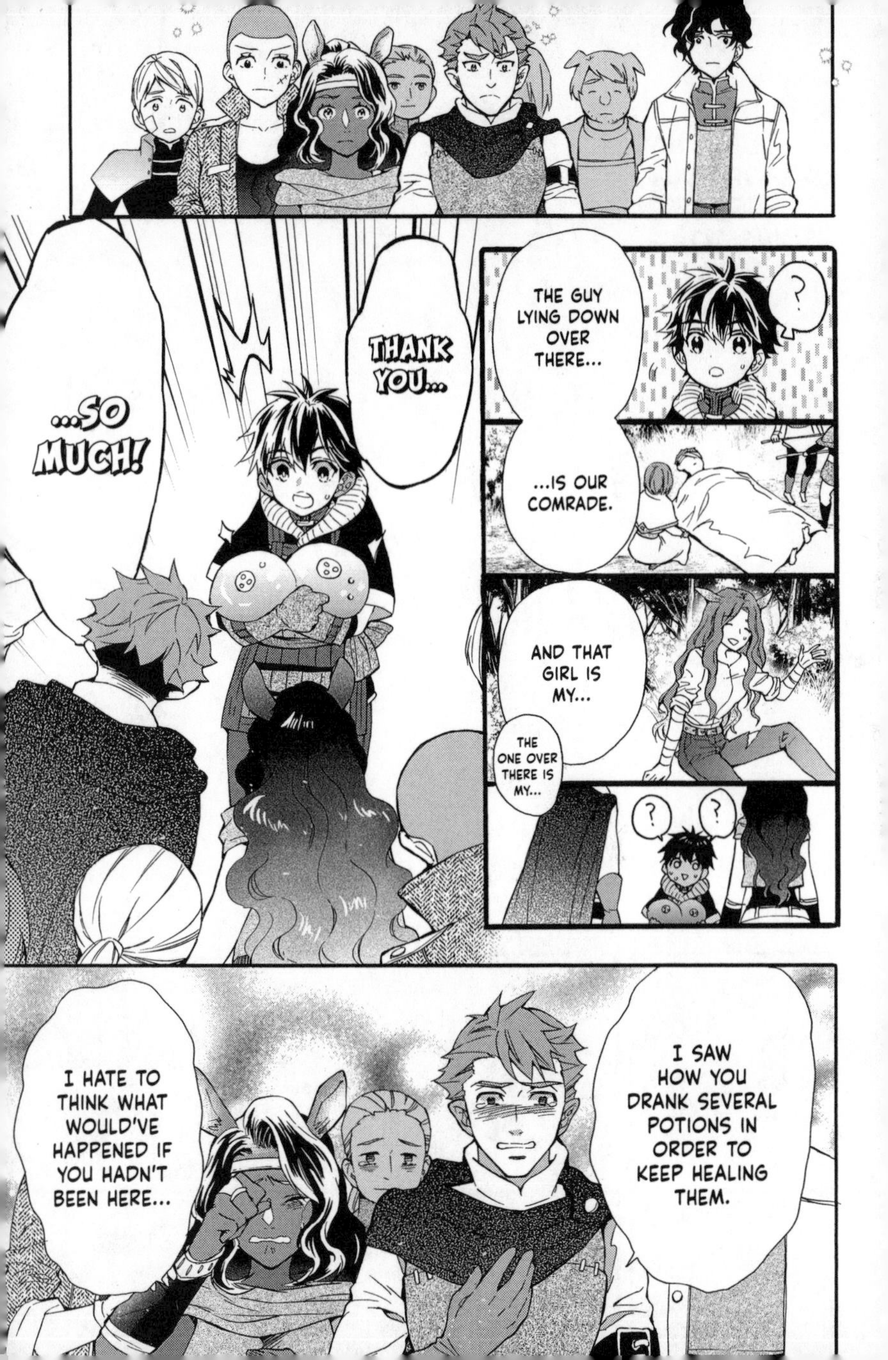
THE GUY LYING DOWN OVER THERE...
?
...IS OUR COMRADE.
AND THAT GIRL IS MY...
THE ONE OVER THERE IS MY...
?
?
THANK YOU...
...SO MUCH!
I SAW HOW YOU DRANK SEVERAL POTIONS IN ORDER TO KEEP HEALING THEM.
I HATE TO THINK WHAT WOULD'VE HAPPENED IF YOU HADN'T BEEN HERE...

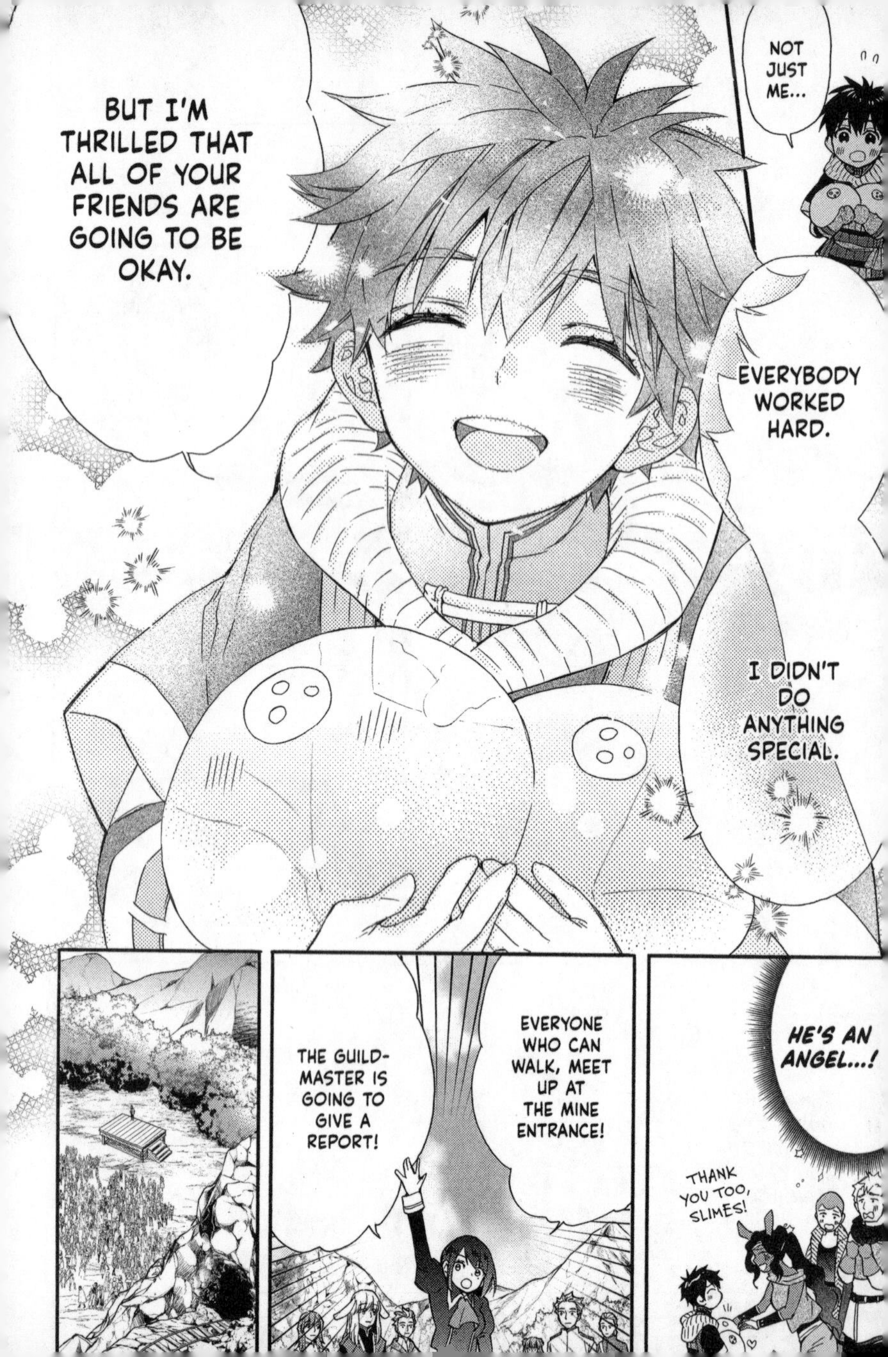
NOT JUST ME...
EVERYBODY WORKED HARD.
I DIDN'T DO ANYTHING SPECIAL.
BUT I'M THRILLED THAT ALL OF YOUR FRIENDS ARE GOING TO BE OKAY.
HE'S AN ANGEL...!
THANK YOU TOO, SLIMES!
EVERYONE WHO CAN WALK, MEET UP AT THE MINE ENTRANCE!
THE GUILD-MASTER IS GOING TO GIVE A REPORT!

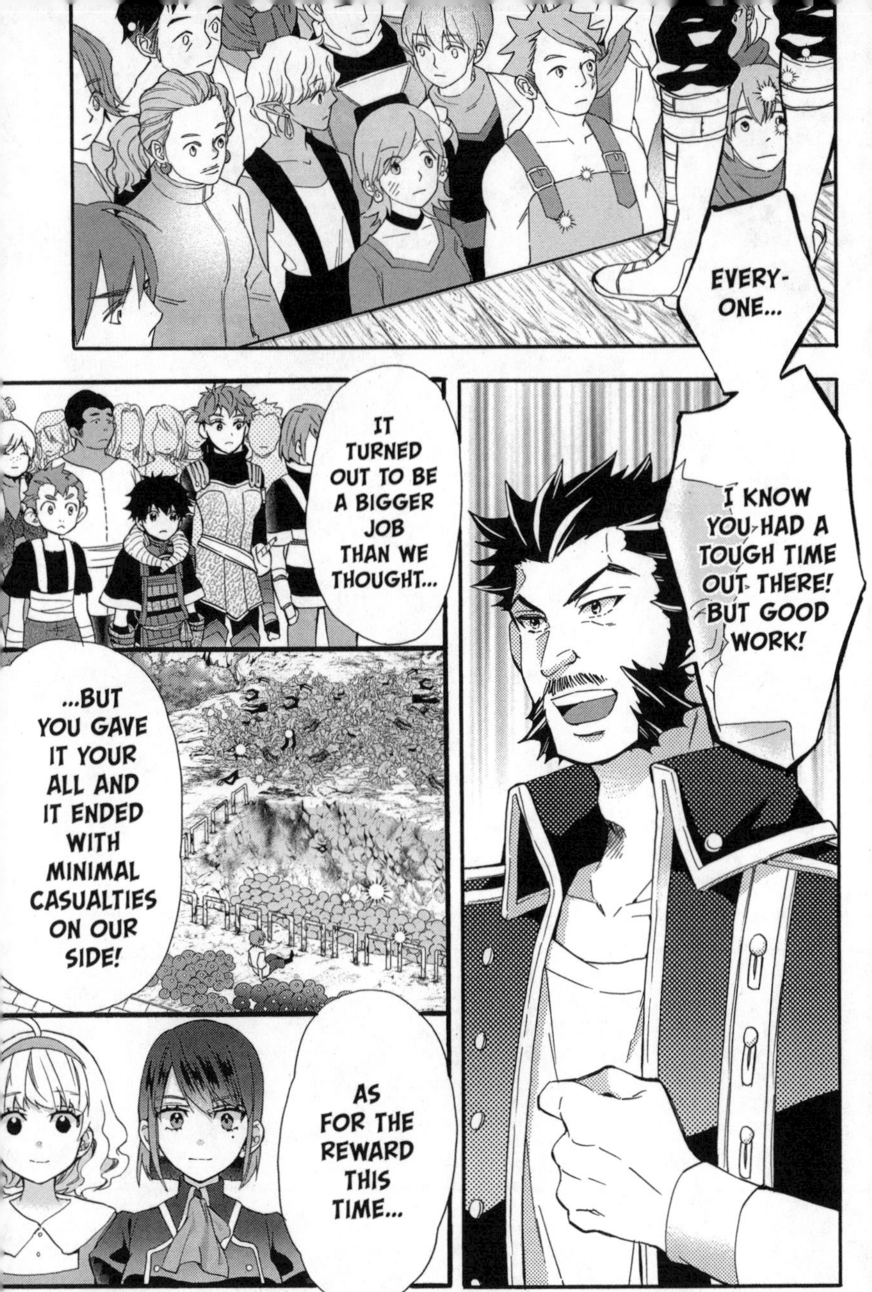
EVERY-ONE...
I KNOW YOU HAD A TOUGH TIME OUT THERE! BUT GOOD WORK!
IT TURNED OUT TO BE A BIGGER JOB THAN WE THOUGHT...
...BUT YOU GAVE IT YOUR ALL AND IT ENDED WITH MINIMAL CASUALTIES ON OUR SIDE!
AS FOR THE REWARD THIS TIME...

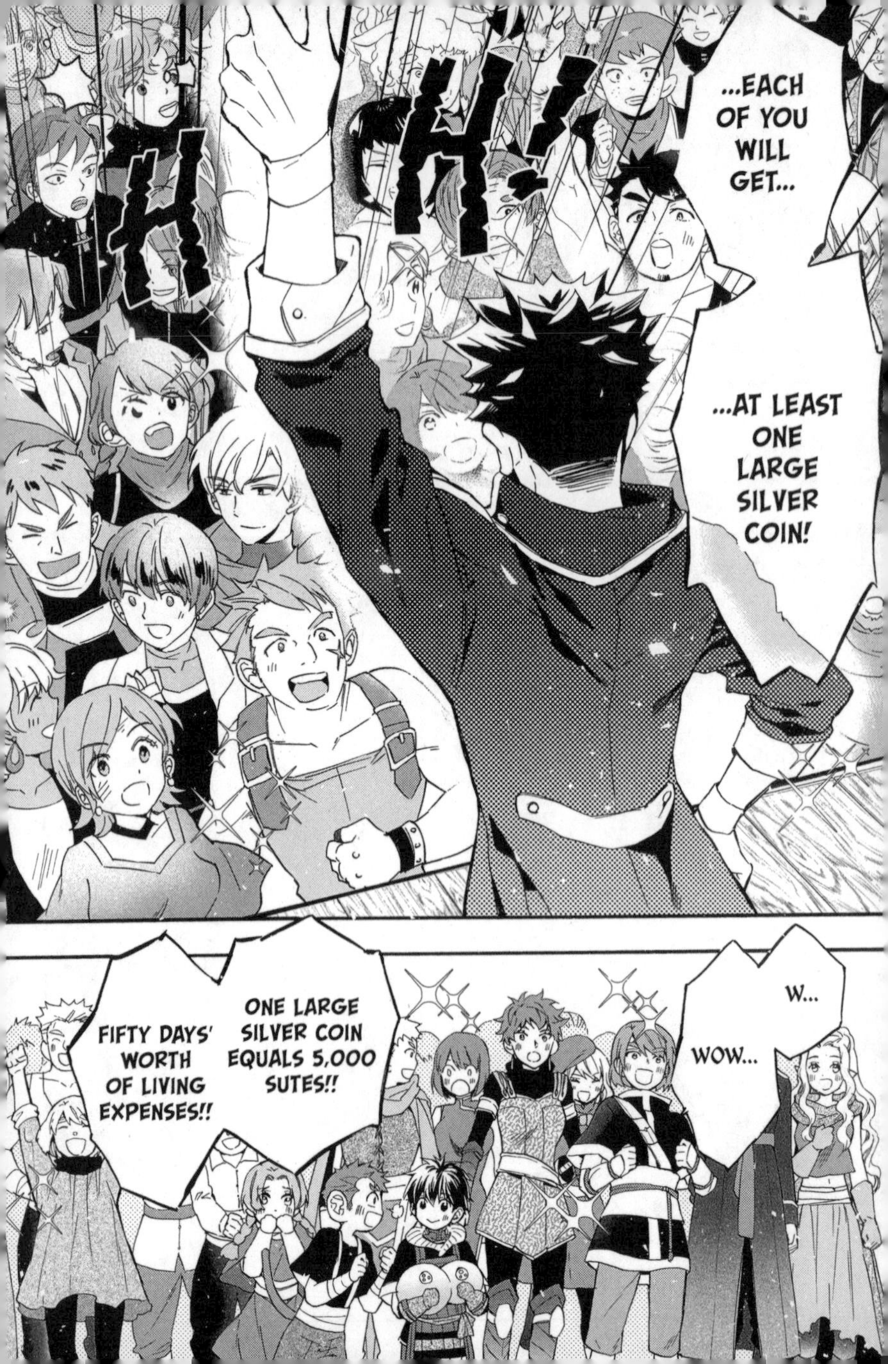
...EACH OF YOU WILL GET...
...AT LEAST ONE LARGE SILVER COIN!
W...
WOW...
ONE LARGE SILVER COIN EQUALS 5,000 SUTES!!
FIFTY DAYS' WORTH OF LIVING EXPENSES!!

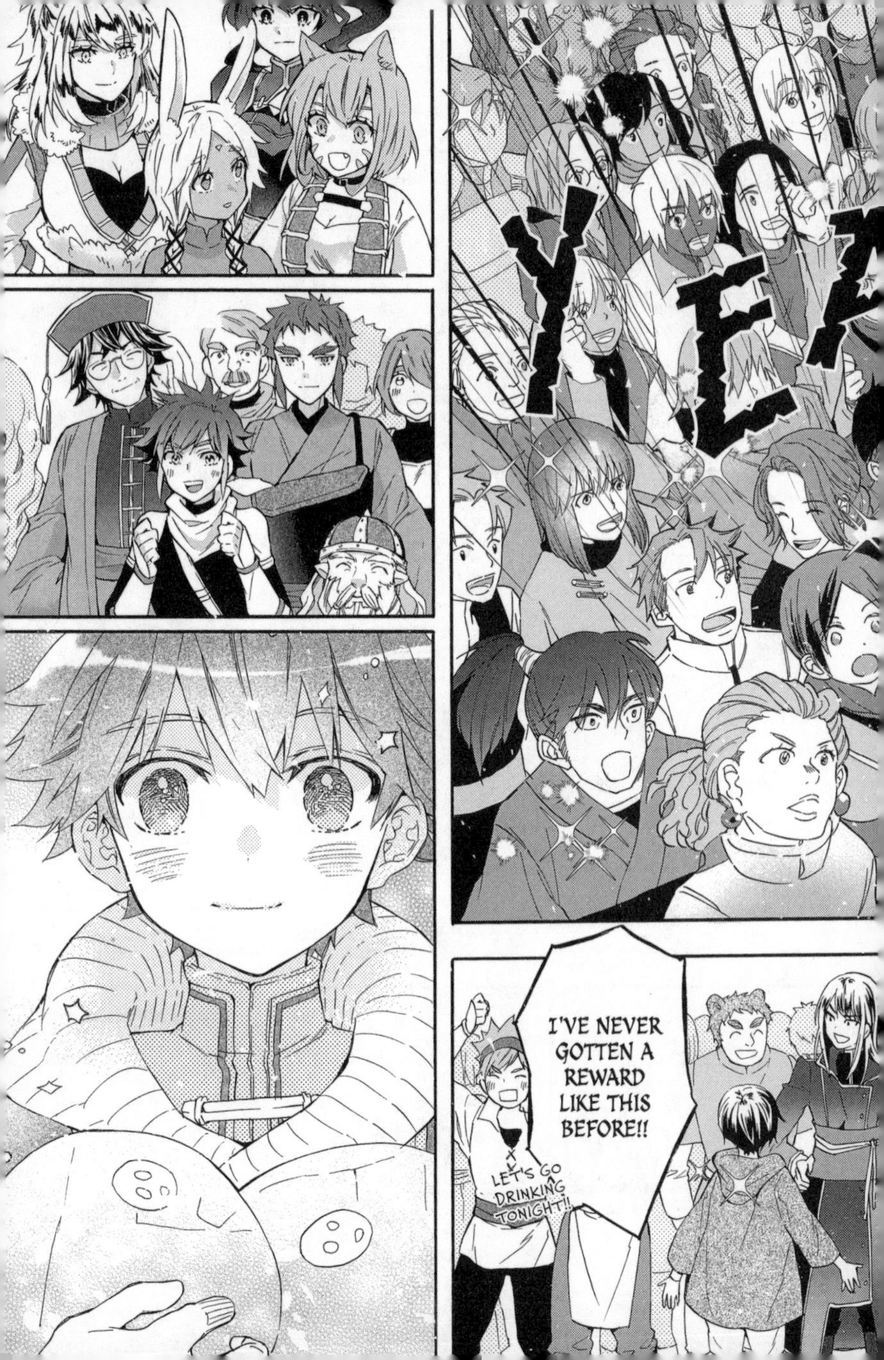
YEA
I'VE NEVER GOTTEN A REWARD LIKE THIS BEFORE!!
LET'S GO DRINKING TONIGHT!!

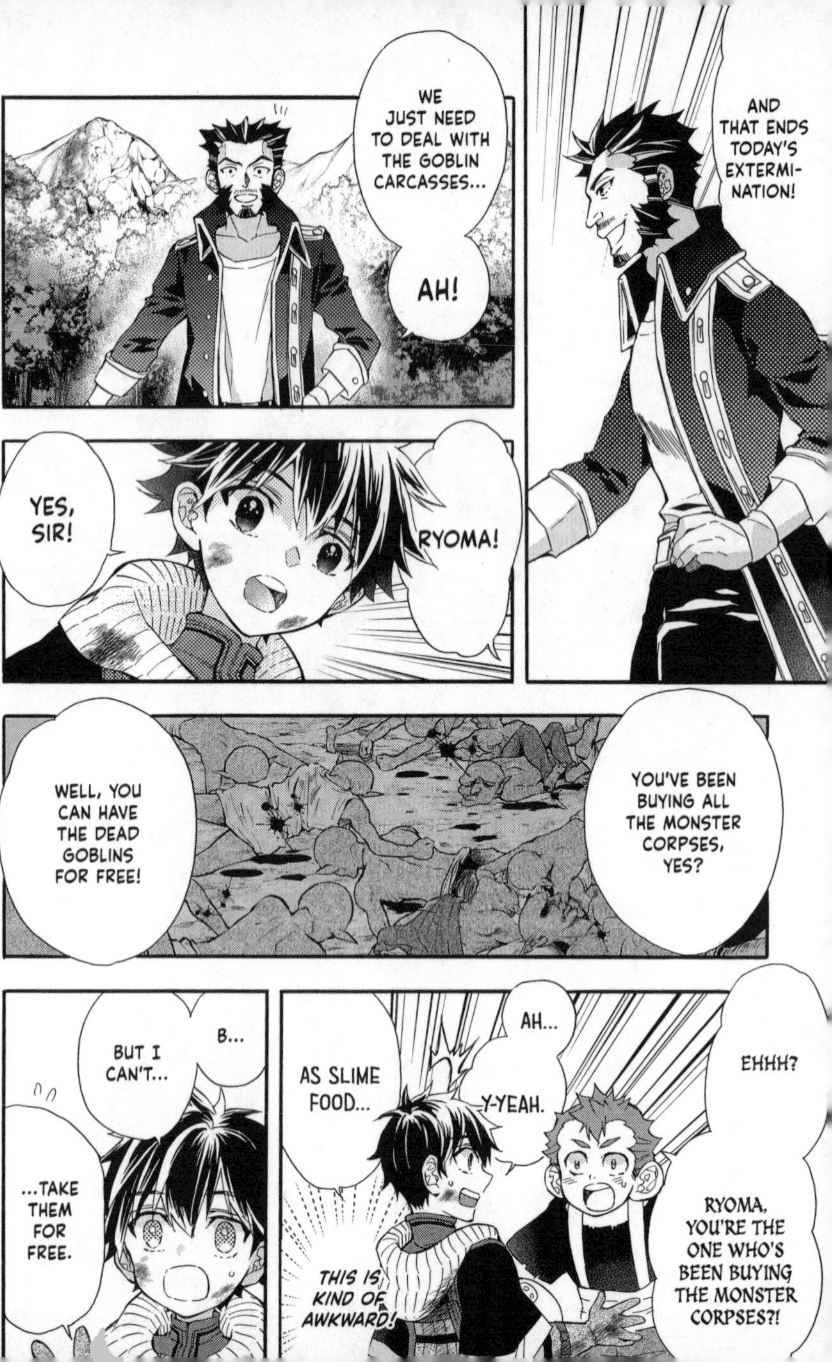
AND THAT ENDS TODAY'S EXTERMI-NATION!
WE JUST NEED TO DEAL WITH THE GOBLIN CARCASSES...
AH!
RYOMA!
YES, SIR!
YOU'VE BEEN BUYING ALL THE MONSTER CORPSES, YES?
WELL, YOU CAN HAVE THE DEAD GOBLINS FOR FREE!
EHHH?
RYOMA, YOU'RE THE ONE WHO'S BEEN BUYING THE MONSTER CORPSES?!
AH...
Y-YEAH.
AS SLIME FOOD...
THIS IS KIND OF AWKWARD!
B...
BUT I CAN'T...
...TAKE THEM FOR FREE.

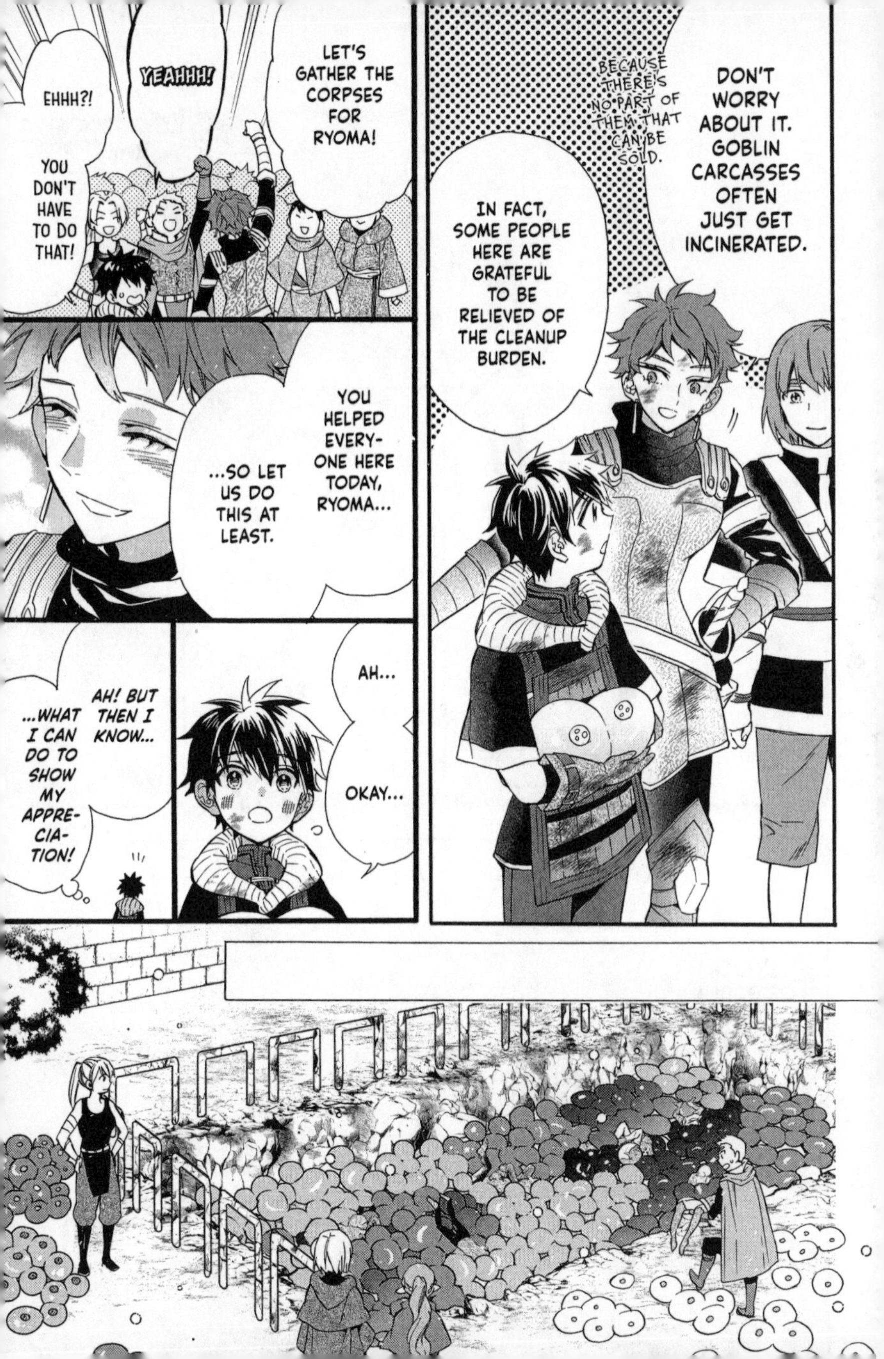
DON'T WORRY ABOUT IT. GOBLIN CARCASSES OFTEN JUST GET INCINERATED.
BECAUSE THERE'S NO PART OF THEM THAT CAN BE SOLD.
IN FACT, SOME PEOPLE HERE ARE GRATEFUL TO BE RELIEVED OF THE CLEANUP BURDEN.
LET'S GATHER THE CORPSES FOR RYOMA!
YEAHHH!
EHHH?!
YOU DON'T HAVE TO DO THAT!
YOU HELPED EVERY-ONE HERE TODAY, RYOMA...
...SO LET US DO THIS AT LEAST.
AH...
OKAY...
AH! BUT THEN I KNOW...
...WHAT I CAN DO TO SHOW MY APPRE-CIA-TION!

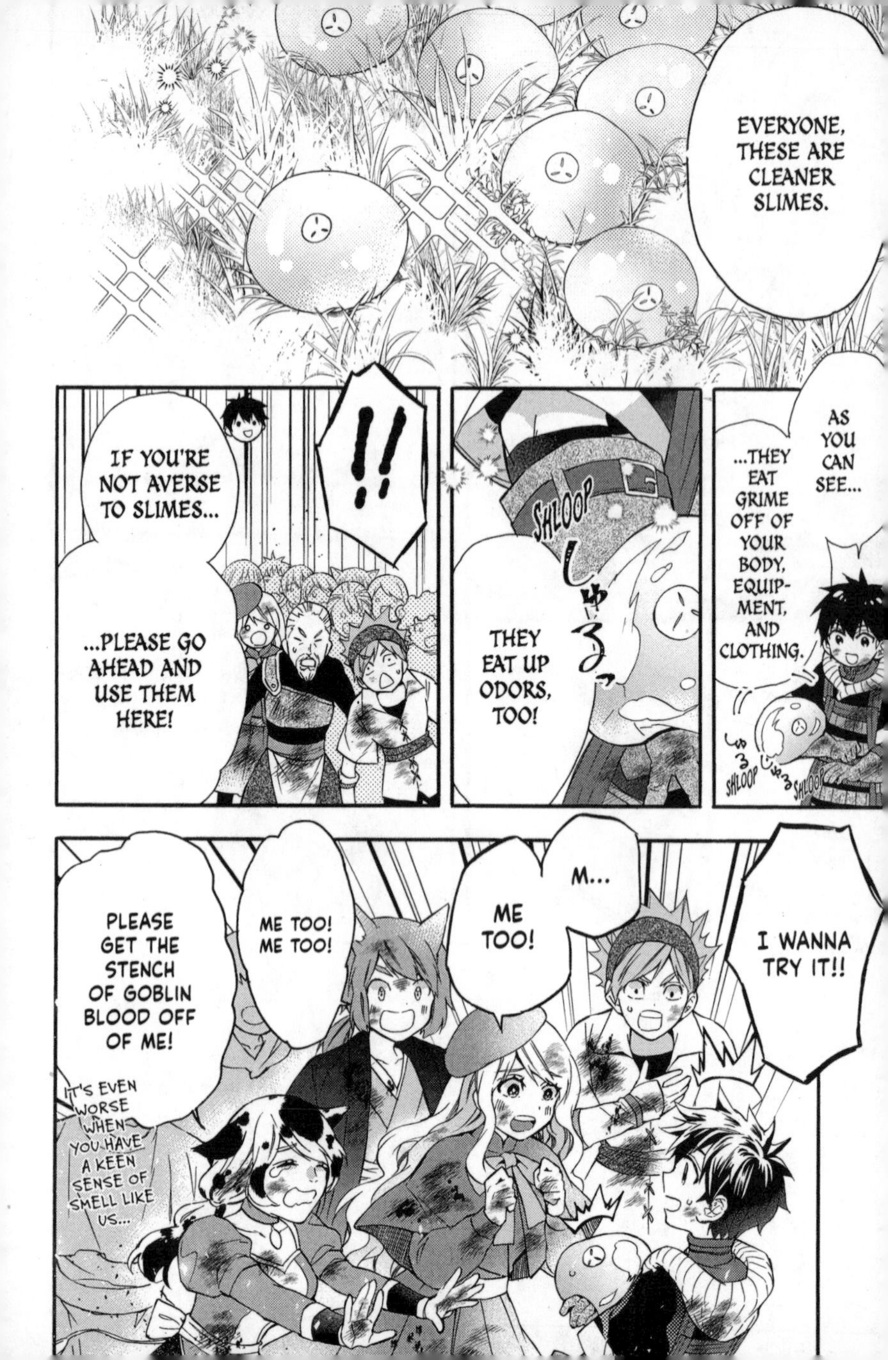
EVERYONE, THESE ARE CLEANER SLIMES.
AS YOU CAN SEE...
...THEY EAT GRIME OFF OF YOUR BODY, EQUIPMENT, AND CLOTHING.
SHLOOP
SHLOOP
SHLOOP
THEY EAT UP ODORS, TOO!
!!
IF YOU'RE NOT AVERSE TO SLIMES...
...PLEASE GO AHEAD AND USE THEM HERE!
I WANNA TRY IT!!
M...
ME TOO!
ME TOO! ME TOO!
PLEASE GET THE STENCH OF GOBLIN BLOOD OFF OF ME!
IT'S EVEN WORSE WHEN YOU HAVE A KEEN SENSE OF SMELL LIKE US...

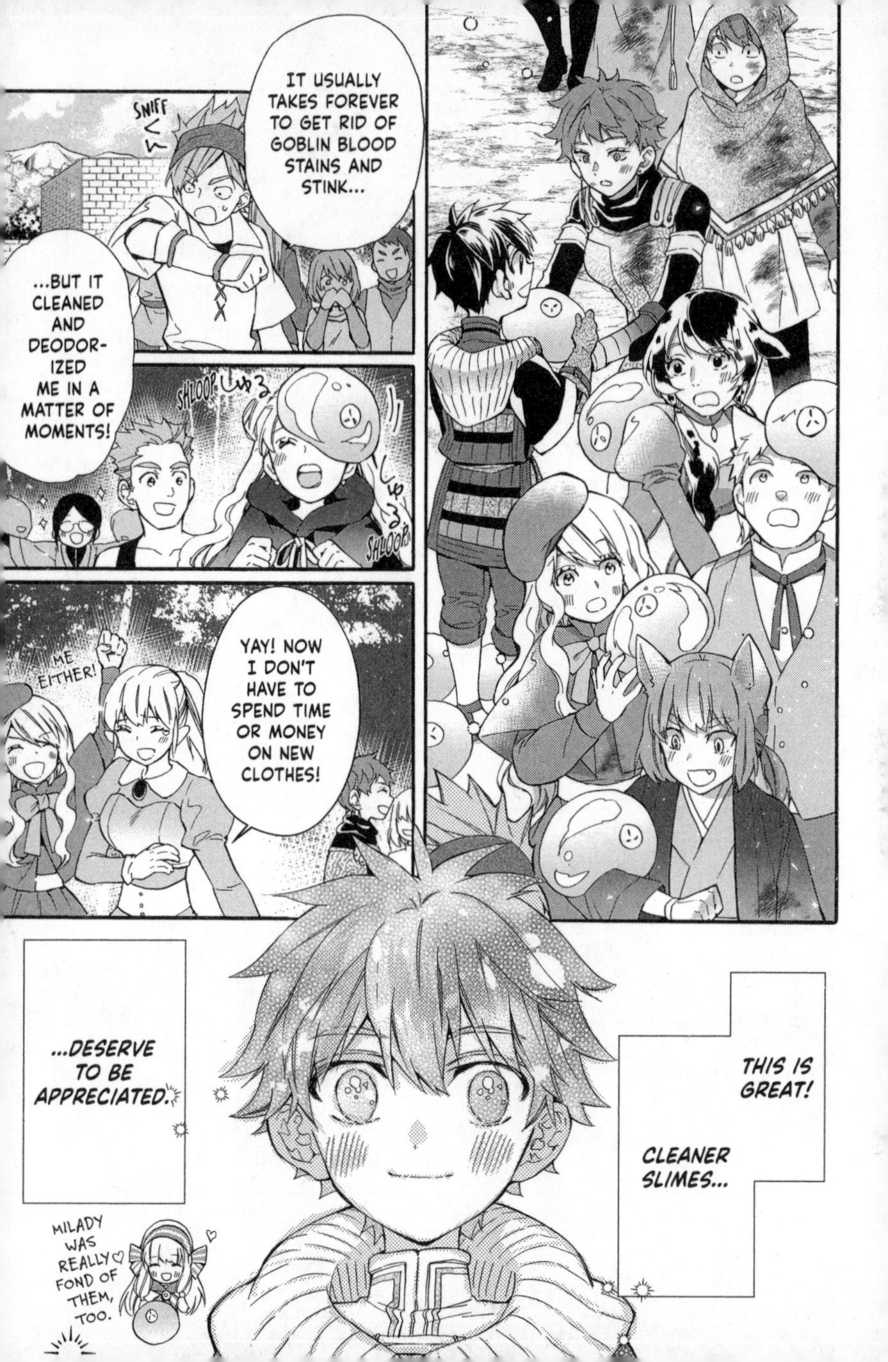

IT USUALLY TAKES FOREVER TO GET RID OF GOBLIN BLOOD STAINS AND STINK...
SNIFF くん
...BUT IT CLEANED AND DEODOR-IZED ME IN A MATTER OF MOMENTS!
SHLOOP しゅる
SHLOOP しゅる
YAY! NOW I DON'T HAVE TO SPEND TIME OR MONEY ON NEW CLOTHES!
ME EITHER!
THIS IS GREAT!
CLEANER SLIMES...
...DESERVE TO BE APPRECIATED.
MILADY WAS REALLY FOND OF THEM, TOO.

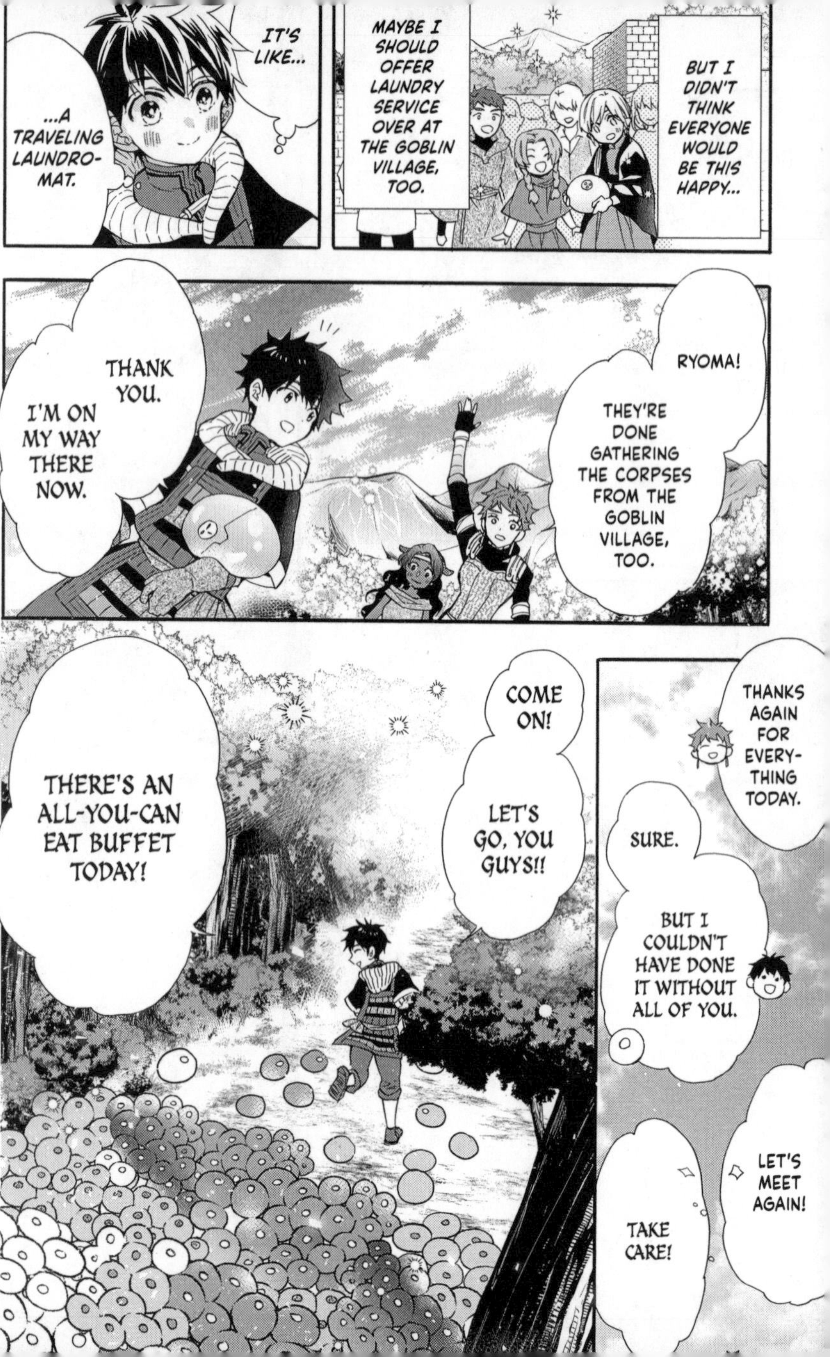
BUT I DIDN'T THINK EVERYONE WOULD BE THIS HAPPY...
MAYBE I SHOULD OFFER LAUNDRY SERVICE OVER AT THE GOBLIN VILLAGE, TOO.
IT'S LIKE...
...A TRAVELING LAUNDROMAT.
RYOMA!
THEY'RE DONE GATHERING THE CORPSES FROM THE GOBLIN VILLAGE, TOO.
THANK YOU.
I'M ON MY WAY THERE NOW.
THANKS AGAIN FOR EVERYTHING TODAY.
SURE.
BUT I COULDN'T HAVE DONE IT WITHOUT ALL OF YOU.
LET'S MEET AGAIN!
TAKE CARE!
COME ON!
LET'S GO, YOU GUYS!!
THERE'S AN ALL-YOU-CAN EAT BUFFET TODAY!

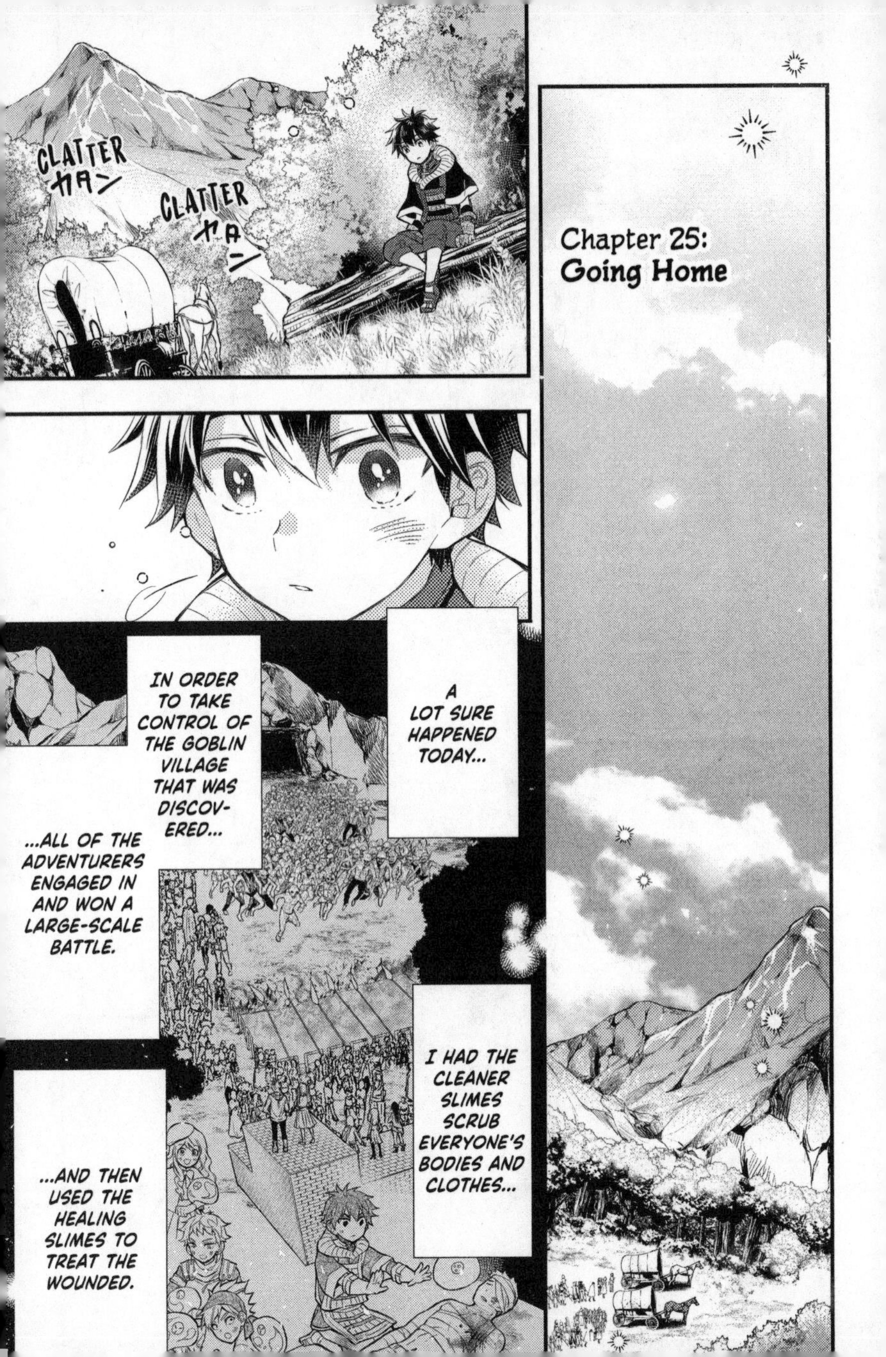
Chapter 25: Going Home
CLATTER カタン
CLATTER カタン
A LOT SURE HAPPENED TODAY...
IN ORDER TO TAKE CONTROL OF THE GOBLIN VILLAGE THAT WAS DISCOVERED...
...ALL OF THE ADVENTURERS ENGAGED IN AND WON A LARGE-SCALE BATTLE.
I HAD THE CLEANER SLIMES SCRUB EVERYONE'S BODIES AND CLOTHES...
...AND THEN USED THE HEALING SLIMES TO TREAT THE WOUNDED.

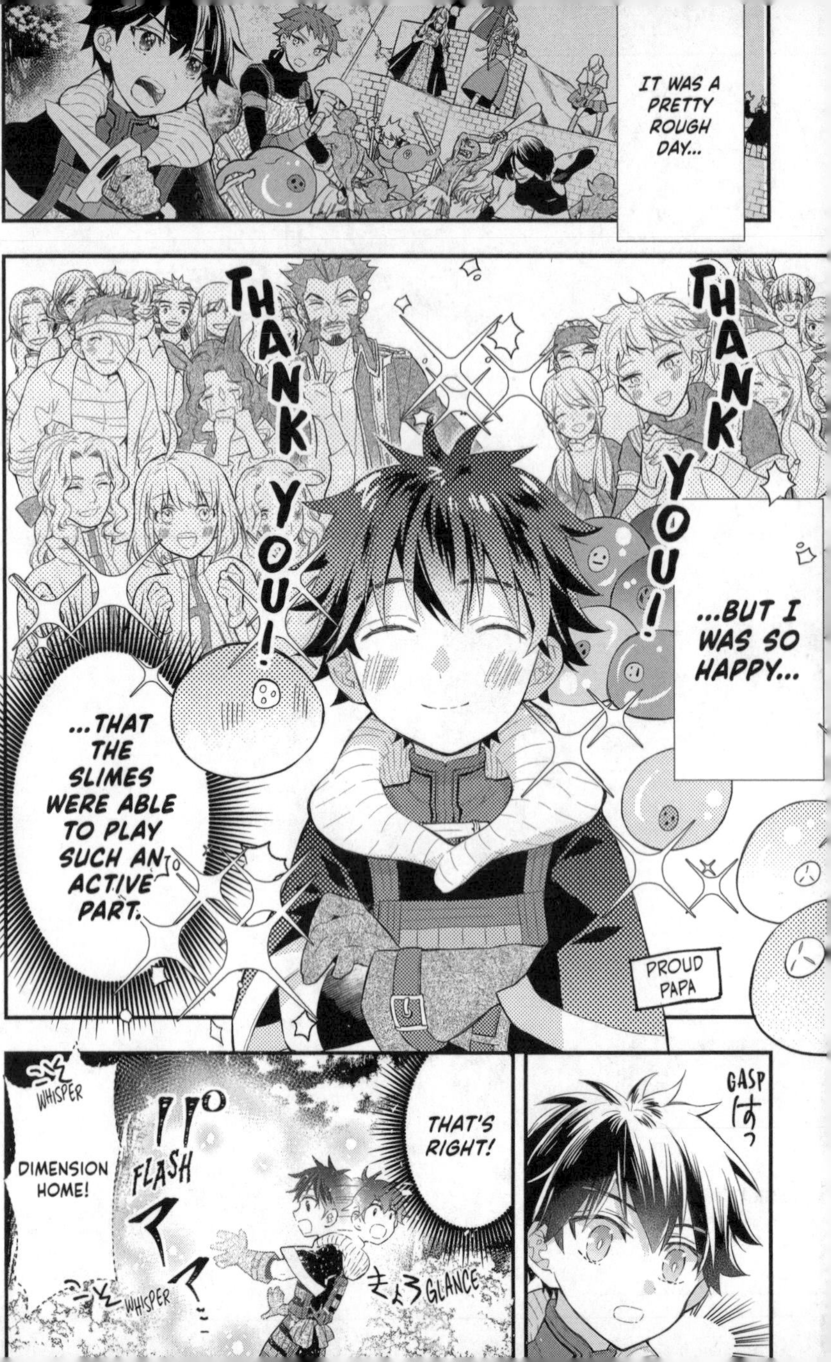
IT WAS A PRETTY ROUGH DAY...
THANK YOU!
...BUT I WAS SO HAPPY...
THANK YOU!
...THAT THE SLIMES WERE ABLE TO PLAY SUCH AN ACTIVE PART.
PROUD PAPA
GASP
はっ
THAT'S RIGHT!
DIMENSION HOME!
WHISPER
FLASH
きょろ
GLANCE
WHISPER

LET'S SEE... SO THIS IS "HIGH HEAL"...

OHHH...

COME HERE, HEALING SLIMES! LET'S CHECK YOUR SKILL LEVEL.

✚	HEALING MAGIC	3
	HEAL, HIGH HEAL	

MY HEALING MAGIC SKILL WENT UP TO LEVEL 2!

RYOMA?

FLASH

MAYBE MY STATUS TOO...

✚	HEALING MAGIC	2
	HEAL	

SO YOUR HEALING MAGIC SKILL ROSE TO LEVEL 3 ALSO.

WELL, I GUESS IF YOU USE IT THAT MUCH...

AH!

WHAT ARE YOU DOING HERE?

EVERY-ONE!

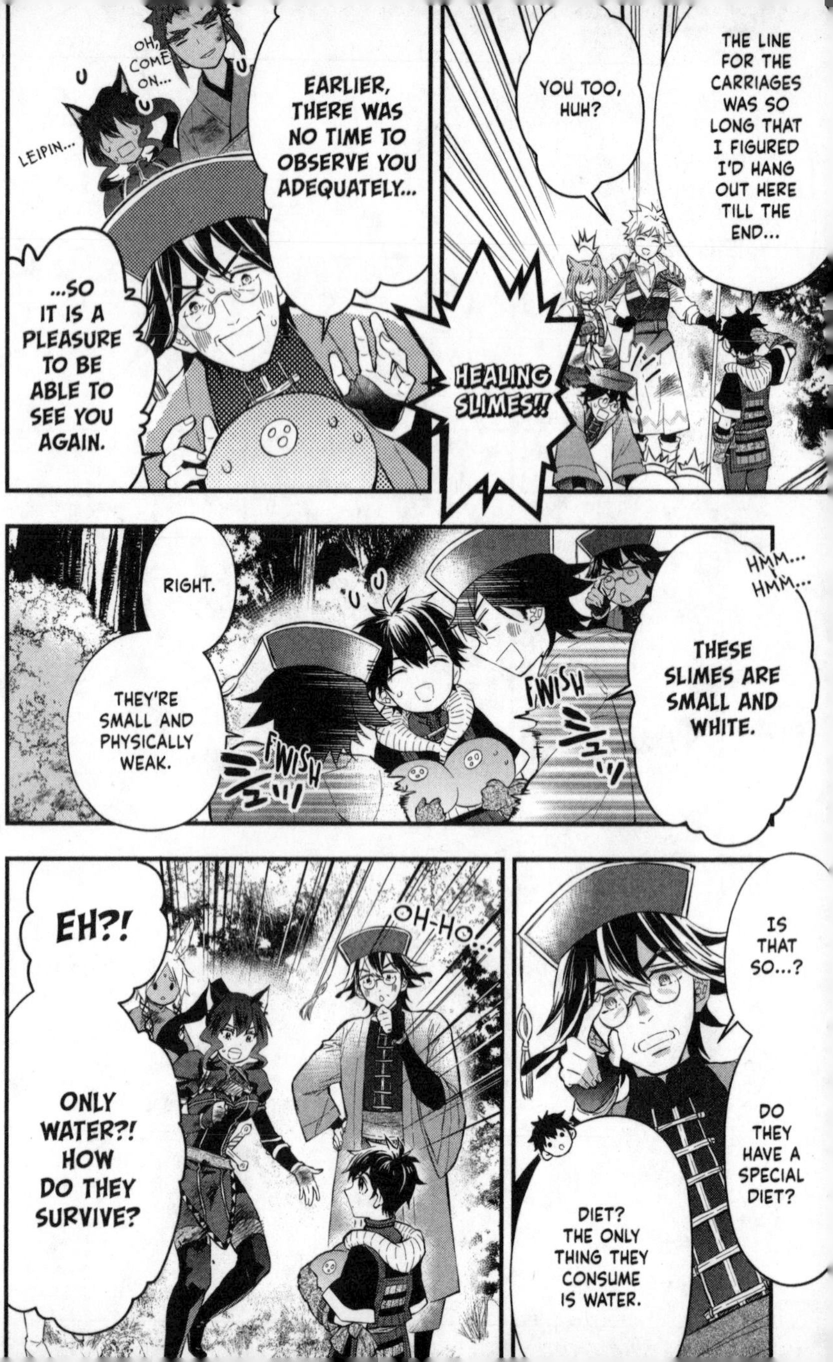
THE LINE FOR THE CARRIAGES WAS SO LONG THAT I FIGURED I'D HANG OUT HERE TILL THE END...
YOU TOO, HUH?
HEALING SLIMES!!
EARLIER, THERE WAS NO TIME TO OBSERVE YOU ADEQUATELY...
OH, COME ON...
LEIPIN...
...SO IT IS A PLEASURE TO BE ABLE TO SEE YOU AGAIN.
HMM... HMM...
THESE SLIMES ARE SMALL AND WHITE.
FWISH
シュッ
RIGHT.
THEY'RE SMALL AND PHYSICALLY WEAK.
FWISH
シュッ
IS THAT SO...?
DO THEY HAVE A SPECIAL DIET?
DIET? THE ONLY THING THEY CONSUME IS WATER.
OH-HO...
EH?!
ONLY WATER?! HOW DO THEY SURVIVE?

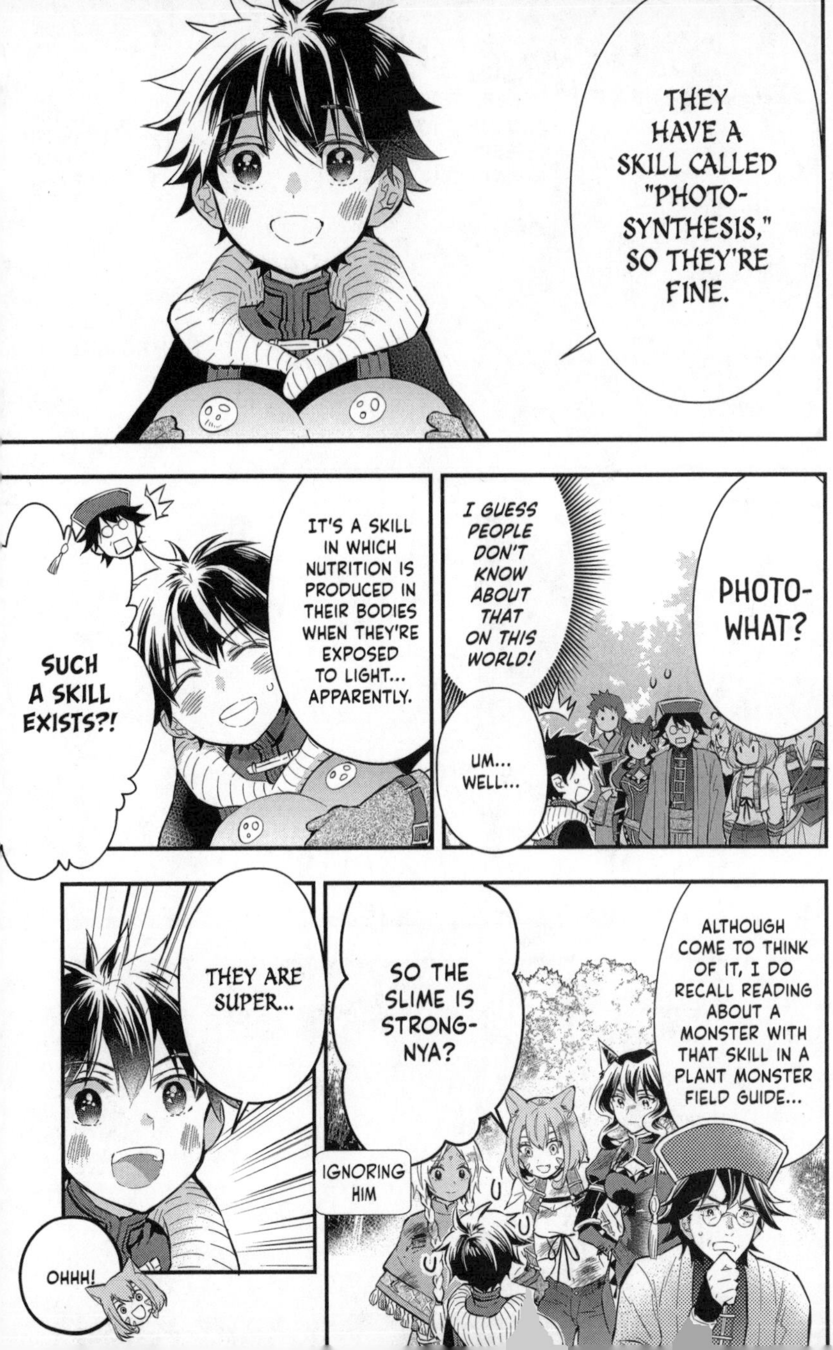
THEY HAVE A SKILL CALLED "PHOTO-SYNTHESIS," SO THEY'RE FINE.
PHOTO-WHAT?
I GUESS PEOPLE DON'T KNOW ABOUT THAT ON THIS WORLD!
UM... WELL...
IT'S A SKILL IN WHICH NUTRITION IS PRODUCED IN THEIR BODIES WHEN THEY'RE EXPOSED TO LIGHT... APPARENTLY.
SUCH A SKILL EXISTS?!
ALTHOUGH COME TO THINK OF IT, I DO RECALL READING ABOUT A MONSTER WITH THAT SKILL IN A PLANT MONSTER FIELD GUIDE...
SO THE SLIME IS STRONG-NYA?
IGNORING HIM
THEY ARE SUPER...
OHHH!

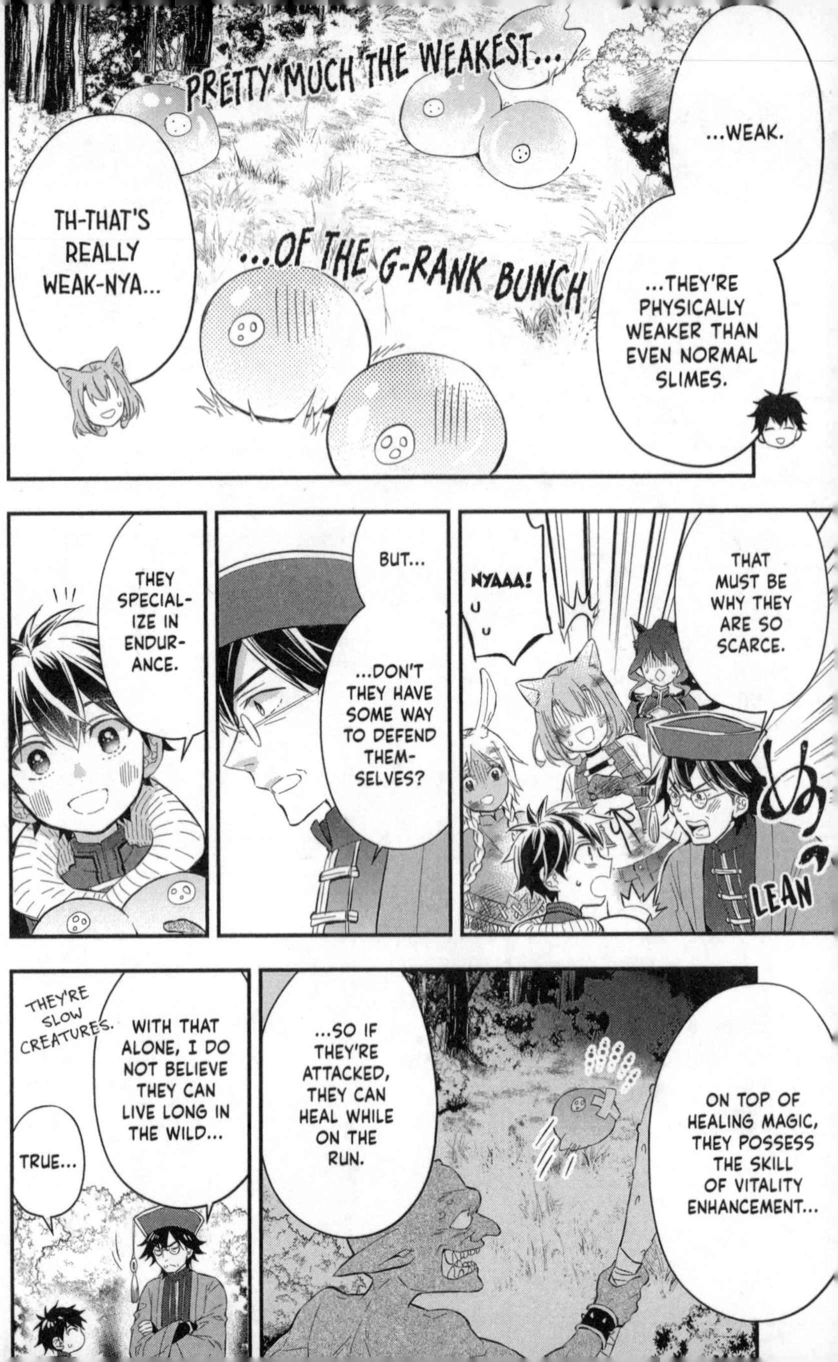
...WEAK.
...THEY'RE PHYSICALLY WEAKER THAN EVEN NORMAL SLIMES.
PRETTY MUCH THE WEAKEST...
...OF THE G-RANK BUNCH
TH-THAT'S REALLY WEAK-NYA...
THAT MUST BE WHY THEY ARE SO SCARCE.
NYAAA!
LEAN
BUT...
...DON'T THEY HAVE SOME WAY TO DEFEND THEMSELVES?
THEY SPECIALIZE IN ENDURANCE.
ON TOP OF HEALING MAGIC, THEY POSSESS THE SKILL OF VITALITY ENHANCEMENT...
...SO IF THEY'RE ATTACKED, THEY CAN HEAL WHILE ON THE RUN.
WITH THAT ALONE, I DO NOT BELIEVE THEY CAN LIVE LONG IN THE WILD...
THEY'RE SLOW CREATURES.
TRUE...

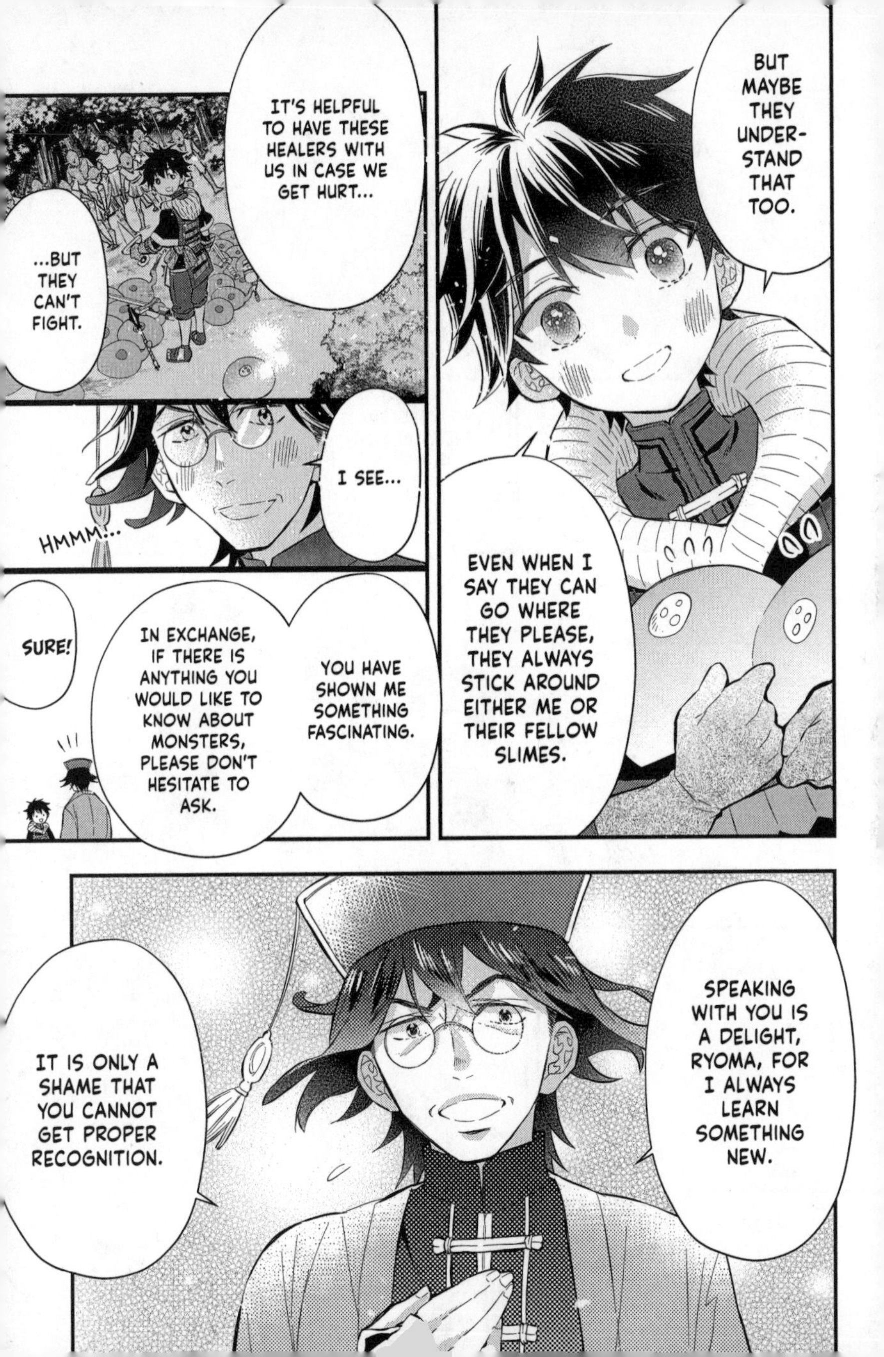
BUT MAYBE THEY UNDER-STAND THAT TOO.
EVEN WHEN I SAY THEY CAN GO WHERE THEY PLEASE, THEY ALWAYS STICK AROUND EITHER ME OR THEIR FELLOW SLIMES.
IT'S HELPFUL TO HAVE THESE HEALERS WITH US IN CASE WE GET HURT...
...BUT THEY CAN'T FIGHT.
I SEE...
HMMM...
YOU HAVE SHOWN ME SOMETHING FASCINATING.
IN EXCHANGE, IF THERE IS ANYTHING YOU WOULD LIKE TO KNOW ABOUT MONSTERS, PLEASE DON'T HESITATE TO ASK.
SURE!
SPEAKING WITH YOU IS A DELIGHT, RYOMA, FOR I ALWAYS LEARN SOMETHING NEW.
IT IS ONLY A SHAME THAT YOU CANNOT GET PROPER RECOGNITION.

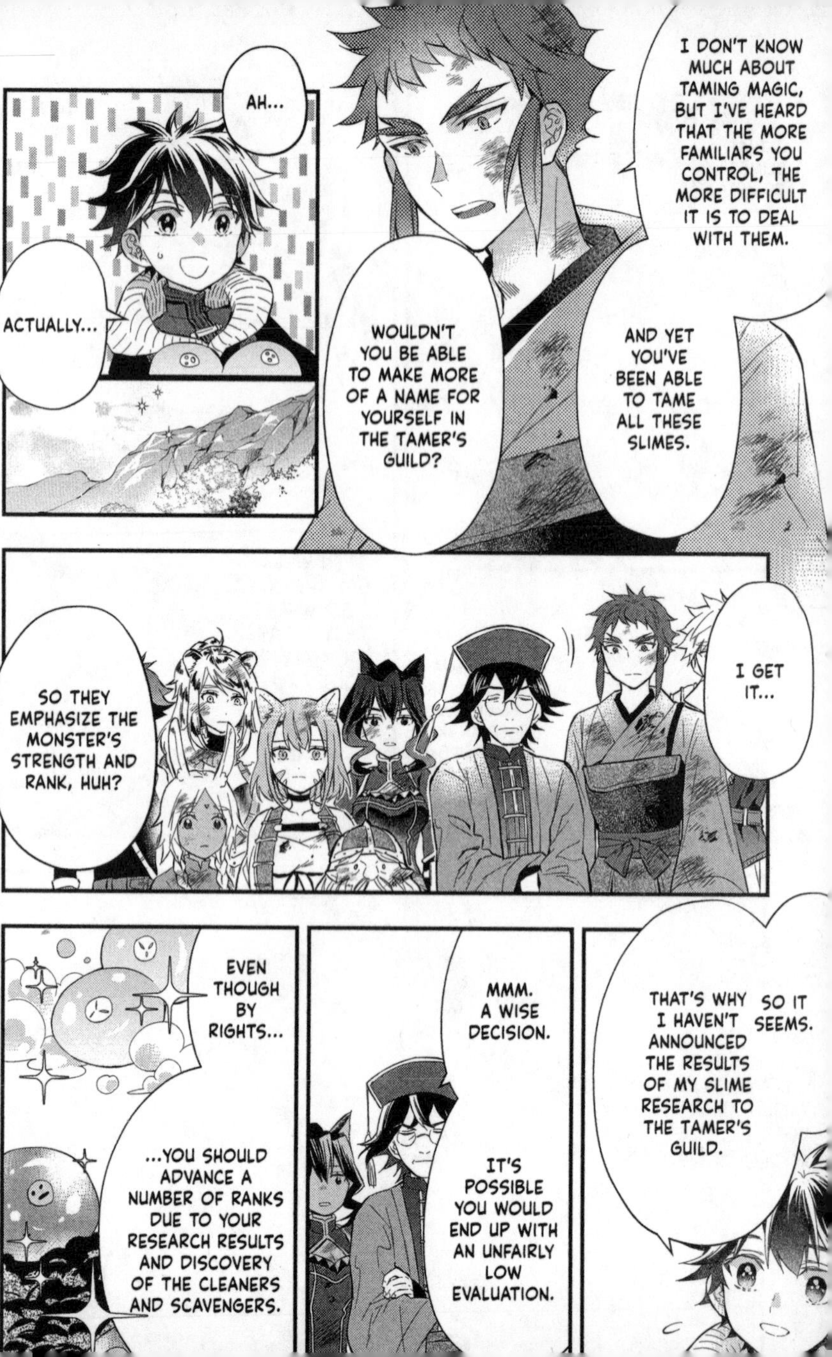
I DON'T KNOW MUCH ABOUT TAMING MAGIC, BUT I'VE HEARD THAT THE MORE FAMILIARS YOU CONTROL, THE MORE DIFFICULT IT IS TO DEAL WITH THEM.
AND YET YOU'VE BEEN ABLE TO TAME ALL THESE SLIMES.
WOULDN'T YOU BE ABLE TO MAKE MORE OF A NAME FOR YOURSELF IN THE TAMER'S GUILD?
AH...
ACTUALLY...
I GET IT...
SO THEY EMPHASIZE THE MONSTER'S STRENGTH AND RANK, HUH?
SO IT SEEMS.
THAT'S WHY I HAVEN'T ANNOUNCED THE RESULTS OF MY SLIME RESEARCH TO THE TAMER'S GUILD.
MMM. A WISE DECISION.
IT'S POSSIBLE YOU WOULD END UP WITH AN UNFAIRLY LOW EVALUATION.
EVEN THOUGH BY RIGHTS...
...YOU SHOULD ADVANCE A NUMBER OF RANKS DUE TO YOUR RESEARCH RESULTS AND DISCOVERY OF THE CLEANERS AND SCAVENGERS.

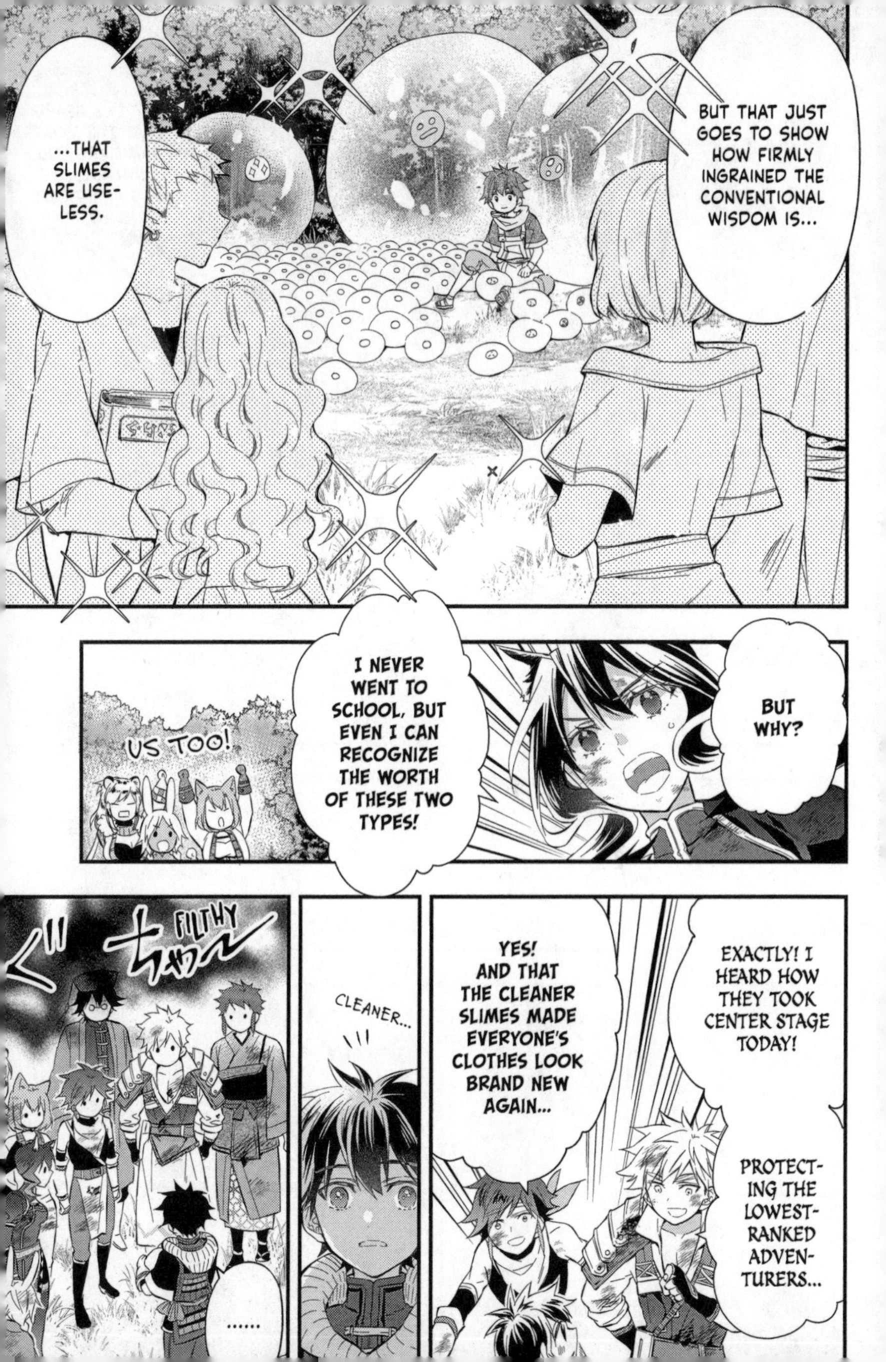
BUT THAT JUST GOES TO SHOW HOW FIRMLY INGRAINED THE CONVENTIONAL WISDOM IS...
...THAT SLIMES ARE USE-LESS.
BUT WHY?
I NEVER WENT TO SCHOOL, BUT EVEN I CAN RECOGNIZE THE WORTH OF THESE TWO TYPES!
US TOO!
EXACTLY! I HEARD HOW THEY TOOK CENTER STAGE TODAY!
YES! AND THAT THE CLEANER SLIMES MADE EVERYONE'S CLOTHES LOOK BRAND NEW AGAIN...
PROTECT-ING THE LOWEST-RANKED ADVEN-TURERS...
CLEANER...
......
FILTHY

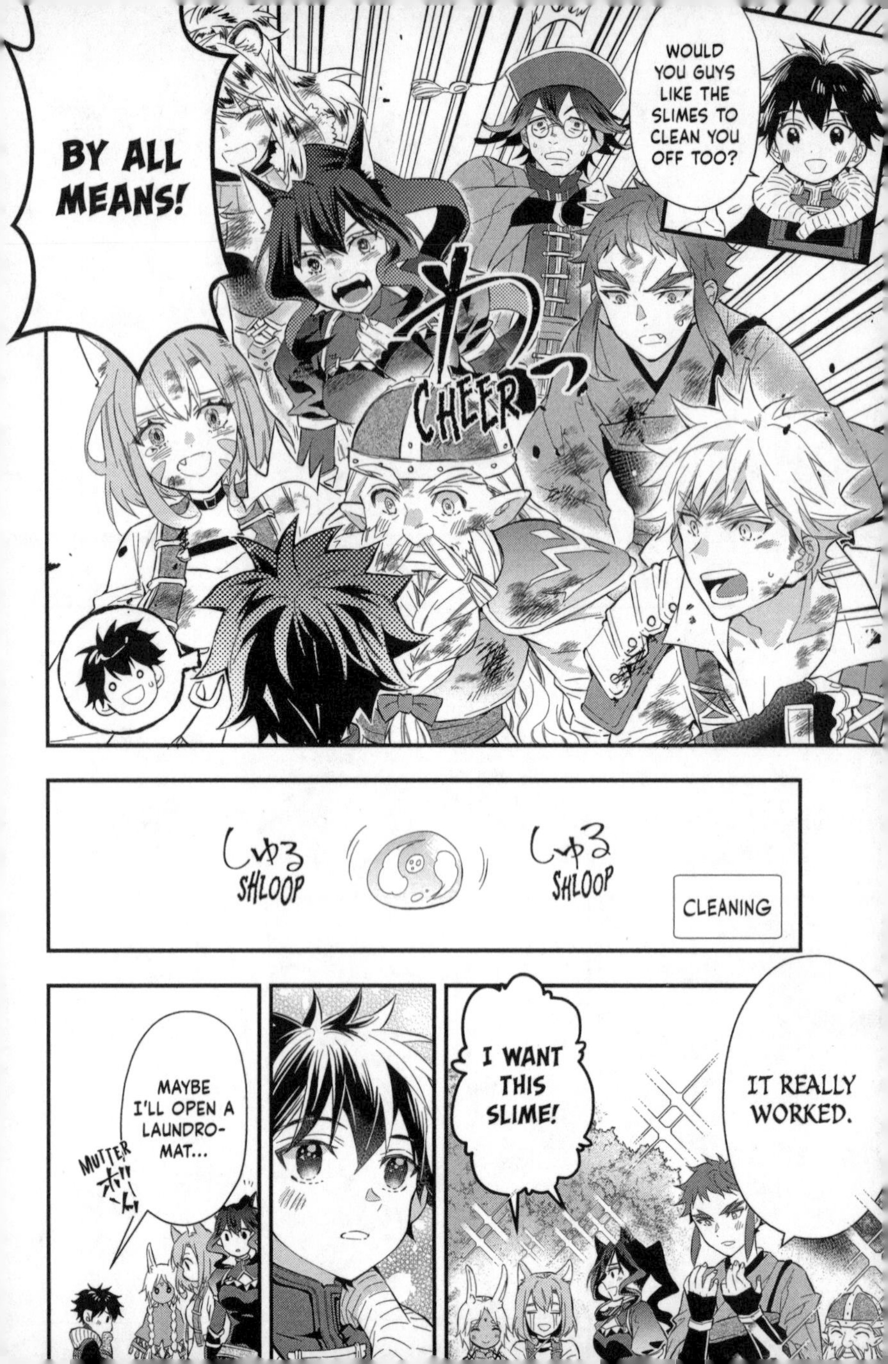
WOULD YOU GUYS LIKE THE SLIMES TO CLEAN YOU OFF TOO?
BY ALL MEANS!
CHEER
CLEANING
しゅる SHLOOP
しゅる SHLOOP
IT REALLY WORKED.
I WANT THIS SLIME!
MAYBE I'LL OPEN A LAUNDRO-MAT...
MUTTER

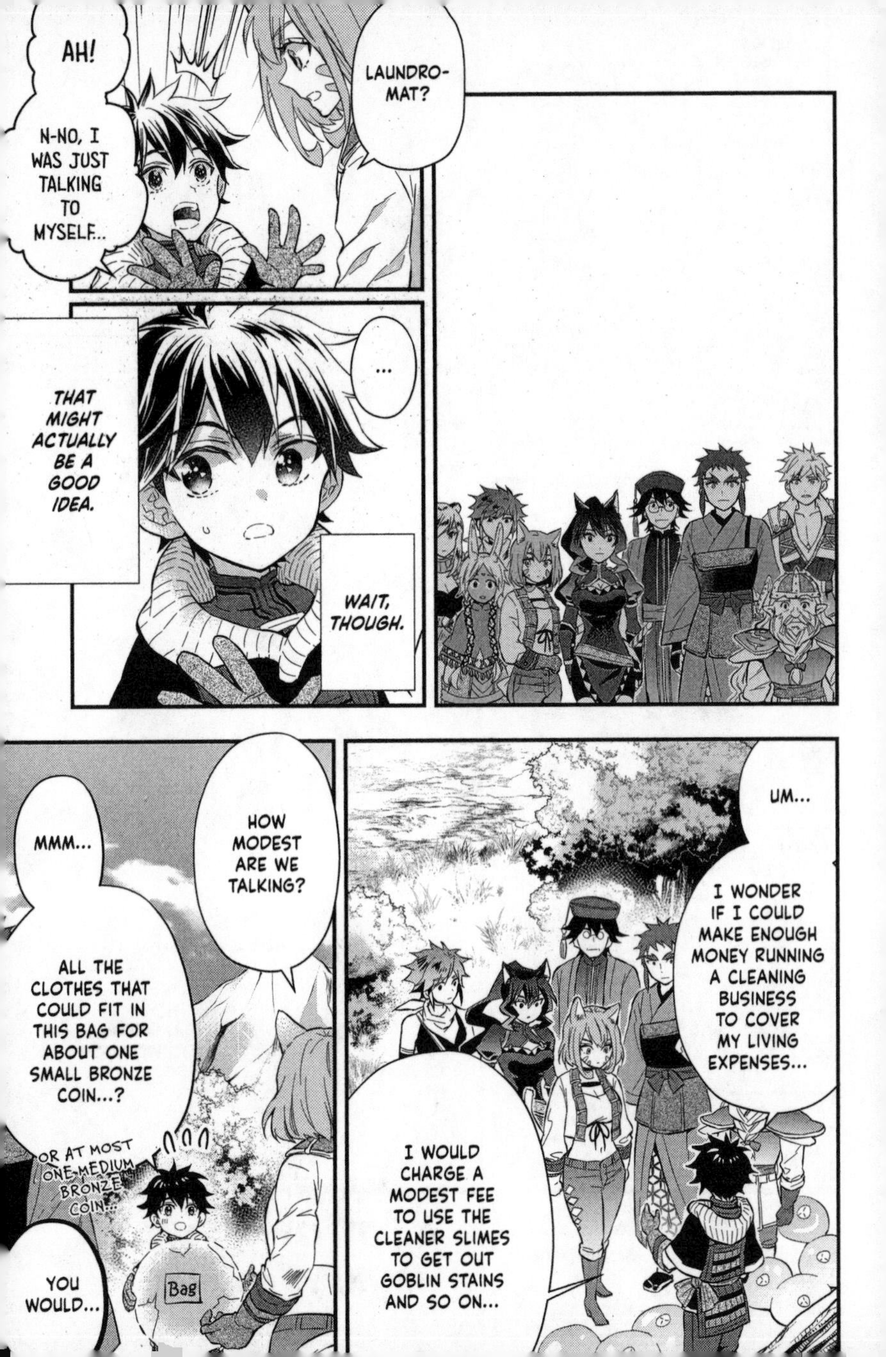
LAUNDRO-MAT?
AH!
N-NO, I WAS JUST TALKING TO MYSELF...
...
THAT MIGHT ACTUALLY BE A GOOD IDEA.
WAIT, THOUGH.
UM...
I WONDER IF I COULD MAKE ENOUGH MONEY RUNNING A CLEANING BUSINESS TO COVER MY LIVING EXPENSES...
I WOULD CHARGE A MODEST FEE TO USE THE CLEANER SLIMES TO GET OUT GOBLIN STAINS AND SO ON...
HOW MODEST ARE WE TALKING?
MMM...
ALL THE CLOTHES THAT COULD FIT IN THIS BAG FOR ABOUT ONE SMALL BRONZE COIN...?
OR AT MOST ONE MEDIUM BRONZE COIN...
Bag
YOU WOULD...

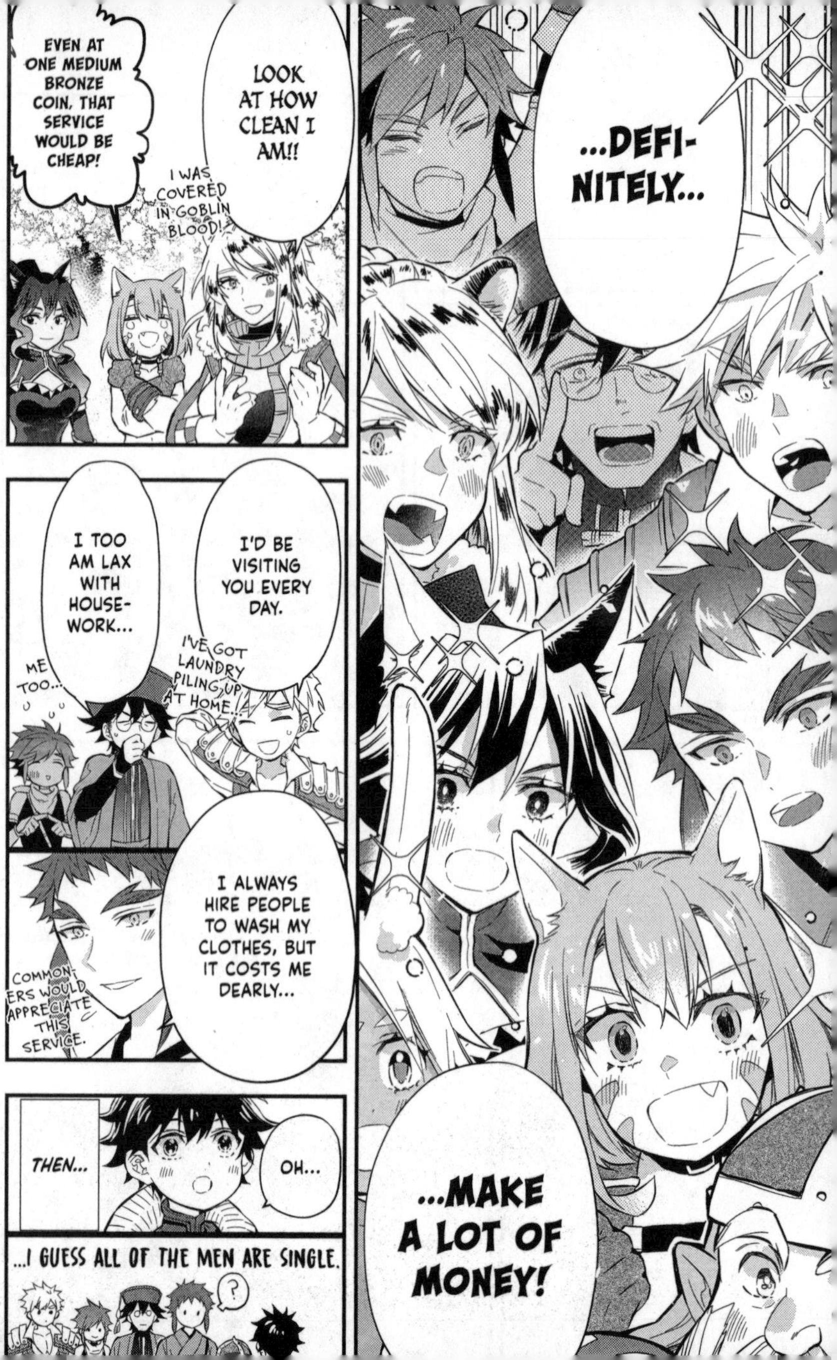
...DEFINITELY...
...MAKE A LOT OF MONEY!
LOOK AT HOW CLEAN I AM!!
I WAS COVERED IN GOBLIN BLOOD!
EVEN AT ONE MEDIUM BRONZE COIN, THAT SERVICE WOULD BE CHEAP!
I'D BE VISITING YOU EVERY DAY.
I'VE GOT LAUNDRY PILING UP AT HOME!
I TOO AM LAX WITH HOUSEWORK...
ME TOO...
I ALWAYS HIRE PEOPLE TO WASH MY CLOTHES, BUT IT COSTS ME DEARLY...
COMMONERS WOULD APPRECIATE THIS SERVICE.
OH...
THEN...
...I GUESS ALL OF THE MEN ARE SINGLE.
?

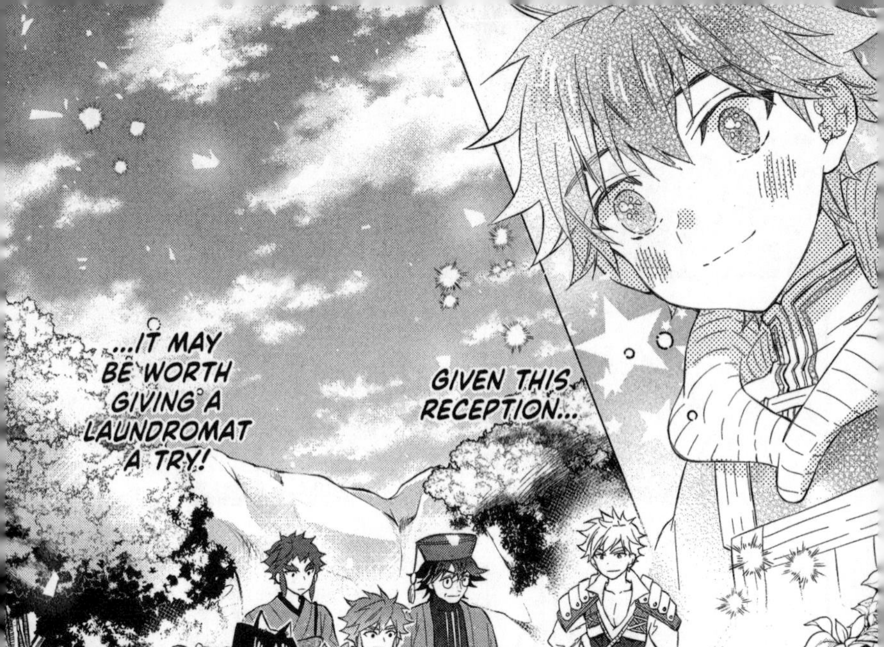
GIVEN THIS RECEPTION...
...IT MAY BE WORTH GIVING A LAUNDROMAT A TRY!
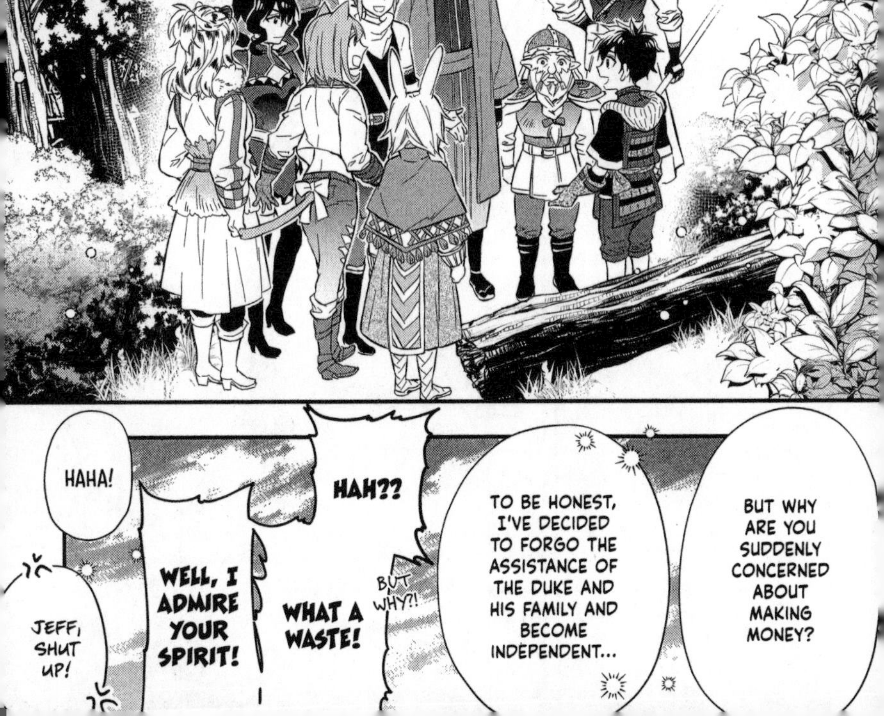
BUT WHY ARE YOU SUDDENLY CONCERNED ABOUT MAKING MONEY?
TO BE HONEST, I'VE DECIDED TO FORGO THE ASSISTANCE OF THE DUKE AND HIS FAMILY AND BECOME INDEPENDENT...
HAH??
BUT WHY?!
WHAT A WASTE!
WELL, I ADMIRE YOUR SPIRIT!
HAHA!
JEFF, SHUT UP!

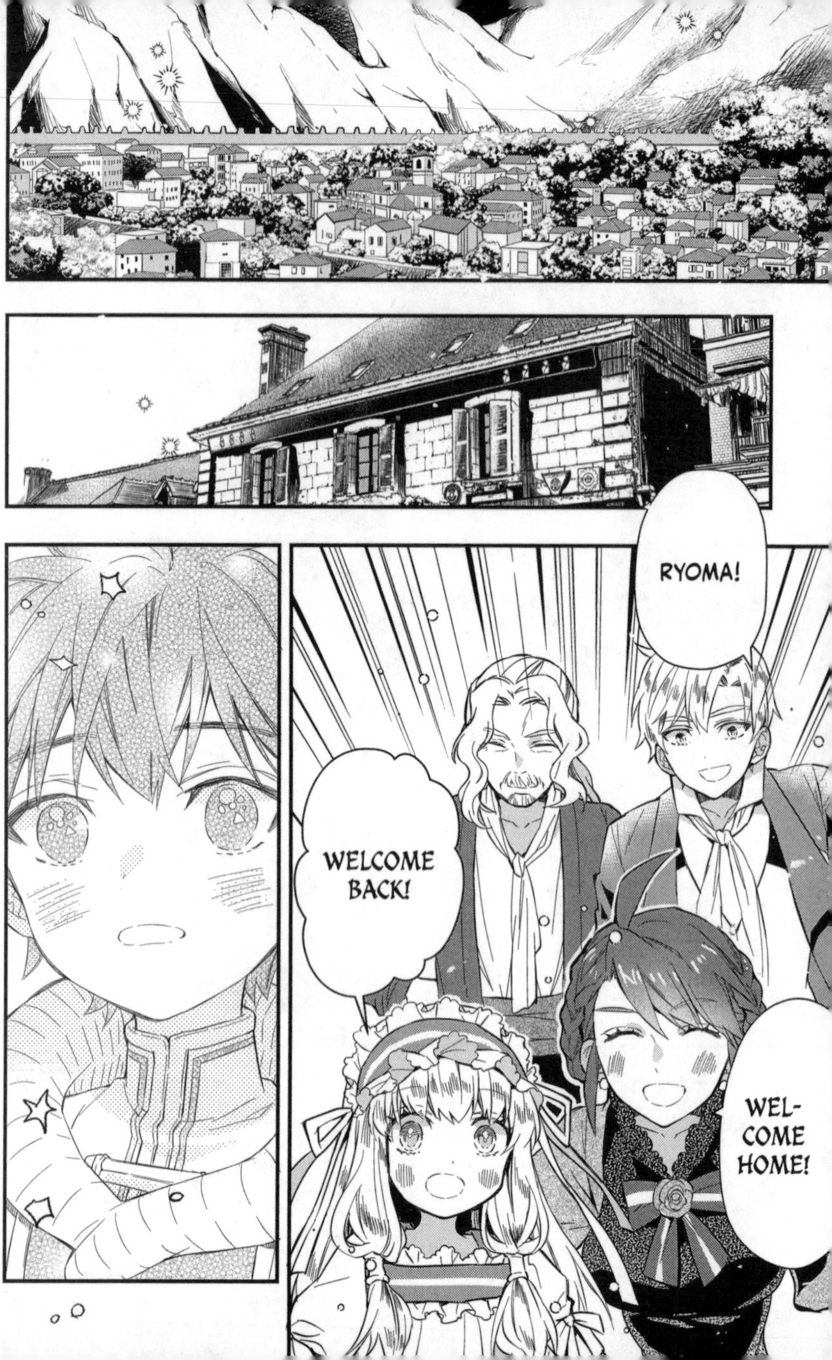
RYOMA!
WELCOME BACK!
WEL-COME HOME!

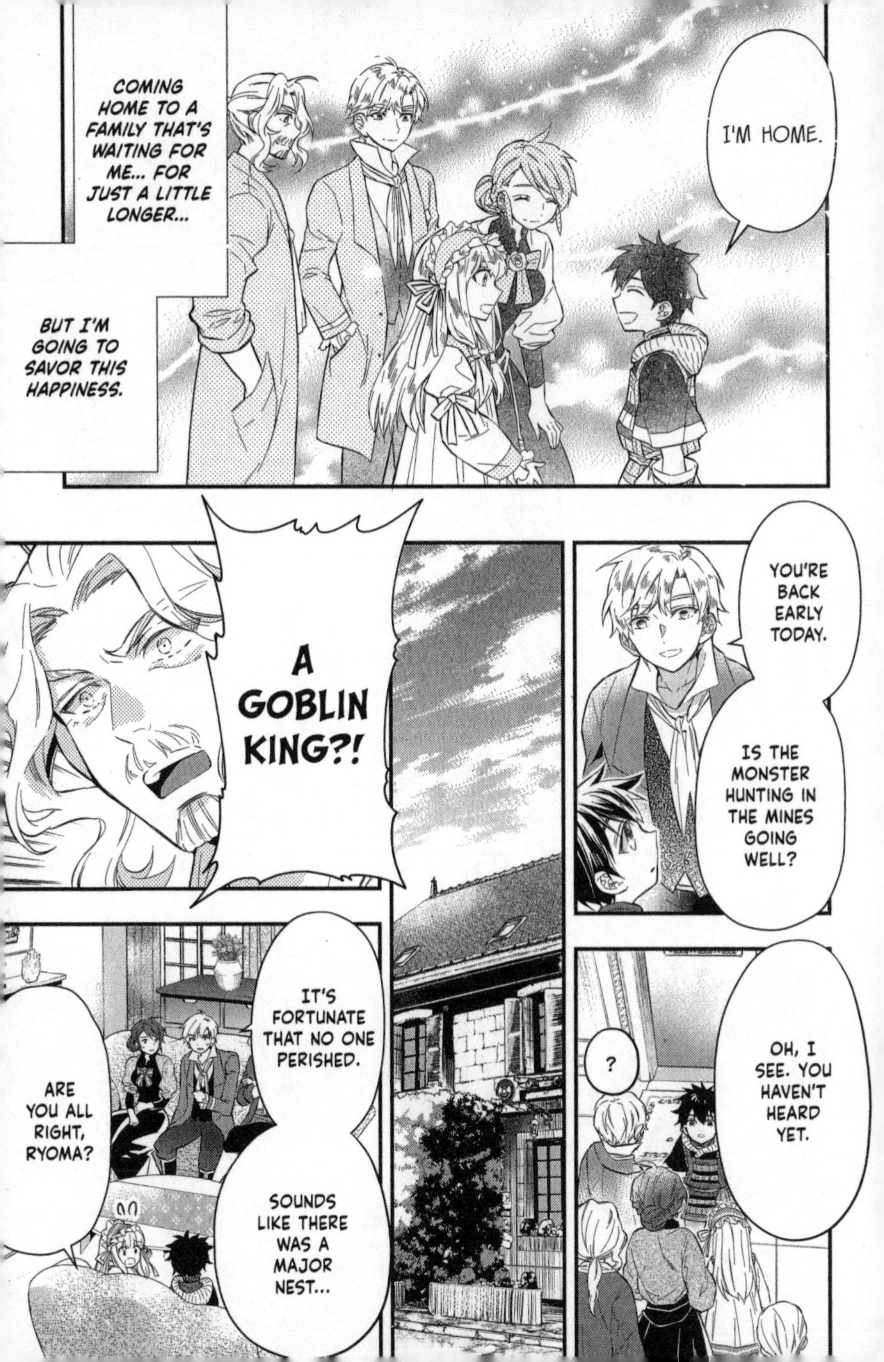
I'M HOME.
COMING HOME TO A FAMILY THAT'S WAITING FOR ME... FOR JUST A LITTLE LONGER...
BUT I'M GOING TO SAVOR THIS HAPPINESS.
YOU'RE BACK EARLY TODAY.
IS THE MONSTER HUNTING IN THE MINES GOING WELL?
OH, I SEE. YOU HAVEN'T HEARD YET.
?
A GOBLIN KING?!
IT'S FORTUNATE THAT NO ONE PERISHED.
SOUNDS LIKE THERE WAS A MAJOR NEST...
ARE YOU ALL RIGHT, RYOMA?

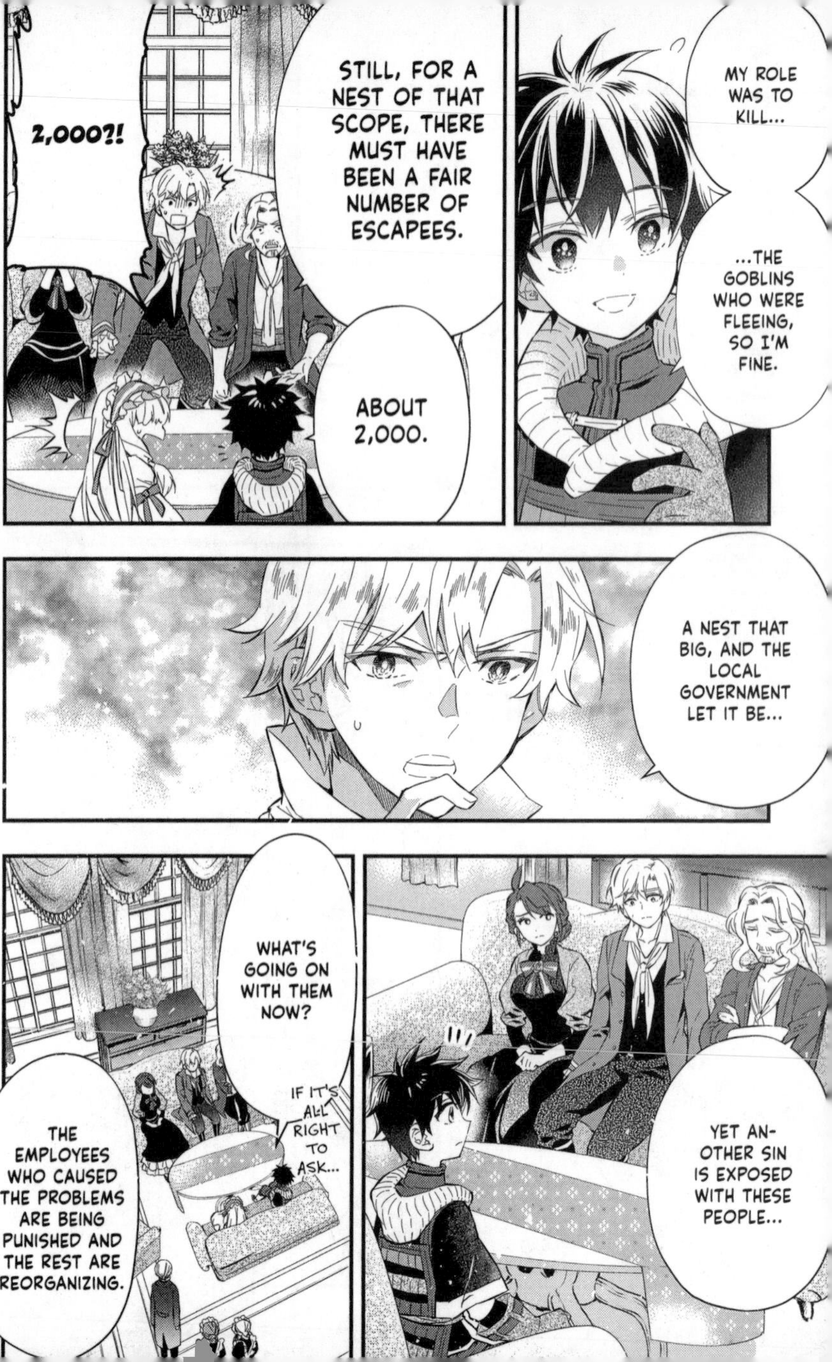
MY ROLE WAS TO KILL...
...THE GOBLINS WHO WERE FLEEING, SO I'M FINE.
STILL, FOR A NEST OF THAT SCOPE, THERE MUST HAVE BEEN A FAIR NUMBER OF ESCAPEES.
ABOUT 2,000.
2,000?!
A NEST THAT BIG, AND THE LOCAL GOVERNMENT LET IT BE...
YET AN-OTHER SIN IS EXPOSED WITH THESE PEOPLE...
WHAT'S GOING ON WITH THEM NOW?
IF IT'S ALL RIGHT TO ASK...
THE EMPLOYEES WHO CAUSED THE PROBLEMS ARE BEING PUNISHED AND THE REST ARE REORGANIZING.

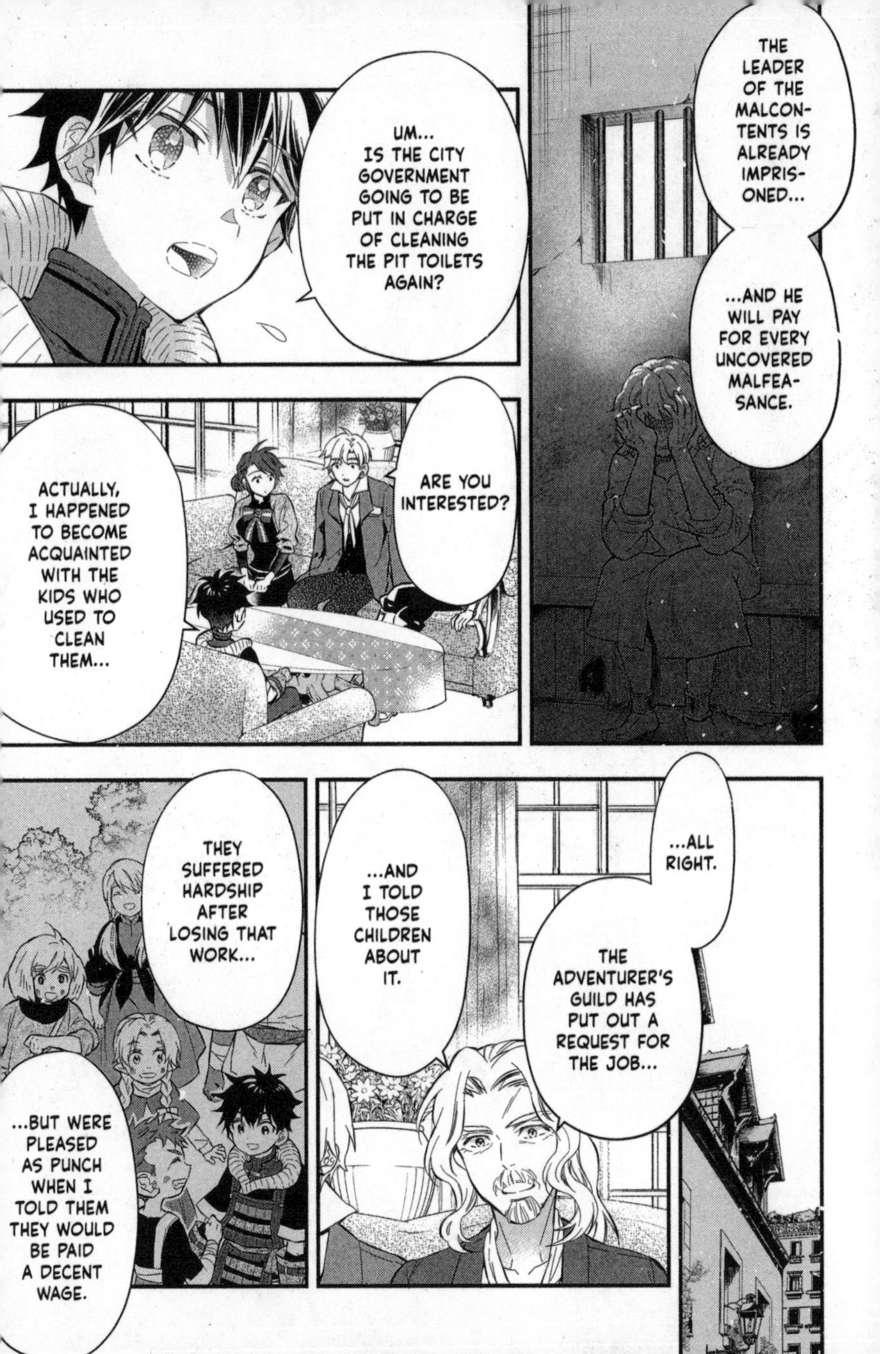
THE LEADER OF THE MALCONTENTS IS ALREADY IMPRISONED...
...AND HE WILL PAY FOR EVERY UNCOVERED MALFEASANCE.
UM... IS THE CITY GOVERNMENT GOING TO BE PUT IN CHARGE OF CLEANING THE PIT TOILETS AGAIN?
ARE YOU INTERESTED?
ACTUALLY, I HAPPENED TO BECOME ACQUAINTED WITH THE KIDS WHO USED TO CLEAN THEM...
...ALL RIGHT.
THE ADVENTURER'S GUILD HAS PUT OUT A REQUEST FOR THE JOB...
...AND I TOLD THOSE CHILDREN ABOUT IT.
THEY SUFFERED HARDSHIP AFTER LOSING THAT WORK...
...BUT WERE PLEASED AS PUNCH WHEN I TOLD THEM THEY WOULD BE PAID A DECENT WAGE.

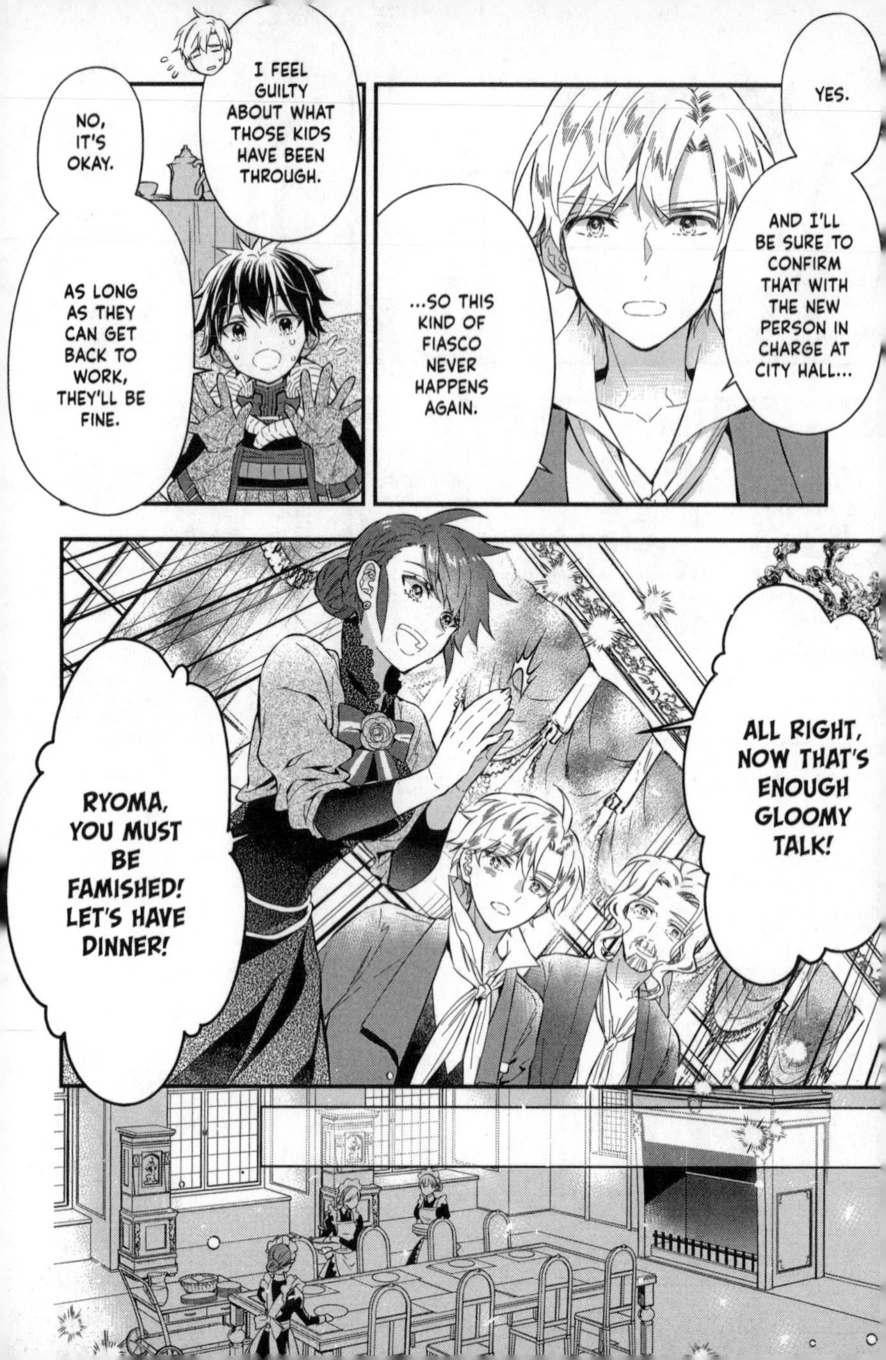
YES.
AND I'LL BE SURE TO CONFIRM THAT WITH THE NEW PERSON IN CHARGE AT CITY HALL...
...SO THIS KIND OF FIASCO NEVER HAPPENS AGAIN.
I FEEL GUILTY ABOUT WHAT THOSE KIDS HAVE BEEN THROUGH.
NO, IT'S OKAY.
AS LONG AS THEY CAN GET BACK TO WORK, THEY'LL BE FINE.
ALL RIGHT, NOW THAT'S ENOUGH GLOOMY TALK!
RYOMA, YOU MUST BE FAMISHED! LET'S HAVE DINNER!

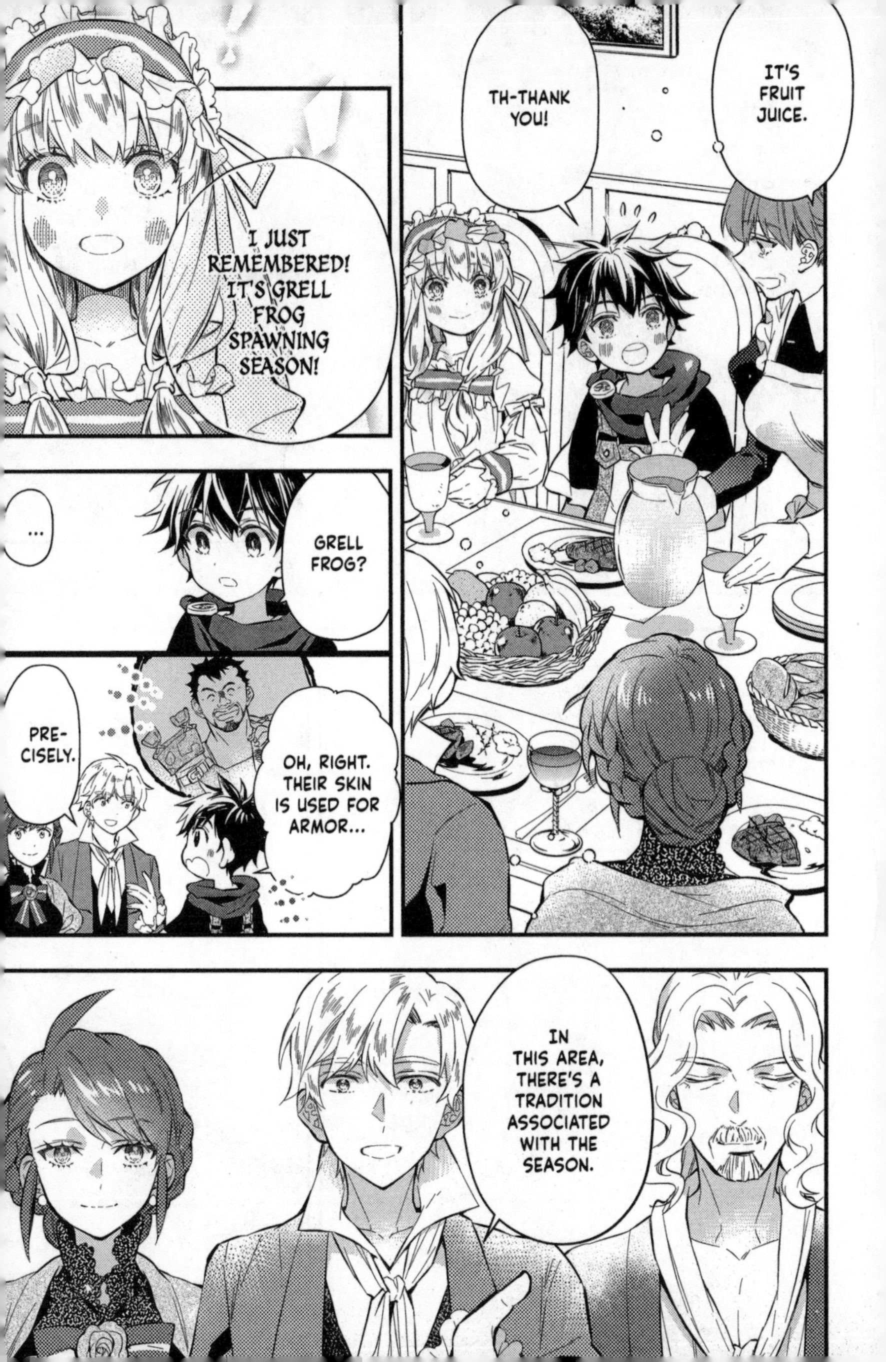
IT'S FRUIT JUICE.
TH-THANK YOU!
I JUST REMEMBERED! IT'S GRELL FROG SPAWNING SEASON!
GRELL FROG?
...
OH, RIGHT. THEIR SKIN IS USED FOR ARMOR...
PRE-CISELY.
IN THIS AREA, THERE'S A TRADITION ASSOCIATED WITH THE SEASON.

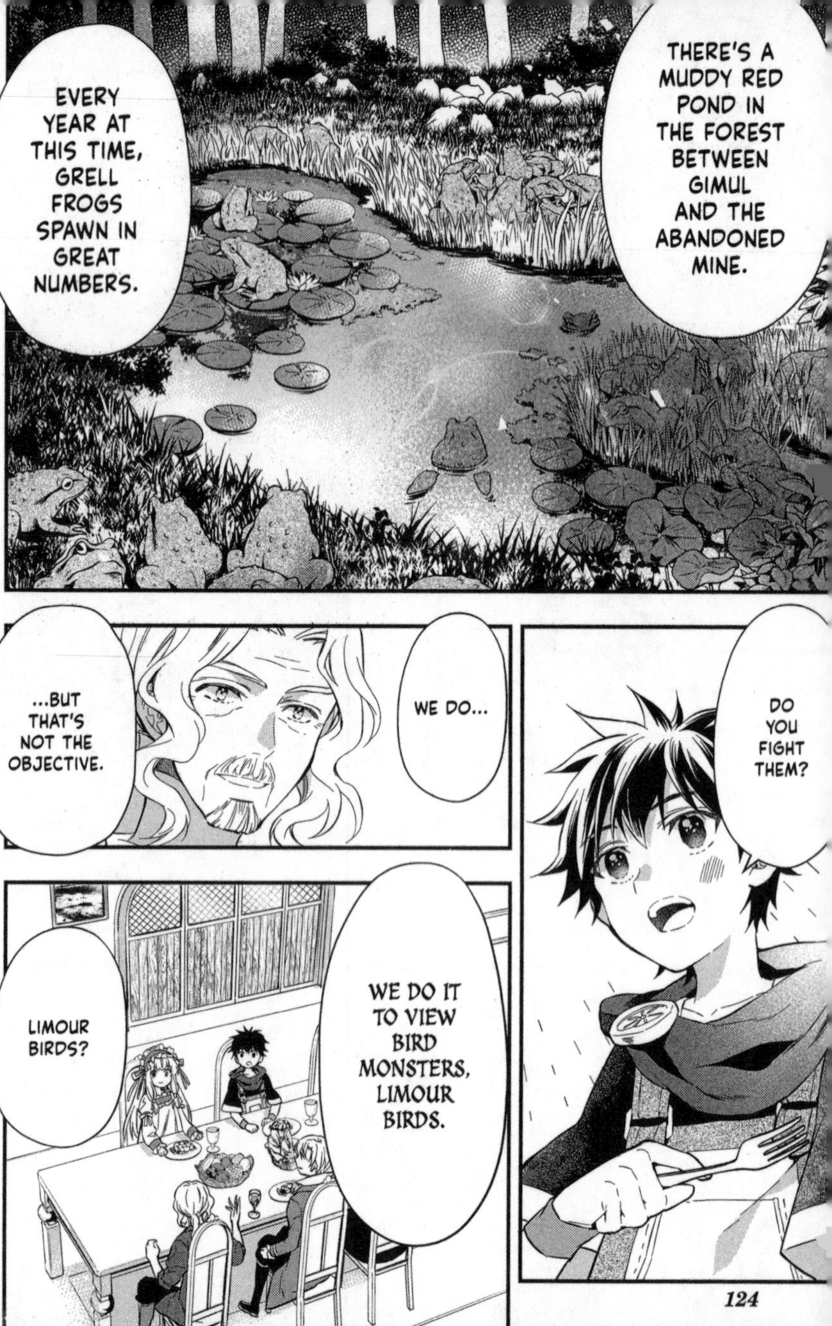
THERE'S A MUDDY RED POND IN THE FOREST BETWEEN GIMUL AND THE ABANDONED MINE.
EVERY YEAR AT THIS TIME, GRELL FROGS SPAWN IN GREAT NUMBERS.
DO YOU FIGHT THEM?
WE DO...
...BUT THAT'S NOT THE OBJECTIVE.
WE DO IT TO VIEW BIRD MONSTERS, LIMOUR BIRDS.
LIMOUR BIRDS?

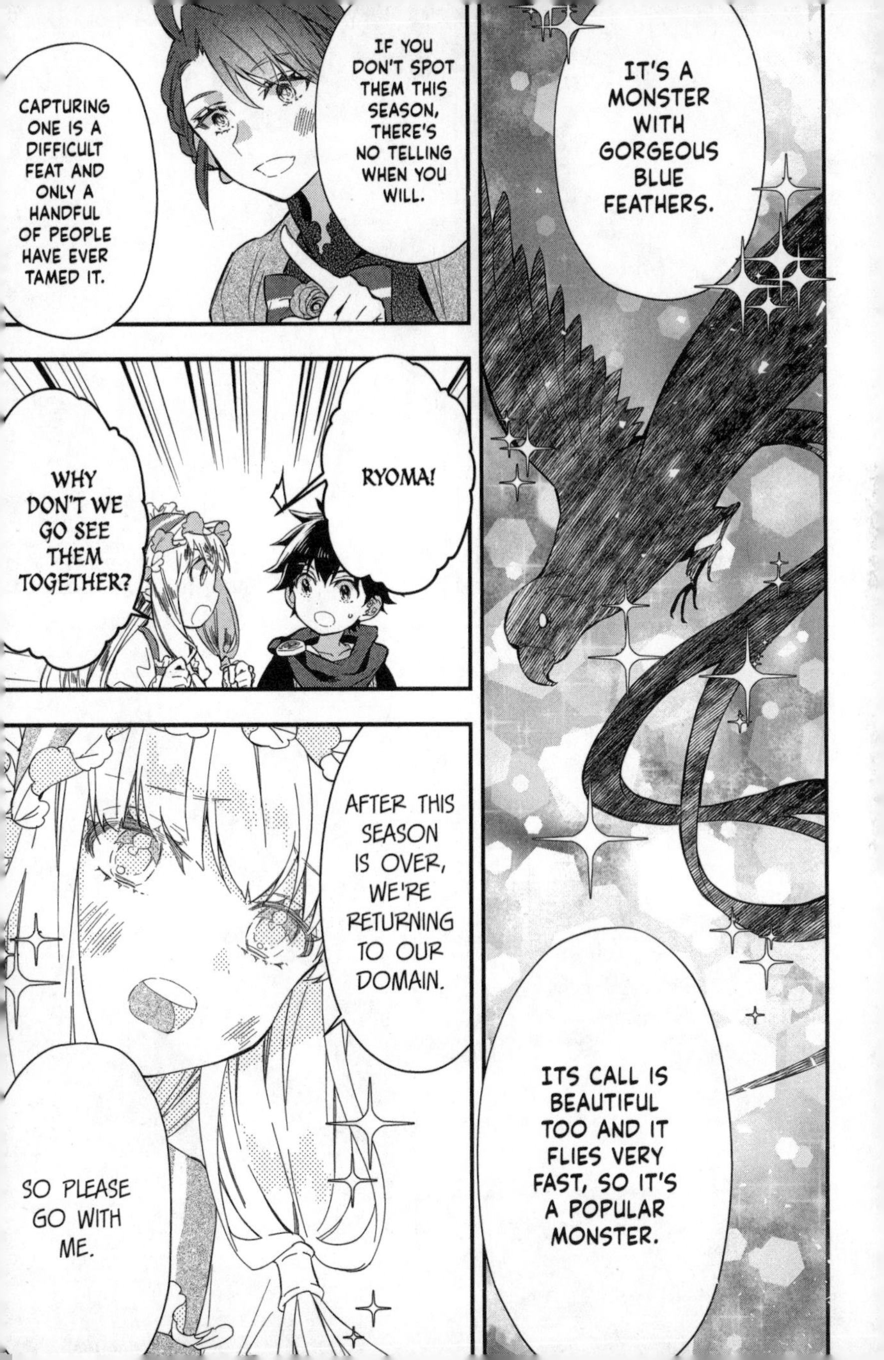
IT'S A MONSTER WITH GORGEOUS BLUE FEATHERS.
ITS CALL IS BEAUTIFUL TOO AND IT FLIES VERY FAST, SO IT'S A POPULAR MONSTER.
IF YOU DON'T SPOT THEM THIS SEASON, THERE'S NO TELLING WHEN YOU WILL.
CAPTURING ONE IS A DIFFICULT FEAT AND ONLY A HANDFUL OF PEOPLE HAVE EVER TAMED IT.
RYOMA!
WHY DON'T WE GO SEE THEM TOGETHER?
AFTER THIS SEASON IS OVER, WE'RE RETURNING TO OUR DOMAIN.
SO PLEASE GO WITH ME.

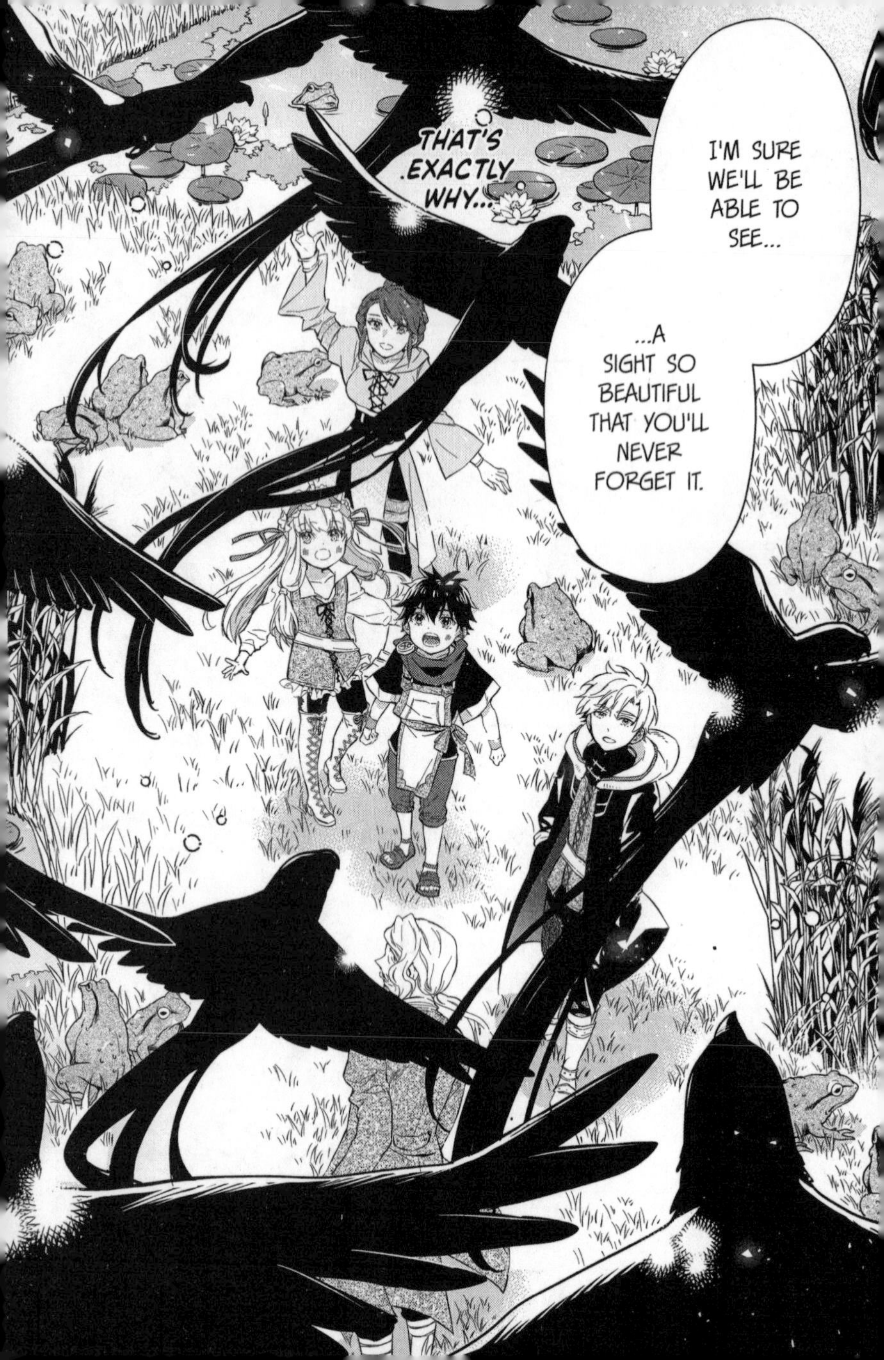
I'M SURE WE'LL BE ABLE TO SEE...
...A SIGHT SO BEAUTIFUL THAT YOU'LL NEVER FORGET IT.
THAT'S .EXACTLY WHY...

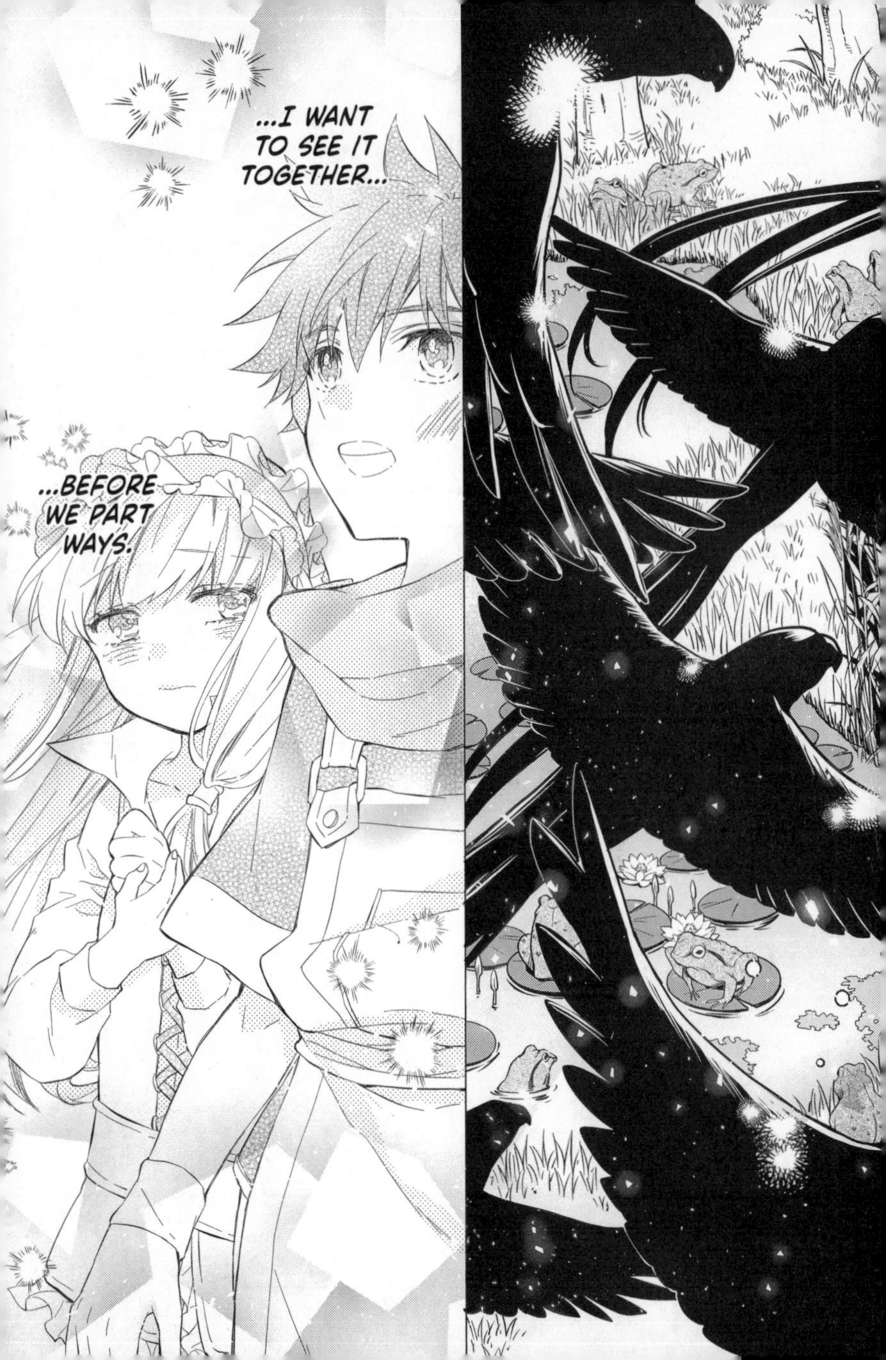
...I WANT TO SEE IT TOGETHER...
...BEFORE WE PART WAYS.

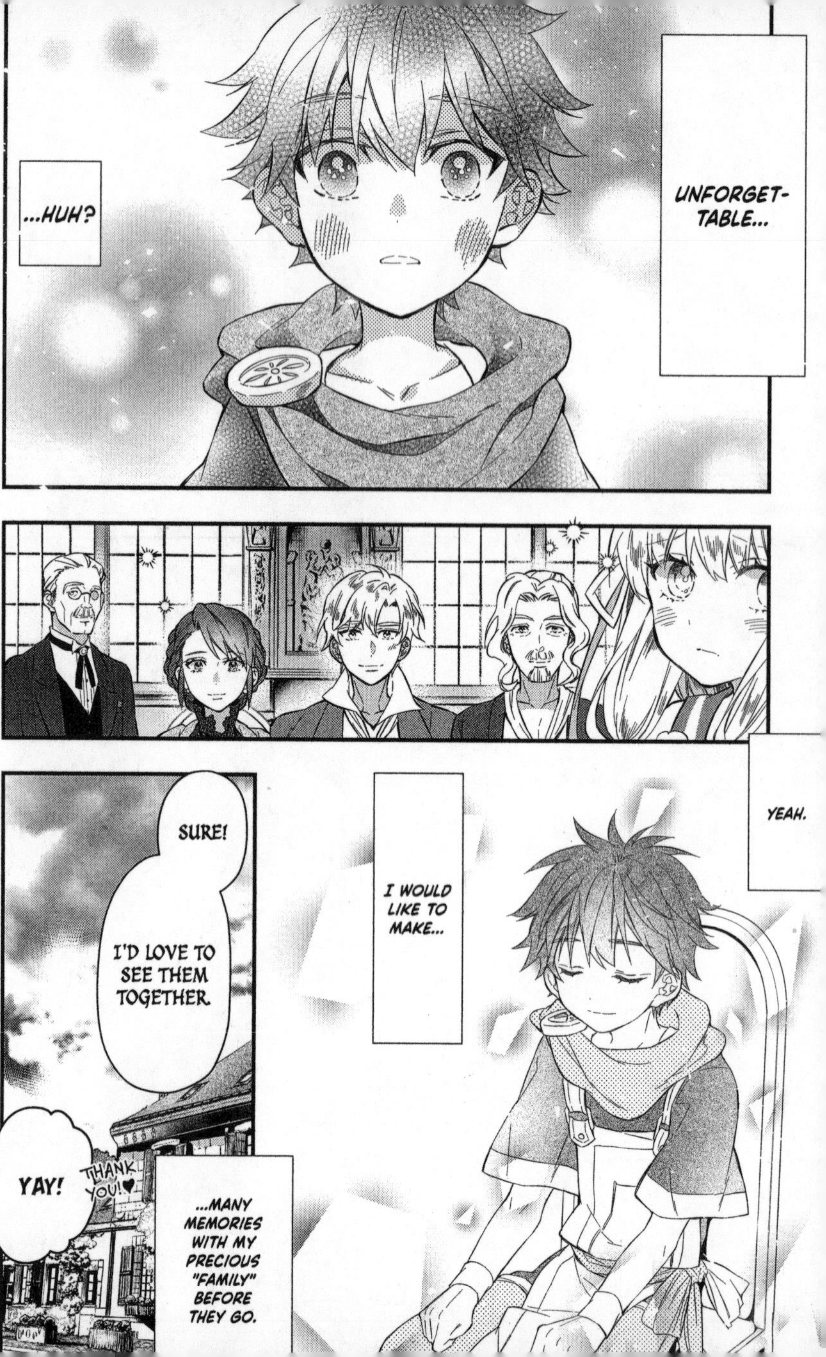
UNFORGET-TABLE...
...HUH?
YEAH.
I WOULD LIKE TO MAKE...
SURE!
I'D LOVE TO SEE THEM TOGETHER.
YAY!
THANK YOU!♥
...MANY MEMORIES WITH MY PRECIOUS "FAMILY" BEFORE THEY GO.

Chapter 26: Advice About Starting a Business

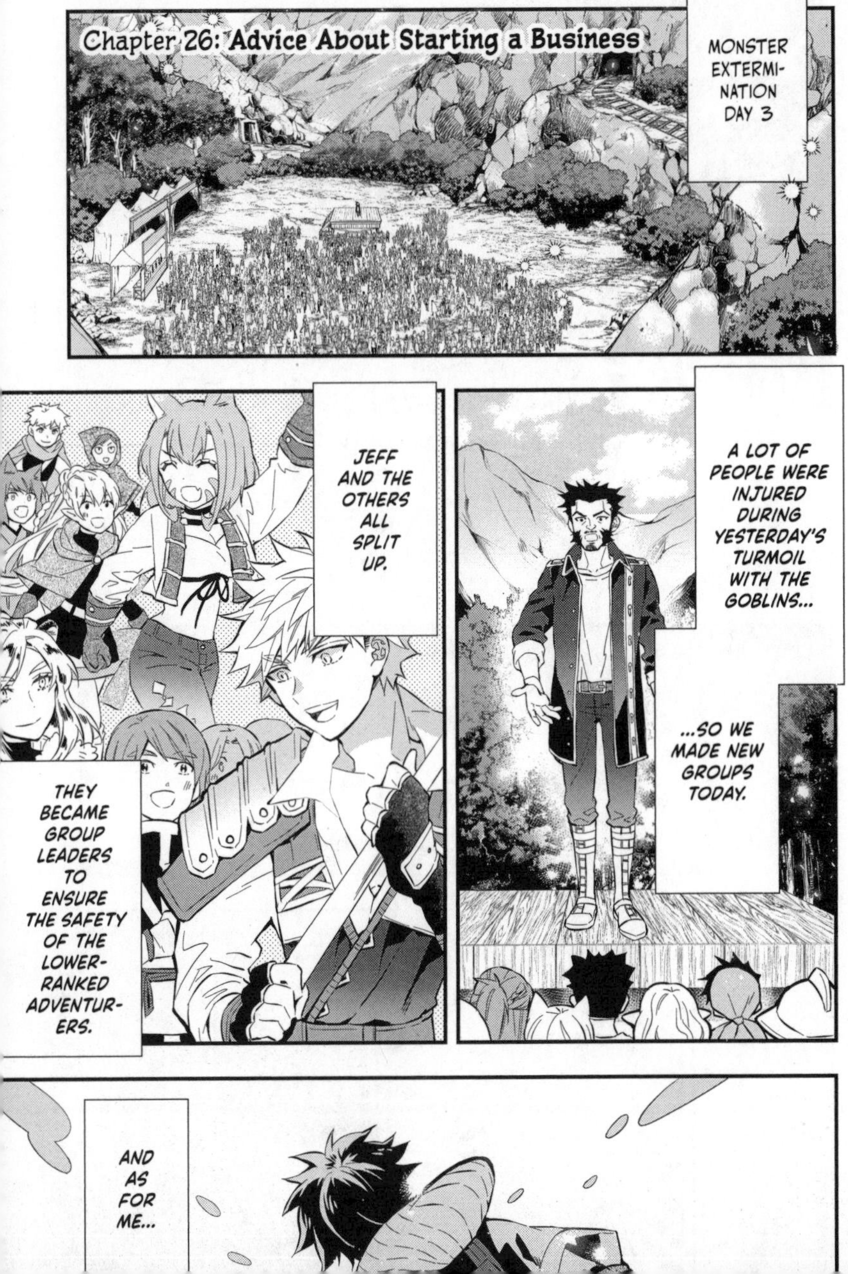
MONSTER EXTERMINATION DAY 3
A LOT OF PEOPLE WERE INJURED DURING YESTERDAY'S TURMOIL WITH THE GOBLINS...
...SO WE MADE NEW GROUPS TODAY.
JEFF AND THE OTHERS ALL SPLIT UP.
THEY BECAME GROUP LEADERS TO ENSURE THE SAFETY OF THE LOWER-RANKED ADVENTURERS.
AND AS FOR ME...

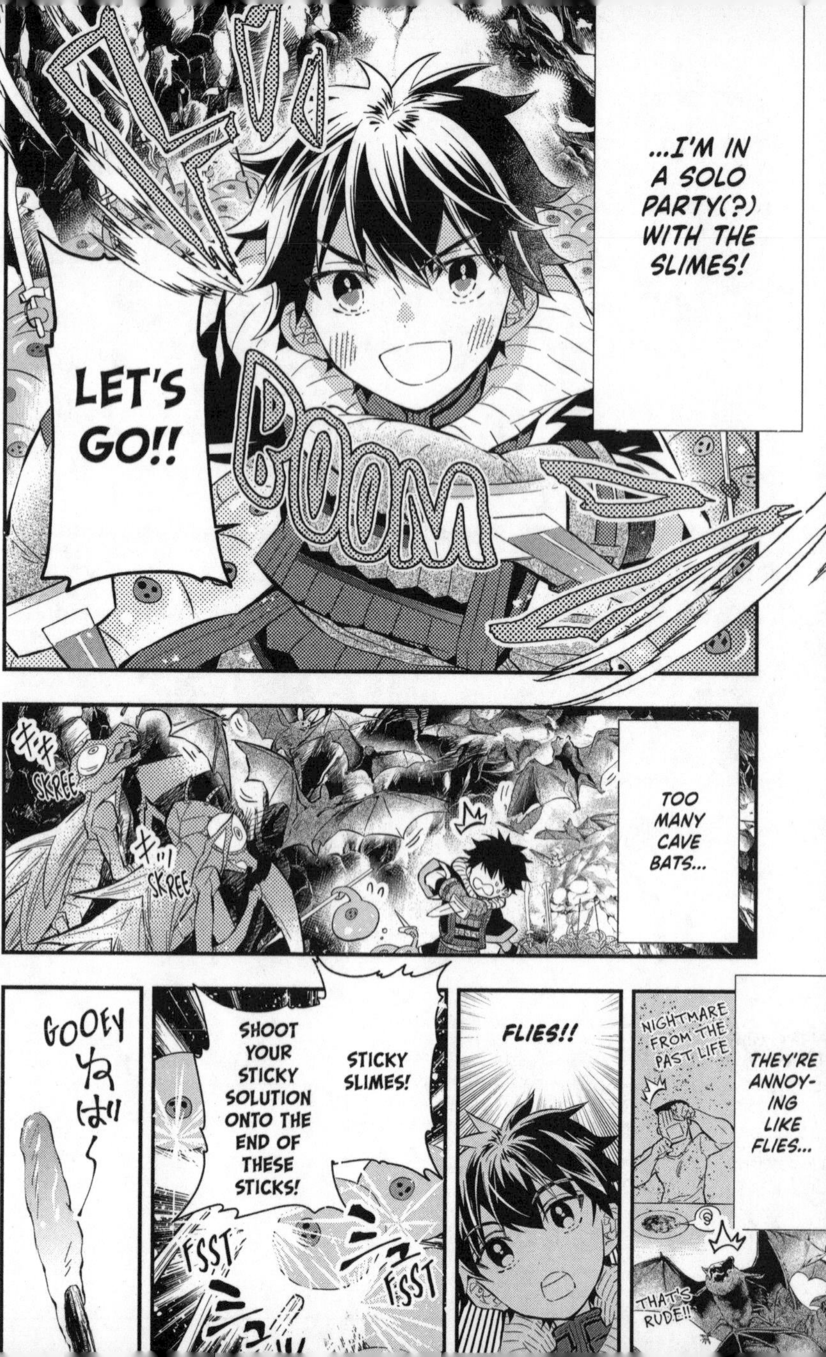
...I'M IN A SOLO PARTY(?) WITH THE SLIMES!
LET'S GO!!
BOOM
TOO MANY CAVE BATS...
SKREE
SKREE
THEY'RE ANNOY-ING LIKE FLIES...
NIGHTMARE FROM THE PAST LIFE
THAT'S RUDE!!
FLIES!!
STICKY SLIMES!
SHOOT YOUR STICKY SOLUTION ONTO THE END OF THESE STICKS!
FSST
FSST
GOOEY

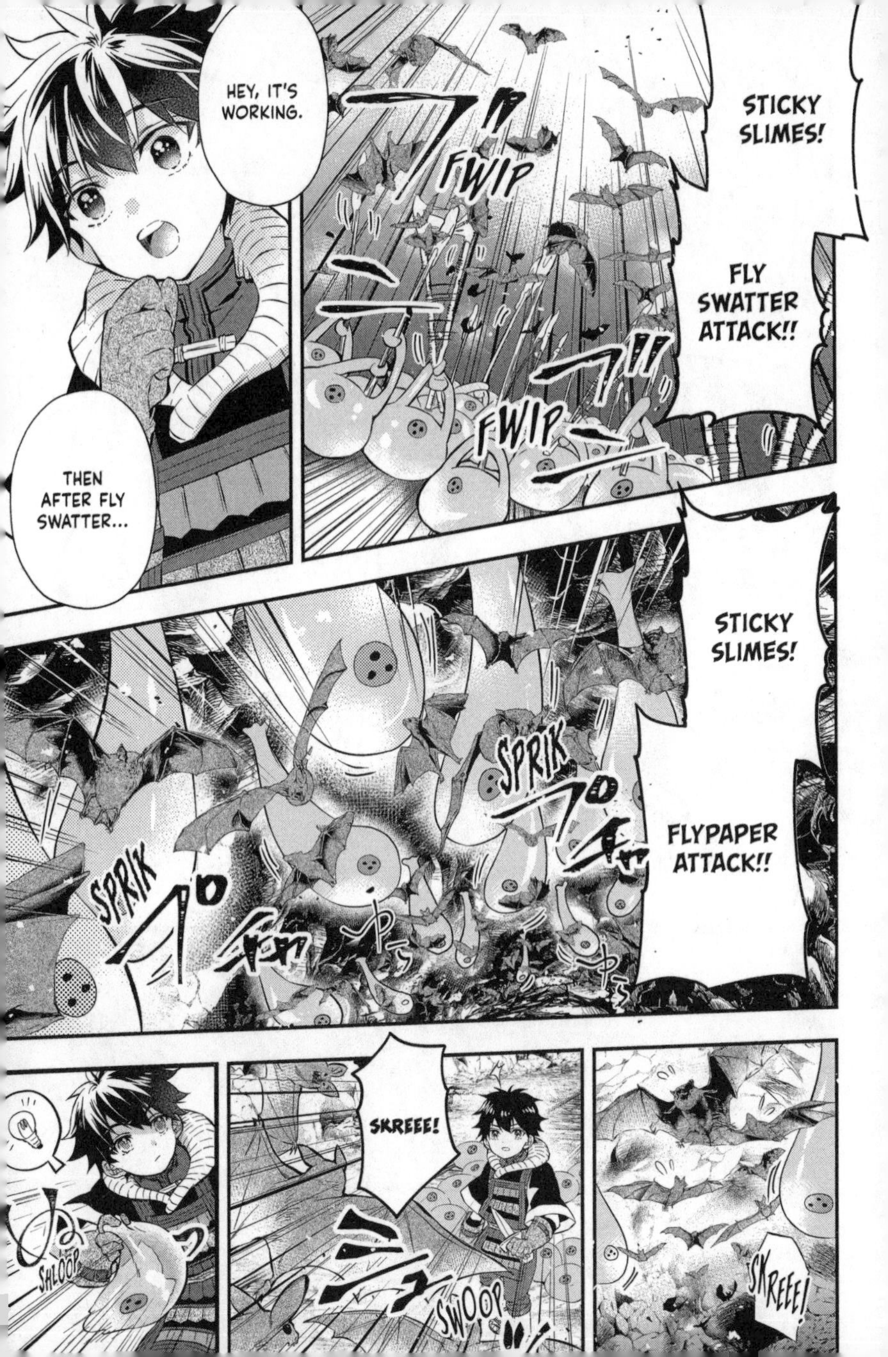
STICKY SLIMES!
FLY SWATTER ATTACK!!
FWIP
FWIP
HEY, IT'S WORKING.
THEN AFTER FLY SWATTER...
STICKY SLIMES!
FLYPAPER ATTACK!!
SPRIK
SPRIK
SKREEE!
SKREEE!
SWOOP
SHLOOP

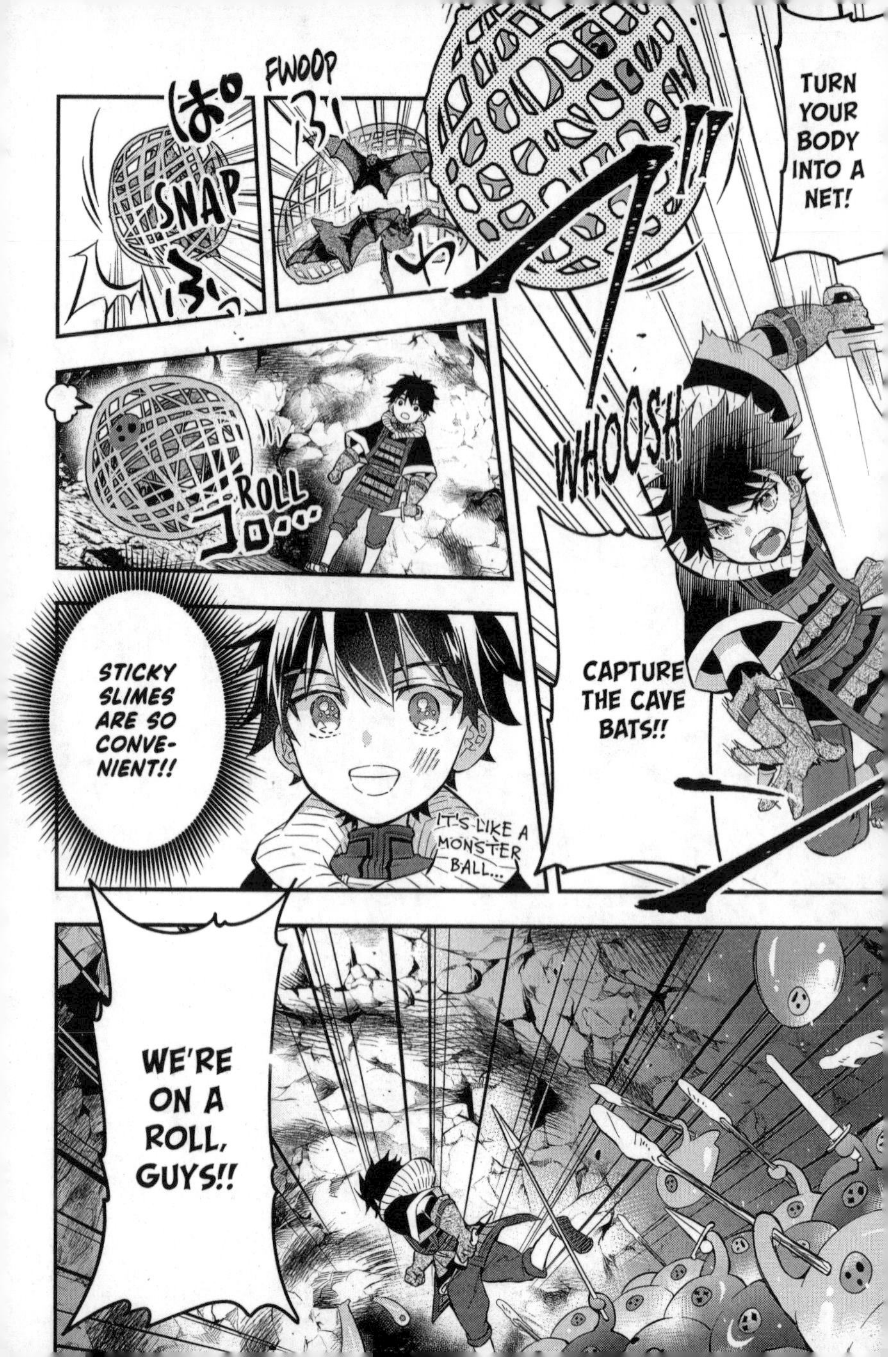

TURN YOUR BODY INTO A NET!
WHOOSH
CAPTURE THE CAVE BATS!!
FWOOP
SNAP
ROLL
STICKY SLIMES ARE SO CONVENIENT!!
IT'S LIKE A MONSTER BALL...
WE'RE ON A ROLL, GUYS!!

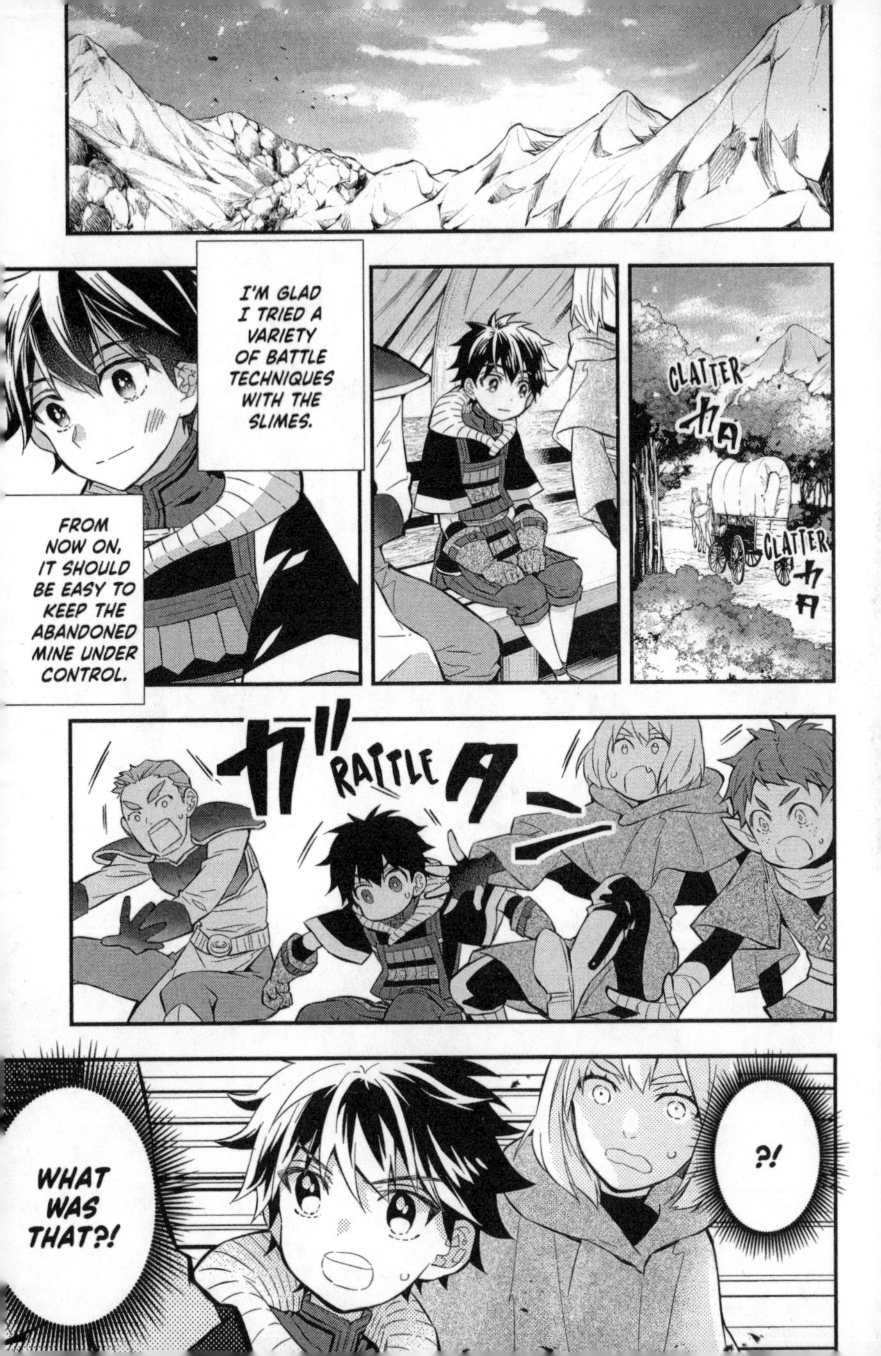

CLATTER
カタ
CLATTER
カタ
I'M GLAD I TRIED A VARIETY OF BATTLE TECHNIQUES WITH THE SLIMES.
FROM NOW ON, IT SHOULD BE EASY TO KEEP THE ABANDONED MINE UNDER CONTROL.
ガタ
RATTLE
ガタン
?!
WHAT WAS THAT?!

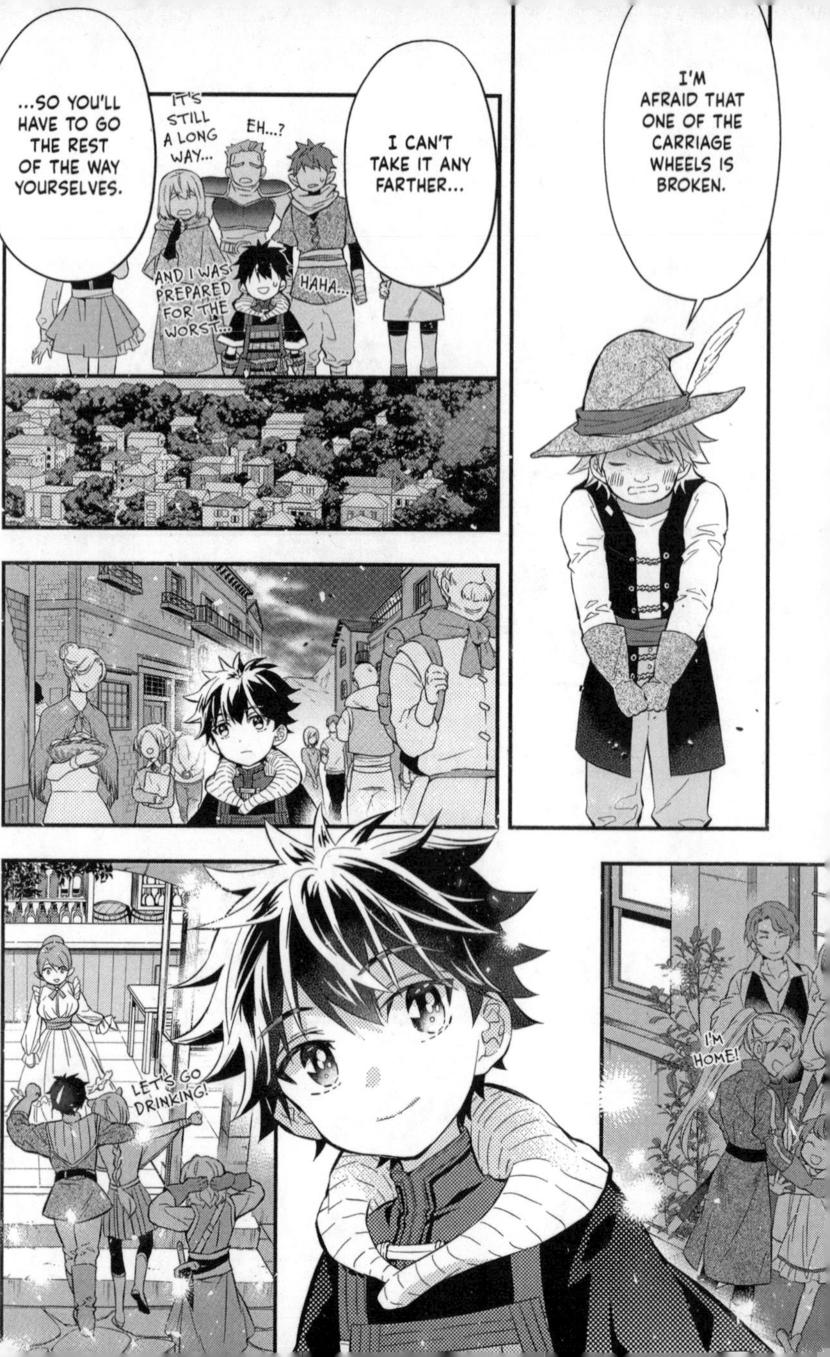
I'M AFRAID THAT ONE OF THE CARRIAGE WHEELS IS BROKEN.
I CAN'T TAKE IT ANY FARTHER...
...SO YOU'LL HAVE TO GO THE REST OF THE WAY YOURSELVES.
EH...?
IT'S STILL A LONG WAY...
HAHA...
AND I WAS PREPARED FOR THE WORST...
I'M HOME!
LET'S GO DRINKING!

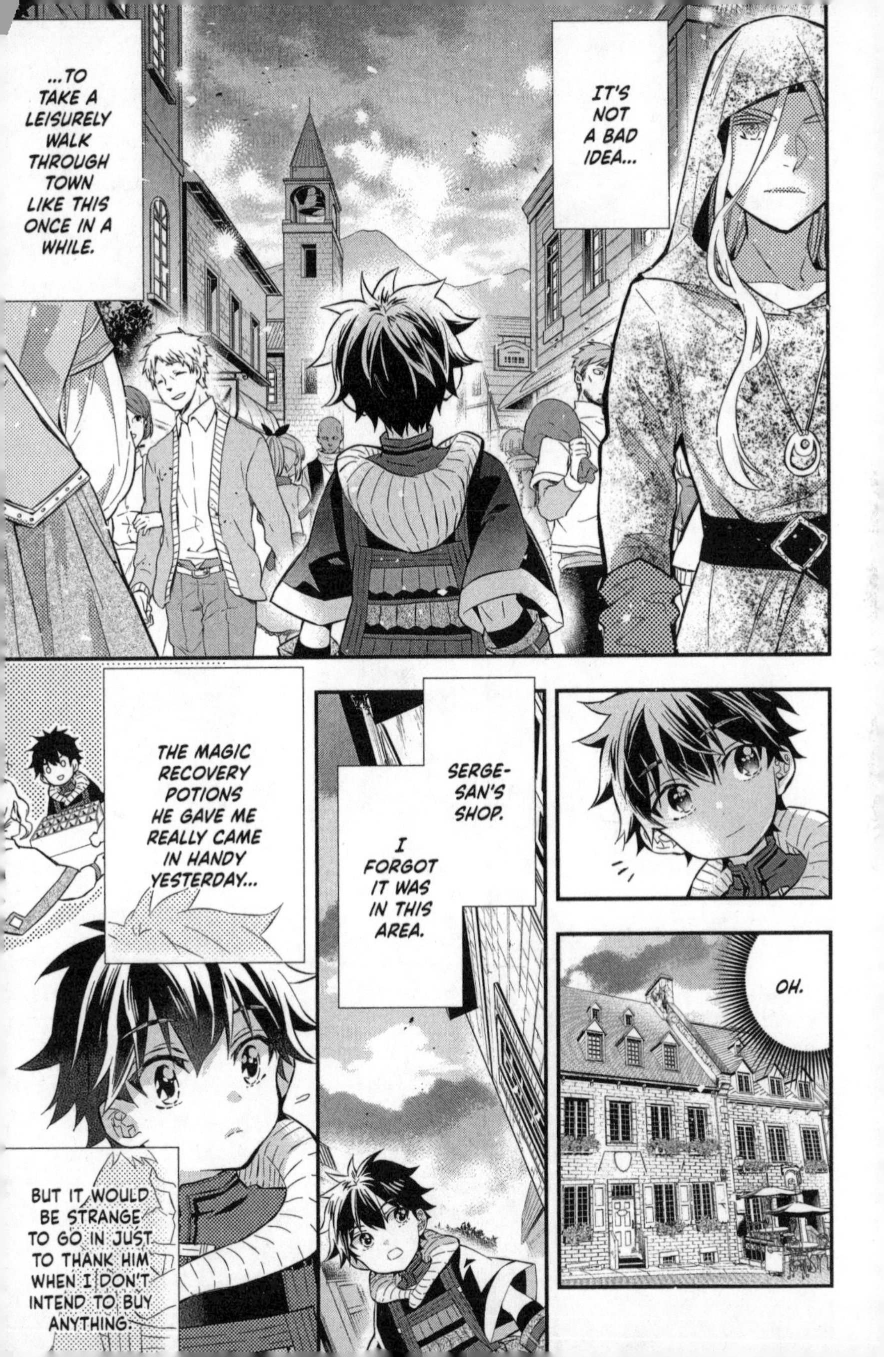
IT'S NOT A BAD IDEA...
...TO TAKE A LEISURELY WALK THROUGH TOWN LIKE THIS ONCE IN A WHILE.
OH.
SERGE-SAN'S SHOP.
I FORGOT IT WAS IN THIS AREA.
THE MAGIC RECOVERY POTIONS HE GAVE ME REALLY CAME IN HANDY YESTERDAY...
BUT IT WOULD BE STRANGE TO GO IN JUST TO THANK HIM WHEN I DON'T INTEND TO BUY ANYTHING.

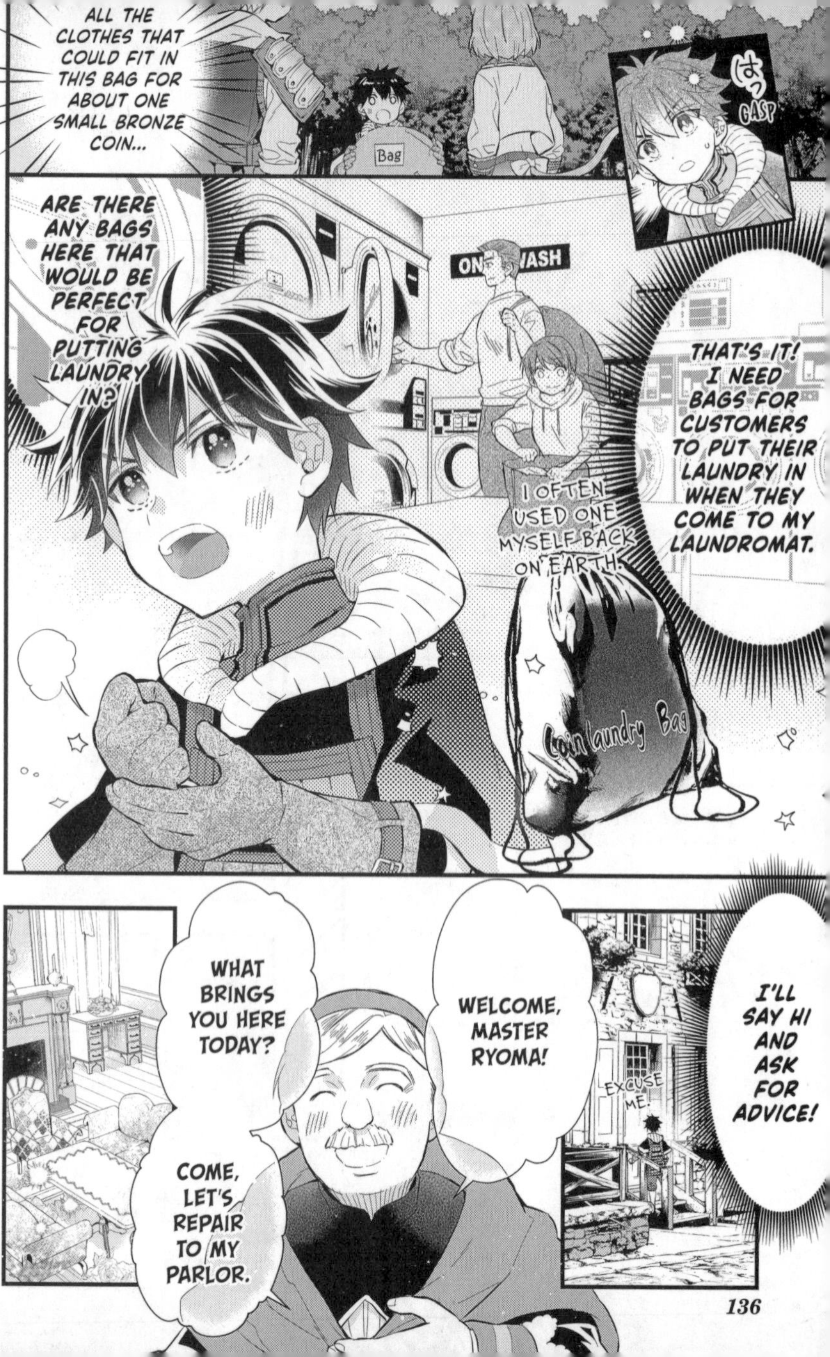

ALL THE CLOTHES THAT COULD FIT IN THIS BAG FOR ABOUT ONE SMALL BRONZE COIN...
Bag
はっ
GASP
THAT'S IT! I NEED BAGS FOR CUSTOMERS TO PUT THEIR LAUNDRY IN WHEN THEY COME TO MY LAUNDROMAT.
I OFTEN USED ONE MYSELF BACK ON EARTH.
ARE THERE ANY BAGS HERE THAT WOULD BE PERFECT FOR PUTTING LAUNDRY IN?
Coin laundry Bag
I'LL SAY HI AND ASK FOR ADVICE!
EXCUSE ME!
WELCOME, MASTER RYOMA!
WHAT BRINGS YOU HERE TODAY?
COME, LET'S REPAIR TO MY PARLOR.

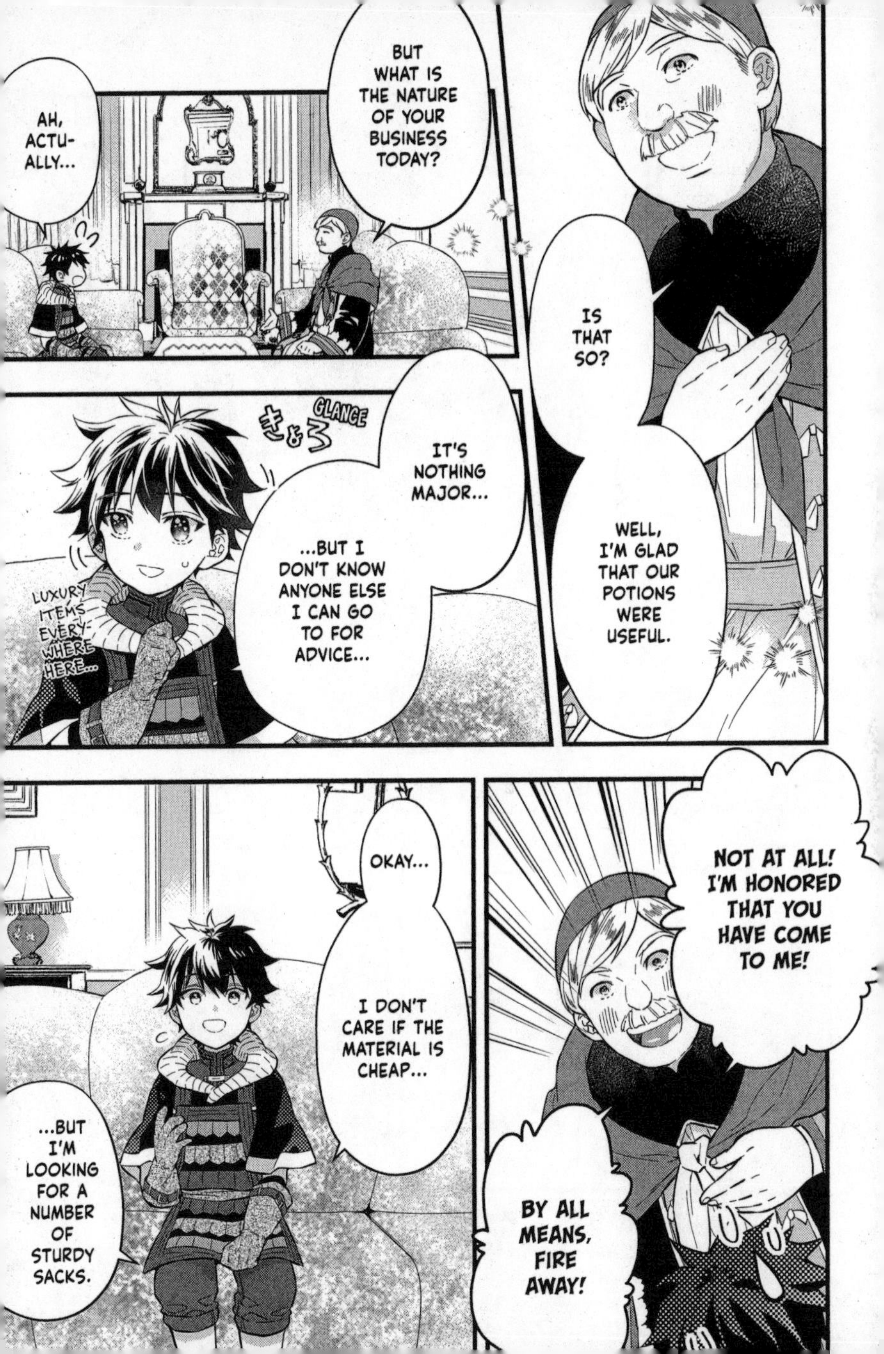
IS THAT SO?
WELL, I'M GLAD THAT OUR POTIONS WERE USEFUL.
BUT WHAT IS THE NATURE OF YOUR BUSINESS TODAY?
AH, ACTU-ALLY...
きょろ GLANCE
IT'S NOTHING MAJOR...
...BUT I DON'T KNOW ANYONE ELSE I CAN GO TO FOR ADVICE...
LUXURY ITEMS EVERY-WHERE HERE...
NOT AT ALL! I'M HONORED THAT YOU HAVE COME TO ME!
BY ALL MEANS, FIRE AWAY!
OKAY...
I DON'T CARE IF THE MATERIAL IS CHEAP...
...BUT I'M LOOKING FOR A NUMBER OF STURDY SACKS.

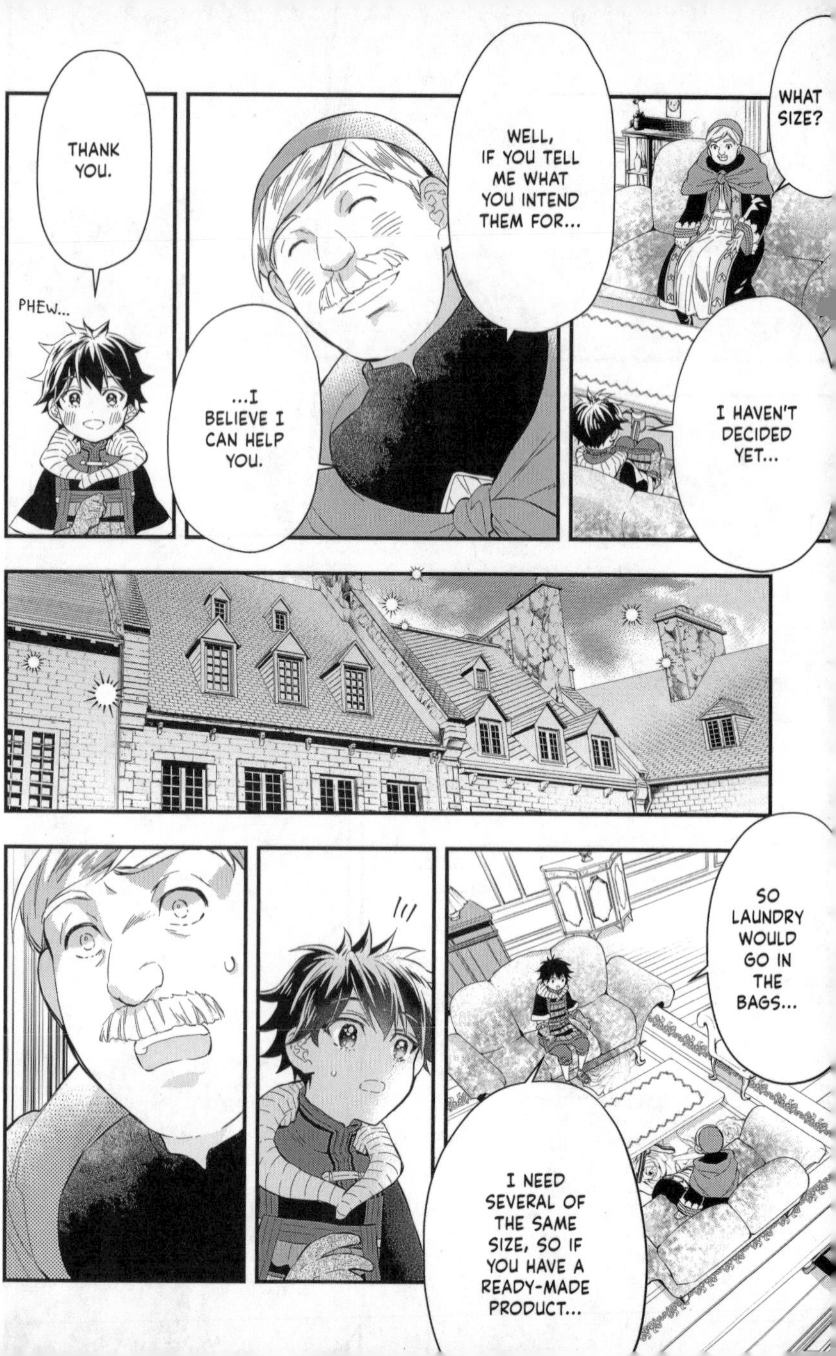
WHAT SIZE?
I HAVEN'T DECIDED YET...
WELL, IF YOU TELL ME WHAT YOU INTEND THEM FOR...
...I BELIEVE I CAN HELP YOU.
THANK YOU.
PHEW...
SO LAUNDRY WOULD GO IN THE BAGS...
I NEED SEVERAL OF THE SAME SIZE, SO IF YOU HAVE A READY-MADE PRODUCT...

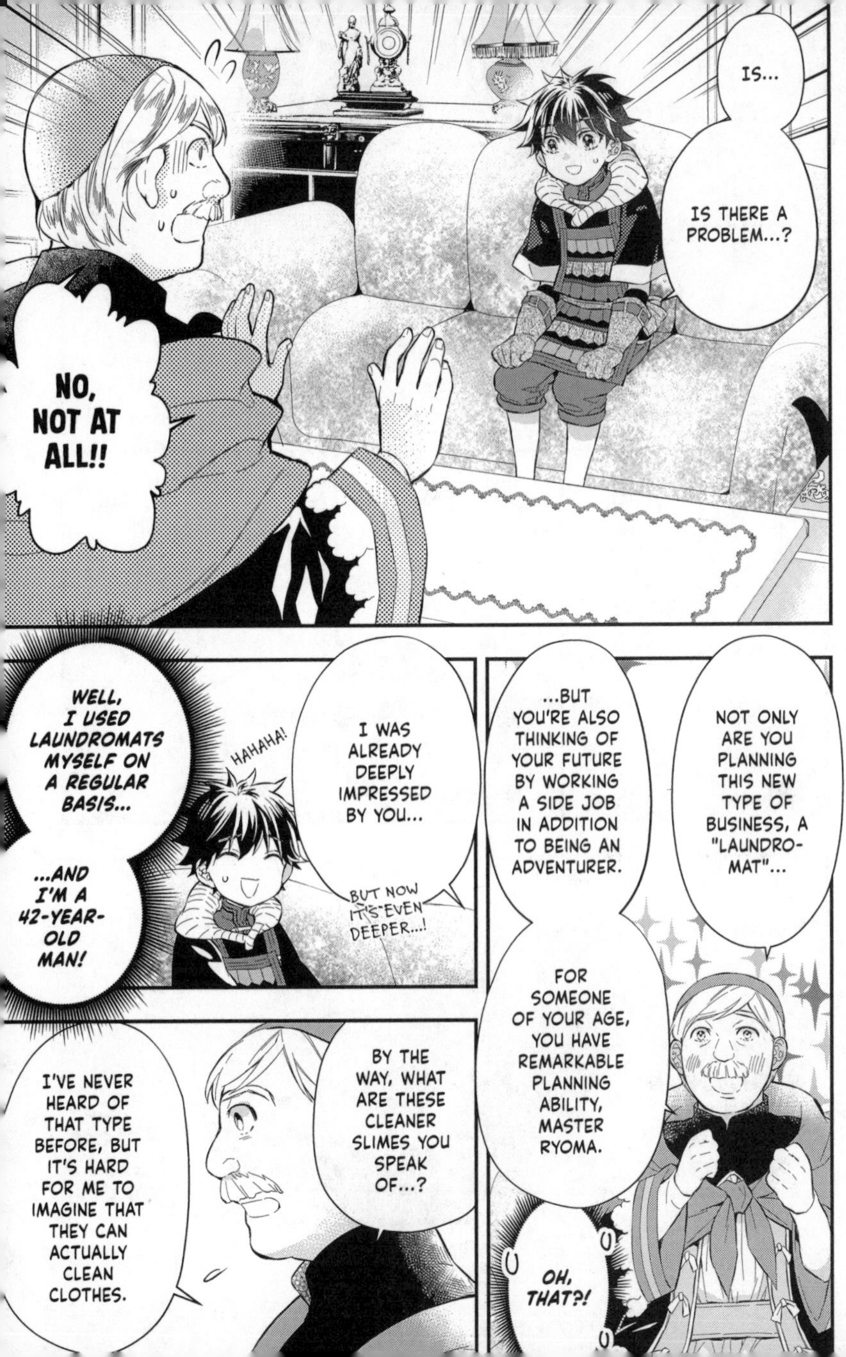
IS...
IS THERE A PROBLEM...?
NO, NOT AT ALL!!
NOT ONLY ARE YOU PLANNING THIS NEW TYPE OF BUSINESS, A "LAUNDROMAT"...
...BUT YOU'RE ALSO THINKING OF YOUR FUTURE BY WORKING A SIDE JOB IN ADDITION TO BEING AN ADVENTURER.
FOR SOMEONE OF YOUR AGE, YOU HAVE REMARKABLE PLANNING ABILITY, MASTER RYOMA.
OH, THAT?!
I WAS ALREADY DEEPLY IMPRESSED BY YOU...
BUT NOW IT'S EVEN DEEPER...!
HAHAHA!
WELL, I USED LAUNDROMATS MYSELF ON A REGULAR BASIS...
...AND I'M A 42-YEAR-OLD MAN!
BY THE WAY, WHAT ARE THESE CLEANER SLIMES YOU SPEAK OF...?
I'VE NEVER HEARD OF THAT TYPE BEFORE, BUT IT'S HARD FOR ME TO IMAGINE THAT THEY CAN ACTUALLY CLEAN CLOTHES.

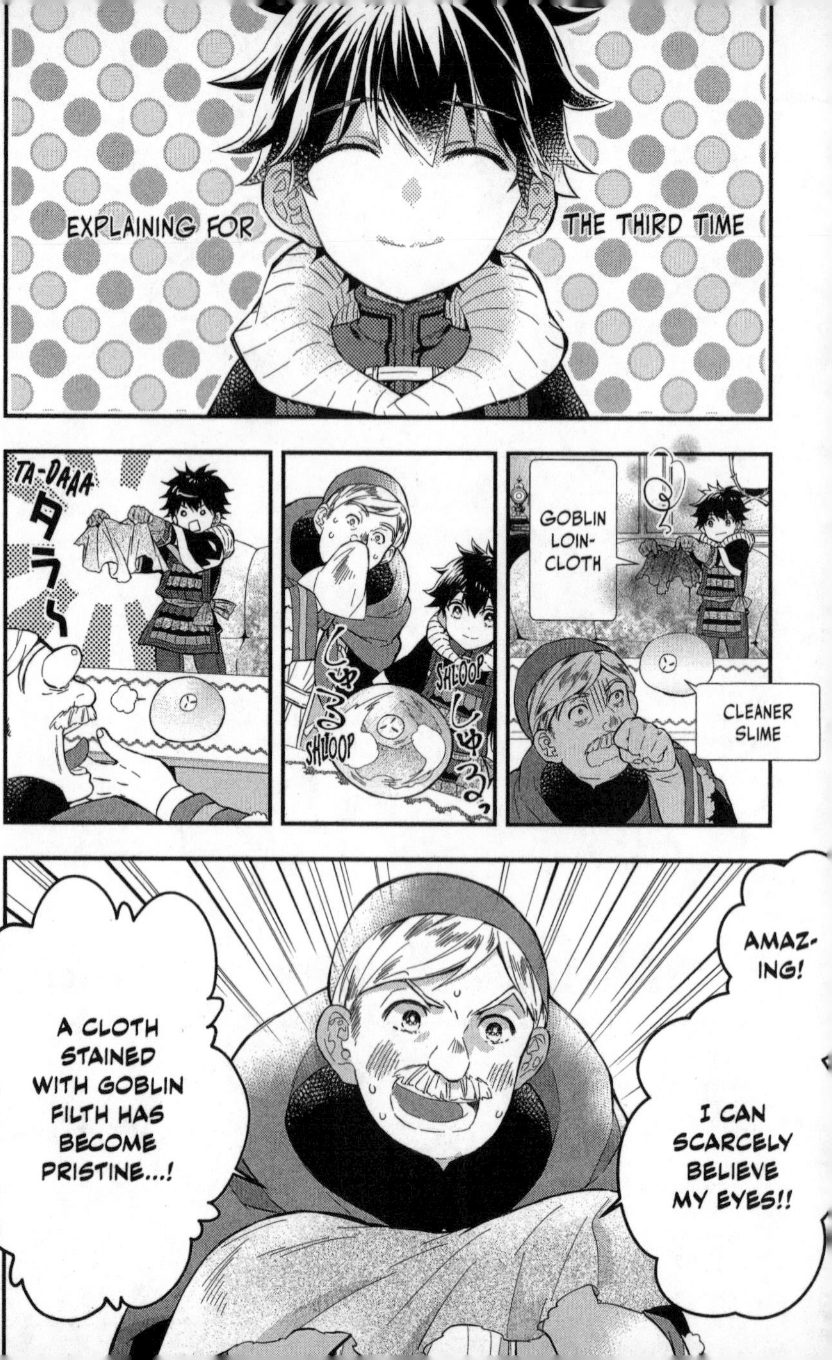

EXPLAINING FOR THE THIRD TIME
GOBLIN LOIN-CLOTH
CLEANER SLIME
SHLOOP
しゅる
SHLOOP
しゅる
TA-DAAA
タラ〜
AMAZ-ING!
I CAN SCARCELY BELIEVE MY EYES!!
A CLOTH STAINED WITH GOBLIN FILTH HAS BECOME PRISTINE...!

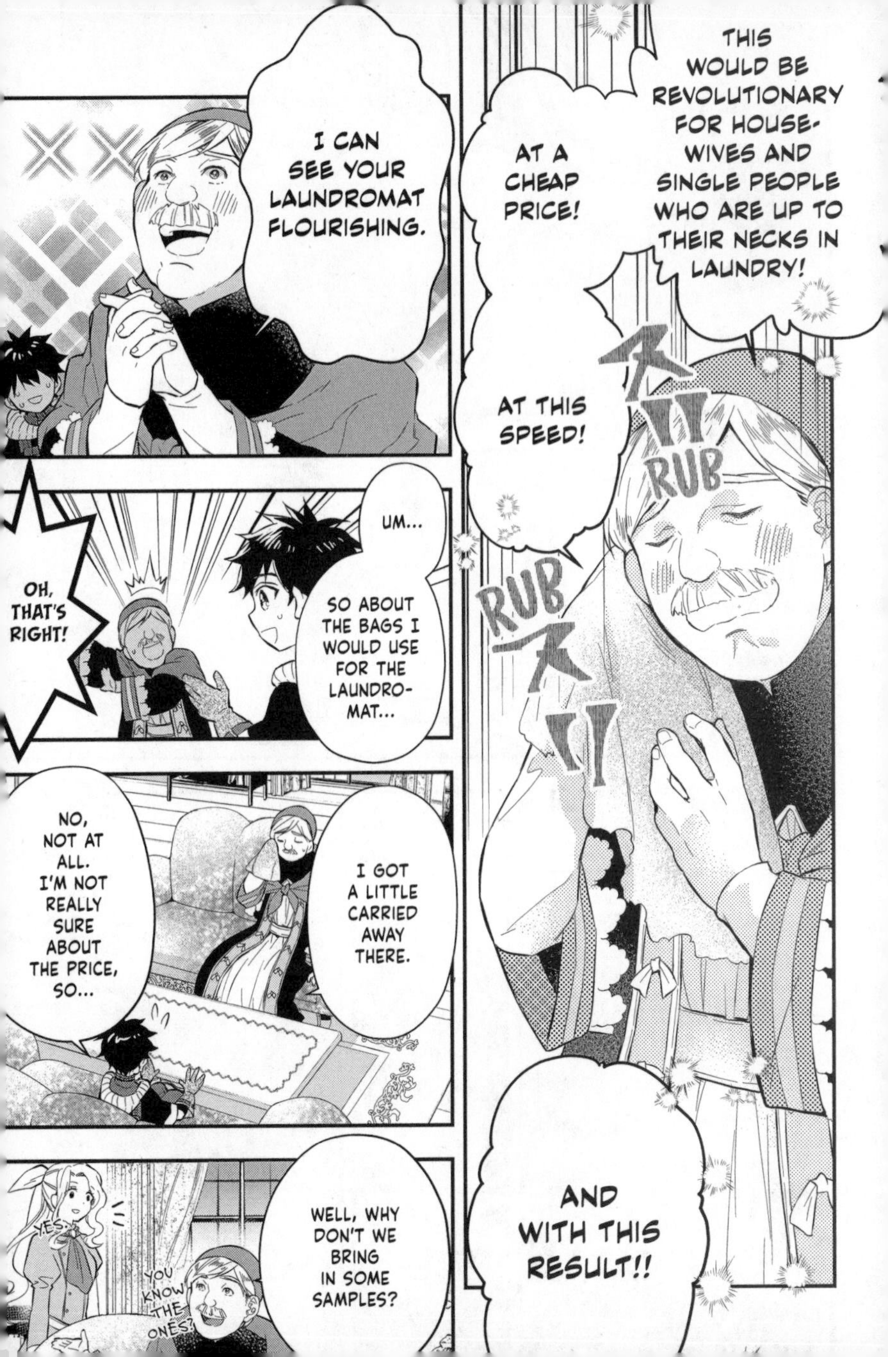
THIS WOULD BE REVOLUTIONARY FOR HOUSE-WIVES AND SINGLE PEOPLE WHO ARE UP TO THEIR NECKS IN LAUNDRY!
AT A CHEAP PRICE!
RUB
AT THIS SPEED!
RUB
AND WITH THIS RESULT!!
I CAN SEE YOUR LAUNDROMAT FLOURISHING.
UM...
SO ABOUT THE BAGS I WOULD USE FOR THE LAUNDRO-MAT...
OH, THAT'S RIGHT!
I GOT A LITTLE CARRIED AWAY THERE.
NO, NOT AT ALL. I'M NOT REALLY SURE ABOUT THE PRICE, SO...
WELL, WHY DON'T WE BRING IN SOME SAMPLES?
YOU KNOW THE ONES?
YES.

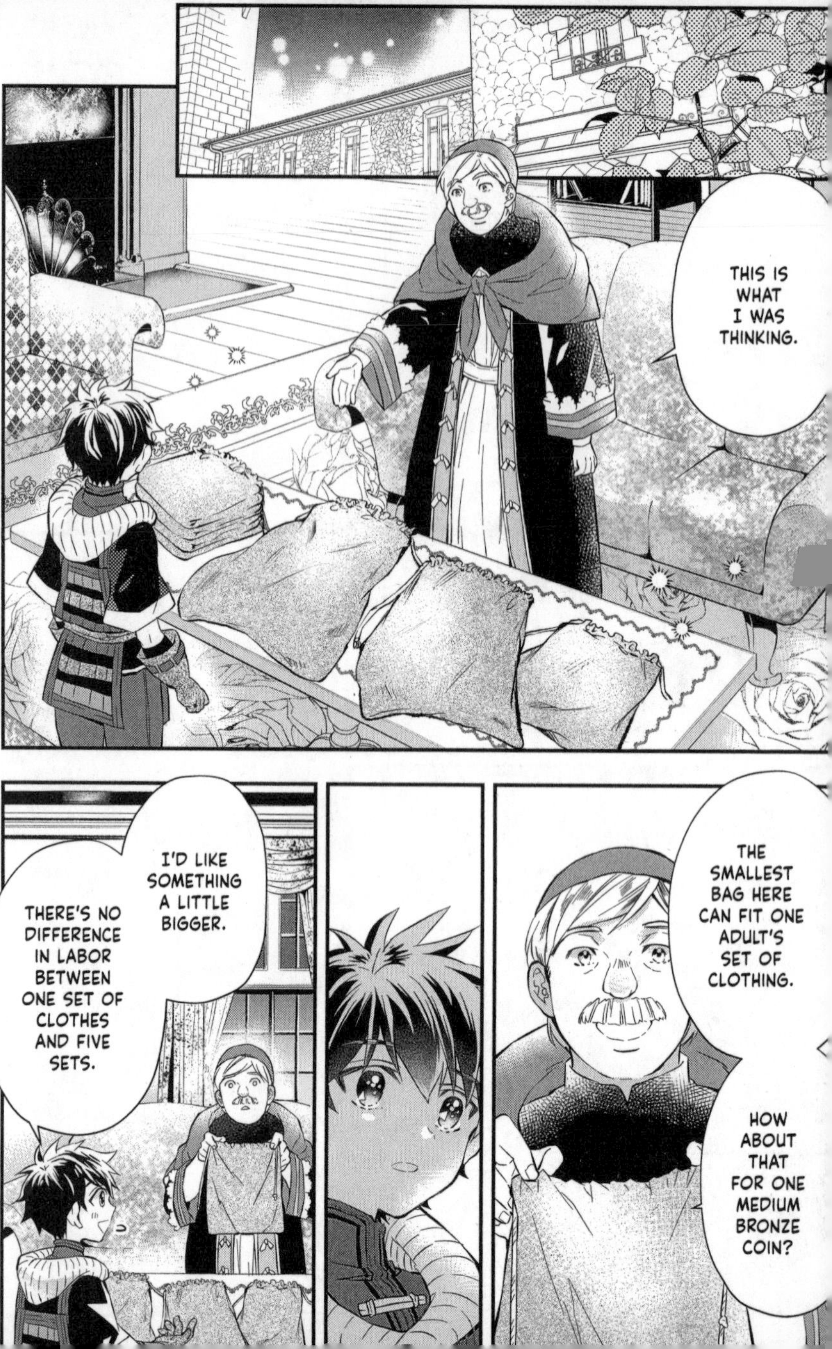
THIS IS WHAT I WAS THINKING.
THE SMALLEST BAG HERE CAN FIT ONE ADULT'S SET OF CLOTHING.
HOW ABOUT THAT FOR ONE MEDIUM BRONZE COIN?
I'D LIKE SOMETHING A LITTLE BIGGER.
THERE'S NO DIFFERENCE IN LABOR BETWEEN ONE SET OF CLOTHES AND FIVE SETS.

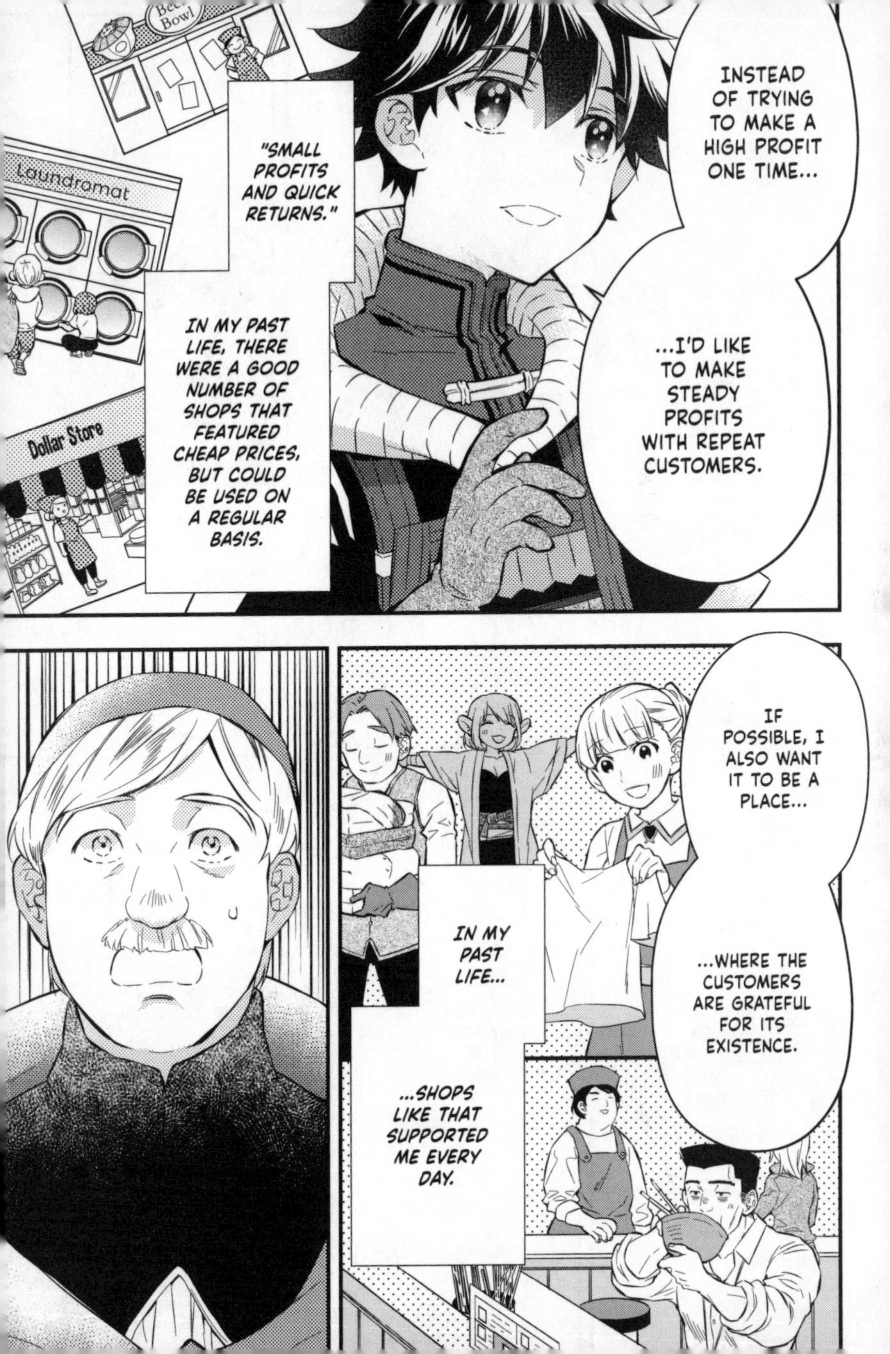
INSTEAD OF TRYING TO MAKE A HIGH PROFIT ONE TIME...
...I'D LIKE TO MAKE STEADY PROFITS WITH REPEAT CUSTOMERS.
"SMALL PROFITS AND QUICK RETURNS."
IN MY PAST LIFE, THERE WERE A GOOD NUMBER OF SHOPS THAT FEATURED CHEAP PRICES, BUT COULD BE USED ON A REGULAR BASIS.
Laundromat
Dollar Store
IF POSSIBLE, I ALSO WANT IT TO BE A PLACE...
...WHERE THE CUSTOMERS ARE GRATEFUL FOR ITS EXISTENCE.
IN MY PAST LIFE...
...SHOPS LIKE THAT SUPPORTED ME EVERY DAY.

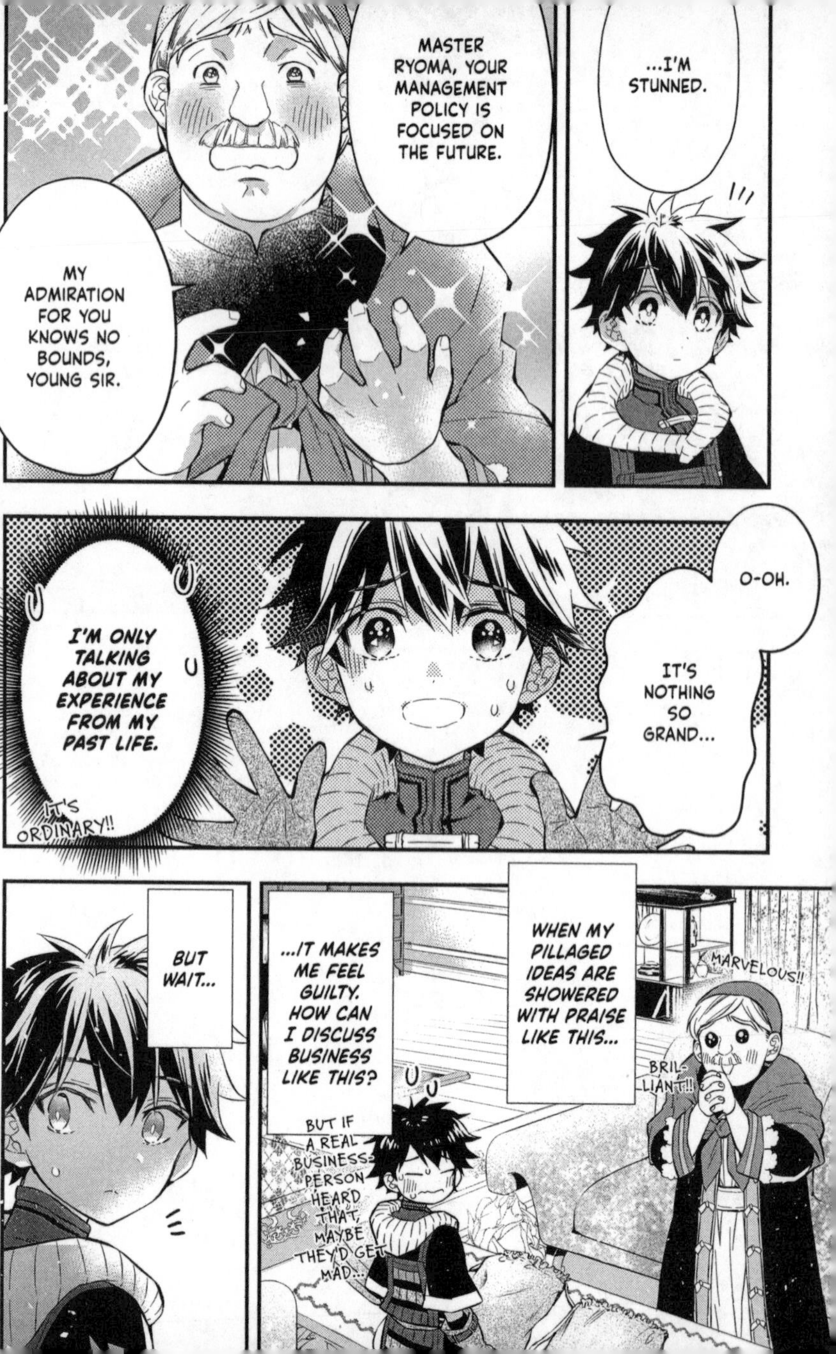

...I'M STUNNED.
MASTER RYOMA, YOUR MANAGEMENT POLICY IS FOCUSED ON THE FUTURE.
MY ADMIRATION FOR YOU KNOWS NO BOUNDS, YOUNG SIR.
O-OH.
IT'S NOTHING SO GRAND...
I'M ONLY TALKING ABOUT MY EXPERIENCE FROM MY PAST LIFE.
IT'S ORDINARY!!
MARVELOUS!!
WHEN MY PILLAGED IDEAS ARE SHOWERED WITH PRAISE LIKE THIS...
BRILLIANT!!
...IT MAKES ME FEEL GUILTY. HOW CAN I DISCUSS BUSINESS LIKE THIS?
BUT IF A REAL BUSINESS-PERSON HEARD THAT, MAYBE THEY'D GET MAD...
BUT WAIT...

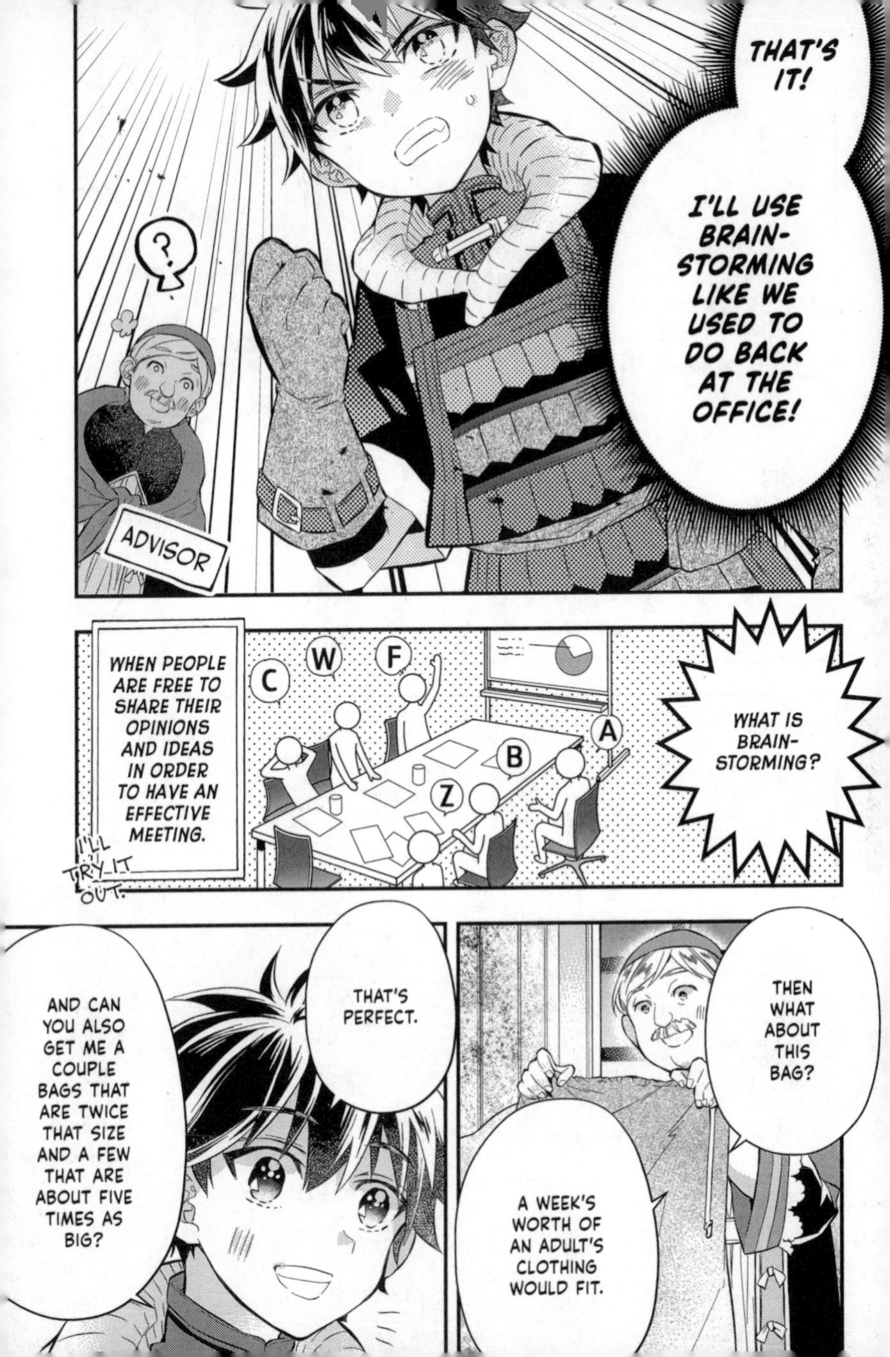
THAT'S IT!
I'LL USE BRAIN-STORMING LIKE WE USED TO DO BACK AT THE OFFICE!
?
ADVISOR
WHAT IS BRAIN-STORMING?
A
B
F
W
C
Z
WHEN PEOPLE ARE FREE TO SHARE THEIR OPINIONS AND IDEAS IN ORDER TO HAVE AN EFFECTIVE MEETING.
I'LL TRY IT OUT.
THEN WHAT ABOUT THIS BAG?
A WEEK'S WORTH OF AN ADULT'S CLOTHING WOULD FIT.
THAT'S PERFECT.
AND CAN YOU ALSO GET ME A COUPLE BAGS THAT ARE TWICE THAT SIZE AND A FEW THAT ARE ABOUT FIVE TIMES AS BIG?

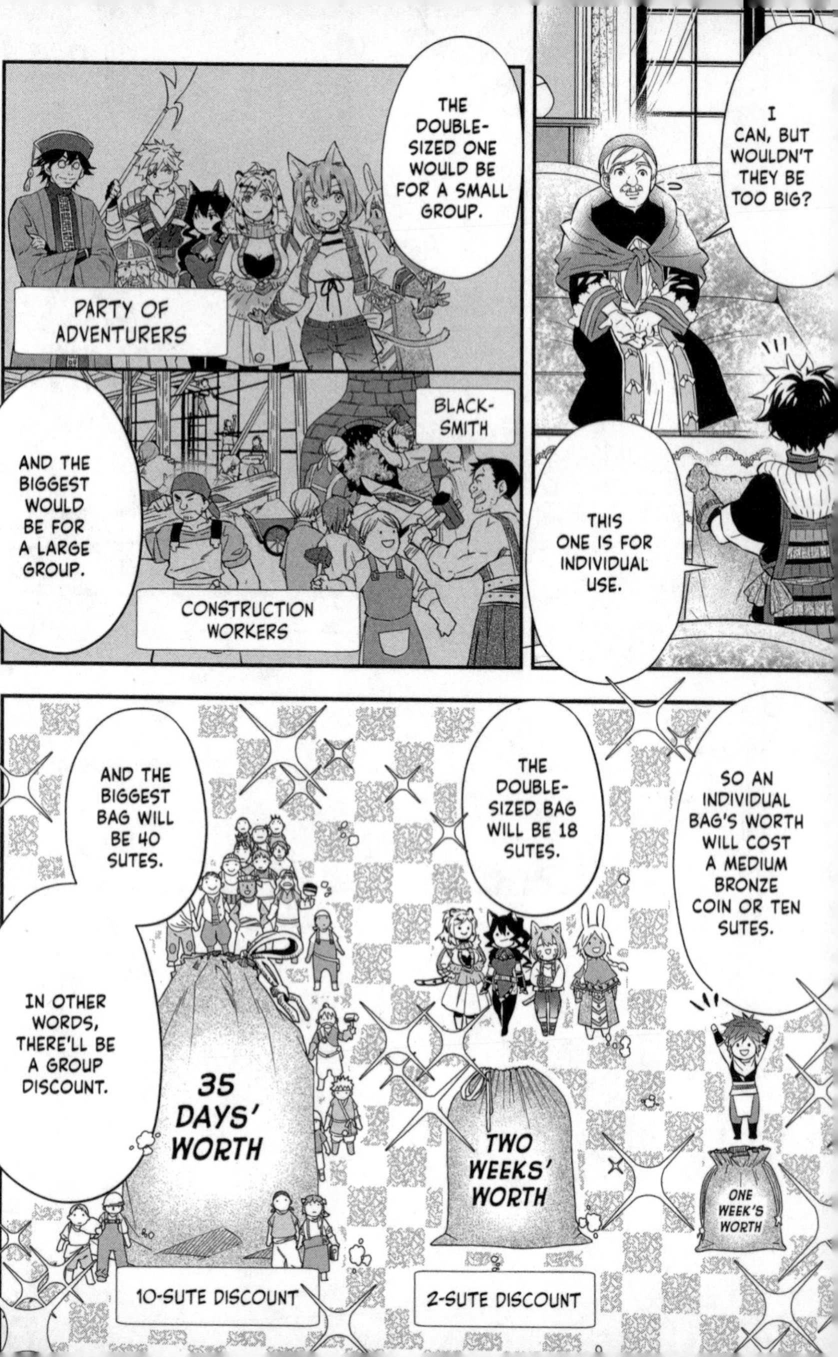
I CAN, BUT WOULDN'T THEY BE TOO BIG?
THIS ONE IS FOR INDIVIDUAL USE.
THE DOUBLE-SIZED ONE WOULD BE FOR A SMALL GROUP.
PARTY OF ADVENTURERS
BLACK-SMITH
AND THE BIGGEST WOULD BE FOR A LARGE GROUP.
CONSTRUCTION WORKERS
SO AN INDIVIDUAL BAG'S WORTH WILL COST A MEDIUM BRONZE COIN OR TEN SUTES.
ONE WEEK'S WORTH
THE DOUBLE-SIZED BAG WILL BE 18 SUTES.
TWO WEEKS' WORTH
2-SUTE DISCOUNT
AND THE BIGGEST BAG WILL BE 40 SUTES.
IN OTHER WORDS, THERE'LL BE A GROUP DISCOUNT.
35 DAYS' WORTH
10-SUTE DISCOUNT

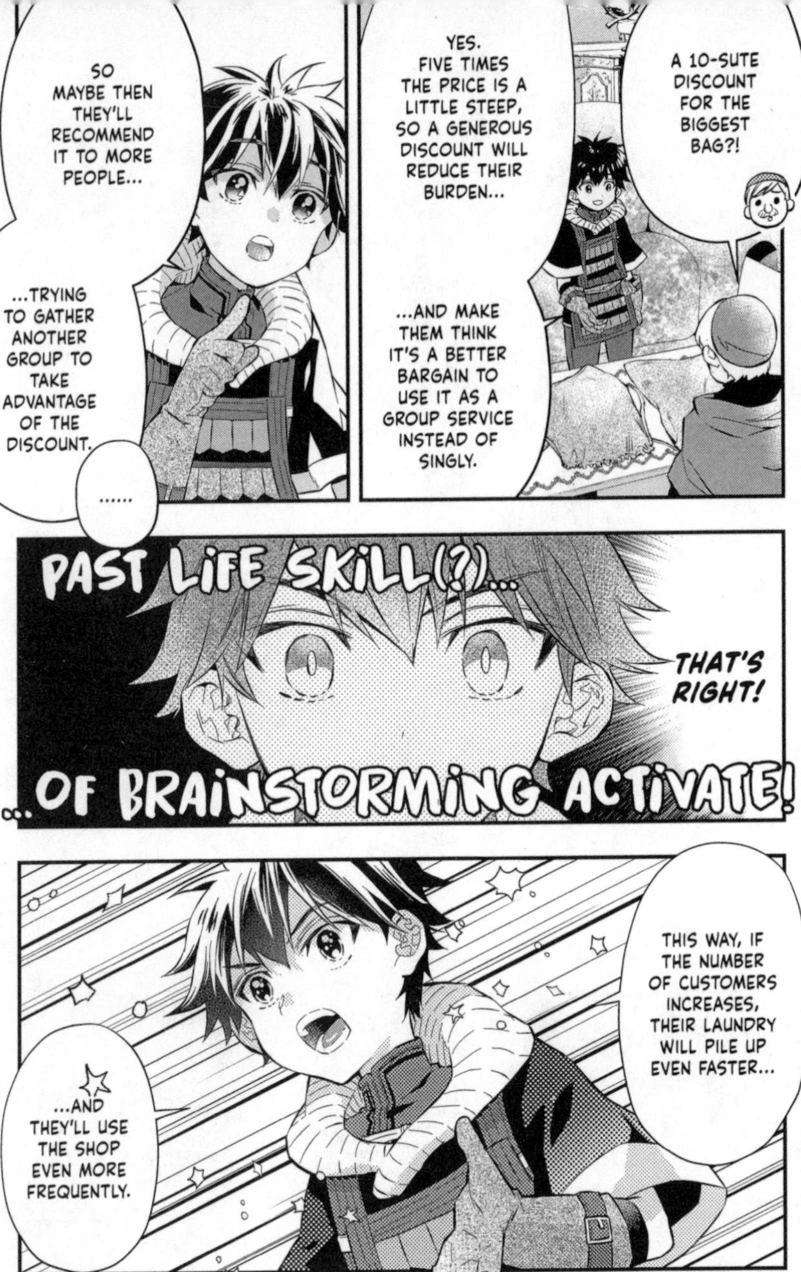
A 10-SUTE DISCOUNT FOR THE BIGGEST BAG?!
YES. FIVE TIMES THE PRICE IS A LITTLE STEEP, SO A GENEROUS DISCOUNT WILL REDUCE THEIR BURDEN...
...AND MAKE THEM THINK IT'S A BETTER BARGAIN TO USE IT AS A GROUP SERVICE INSTEAD OF SINGLY.
SO MAYBE THEN THEY'LL RECOMMEND IT TO MORE PEOPLE...
...TRYING TO GATHER ANOTHER GROUP TO TAKE ADVANTAGE OF THE DISCOUNT.
......
PAST LIFE SKILL(?)...
THAT'S RIGHT!
...OF BRAINSTORMING ACTIVATE!
THIS WAY, IF THE NUMBER OF CUSTOMERS INCREASES, THEIR LAUNDRY WILL PILE UP EVEN FASTER...
...AND THEY'LL USE THE SHOP EVEN MORE FREQUENTLY.

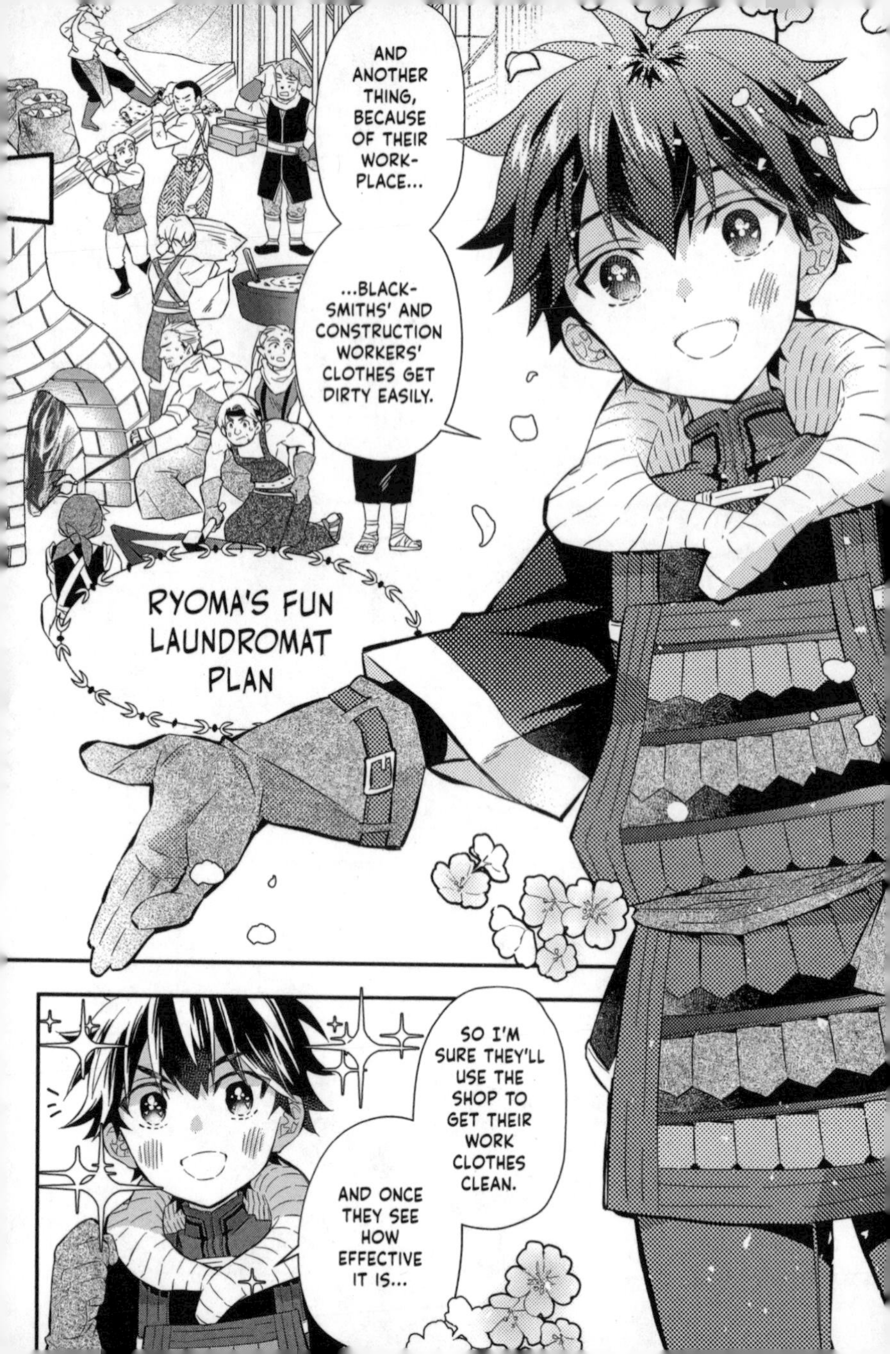
AND ANOTHER THING, BECAUSE OF THEIR WORK-PLACE...
...BLACK-SMITHS' AND CONSTRUCTION WORKERS' CLOTHES GET DIRTY EASILY.
RYOMA'S FUN LAUNDROMAT PLAN
SO I'M SURE THEY'LL USE THE SHOP TO GET THEIR WORK CLOTHES CLEAN.
AND ONCE THEY SEE HOW EFFECTIVE IT IS...

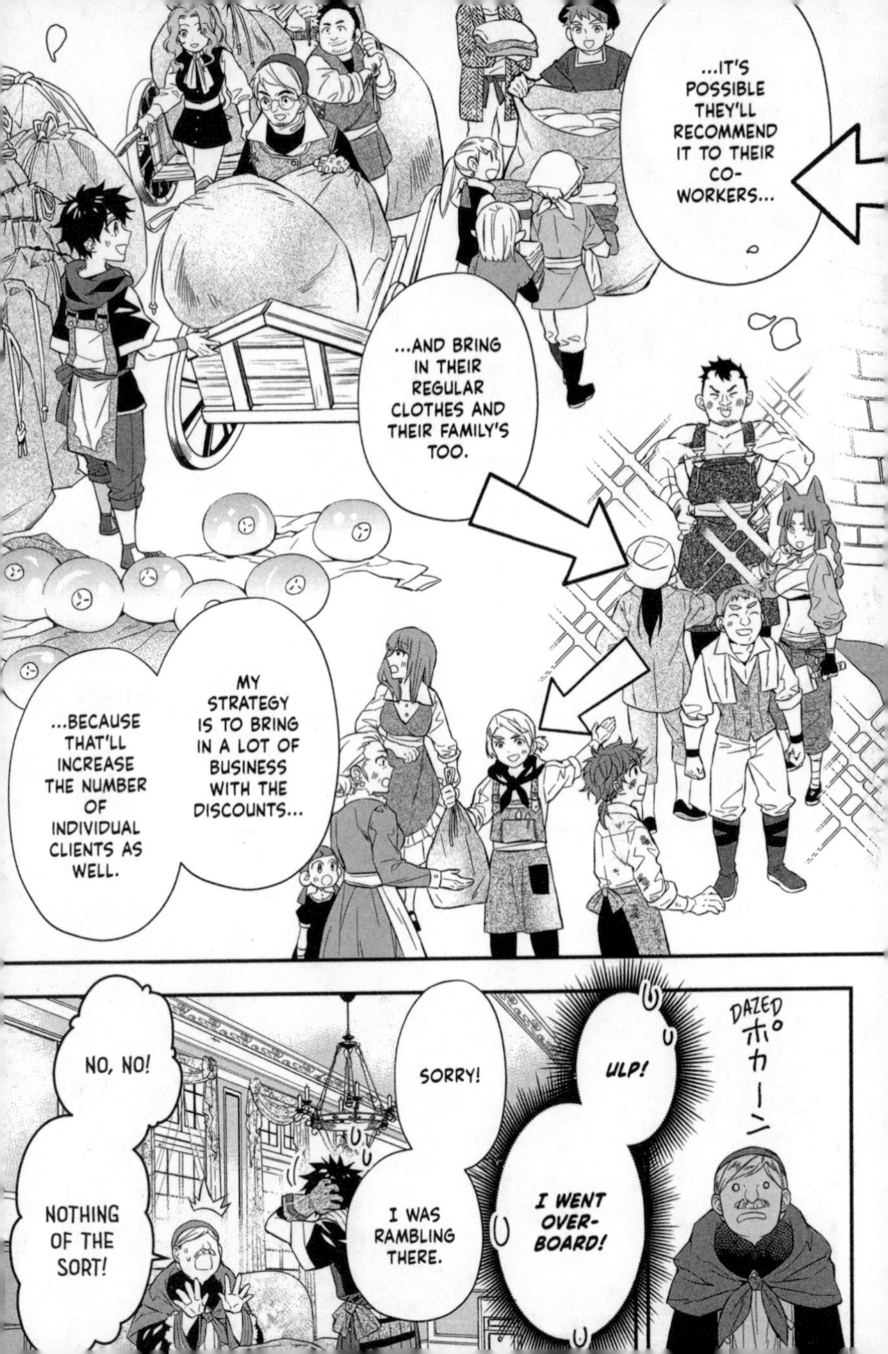
...IT'S POSSIBLE THEY'LL RECOMMEND IT TO THEIR CO-WORKERS...
...AND BRING IN THEIR REGULAR CLOTHES AND THEIR FAMILY'S TOO.
MY STRATEGY IS TO BRING IN A LOT OF BUSINESS WITH THE DISCOUNTS...
...BECAUSE THAT'LL INCREASE THE NUMBER OF INDIVIDUAL CLIENTS AS WELL.
DAZED
ポカーン
ULP!
I WENT OVER-BOARD!
SORRY!
I WAS RAMBLING THERE.
NO, NO!
NOTHING OF THE SORT!

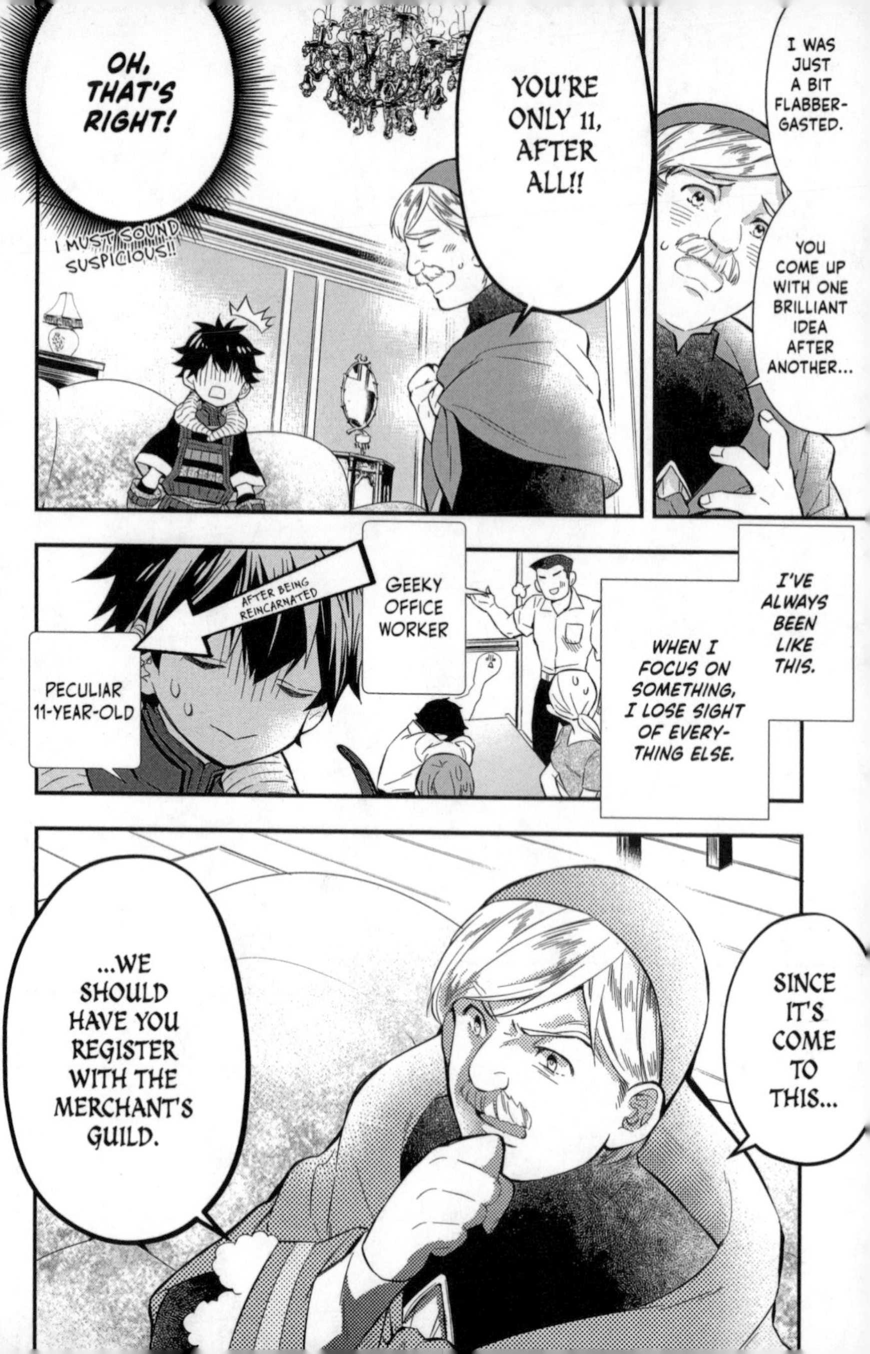
I WAS JUST A BIT FLABBER-GASTED.
YOU COME UP WITH ONE BRILLIANT IDEA AFTER ANOTHER...
YOU'RE ONLY 11, AFTER ALL!!
OH, THAT'S RIGHT!
I MUST SOUND SUSPICIOUS!!
I'VE ALWAYS BEEN LIKE THIS.
WHEN I FOCUS ON SOMETHING, I LOSE SIGHT OF EVERY-THING ELSE.
GEEKY OFFICE WORKER
AFTER BEING REINCARNATED
PECULIAR 11-YEAR-OLD
SINCE IT'S COME TO THIS...
...WE SHOULD HAVE YOU REGISTER WITH THE MERCHANT'S GUILD.

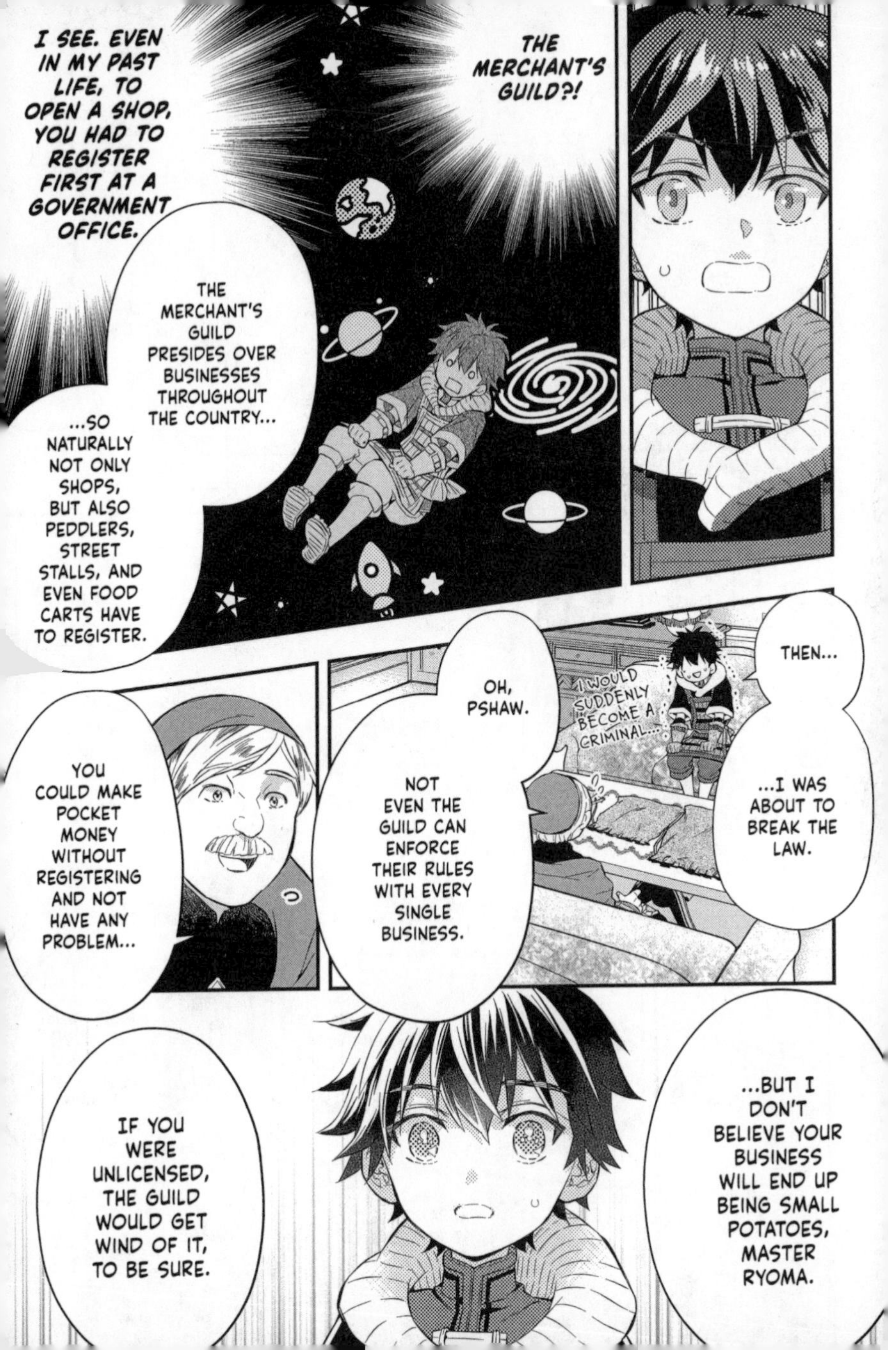
THE MERCHANT'S GUILD?!
I SEE. EVEN IN MY PAST LIFE, TO OPEN A SHOP, YOU HAD TO REGISTER FIRST AT A GOVERNMENT OFFICE.
THE MERCHANT'S GUILD PRESIDES OVER BUSINESSES THROUGHOUT THE COUNTRY...
...SO NATURALLY NOT ONLY SHOPS, BUT ALSO PEDDLERS, STREET STALLS, AND EVEN FOOD CARTS HAVE TO REGISTER.
THEN...
I WOULD SUDDENLY BECOME A CRIMINAL...
...I WAS ABOUT TO BREAK THE LAW.
OH, PSHAW.
NOT EVEN THE GUILD CAN ENFORCE THEIR RULES WITH EVERY SINGLE BUSINESS.
YOU COULD MAKE POCKET MONEY WITHOUT REGISTERING AND NOT HAVE ANY PROBLEM...
...BUT I DON'T BELIEVE YOUR BUSINESS WILL END UP BEING SMALL POTATOES, MASTER RYOMA.
IF YOU WERE UNLICENSED, THE GUILD WOULD GET WIND OF IT, TO BE SURE.

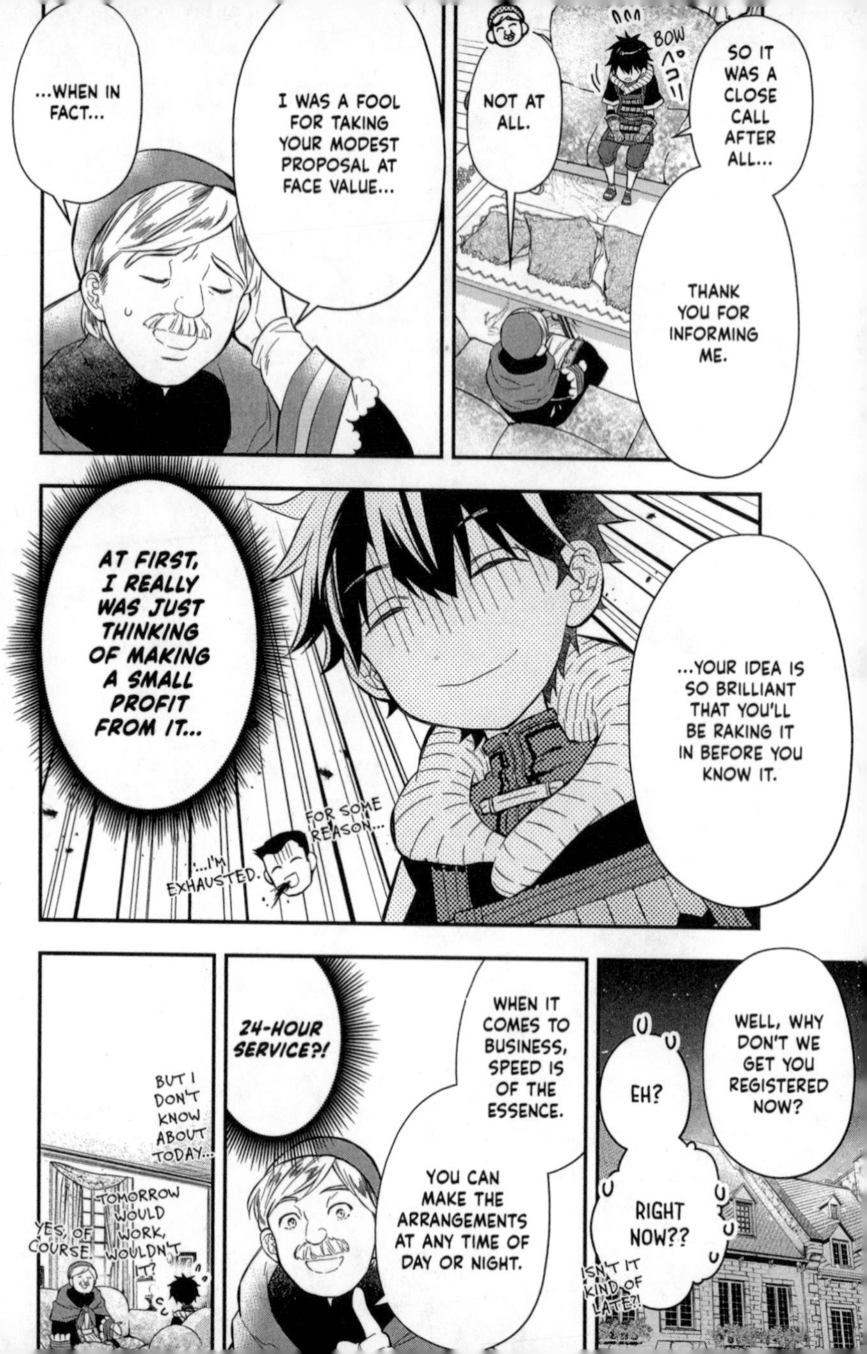
SO IT WAS A CLOSE CALL AFTER ALL...
BOW
THANK YOU FOR INFORMING ME.
NOT AT ALL.
I WAS A FOOL FOR TAKING YOUR MODEST PROPOSAL AT FACE VALUE...
...WHEN IN FACT...
...YOUR IDEA IS SO BRILLIANT THAT YOU'LL BE RAKING IT IN BEFORE YOU KNOW IT.
AT FIRST, I REALLY WAS JUST THINKING OF MAKING A SMALL PROFIT FROM IT...
FOR SOME REASON...
...I'M EXHAUSTED.
WELL, WHY DON'T WE GET YOU REGISTERED NOW?
EH?
RIGHT NOW??
ISN'T IT KIND OF LATE?!
WHEN IT COMES TO BUSINESS, SPEED IS OF THE ESSENCE.
YOU CAN MAKE THE ARRANGEMENTS AT ANY TIME OF DAY OR NIGHT.
24-HOUR SERVICE?!
BUT I DON'T KNOW ABOUT TODAY...
TOMORROW WOULD WORK, WOULDN'T IT?
YES, OF COURSE.

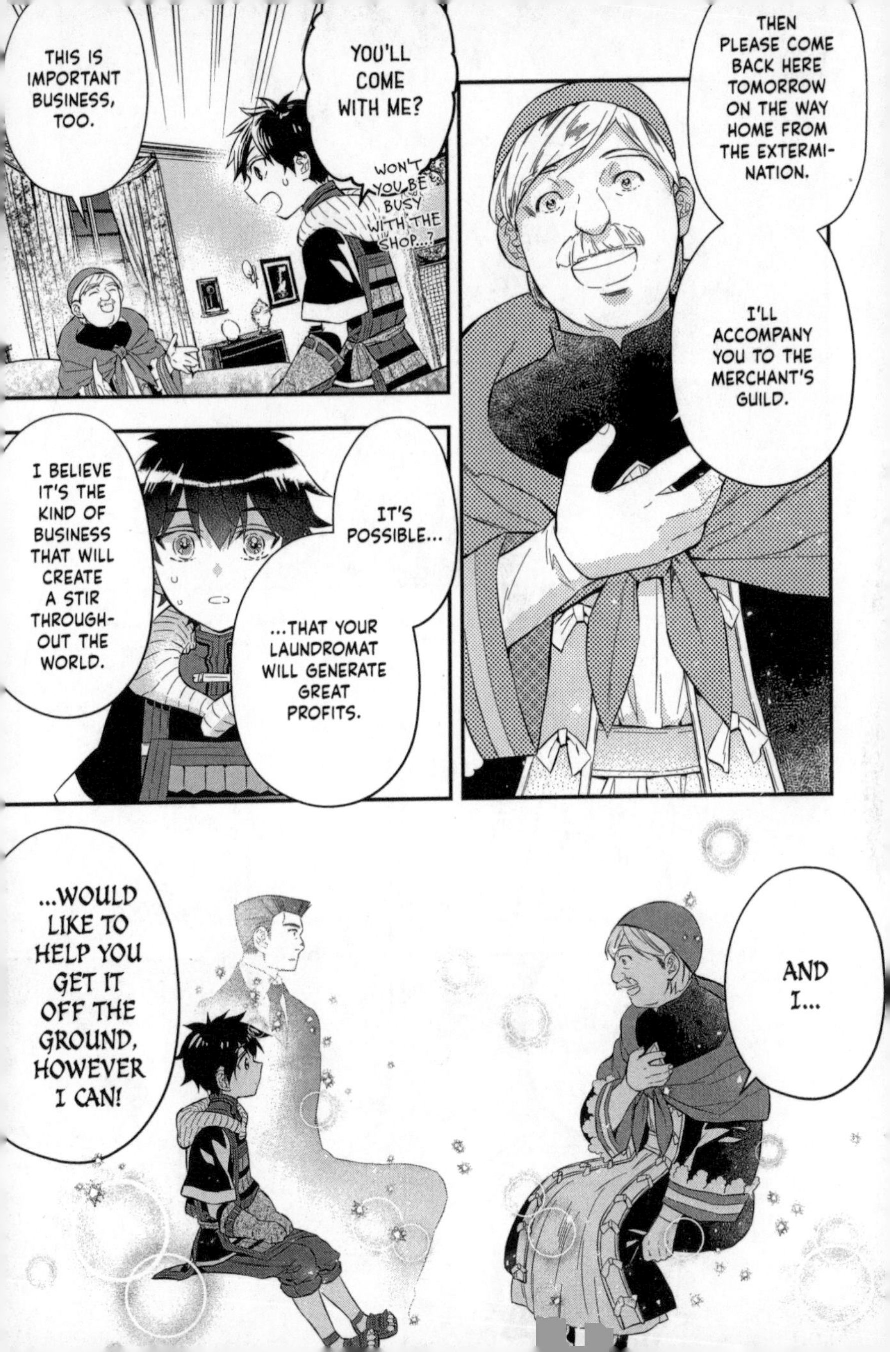

THEN PLEASE COME BACK HERE TOMORROW ON THE WAY HOME FROM THE EXTERMINATION.
I'LL ACCOMPANY YOU TO THE MERCHANT'S GUILD.
YOU'LL COME WITH ME?
WON'T YOU BE BUSY WITH THE SHOP...?
THIS IS IMPORTANT BUSINESS, TOO.
IT'S POSSIBLE...
...THAT YOUR LAUNDROMAT WILL GENERATE GREAT PROFITS.
I BELIEVE IT'S THE KIND OF BUSINESS THAT WILL CREATE A STIR THROUGHOUT THE WORLD.
AND I...
...WOULD LIKE TO HELP YOU GET IT OFF THE GROUND, HOWEVER I CAN!

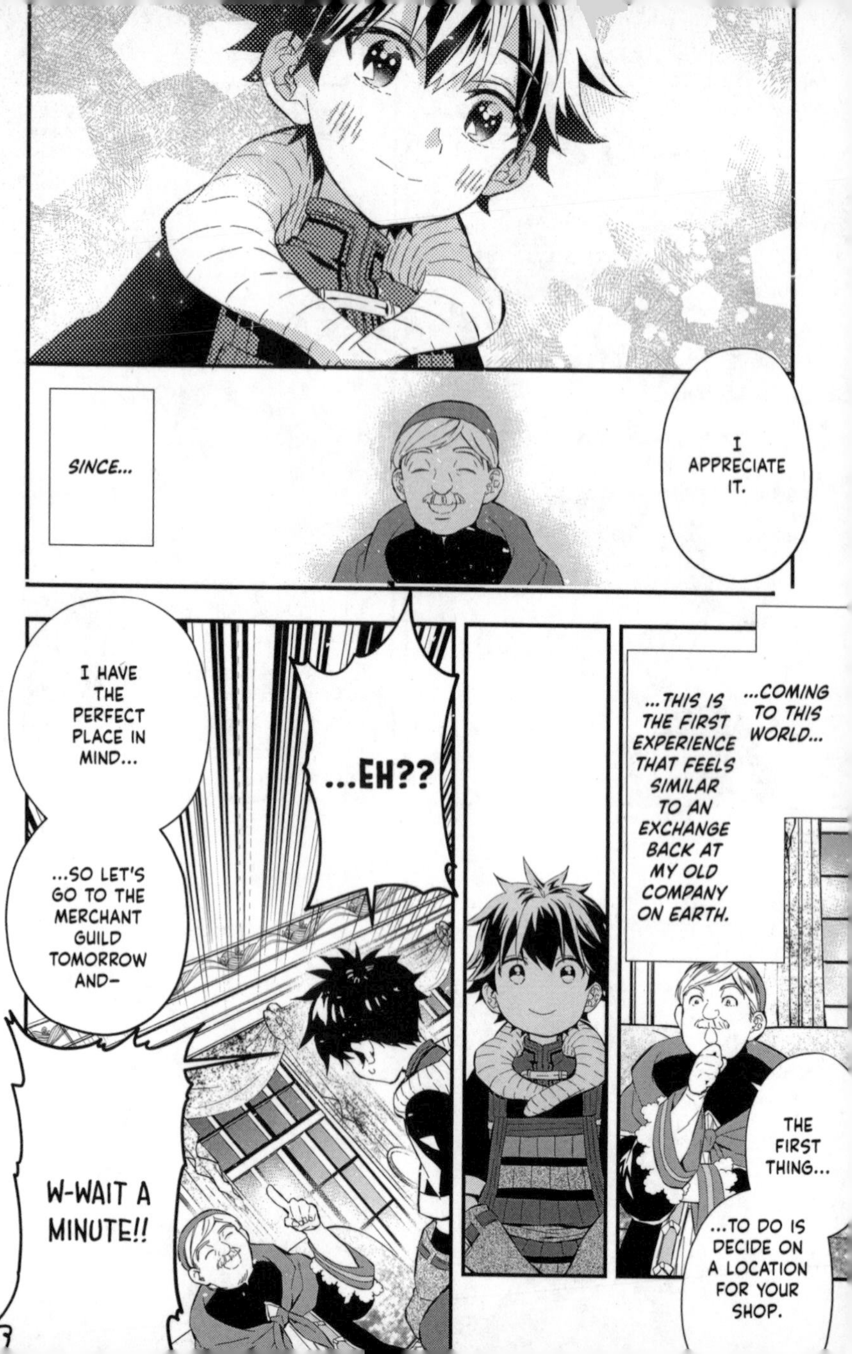
I APPRECIATE IT.
SINCE...
...COMING TO THIS WORLD...
...THIS IS THE FIRST EXPERIENCE THAT FEELS SIMILAR TO AN EXCHANGE BACK AT MY OLD COMPANY ON EARTH.
THE FIRST THING...
...TO DO IS DECIDE ON A LOCATION FOR YOUR SHOP.
...EH??
I HAVE THE PERFECT PLACE IN MIND...
...SO LET'S GO TO THE MERCHANT GUILD TOMORROW AND–
W-WAIT A MINUTE!!

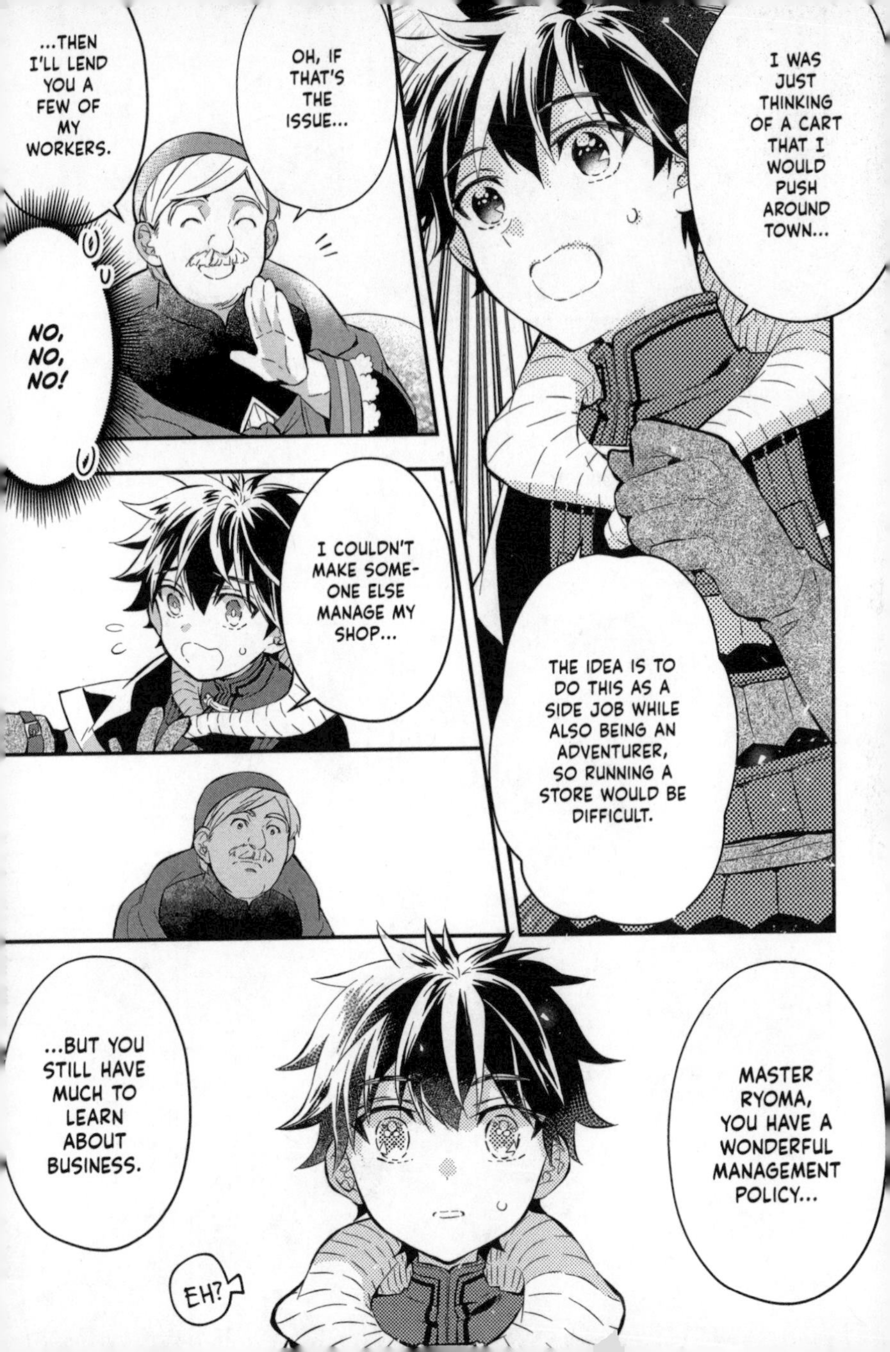
I WAS JUST THINKING OF A CART THAT I WOULD PUSH AROUND TOWN...
THE IDEA IS TO DO THIS AS A SIDE JOB WHILE ALSO BEING AN ADVENTURER, SO RUNNING A STORE WOULD BE DIFFICULT.
OH, IF THAT'S THE ISSUE...
...THEN I'LL LEND YOU A FEW OF MY WORKERS.
NO, NO, NO!
I COULDN'T MAKE SOME-ONE ELSE MANAGE MY SHOP...
MASTER RYOMA, YOU HAVE A WONDERFUL MANAGEMENT POLICY...
...BUT YOU STILL HAVE MUCH TO LEARN ABOUT BUSINESS.
EH?

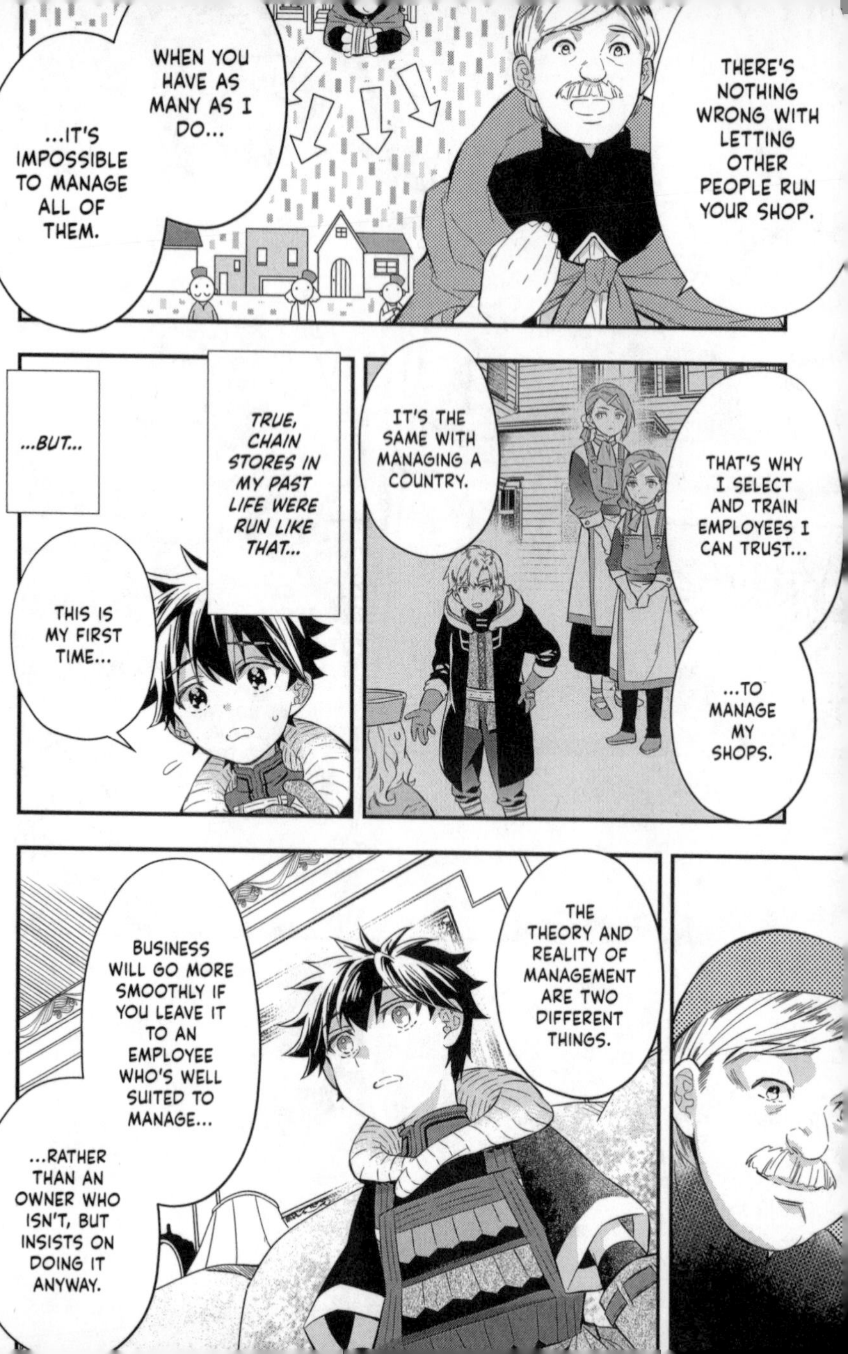

THERE'S NOTHING WRONG WITH LETTING OTHER PEOPLE RUN YOUR SHOP.
WHEN YOU HAVE AS MANY AS I DO...
...IT'S IMPOSSIBLE TO MANAGE ALL OF THEM.
THAT'S WHY I SELECT AND TRAIN EMPLOYEES I CAN TRUST...
...TO MANAGE MY SHOPS.
IT'S THE SAME WITH MANAGING A COUNTRY.
TRUE, CHAIN STORES IN MY PAST LIFE WERE RUN LIKE THAT...
...BUT...
THIS IS MY FIRST TIME...
THE THEORY AND REALITY OF MANAGEMENT ARE TWO DIFFERENT THINGS.
BUSINESS WILL GO MORE SMOOTHLY IF YOU LEAVE IT TO AN EMPLOYEE WHO'S WELL SUITED TO MANAGE...
...RATHER THAN AN OWNER WHO ISN'T, BUT INSISTS ON DOING IT ANYWAY.

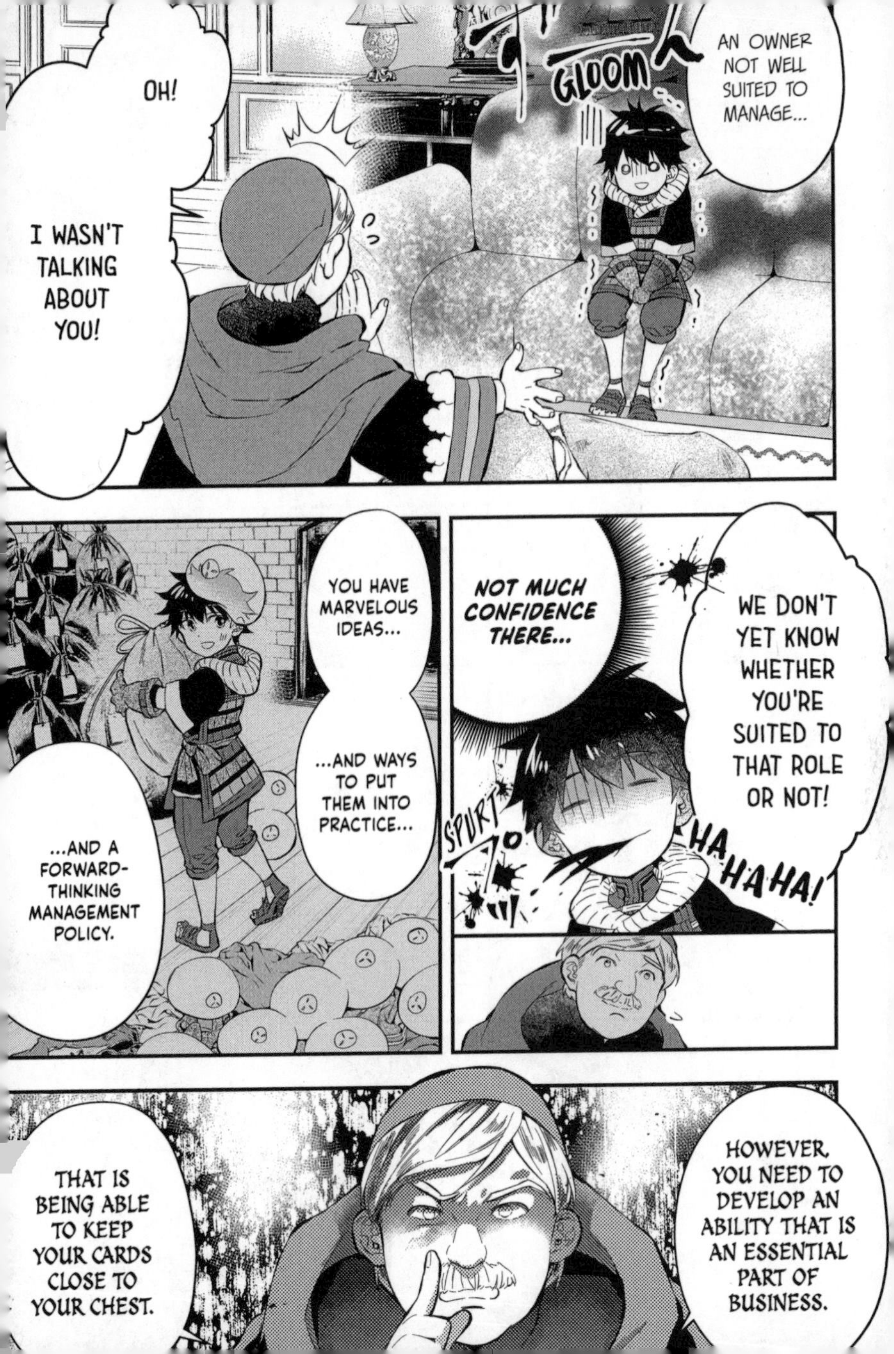
AN OWNER NOT WELL SUITED TO MANAGE...
GLOOM
OH!
I WASN'T TALKING ABOUT YOU!
WE DON'T YET KNOW WHETHER YOU'RE SUITED TO THAT ROLE OR NOT!
HA HA HA!
NOT MUCH CONFIDENCE THERE...
SPURT
YOU HAVE MARVELOUS IDEAS...
...AND WAYS TO PUT THEM INTO PRACTICE...
...AND A FORWARD-THINKING MANAGEMENT POLICY.
HOWEVER, YOU NEED TO DEVELOP AN ABILITY THAT IS AN ESSENTIAL PART OF BUSINESS.
THAT IS BEING ABLE TO KEEP YOUR CARDS CLOSE TO YOUR CHEST.

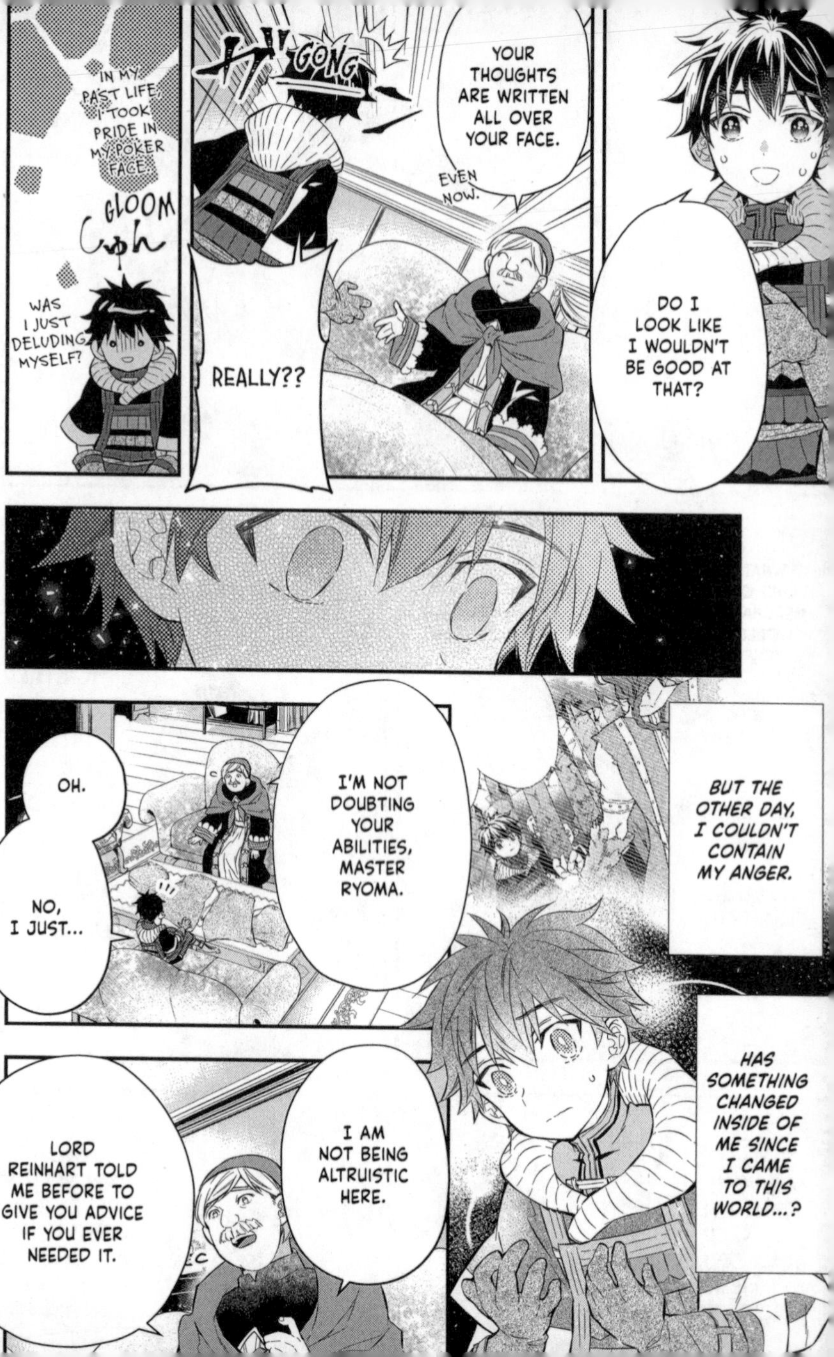
DO I LOOK LIKE I WOULDN'T BE GOOD AT THAT?
YOUR THOUGHTS ARE WRITTEN ALL OVER YOUR FACE.
EVEN NOW.
GONG
REALLY??
IN MY PAST LIFE, I TOOK PRIDE IN MY POKER FACE.
GLOOM
WAS I JUST DELUDING MYSELF?
BUT THE OTHER DAY, I COULDN'T CONTAIN MY ANGER.
HAS SOMETHING CHANGED INSIDE OF ME SINCE I CAME TO THIS WORLD...?
I'M NOT DOUBTING YOUR ABILITIES, MASTER RYOMA.
OH.
NO, I JUST...
I AM NOT BEING ALTRUISTIC HERE.
LORD REINHART TOLD ME BEFORE TO GIVE YOU ADVICE IF YOU EVER NEEDED IT.

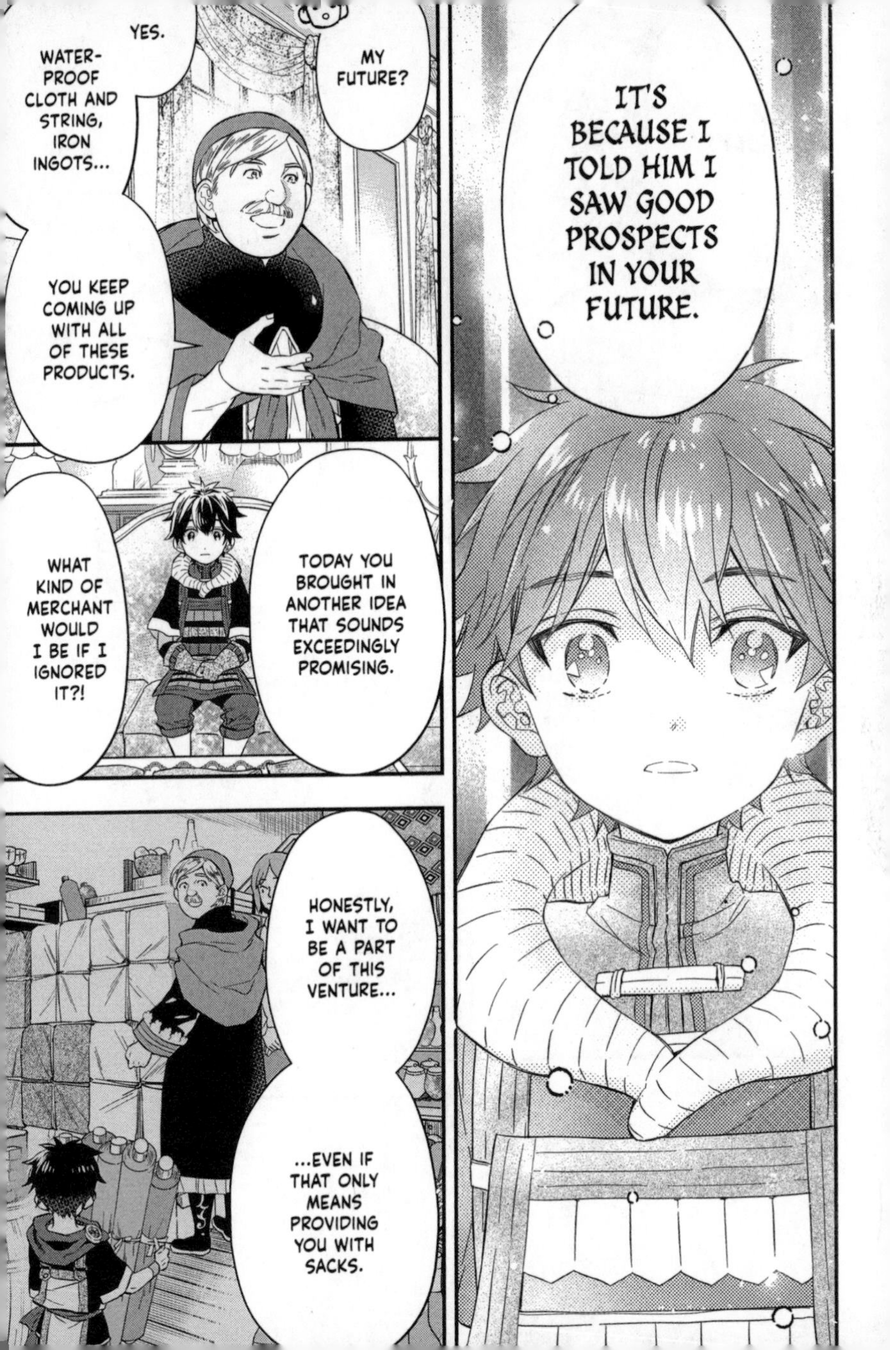
IT'S BECAUSE I TOLD HIM I SAW GOOD PROSPECTS IN YOUR FUTURE.
MY FUTURE?
YES.
WATER-PROOF CLOTH AND STRING, IRON INGOTS...
YOU KEEP COMING UP WITH ALL OF THESE PRODUCTS.
TODAY YOU BROUGHT IN ANOTHER IDEA THAT SOUNDS EXCEEDINGLY PROMISING.
WHAT KIND OF MERCHANT WOULD I BE IF I IGNORED IT?!
HONESTLY, I WANT TO BE A PART OF THIS VENTURE...
...EVEN IF THAT ONLY MEANS PROVIDING YOU WITH SACKS.

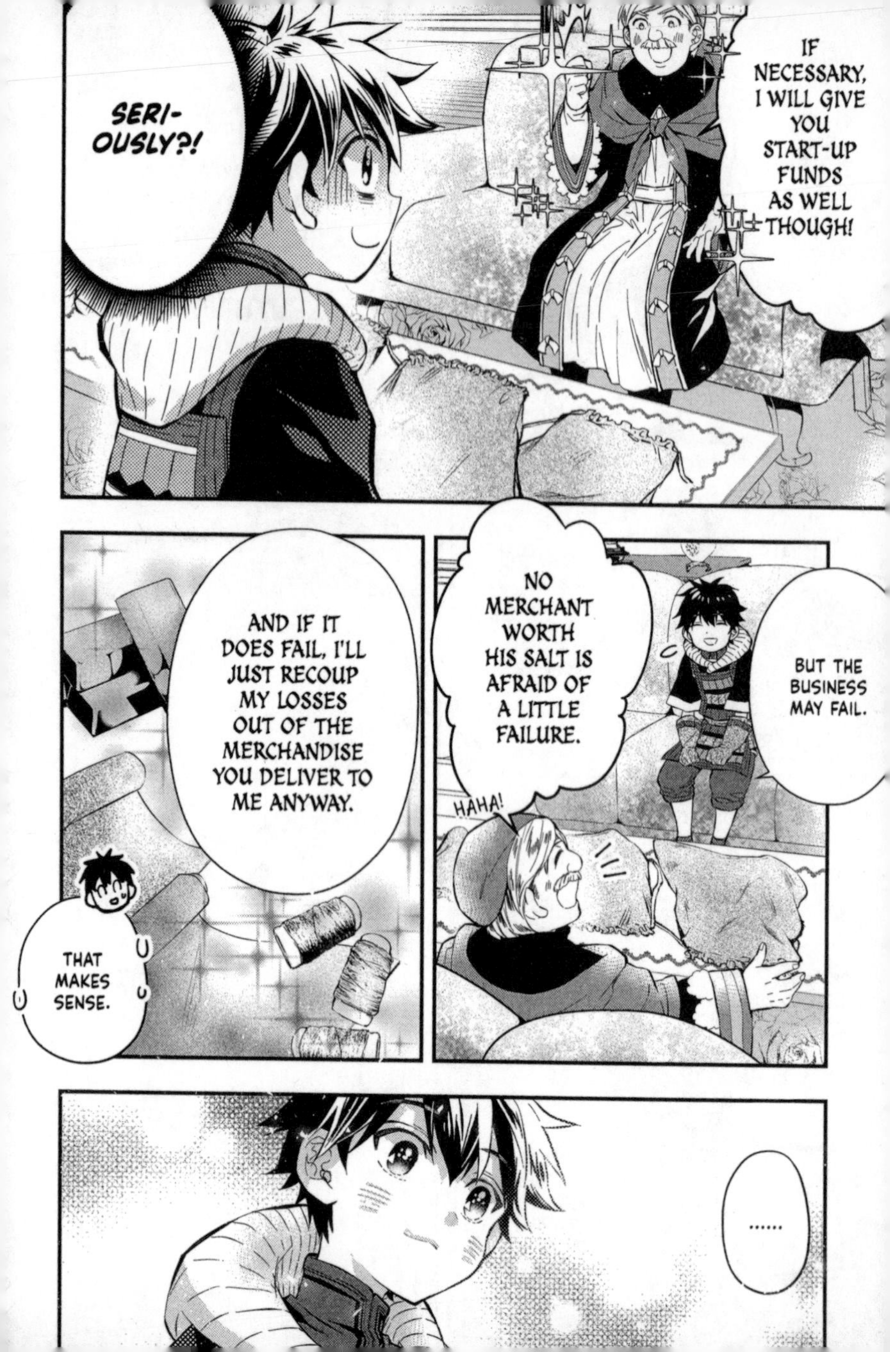
IF NECESSARY, I WILL GIVE YOU START-UP FUNDS AS WELL THOUGH!
SERI-OUSLY?!
BUT THE BUSINESS MAY FAIL.
NO MERCHANT WORTH HIS SALT IS AFRAID OF A LITTLE FAILURE.
HAHA!
AND IF IT DOES FAIL, I'LL JUST RECOUP MY LOSSES OUT OF THE MERCHANDISE YOU DELIVER TO ME ANYWAY.
THAT MAKES SENSE.
......

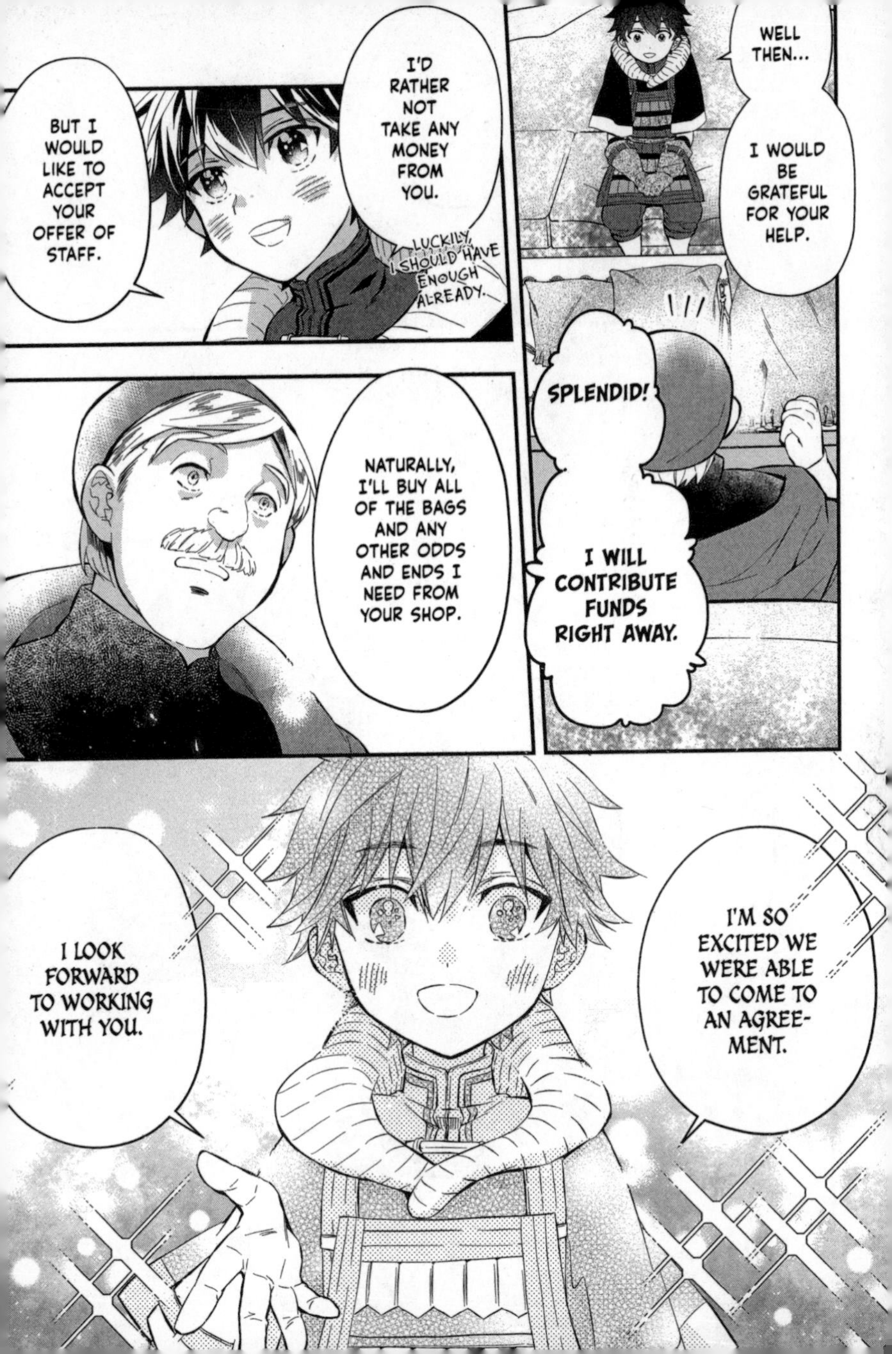
WELL THEN...
I WOULD BE GRATEFUL FOR YOUR HELP.
SPLENDID!
I WILL CONTRIBUTE FUNDS RIGHT AWAY.
I'D RATHER NOT TAKE ANY MONEY FROM YOU.
LUCKILY, I SHOULD HAVE ENOUGH ALREADY.
BUT I WOULD LIKE TO ACCEPT YOUR OFFER OF STAFF.
NATURALLY, I'LL BUY ALL OF THE BAGS AND ANY OTHER ODDS AND ENDS I NEED FROM YOUR SHOP.
I'M SO EXCITED WE WERE ABLE TO COME TO AN AGREE-MENT.
I LOOK FORWARD TO WORKING WITH YOU.

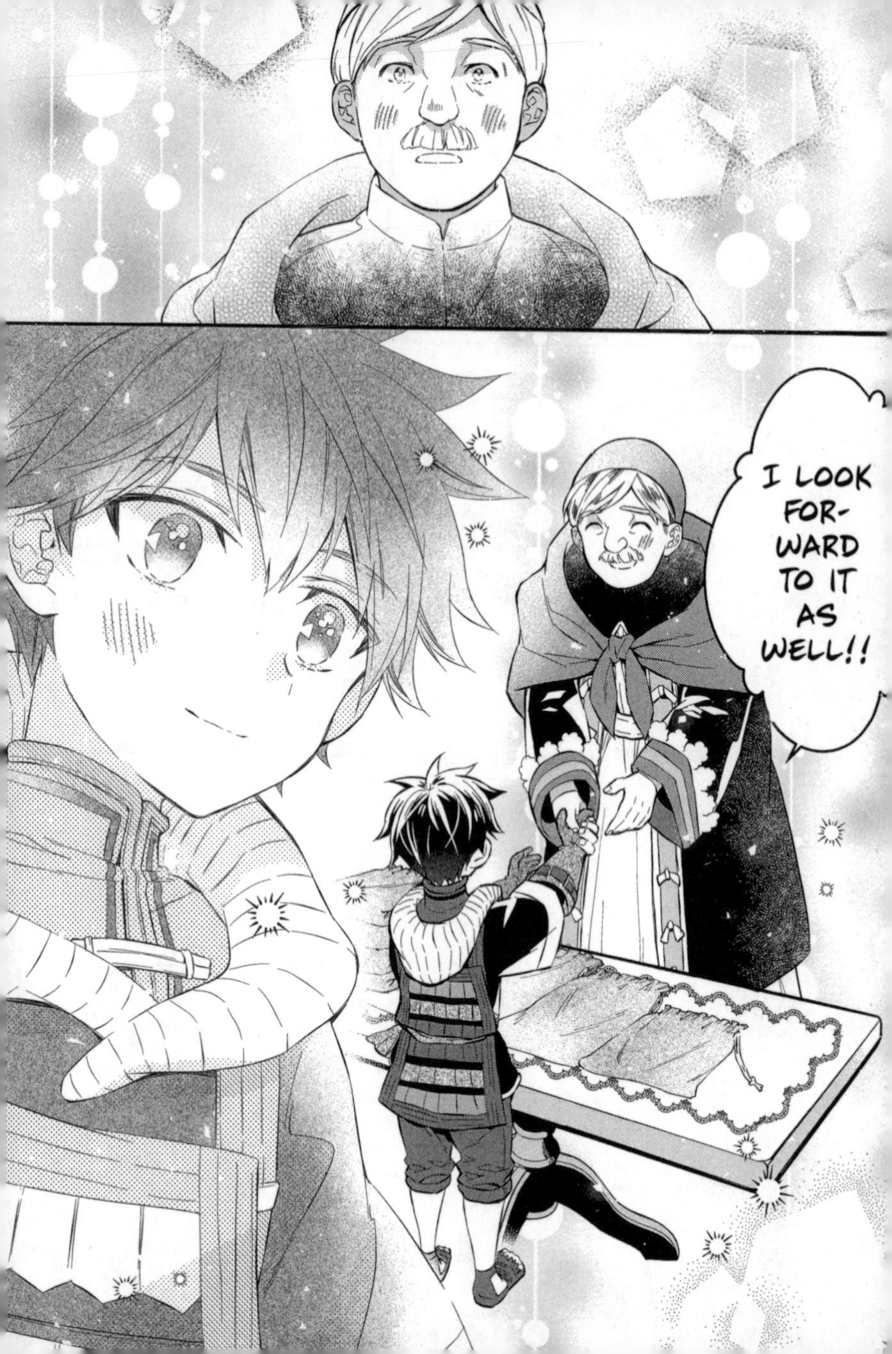
I LOOK FOR-WARD TO IT AS WELL!!

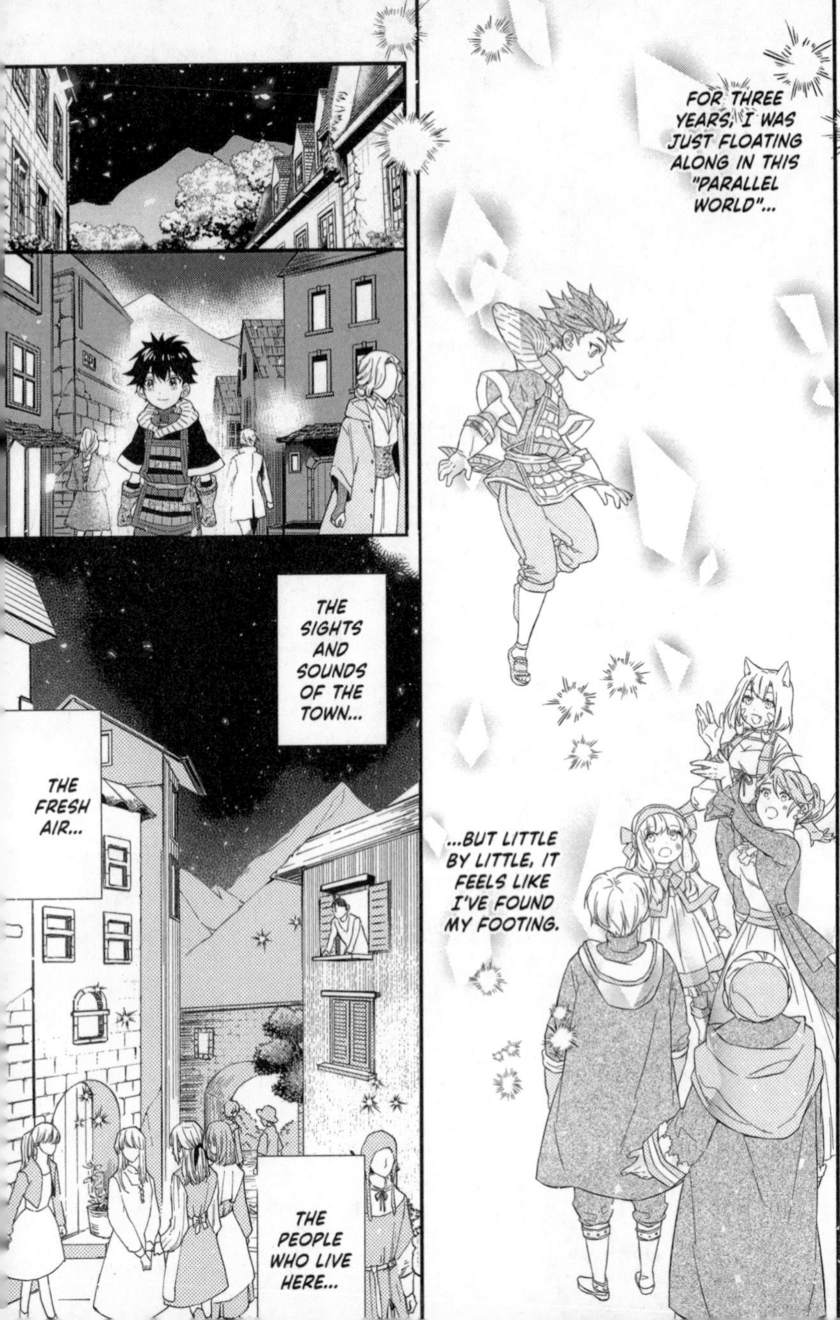
FOR THREE YEARS, I WAS JUST FLOATING ALONG IN THIS "PARALLEL WORLD"...
...BUT LITTLE BY LITTLE, IT FEELS LIKE I'VE FOUND MY FOOTING.
THE SIGHTS AND SOUNDS OF THE TOWN...
THE FRESH AIR...
THE PEOPLE WHO LIVE HERE...

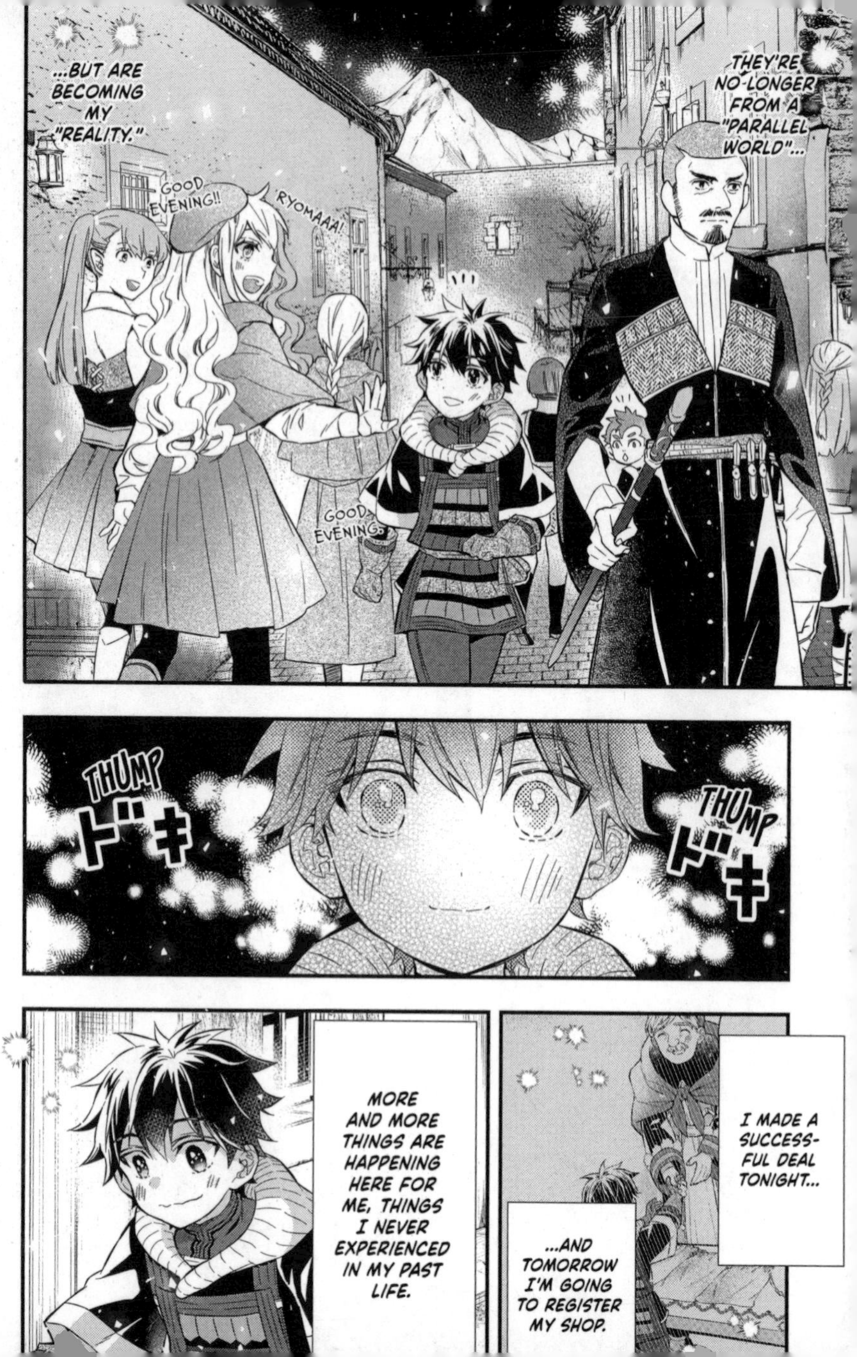
THEY'RE NO-LONGER FROM A "PARALLEL WORLD"...
...BUT ARE BECOMING MY "REALITY."
RYOMAAA!
GOOD EVENING!!
!!
GOOD EVENING
THUMP
ドキ
THUMP
ドキ
I MADE A SUCCESS-FUL DEAL TONIGHT...
...AND TOMORROW I'M GOING TO REGISTER MY SHOP.
MORE AND MORE THINGS ARE HAPPENING HERE FOR ME, THINGS I NEVER EXPERIENCED IN MY PAST LIFE.

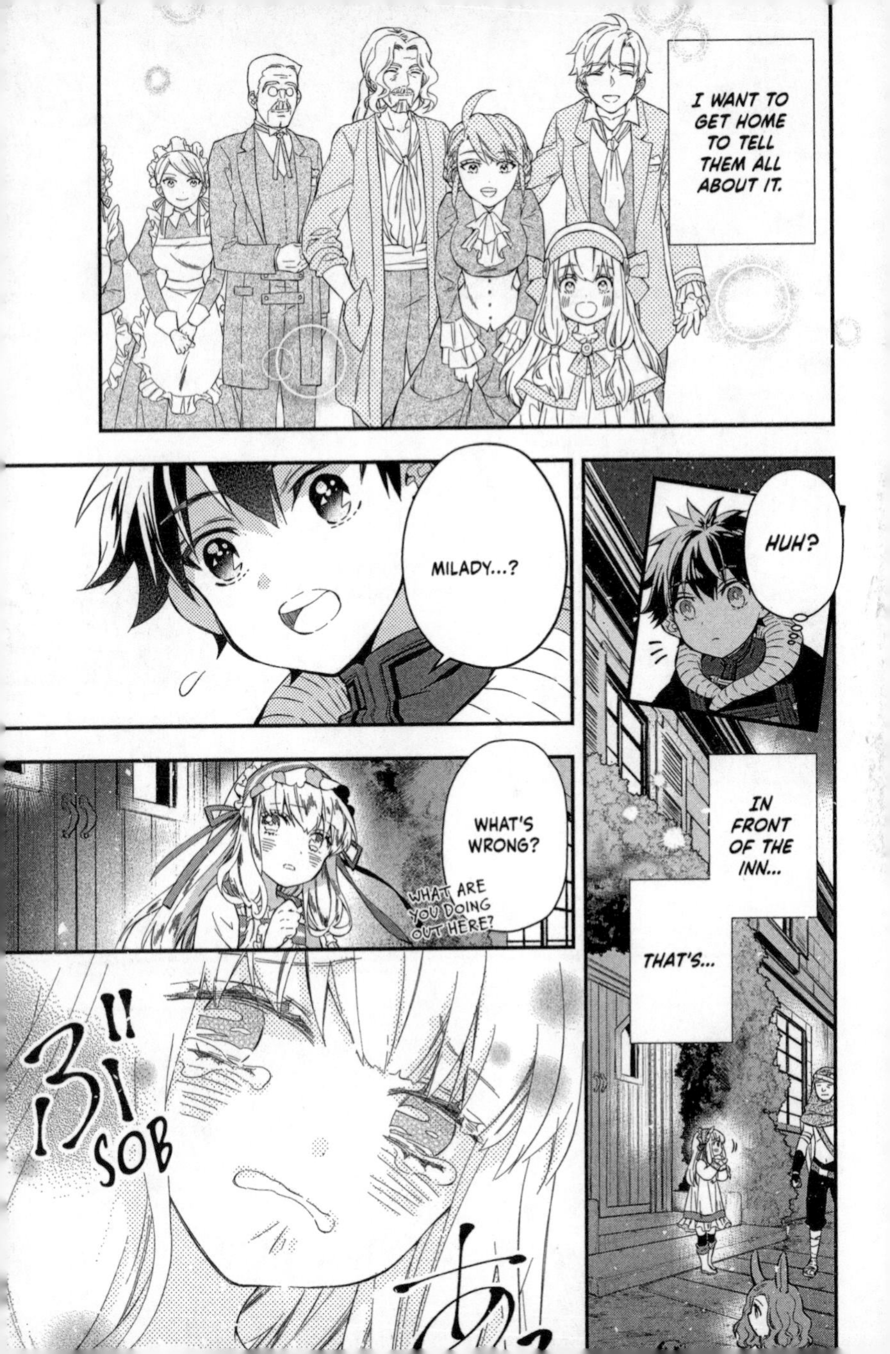
I WANT TO GET HOME TO TELL THEM ALL ABOUT IT.
HUH?
IN FRONT OF THE INN...
THAT'S...
MILADY...?
WHAT'S WRONG?
WHAT ARE YOU DOING OUT HERE?
SOB

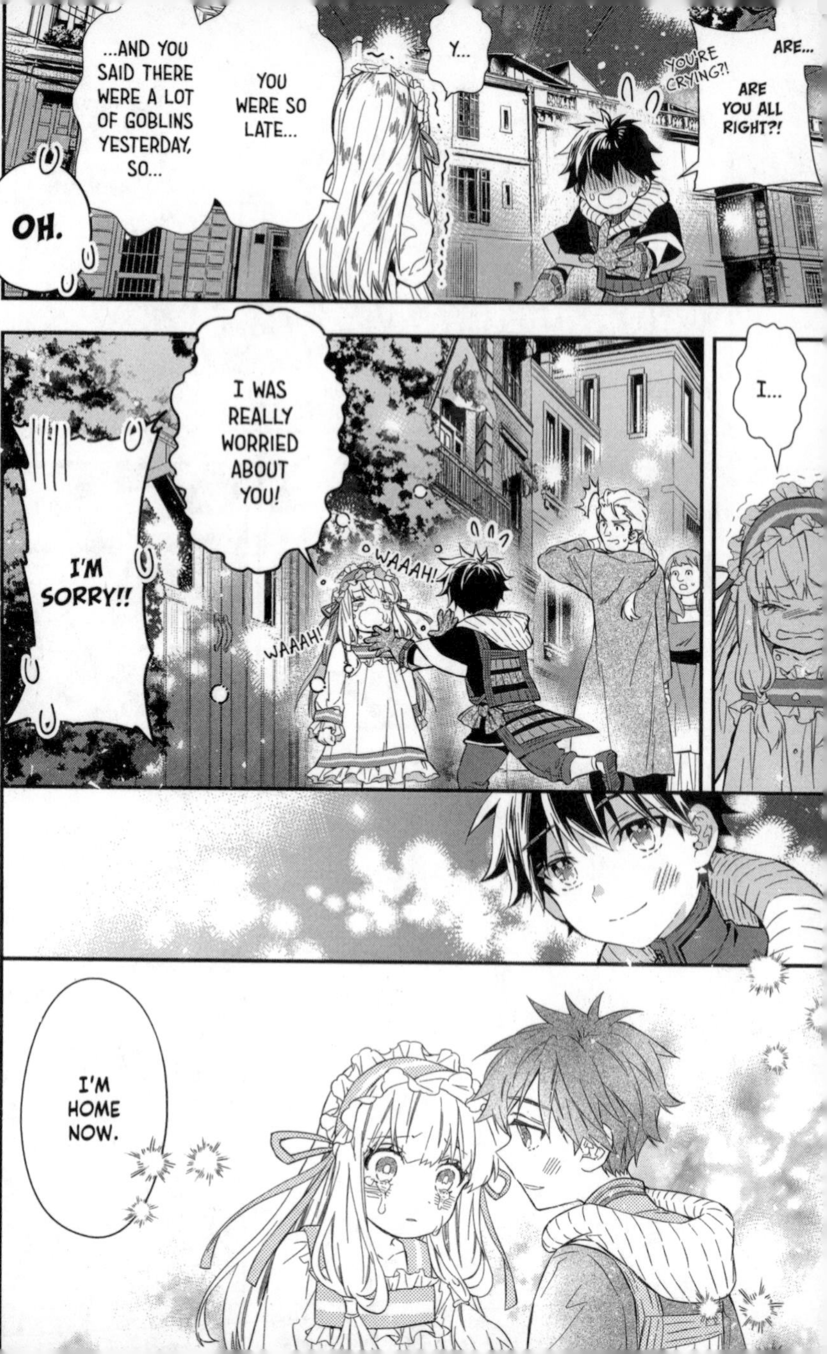
ARE...
ARE YOU ALL RIGHT?!
YOU'RE CRYING?!
Y...
YOU WERE SO LATE...
...AND YOU SAID THERE WERE A LOT OF GOBLINS YESTERDAY, SO...
OH.
I...
I WAS REALLY WORRIED ABOUT YOU!
WAAAH!
WAAAH!
I'M SORRY!!
I'M HOME NOW.

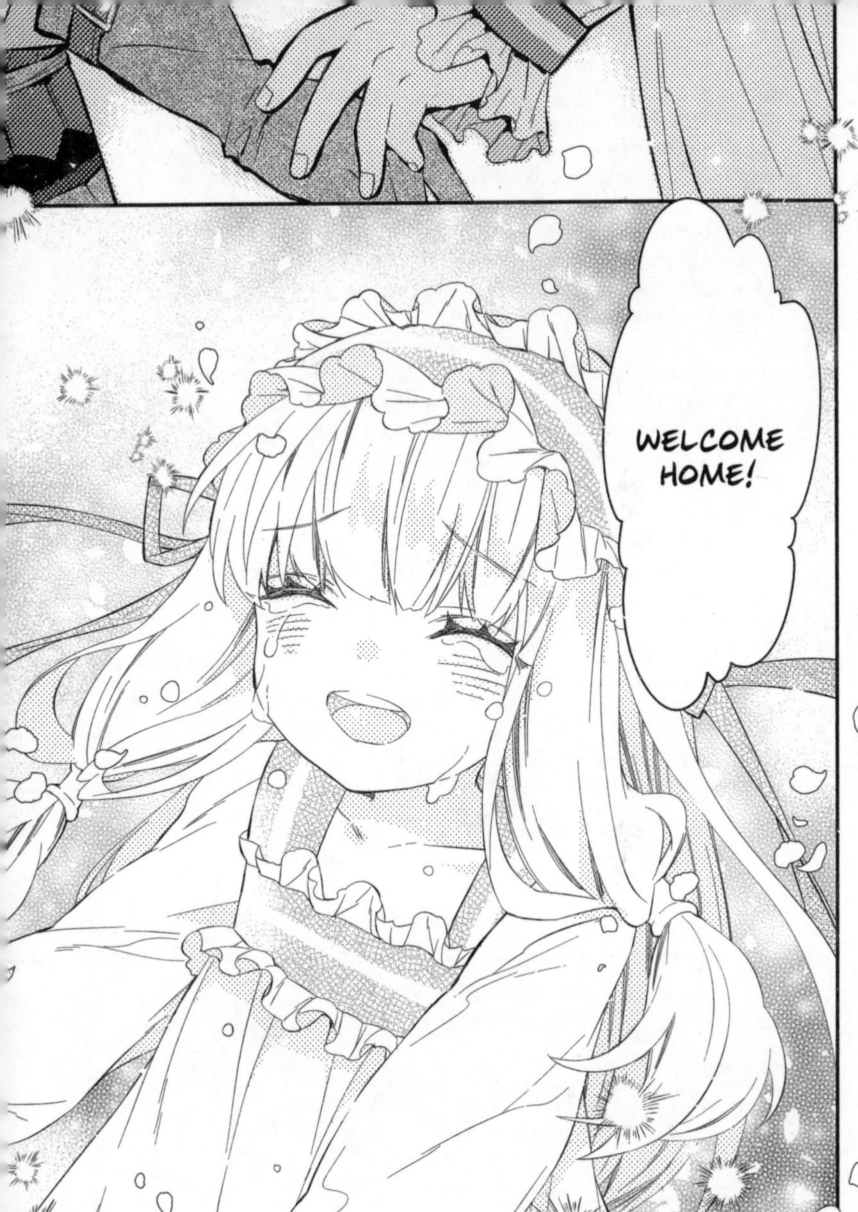
WELCOME HOME!

BY THE GRACE OF THE GODS Volume 5: The End

in which the researcher manages to survive and learns some kind of great truth or becomes able to use some incredible form of magic, but the cost is high. And the nastier among them don't gamble with their own lives, but conduct experiments using other people. Henceforth, if you decide to apprentice yourself to someone for the sake of studying magic, be careful not to choose someone like that. Anyone who obviously exposes another to danger and labels it training is not a decent teacher. Even with attack magic, a true teacher will have carefully considered the risks before training their student in it."

True, if I couldn't learn something on my own, I would need someone to teach me. Maybe that would take the form of a conversation, like today's with Leipin, or maybe I would have to become someone's disciple. In that case, I would heed Leipin's warning not to be taken in by a strange person.

At last, the carriages arrived. As our destinations in Gimul were different, we would be taking separate carriages. So, in the end, I said,

"Thank you, Leipin."

"Oh, I did nothing but pass the time with you. And besides, it's not often that I get the opportunity to speak of research and learning with a fellow adventurer. It was stimulating."

For my part, I was especially grateful for the helpful conversation and Leipin's consideration for me.

To read a brand-new short story by **ROY**, the author of *By the Grace of the Gods*, please turn to page 177 of this book, where you'll find the story presented in left-to-right reading order.

THE END

"Well, let's see... I suppose it's safe to say that I study the special characteristics of the elements."

"Special characteristics of the elements. That's what you mentioned earlier."

"Yes. Simply put, I'm plumbing the depths of the elements. Really, anyone who uses magic cannot avoid them. Take my specialty, 'fire.' It can produce an explosion, as with 'Flame Bomb,' as well as spread a fire that already exists. With the other example that I brought up, 'Flame Carpet,' you could say it is magic in which magic energy is used to recreate the phenomenon of 'the spread of fire.'"

"I see!"

It reminded me of the conversation about alchemy with the Duke's family at the Morgan Trading Company the other day.

"Magic is an art in which one uses magic energy to distort the physical rules laid down by the gods and make the impossible possible. The greater the distortion, the more difficult it is to use and the greater the consumption of magic energy."

"It's said that magic that hews to the laws laid down by the gods is the easiest, most efficient, and ideal kind of magic, but it is no simple task to uncover those unseen, complicated laws."

That's what Sebas and Lord Reinbach were saying, and I thought it might be the same thing here.

"Yes, exactly. If there is something flammable near a fire, the flames spread. That's an ordinary thing, a matter of course. 'Flame Carpet' is magic that adheres to the normal properties of fire. It's the same thing with water. Earth as well. Deepening understanding of the elements you use is very important when it comes to researching magic and improving as a magician."

That being the case, my scientific knowledge from Earth should continue to serve me well here!

"However, it is never a good idea to do anything reckless or dangerous in the name of understanding."

"What do you mean?"

"...I mentioned it while talking about history, but every once in a while, you'll find a researcher like that. One whose thirst for knowledge gets the better of him, to the point of losing any sense of ethics."

It sounded like Leipin was talking about "mad scientists." He said that in order to understand the elements, they abandon themselves to the elements. For example, they might jump into flames, drown themselves, bury themselves, or get struck by lightning.

"Suffering a light injury is one thing, but I am against any research or experiments that unnecessarily put lives at risk. There are instances begun speaking. We probably had a little while longer before it was our turn.

"Well then, let's continue... During the war, the nobility and governments had control of magic, but some magicians survived by escaping from the battlefield and secretly settling in towns. Perhaps because of that, as time passed, there was an increase in the number of people in towns who had a grounding in magic as well as those who did magic in secret. Naturally, the aristocracy and governments made moves to stamp them out time and again, but commoners vastly outnumbered noblemen, so policing or no, the fugitive magicians had children, who grew up learning about magic. It was a game of cat and mouse. However, in some areas, the crackdown was too fierce. These governments were so strict about maintaining their monopoly over magic that they even became suspicious of people who had nothing to do with it."

It reminded me of seventeenth century witch hunts, and as Leipin explained it, people rose up in revolt as a result. In the end, some nations were even destroyed.

"So now an average person like me can use magic and not get punished, but there was a long history to get to this point, huh?"

"Indeed. However, I hesitate to say that the oppression of the past no longer exists."

Leipin mentioned the nobility that still clung to old-fashioned ways of thinking and radical anti-magic religious leaders.

"There seem to be many people like that in the magic research institution, people who are very secretive at heart. And beyond that, though rare, there have been cases of researchers dying suspicious deaths."

"That's kind of scary."

"I sense that you get caught up in details and concern yourself with uncovering the truth. In other words, I believe you have what it takes to be a researcher, Ryoma. And I myself am not an unconcerned third party. We should both be careful."

"Thank you for worrying about me."

Well, it appeared our time had come.

"It looks like there will be space for us now."

"Yes. Should we get over there?"

We stood up and ambled over to the shortened carriage line.

It looked like we had a couple more minutes to talk, so...

"Oh, right. One last question. You said we should both be careful. What kind of magic research do you usually do?"

served the wealthy and powerful. Eventually, even magicians' bloodlines became subsumed by the aristocracy, until magic itself became the symbol of aristocratic power. So at that point in time, the nobility had a monopoly on magic. An individual could conduct research, but it would have to be done in secret at home. Until one day, all of a sudden, a message from the gods came down, granting permission for magic research to everyone."

"The gods gave blanket permission?"

"It appears that until that time, humans were under the kind protection of the gods, but humans had developed a certain degree of intelligence and skills over the years. Humans were no longer beings who needed everything to be given to them. They could search for or produce what they needed under their own power. It was like a child had become an adult. The message the gods gave was that they would continue to watch over us, but would refrain from communicating or meddling in our lives except for some extraordinary reason."

Doting parents to children who have already grown up... I knew people like that back at the company in my past life. I always thought that was a little weird. But imagine the human race after they suddenly got that message...

"The expression on your face tells me you have guessed what happened next."

"I suspect there was considerable confusion."

"Correct. After no longer receiving new teachings from the gods, people held on to the knowledge they were given up to then and continued to search for more on their own in order to survive. Through that process, they made mistakes, and where there were many groups, there was antagonism between them. Being humans, that is to be expected...but this is where it gets complicated, so I'm going to stop here. After all, if you look at a history book under a microscope, you'll see that it's full of holes. In this case, we have a thousand-year period devoid of details, an incalculable loss of materials due to the maelstrom of war. There are many far-fetched rumors, of magic that was lost in war, of an ancient civilization that was even more advanced than our own, of nations collaborating to keep the truth of what really happened hidden... But I am no historian, so if I have piqued your interest, you should dig further on your own."

"Understood."

I was somewhat interested, but knew that if I got into a deep conversation on the topic, there would be no end to it. Perhaps thinking the same thing, Leipin shifted his gaze toward the carriage boarding area. There were considerably fewer people waiting than when we had

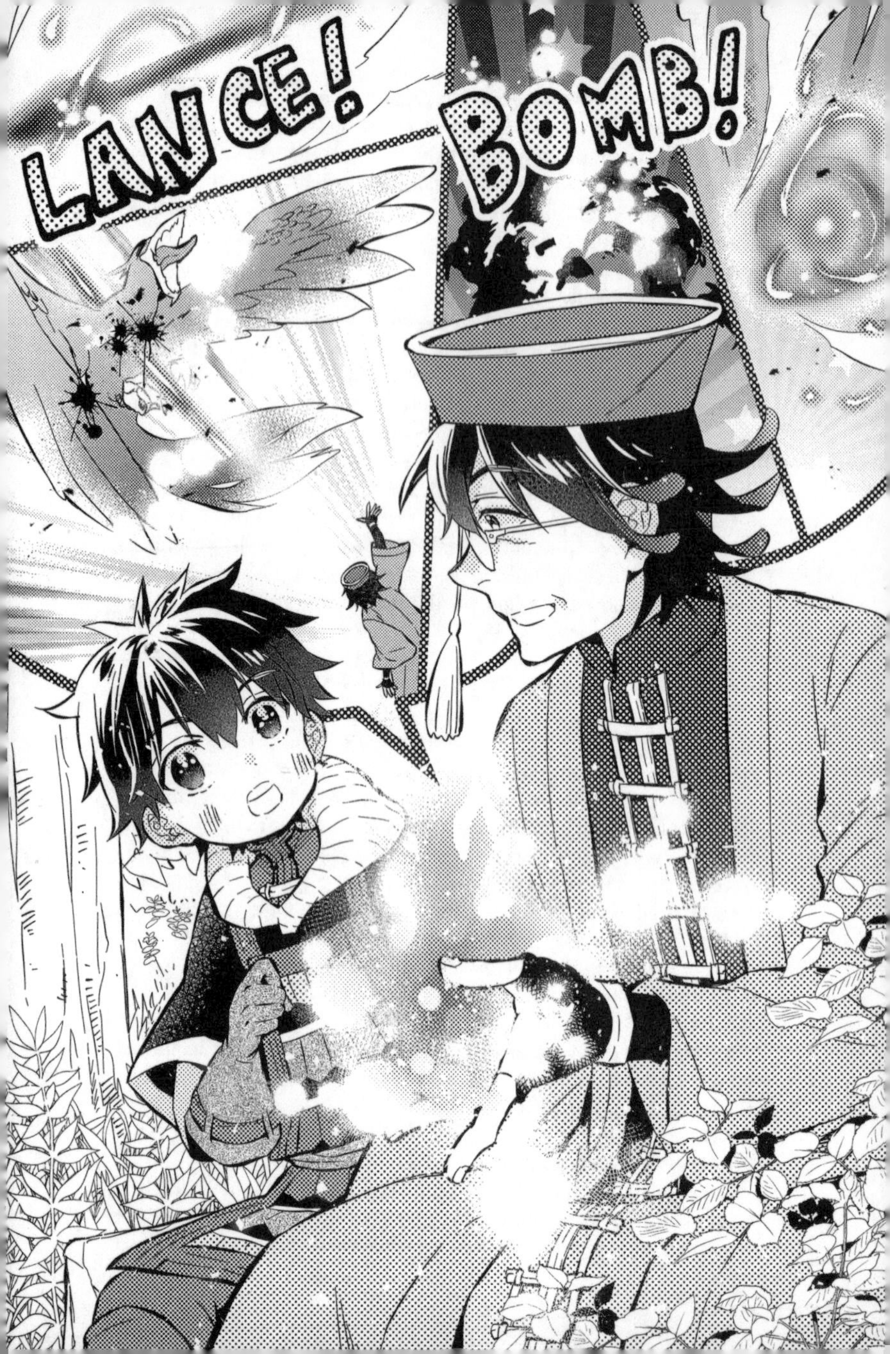
BOMB!
LANCE!

"Rituals... This sounds like an important story."

"Indeed. If there was a drought, they would perform a rainmaking ritual. If the sea was rough, a calming ritual. People were performing rituals all over the world, and by doing so, they survived calamities... These rituals were actually magic. But unlike now, when someone can use it freely with their individual will, back then magic was activated by a group of people."

"...On my own, I can produce drinking water, but I can't change the weather and make it rain. But that kind of magic is possible if many people get together and pool their magic energy?"

"Yes. One ritual would accomplish one magic spell. The gathered people would share their meager amounts of magic energy, and it was enough together to activate the spell. Since people at the time didn't have the techniques to manipulate magic energy on a personal level, the rituals were necessary to control it. It was the role of clergymen to oversee and lead the rituals."

"Huh... I didn't know the history of magic, but that's interesting. So those gods-given rituals were the world's first magic. But then how did it reach its current form?"

"They say a long time passed like that, at least thousands of years. Now we call this primordial magic that the gods gave us 'religious rites.' However, we don't have research on any of this. You seemed to be thinking about unlocking the meaning of those 'rites,' but supposedly even pondering that was an affront to the gods."

"Oh... I see."

"Now there is no ban on magic research, but it was forbidden back then. In the first place, magic was believed to be 'demonic laws,' demons being creatures at odds with the gods, who violated the rules set down by the gods. You see, in ancient times, the rites presided over by the clergy were legal, but all other magic was prohibited...even if the effects were the same."

Ryoma wondered what had happened to make them legalized.

"A new menace that threatened the human race was born. They were the ancestors of what are now common monsters. They and humans hunted each other. On top of that, there must have been people, as there are in every age, whose hunger for knowledge was insatiable. Was there a war against the monsters? Not much data remains from that period... But it's clear that from some point on, humans began to secretly research magic and use it as a weapon—although only a select number of people were able to use magic back then. Those ancient magicians were embraced by the aristocracy. And magicians found that conducting magic research could be convenient and safe when they of difficulty for magic that uses a lot of magic energy is higher than that for magic which doesn't use much magic energy. Furthermore, in the case of attack magic, as the force increases, you can widen the range of its effect. To cite an example from my own specialty, fire magic, there are intermediate level spells such as 'Flame Bomb,' 'Flame Lance,' and 'Flame Carpet.' 'Flame Bomb' is attack magic. After it flies into the target or specified area, it violently explodes and engulfs the area. 'Flame Lance' is the opposite. It compresses flames and heat into the form of a lance and then lets fly. Naturally, the range of its effect is limited, but it makes up for it with a high degree of penetrating power and force at the point of contact."

"You use them for different purposes, depending on the situation, right?"

"Exactly. Now you said that your healing slimes learned intermediate magic on their own, but there's nothing especially unusual about that. There is upward compatibility with elementary magic. If you have the required magic energy and the ability to regulate it, there is magic you can use that has the same tenets as elementary magic.

"With fire magic, there is 'Fireball,' which is just 'Big Fire,' but with more magic energy put into it to increase the impact. 'Heal' and 'High Heal' are along the same line."

That made sense. It reminded me of what Sebas had once taught me, that the intermediate space magic, "Warp," essentially worked the same way as the elementary "Teleport."

"It seems you get my point. Incidentally, if you can use intermediate magic, you're a full-fledged magician… Well, perhaps that is overstating it, but at least I can say with confidence that you are no longer a beginner. Elementary magic doesn't consume much magic energy, so these days there are a fair number of people who can use it."

"'These days'? You mean it was different a long time ago?"

What he said made me very curious, so I couldn't help but ask.

"Yes. That's a slice of history… But in the first place, do you know how magic came to be?"

"The origin of magic? …I don't believe I do."

"I see. Well, then I shall get right to it. Magic came about from a miracle of the gods."

"Miracle of the gods?"

"I only know what I've heard, but long, long ago, humans couldn't use magic. Back then, their technology wasn't as developed as it is now either, so they led fragile existences. But humans were blessed by the gods and came into possession of a number of miracles. They were in the form of rituals performed by members of the clergy."

emphasize controlling the magic. My grandfather's martial arts training really took precedence over that..."

"Then perhaps you should begin by deepening your understanding of magic, Ryoma."

"My understanding of magic?"

"Of course actual practice is important, but you trained yourself in magic naturally through using it on a daily basis, yes? From what I've seen of your earth magic, there's not much useful advice I can give you. And growing up in the forest as you have, learning martial arts, you already have plenty of strength, stamina, and concentration. On top of that, Miya and the others told me all about your skills. So if there is anything that you lack, Ryoma, I believe it would be knowledge and understanding. If you have fundamental knowledge about magic, apply it. Appy it to existing magic. Apply it to the characteristics of the elements. And if you have a good understanding of history and traditions, it will often come in handy. For there is much to learn from the failures of our forebears and what they did to keep from making the same mistakes."

"Certainly, I only know a small part of all existing magic, and hardly anything of the history and traditions."

Up until then, I had always used simple magic and my own style. I had managed to get by, but if my goal was to improve, I would need to study hard here.

"If you like, I could teach you a bit."

"Really?!"

"We have time and I don't mind."

"Yes, please! I'd be very grateful."

"Then where shall we begin?"

"Well, let's see... I really only know the basics. Beyond that, I don't know what I don't know."

"Then perhaps I shall just pick something at random. If you know the basics... All right, how about intermediate magic?"

"Intermediate magic! That reminds me. The other day, my healing slimes suddenly learned intermediate healing magic, 'High Heal.'"

"Then we'll start with the fundamentals of classifying elementary, intermediate, and advanced magic...but simply put, one of the important things about activating this magic is the amount of magic energy. The other two important things that go along with it are the effect and degree of difficulty. For example, it takes more strength to carry something that's heavy than something that's light, yes? Likewise, in order to manipulate a lot of magic energy, a corresponding amount of the ability to control it is required. Accordingly, the degree

"I'm good either way, but I have a feeling that maybe you found yourself in an odd group today, Leipin?"

"Actually, it was… I mean, they were all serious, but 'too serious,' I guess you could say."

Listening to Leipin's recounting of the day's travails, I picked up that:

Leipin had led a group of young adventurers who were all E- and F-ranked.

The members were all in their late teens.

Four out of five of them wanted to become magicians. The fifth couldn't use any magic whatsoever.

"They were so serious about fighting monsters all day long that they became careless about other things. For example, they would mistakenly use the wrong amount of magic and end up running out. If I had to sum them up in a word, it would be 'inexperienced.' And every mistake that one or the other made would spark an endless argument between them."

"It sounds like you had your hands full…"

"Mmm… The arguments were about the errors and what caused them, and what to do to prevent them from happening again, so it was productive in a sense. Perhaps I should just chalk it up to their naturally hot-blooded youth."

"I imagine they insulted each other and didn't take constructive criticism well."

"Yes, exactly. But that's to be expected at their age. And their desire to improve themselves is admirable."

Maybe that stirred a memory in Leipin's mind, because he gave a bitter smile.

"By the way, Leipin, not to change the subject, but what do you think is an important thing for magicians to know or have?"

"That is a bit out of the blue. And a difficult question to answer succinctly. Because there are many different types of magicians."

"I see… Actually, I pretty much used magic in my own way and just to support my lifestyle. With the exception of some forms of attack magic, I've only recently really started training."

"Oh, so that's why you wanted to ask about the important points of being a magician."

He folded his arms and looked like he was pondering the question.

"That earth magic you just did had a lot of finesse."

"Um, well, my grandmother could use magic. She just taught me the basics of using it, and gave me some advice, like how I should

By the Grace of the Gods

ORIGINAL SHORT STORY

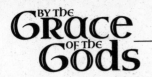

A Chat Between Magicians

While waiting in the line for the carriage ride home after another long day slaying monsters…

"Good work today, Ryoma."

"Oh, you too."

It was Leipin, researcher of monsters.

"Crowded again, eh?"

"Well, it can't be helped. Almost everyone who came for the hunt is using this transportation. I'm sure they've got families waiting for them and things to do back home, and this is the quickest way."

"Certainly, I can empathize with the desire to get home quickly."

Huh? He seemed somewhat tired.

"Did something happen?"

"Mm, is my fatigue that obvious? That won't do."

"Oh, it's fine. The day is done, so you should relax a bit."

There were adventurers as far as the eye could see, all warriors who exterminated monsters from the depths of the abandoned mine. Though we were on the outskirts of town, it was relatively safe.

After I used earth magic to create a stone chair, Leipin sat down weaily.

"I have water too."

"Please… Whew. It is nice to take a load off… So how was your group today, Ryoma?"

"Oh, I was alone today, just me and my slimes."

"Ah, really? Do you prefer it that way?"

BY THE GRACE OF THE GODS 5

Story:
Roy

Art:
Ranran

Character Design:
Ririnra

Translation: Sheldon Drzka
Lettering: Elena Pizarro
Cover Design: Andrea Miller
Editor: David Yoo

BY THE GRACE OF THE GODS Volume 5
© Roy
© 2020 Ranran / SQUARE ENIX CO., LTD.
First published in Japan in 2020 by SQUARE ENIX CO., LTD.
English translation rights arranged with
SQUARE ENIX CO., LTD. and SQUARE ENIX, INC.
English translation © 2022 by SQUARE ENIX CO., LTD.

ISBN: 978-1-64609-089-1

Library of Congress Cataloging-in-Publication
Data is on file with the publisher.

Printed in the U.S.A.
First printing, August 2022
10 9 8 7 6 5 4 3 2 1

SQUARE ENIX
MANGA & BOOKS
www.square-enix-books.com